To Grandma,

Wishing you lots of smiles in your future.

CW00863429

SMILE

SMILE

SCOTT MCCLAIN

ISBN: 978-1511504355

A big thank you to my dad and my wife for being the first two people to read this novel and for offering their insight and feedback to make it even better.

I'd also like to thank John Amy who did a marvellous job with designing the cover. Find him at www.ebookdesigner.co.uk for further examples of his work. He was prompt, helpful and sorted out all the technical bits for both ebook and paperback versions and I can't commend him highly enough.

DISCLAIMER:

This book is dedicated to:

My wife, Sarah, for giving me the belief to follow my dreams and supporting me throughout all the times my belief wavered.

My children, Amber and Noah, for giving me a reason to write this book in the first place.

And my friend, Helen, for inspiring me to make the most of what I have and making me realise that time is precious. I hope there's a library in Heaven where you could perhaps read this someday.

CHAPTER ONE

16ᵗʰ September 1994, late evening

There was a loud knock on the door of his study.

"Come in!" he summoned.

A stern-looking woman in her fifties, hair tied up in a crisp bun and looking more drained than normal, entered the study.

"Yes?" the man behind the desk said, without looking up. He was busy scrawling on some printed notes very intently and the woman who had entered looked around awkwardly.

"Sir, you need to come with me," she said impatiently.

The man she was speaking to looked up from his desk with a frown. "Excuse me?"

"No questions, sir, please. I must insist. Come with me."

The man sighed and screwed the top back on to his fountain pen, placing it gently on his desk. "I see. Very well, Mrs Forbes, very well."

He followed Mrs Forbes out of the room and they headed into the depths of the house. He was walking slightly behind her, but not looking at her, and was fervently hoping the atmosphere between them wouldn't get any more awkward.

"Is it Laura, Mrs Forbes?" he asked trying to break the silence.

She looked over her shoulder and looked deep into his eyes. "Yes, sir."

"I see." He frowned again. "Isn't this a little earlier than planned?"

"Two weeks, sir. But she can't wait any longer."

"Right, of course," he said quietly.

They returned to the awkward silence. The tension in the air between them thickened with every step. He thought she was holding herself back from saying something. Her shoulders seemed very tense, but then it hadn't been an easy few weeks for anybody in the house.

A few moments of further silence elapsed before he could hear a faint sound in the distance. It sounded like somebody was being tortured right in the depths of the house. Mrs Forbes turned around to look at him again.

He was trying extremely hard to keep his face as impassive as possible. Inside he was swirling with mixed emotions. Nervousness. A little bit of fear. Guilt. Even a twinge of excitement. He realised he was gnawing at his bottom lip; he only did that when something was really bothering him.

She snorted, her face looking furious before she went back to concentrating on where she was going.

Turning into the bottom corridor in the house, the faint noise was becoming louder. It was a sound of frustration, mixed with some anger and pain. It wasn't nice on the ears.

He sighed inwardly. All of this was happening because he had made one mistake.

Mrs Forbes paused for just a second outside the last door in the corridor. There was nowhere else to go, he realised. The stone floor and walls made the cries and screams echo and this sent chills down his spine.

"This is it, sir," Mrs Forbes said, still with a stern tone like she was grinding her back teeth as she said it.

"Thank you, Miranda," he said softly.

She raised a quizzical eyebrow at him, the informality surprising her.

He was past caring what she thought.

The crying had ceased for a few moments, but a loud wail followed by a scream came from the other side of the door. He winced, but grabbed hold of the door handle and, telling himself that it was all going to be alright, he pulled the handle down and slowly pushed the door open.

It creaked loudly and opened into a dimly lit, but comfortably furnished room. There was a hospital bed in the corner of the room with a middle-aged woman in a royal blue midwife's uniform crouched over the person proving to be the source of the screaming and wailing. The patient was in her late teens, wearing a loose-fitting gown that was drenched in sweat.

There was a large gas canister on one side of the bed, connected to a long pipe and a mouthpiece that the girl was taking big gulps from. Aside from the bed there was only a chair in the far corner laden with what appeared to be sheets and blankets and some kind of potted plant in the opposite corner to give the room a bit of homeliness. Plants and vegetation weren't really his thing. Or furnishing rooms either for that matter. That had been his wife's passion.

"What's the latest?" Mrs Forbes asked, her voice sounding tense. "Have I missed anything?"

The midwife turned to look at the visitors. She looked rather pallid and a light sheen of perspiration covered her face. She gave an exasperated glance, shook her head and went back to looking at her patient on the bed.

"It's not looking good," came the snapped response in a guttural Glaswegian accent. "I doubt we'll be able to save both of them. She has pretty severe pre-eclampsia."

"And the baby?" Mrs Forbes enquired, her voice bordering on hysterical.

"Seems healthy at this stage, as far as I can tell. There aren't any obvious signs of distress so far. But the difficult part is still to come," the midwife said without looking at them.

"Is there anything I can do to help?" Mrs Forbes asked.

"Apart from trying to keep this lassie focused on pushing when she has a contraction, you can try to keep her as comfortable as possible."

Mrs Forbes gulped and wiped her brow with a sleeve. "That doesn't sound promising," she said, under her breath.

The midwife turned around again, a stern expression on her face. "It wasn't meant to. Listen, this young lady could be struggling for her life in the next hour or two unless we can get this baby delivered. She's not in the best of shape, her contractions don't appear to be that regular or strong, but the baby is in the right position to come out. Normally, I wouldn't even try and deliver a baby in these conditions, but, as I've been told *so* many times already, this is the only option."

His heart leapt into his mouth. He had never expected it to come to this.

Mrs Forbes stepped in front of him and jabbed him in the chest. Hard.

"Now do you understand what you've done, sir?"

He could feel the guilt begin to churn in his stomach. He wondered if he could ever reveal to anybody what he had done. He shook that thought off. It wouldn't only cost him emotionally, but his whole world could be at risk. He noticed the patient on the bed, on just finishing another minute or so of wailing, was struggling to catch her breath. She was taking very deep breaths in large gulps and periodically breathing through the mouthpiece. He didn't know if there was anywhere that was safe to look.

"That's it, hen. You're doing really well. On your next contraction you need to push," the midwife said to her patient, sternly but not unkindly.

The girl looked up at the midwife with fear in her eyes.

"I know it hurts, hen. It really does, I can tell. But if you want this baby out any time soon, you need to keep pushing."

A grim and determined look came over the girl's face. Her eyes were brimming with tears and she was more than a little wild-eyed. She looked over the midwife's shoulder and noticed him for the first time. The tears seemed to well up in her a little more and her bottom lip began to tremble. Then something inside her seemed to take over and she let out a frustrated roar of pain that once again set his spine tingling. This went on for several seconds and then the midwife grabbed hold of her shoulders and pinned her to the bed.

"Go on, hen, push!"

Her whole body was tense as she strained. She had the soles of her feet pressed together with her knees as far apart as possible. He looked over at the strange sight and immediately wished he hadn't. His hand came up to his mouth and he thought he was going to be sick. He swallowed hard, and he could taste the bile in his throat.

"She's been in early labour since yesterday, sir," Mrs Forbes said quietly in his ear.

"Really? She's been like this for that long?" he replied, concern evident in his voice.

"No, sir. She's been in the latter part of labour like this since early this afternoon."

"Oh," he replied, feeling stupid. "I didn't realise…" He didn't really know what to say. He didn't have a clue about what was going on, or even why. He barely had any memory of how it had all happened originally.

Mrs Forbes didn't appear forthcoming with any sympathy. She had four children of her own. The youngest was on the bed in front of them.

"Yes, well… If you could have kept your dignity to yourself, instead of knocking up other people's daughters, we wouldn't be here in this situation now." Another stern look crossed Mrs Forbes' face as her daughter let out a small whimper and then Laura's face contorted again as another contraction washed over her.

From the little he could remember, it had been New Years Eve, and he had thrown a huge party for all of the staff working for him. There was lots of alcohol splashing about, and as he was hosting, he was footing the bill. He had even opened his wine cellar and uncorked some distinguished vintages.

It had been a tough year for him with his wife having two further miscarriages and the chances of them being able to conceive were looking more and more remote. His business had gone from strength to strength, though, and with all of his problems in his personal life he had thrown himself deeper into his work. He had put in a lot of eighteen-hour days and he found himself becoming addicted to his work. But a few weeks before Christmas, he had received some very unexpected news. His wife hadn't been feeling very well in the few months previous, had lost a lot of weight, and by the time the doctors had found out she had contracted breast cancer, it was too late. Her life had been ticking away ever since that day; the prognosis was six months to a year. In the end, she degenerated so quickly she didn't even survive five months.

Determined to enjoy himself following her diagnosis, he had spent New Years Eve drinking and socialising with his staff. His wife had gone to spend the New Year with her parents, in the West Country, away from the humdrum of his busy life. He had been disappointed initially, but eventually understood that she didn't have long left, and wanted to make the most of what was left of her life; she had every right to spend the New Year with her family.

It came as a complete shock to him to wake up the following morning with a thick head and a young, nubile member of his housekeeping staff in bed alongside him. To this day, he still couldn't remember how those circumstances had come about. He hadn't even realised who she was when he had rolled over the next morning until she picked her clothes up off the floor and fled, looking very ashamed.

It had also been a complete shock to him when he awoke to Mrs Forbes, his chief housekeeper for many years, practically banging his bedroom door down a few weeks later demanding he explain himself. He was stunned when she revealed a doctor's letter showing the pregnancy test had been positive.

He'd stammered and spluttered but he wasn't fooling anybody. He had invited Mrs Forbes in, shut the door quickly behind her, and explained as much as he could. He vehemently insisted that his wife couldn't find out; he didn't want her last few months on the planet to be ruined because he had made one mistake in a drunken moment that he would have to live with for the rest of his life. Mrs Forbes wasn't impressed, but reluctantly agreed in exchange for a few terms of her own.

The outcome of it all had been to ensure that Laura had the best possible care throughout her pregnancy in return for nobody letting slip that the baby was actually his. If anybody asked, Laura would say that she didn't know who the father was. There had been some talk of terminating the baby, but Mrs Forbes had had a strict Catholic upbringing, so they dismissed that idea very quickly.

He was adamant as well that the child could not remain in the house once born. He didn't want an illegitimate son to tarnish his memories of his wife, particularly with the circumstances surrounding the conception of the child. He was certain that as soon as the baby was born, it would be transported out of the manor to a family where it would be loved and be brought up without any knowledge of its auspicious beginnings. He had left it up to Laura and her mother if they decided to go too, with a suitable pay out of course, to allow them to bring the baby up without any financial concerns. He had too much to lose if anybody found out.

In the end they had decided that the child would be given up for adoption; it would be best for everybody involved as Laura herself wasn't even sure she could cope with living with a baby that she couldn't tell anybody about.

He also refused to have anything to do with Laura throughout the pregnancy. It had all been a mistake right from the start, and he couldn't make any guarantees, due to his work, that he would be available for doctors and midwife appointments. However, he had promised that he would be there for the actual birth and to supervise the safe transportation of the child away from the house.

He felt so useless throughout the term of the pregnancy, but tried to justify his lack of morality, by telling himself he had never wanted the child, and he had never made the first move. He effectively told himself that it was all Laura's fault. Why hadn't she insisted on using contraception when he was clearly too inebriated to think of such things? However, deep down, he knew he had been as much to blame, for letting himself get into that state and it was only right he should be facing these consequences.

He was aware that Mrs Forbes had come up with the solution for finding some suitable guardians. Two distant friends of another of the housekeeping staff had also not been able to conceive, and, on being approached by the Forbes family, they arranged to bring the baby up as their own. He had never met them, he didn't want to even know what their names were and he never wanted to in the future either. The Forbes' had arranged it all. Strictly speaking, the child would be adopted and the new parents were promised, under the terms of the adoption, that Laura would never have any contact with them. As far as they were aware the father of the baby had been unknown and was unable to be traced.

Laura had wanted it that way, almost as if she wanted to draw a line under the whole episode. Although her mother went along with her wishes (she had tried on several occasions to get her to reconsider letting him off with no apparent consequences), Laura was determined to not make things any worse for him. He had been regarded as a generous employer and she hoped to carry on as part of the housekeeping staff as soon as she felt able to go back to work. She had been allowed a lot of leeway whilst being pregnant, especially being allowed the current room that she was in. She didn't want to rock the boat for him; she just wanted to protect her own job and also for her mother and many of her friends, in whom she couldn't even confide her terrible secret. Revealing herself to be the mother of the only child ever conceived by one of Britain's most public faces would bring his empire crashing down around him, particularly as it had been built on a wave of universal sympathy. To reveal this to the world was never an option available to her, as far as she was concerned.

Throughout the whole pregnancy Mrs Forbes had been remarkably restrained about confronting him. In some ways he was grateful for that. However, he was still expecting some hostility, particularly as she wasn't even going to see her first grandchild grow up. There was still so much that could go wrong.

Shaking his head, and returning from his reverie, he looked at Mrs Forbes a little reluctantly. He tried to think of something to say, but the words didn't come.

"I need some help over here!" the midwife shouted suddenly.

Mrs Forbes looked at him. She saw that he had frozen in place. Giving him a disgusted look, she rushed to be by her daughter's side.

He felt it was safest to stay by the door. He hadn't been involved the whole way through, and he thought it best to not change his stance now in case a maelstrom of emotion caught up with him, which would put his plans at risk. Every step had been carefully worked out. He had to remain fully focused.

Once again, he looked at Mrs Forbes. She was now whispering words of encouragement in Laura's ear while the midwife had put on a pair of latex gloves.

"Well, your cervix isn't as dilated as I'd hoped it would be by now, hen," the midwife said, looking up from between Laura's legs.

Laura, her belly extremely swollen, hands and feet almost twice their regular size as well, let out a small whimper and lay back on the bed exhausted. Her breaths came in big gulps again and she was looking even paler than when he'd first seen her this evening. If he didn't know any better, it looked like she was going to throw in the towel.

"I can try another stretch and sweep, and see if I can move those membranes out the way, hen," the midwife offered hopefully. "It might just trigger something."

Laura nodded and braced herself as the midwife's hand went to work. Her face contorted into all sorts of expressions as another contraction arrived at the same moment.

He was still stood by the door becoming incredibly interested in the plant in the corner. He didn't even know what type of plant it was but it was giving him a welcome distraction.

When the process was completed the midwife withdrew her hand. It was covered in thick blood. Mrs Forbes looked concerned.

"Surely there shouldn't be that much blood for a sweep?" she asked.

The midwife's eyebrows knitted together. "No, hen, there shouldn't," she murmured. She turned to him, still stood awkwardly by the door. "If this goes on much longer we're going to have to send this poor lassie to hospital," she said.

He cleared his throat. "It isn't really an option. Do what you can here. But transporting to hospital is the absolute last resort." He had been reticent to deal with a hospital due to the paperwork involved and the questions that would have been asked if he'd attended the birth as he planned to. Having the baby born in the house was the only way he had envisaged being there at the birth of his child.

The midwife rolled her eyes again and muttered something about celebrities and putting other people's lives at risk, but turned back to Laura who was looking at her expectantly.

"Come on then, hen. I could feel the baby's head on that last sweep so he or she is all ready to drop out, you just need to…"

"Push?" came the whisper.

The midwife almost broke into a grin. "You've got it, hen. Now come on, one last effort."

Another twenty minutes or so passed, with very little progress. The midwife had given Laura another examination, which resulted in more blood, which was becoming runnier, and more concerned looks. There was plenty of straining, gasping for breath, screams, wails and pleading for the pain to stop without ever seeming to have any progress.

And then the midwife smiled, a big beaming smile, and the world seemed like a better place. The room felt brighter, the tension in the air had lifted and there was hope on Mrs Forbes' face, replacing the stern expression she had been wearing since she had walked into his study earlier.

"Can you see that, sir?" Mrs Forbes said excitedly and pointing between her daughter's legs.

It took a few moments, but he finally plucked up the courage to look. The world seemed to stop, and all that was important was that view. He could see a pale patch of flesh amongst all the congealed blood and pubic hair, and it was the most amazing piece of skin that he had ever seen.

"Right then, hen, that's some serious progress! The baby's head is crowning!" the midwife exclaimed, suddenly looking more business-like.

Mrs Forbes clapped her hands together and let out a squeal like a child opening a new toy at Christmas. He wondered why she was getting so excited, bearing in mind she'd never get to see the baby after tonight, but it dawned on him that it was the first view of her first grandchild and that had to mean something to her.

Another half an hour went by, amidst much grunting and pushing from Laura and eager encouragement from both the midwife and Mrs Forbes with more and more of the baby's head being revealed. He was fascinated now and couldn't tear his eyes away from Laura's waist, where another human being was gradually appearing. He felt his eyes well up and he struggled to keep his emotions in check.

He had a child. It definitely wasn't in the circumstances that he wanted, but after the events of the past year, with his wife miscarrying twice, then her cancer diagnosis and subsequent death, witnessing the birth of a child had, at times, seemed rather improbable. He was trying not to think about not seeing the child grow up; it made his eyes prick with tears every time.

With one last push, the baby was on the bed, wriggling and covered in blood and a whole range of other fluids he didn't want to think about. The midwife, who had grabbed a towel from the chair, scooped it up. She dried the baby off before placing it on Laura's chest. Laura had ripped her gown off, and was busy crying uncontrollably with the emotion of it all.

"Congratulations," the midwife said to him, without any emotion. "You have a beautiful little boy."

"Hello you," Laura was saying to the baby, tears streaming down her face. "I'm your mummy, but you'll never get to know who I am."

He felt a large lump in his throat and that guilty feeling rose to the surface again.

The midwife had returned to looking concerned, however. He had thought it was all over. The midwife had snipped the cord now but had returned to looking between Laura's legs. There was still a lot of fresh blood, oozing from somewhere.

Mrs Forbes, who had been busy stroking Laura's face and telling her how proud she was of her, looked up at him and saw the confused look on his face.

"It's the placenta; it's still to come out," she said helpfully.

He nodded without truly understanding what she meant. He could barely rip his gaze away from the tiny human that was snuffling on Laura's chest. He wanted to go over and offer everybody a hug or some congratulations, but his feet felt like they had been concreted to the floor.

Laura then gave birth to a large bloody mass of tissue a few moments later, which took him aback and his stomach churned again.

Everything happened really quickly from then on. There were a lot of raised voices and then the baby was bundled into his arms and Mrs Forbes pushed him out of the door.

"Go, sir. Take the baby to the car. Derek knows where he's going."

He noticed Mrs Forbes struggling to hold back the tears.

"But, Miranda, what's happening to Laura?" he asked, fearing what the answer might be.

"She's got a bleed somewhere. The midwife thinks part of the placenta may still be inside as well. It's not looking good at this stage, sir. We're going to need that ambulance."

He didn't know what to say. He had no words to offer as a crumb of comfort to his housekeeper of many years and her youngest child who he had knocked up in a drunken stupor those nine-or-so months ago.

Instead, he swept his way out of the room. The precious bundle was all he could think about. He wanted to run, but was terrified of dropping the baby, who had his eyes closed now, but was starting to find his little voice, emitting tiny squeaks, as his father led him through the house, looking for the nearest way up and out to the big, wide world.

He was then in the fresh air running across the gravel drive to the garage where Derek, Mrs Forbes' husband, was sat in the car reading a newspaper. On seeing him approach, holding the blanketed bundle, Derek tossed his paper aside, started the engine, and leapt out to open the car door. He took the baby off his employer and strapped it into the car seat.

It all happened so quickly, he realised, as he watched the rear lights of the car disappear down the drive. He had never had a chance to say hello, or even goodbye. A solitary tear rolled its way down his cheek, which he wiped away angrily with the back of his hand. His feet had found themselves fixed to the floor again, and he had no idea how long he was stood there, staring at where the car had disappeared from view.

It was the blue flashing lights of the ambulance that brought him out of his trance, and he immediately felt a jolt of horror as he realised that the night's events might not yet be over.

As he stood in the garage, he saw Laura, now strapped to a gurney, ready to be taken to the hospital. She seemed very pale and still, and all he could see before the doors closed was Mrs Forbes glaring at him.

It was an image that he would see every time he closed his eyes until the day he died.

CHAPTER TWO

Saturday 7th April 2012, late morning
Beans and Banter, Huntingham

"Joel?"

"Yes, Ma?" Joel called back.

"Can you clear the two window tables for me? We've got the lunchtime rush coming soon."

Joel sighed and put the cup he was drying down. "Yes, Ma, on my way," he muttered to himself. His mother was in her forties, her normally brown hair starting to show flecks of grey. She was a diminutive woman, usually wearing an apron and was quite strict in her demeanour with people. She had the air of a Victorian headmistress, so whatever she said had to be obeyed.

"Thanks, son," his mother said, on his way past the counter. Joel's dad, Ted, was there too, cleaning the coffee machine, and he shot Joel a sympathetic smile. Joel knew his mother was strict and he sometimes couldn't imagine how his dad had put up with her for so long. His dad was tall, extremely thin, and was renowned for his sense of humour. His hair was almost all white but thinning on top. The joke was often made that it was being married to Alyssa, for so many years, that was causing his hair to 'run away in fright'.

Joel Wright was seventeen years old and tall like his dad. He considered himself to be fairly handsome for his age, with a scruffy mop of dark hair and shrewd ice blue eyes. He was working in his parents' coffee shop, Beans and Banter, at evenings and weekends to fund a year abroad travelling once he finished college. He didn't mind too much, it wasn't particularly difficult work, and his parents were quite happy with him having one of the tables near the back of the shop where he could sit with his friends.

Beans and Banter wasn't your ordinary coffee shop. The ethos behind the shop was to provide an alternative to the pub culture in Huntingham, an old market town in the East Midlands. Beans and Banter had once been a pub itself, and the layout hadn't changed a lot. Brighter colours on the walls, a few more comfy chairs and softer furnishings had softened the appearance of the former Red Lion Inn. It stayed open until midnight on Fridays and Saturdays, and ten o'clock for the rest of the week. It opened again at eleven every morning for the breakfast runs. Joel's dad had also recently started asking local bands and solo acts perform one night a week, and Joel, as a keen guitarist and pianist himself, had seized on the opportunity to gain some performing experience.

As a result, it wasn't too uncommon for regular punters to approach him whilst he was working and offer him some tips, or recommendations to add to his set list. It therefore didn't concern him too much when one elderly lady, sat in a large group of other similarly aged women, was openly staring at him. He'd had all types stare at him since he'd completed his first set a few weeks ago.

He smiled at the old dear from across the room. She turned away and, after a few moments of consideration, rummaged in her bag for her mobile phone.

Joel cleared the plates and cups from the window tables and was about to turn around and head back to the kitchen, when a knock on the window startled him.

"Hey, Joel!" came the chorus from the three waving people stood in the street. He smiled back at them and beckoned them in.

They were Amie and Hannah French, and Alan Proctor.

Joel and Alan had been best friends since they first sat together as six-year-olds at school and had grown up together since. They were so close they were practically brothers and had often been mistaken as being related. Alan had a similar build and features to Joel, apart from close-cropped hair and warm brown eyes framed behind the latest designer glasses. Alan was from a more privileged background than the rest of the group. He did his best to dumb it down, but Joel had become accustomed to the designer labels, trendy eyewear and the odd moment of upper class twang.

Amie and Hannah were identical twins, of average height with straight red hair and crystal blue eyes. Both of them were a spitting image of their mother, with freckles punctuating their almost perfectly oval faces. They lived opposite the coffee shop, and were a year older than the two boys. They were regular customers in the shop, which was how they had all met, before realising they all went to the same college.

Amie was the more outgoing of the two, was very chatty and wore very flamboyant clothes. She loved bright colours and had taken to expressing this in paintings and drawings that she loved to do.

Hannah was a lot more reserved, dressed in very bland, baggy clothes and had a far away stare in her eyes much of the time. She was quite open about the fact she had depression and her treatment of it, which the group all made allowances for. Hannah had attempted suicide nine months ago and had survived, after being found by the emergency services at her house.

She was taking anti-depression tablets now and had had a strict course of counselling sessions to try and get to the bottom of the root cause of her suicide attempt. The group tended not to ask her about the incident in fear of sparking off another attempt to take her own life. Amie had been incredibly supportive of her sister, and very defensive of her too. She was older by twenty minutes and took her duty as being the older sister very seriously.

They spent a lot of time together as a group, although one member was currently missing. This was Tim Pointer, who went to college with Alan and Joel. He had applied for a television talent show over six months ago, and had made it all the way to the televised finals. He was an extremely talented saxophonist, and had wowed the nation with his youthful charm and emotional saxophone tracks that he'd covered or written himself. Week on week, the regulars of Beans and Banter had been watching the big screen in disbelief as the scruffy-looking, curly-haired, local lad had made it through every round and was now in the top three.

As a result, Hannah, who had found she was becoming quite close with Tim over recent months, had become more withdrawn from the group the longer Tim was away. She had tried to talk to Alan more and more in recent weeks, to try and stop becoming isolated, but a crippling lack of self-confidence held her back. Joel often felt that she didn't think she could measure up to Alan's standards.

Joel, himself, was seemingly oblivious to the fact that Amie was always trying to get his attention; he just thought that was the way she was.

Joel's parents often wondered if any of the teenagers would realise that there was more than just friendship in the air between them.

"Hey, guys, everyone alright?" Joel asked when his closest friends had made their way into the shop.

"We're great, thanks, Joelly!" Amie replied as the natural spokesperson for the group. "How's business today?"

"Yeah, it's been a little slow again, but it's Easter weekend, so I'm guessing everybody's with their families or something." Business had tailed off a bit since the start of the year, in comparison with the last, hence one of the reasons for offering live music once a week and the investment in a large TV screen.

"Oh well, any more gigs coming up?" Alan asked, sitting down at their table.

Joel smiled. "A couple in the next few weeks, but Ma and Pops want to rotate the acts as much as possible."

"Perfectly understandable," Alan agreed.

"So, what are we having? The usual?" Hannah asked quietly, changing the subject.

"Sure, give me a minute, I'll sort them out." Joel headed behind the counter. "Ma, the gang's here, will you be OK for a few minutes?"

"Yes, no problem, make sure it's no more than twenty, though," came the reply.

Joel busied himself with preparing the drinks; it was one of the reasons the group spent a lot of time in the shop. They usually had a couple of drinks a day, mostly tea or instant coffee between them, but made sure they paid for anything fancier. Joel was grateful for that, as it made him realise there was more to their friendship than free drinks.

Joel returned to their table carrying a tray. There was the usual scramble for the sugar bowl, which Amie tended to win. Once they had stirred in their respective sugars and sweeteners and had the first sip, they all settled back into their seats.

"Anybody heard from Tim at all?" Hannah asked suddenly.

They all looked at her in surprise. Joel shook his head and looked at Amie and Alan, who were both giving Hannah a blank look. If anybody was likely to hear from Tim, it was Hannah, not the rest of them.

Hannah sighed and looked down at the table. "I haven't heard from him now for a couple of months. I know he's busy, but I was hoping he wouldn't forget about us."

Amie looked hard at her sister. "Don't be ridiculous, Han. As you said, he's a busy boy now. He has to be rehearsing pretty much every second he's awake at the moment."

"Not even a message, though, Amz. I don't get it. Why can't I get a text from him?"

"Have you messaged him, Han?"

"Not since he first disappeared. I messaged him before we knew he was on Talent UK. I just thought he'd get back to me eventually."

Amie snorted, but didn't say anything further.

Joel felt a bit sorry for Hannah. She had gone some way in forming a bond with Tim, but when he'd disappeared quite suddenly and then shown up on a talent show, she'd taken it quite hard, presumably angry that he couldn't have told her, or given her some kind of warning. Now she was practically being ridiculed for daring to ask if anybody had heard from him. Joel pinched Amie's arm, making her squeal.

"Hey! What was that for?" she yelped, making a mock sad face.

Joel noticed Hannah trying to hide a smile. "Come on, Amz, leave your sister alone. She was only asking," he pointed out.

"It was a stupid question," Amie muttered under her breath.

"Now, now, children," boomed Alan, sending the group into fits of giggles.

Once everyone had calmed down, Joel stood up. "Right then, guys and gals, I must love you and leave you; tables to clean, dishes to wash."

He headed behind the counter again, grabbing the spray and a cloth to wash some recently vacated tables. The elderly lady who had been staring at him earlier appeared from the ladies toilet, and caught his eye once again. Joel, half expecting her to come and speak to him, decided to be proactive.

"Hello, was there anything I can help you with?" he asked innocently.

She looked at him closely and snorted. "You *do* look like him. Can't be a coincidence. I'll have to tell Elsie."

Joel looked at her, feeling a bit lost. "I'm sorry, I don't understand, I look like who?"

"You know, I can't be the only one who has said it to you." She glared at him, shrugging her bag over her shoulder. "Oh come on, boy. The famous author. Andrew whatshisname… The one who writes about depression and all that gubbins."

Joel frowned. "Sir Andrew Anderson?"

Her face lit up. "Yes, that's him. You've got the same sort of facial features. You must have had people tell you."

Joel shook his head. "Sorry, you're the first one," he said.

She turned away, shaking her head sadly and muttering something under her breath about the state of the nation. Joel just stared after her, not quite sure what to make of it all. Was she mentally deranged? He'd never heard that comparison before. He felt a hand on his shoulder and turned around.

"What's up, mate? Getting bother from someone?" Alan enquired.

Joel grimaced. "Not exactly," he said. "Just been told I look like someone famous. That author, Andrew Anderson." He headed over to the newly vacated table and began clearing the cups and plates, with Alan in close pursuit.

"Oh yeah, the guy who wrote that book. What's it called… 'Smile'?"

"I think that's what it's called, that rings bells," Joel admitted.

"Isn't he the one on the front cover? He's got those really piercing blue eyes, a bit like yours. Plus when you see him on telly he's quite tall, a bit like you. He does have a beard, though. You can only grow fluff."

Joel turned round and glared at him. "Don't start, buddy. If I look like him, then the same could be said for you too."

Alan smiled back at him. "Apart from the eyes, Joelly. But at least I can grow a beard," he added, trying to wind Joel up further.

Joel frowned. He didn't have an answer to that.

Joel's mum then appeared from the kitchen. "There's not much work going on here; what's wrong, you two?"

"Joel's been told he looks like Andrew Anderson, that guy who deals with depression in his books," Alan nipped in before Joel could even compose a response. Joel glared at him again.

"Oh really? That's a bit strange. Well, I suppose, they may have a point…" Alyssa said, tailing off and looking thoughtful.

"Come on, Ma, not you as well!" Joel exclaimed, looking annoyed.

CHAPTER THREE

Saturday 7th April, mid-afternoon
Great Bournestone Manor

Sir Andrew Anderson was leaning back in his office chair, eyes closed, listening intently as the warm reedy sound of the saxophone washed over him. He had a penchant for jazz. It gave him the sensation of having a warm light spread into all the corners of his mind. He always tried to make twenty minutes during his day to shut his mind off and lose himself in the music.

There was a knock on his study door. He came out of his trance, taking a few seconds to discover he was still in his office at home.

"Come in," he summoned reluctantly, turning the volume down on his computer.

His assistant, Isabella, popped her head around the door. "Sorry to bother you, sir, but I have Bill and Christina here to see you. They're your two-thirty appointment."

A quick glance at the clock in the corner of his computer screen confirmed he was running ten minutes behind. He must have been lost in his safe place for longer than he thought.

He sighed. "Very well, Izzy, thank you for disturbing me," he said. "As you so often do you've kept me on the straight and narrow," he added hastily when he saw a dark look begin to cross her face.

"Thank you, sir," she replied, smiling sweetly. "I know you hate being interrupted. I'll send them straight in."

Sir Andrew reached for his tour file lying on his desk. Bill Grant and Christina Miles were managing his new tour, known just as 'Smile :D', which was starting at the beginning of July. He wasn't totally sure whether the 'D' was pronounced, but had been assured it would attract a different demographic from his previous tours.

He looked up as a wiry gentleman in his forties and a younger-looking woman of Caribbean descent entered his office. He stood up to greet them and ushered them into the chairs on the opposite side of his desk.

"And what a pleasure it is to see you both," Sir Andrew said, keeping his face neutral, looking closely between the two of them. "What do you have for me?"

"Just an update on the tour, sir," Christina said.

"We like to keep you informed, as we know you like to be," Bill added.

"Very well, continue," Sir Andrew said calmly, leaning back in his chair as he listened.

Bill and Christina proceeded to inform him of how the tour was selling, which locations could perhaps use a bit more advertising and which venues had already been sold out.

It never ceased to amaze him how many people would spend their hard earned money to listen to him talk about his experiences in life and how he'd learned to deal with his depression. He had received an overwhelming response to his first book that he'd published over thirty years ago when he had been working as a GP in a small village medical practice. It had been written in response to an increasing number of patients in whom he had noticed increasingly common symptoms, but couldn't formally give a diagnosis of any medical condition. Instead he had tried to encourage patients to change the way they thought, rather than change who they were. He then managed to draft these techniques into print and tried to raise awareness of depression, its impact on people's lives and how best to deal with it. The global perception of depression had certainly changed in the recent decades, generally brought on by a whole number of events; wars, financial market crashes and even terrorism to name a few. His tours gave him an opportunity to go out to the corners of the globe to meet people struggling to survive normal day-to-day life and it always left him feeling quite humbled to hear about the agony and strife that some people had experienced; it certainly put things in perspective.

Sir Andrew shut his eyes, leaning forward on to his hands steepled beneath his bearded chin. He was a giant of a man, with tidy dark hair, speckled with white these days, but he was fortunate to still appear to have time on his side, in spite of the fact he was due to turn sixty next year. He had always been very keen on details from a young age and not a lot, if anything, got past his shrewd, ice-blue eyes, without him knowing. He was also a calculated reader of people, and his ability to read accurately between the lines often stunned people, especially Izzy. She had learnt very early on to tell him how it was, rather than to try and put a positive spin on what she was saying. He always knew.

"Is everything OK, sir?" Christina asked, after a few moments. She and Bill had been discussing Sir Andrew's recent behaviour, noting it had been very unlike him to be so reserved. He was normally extremely focused, buzzing with positive energy. He almost seemed distracted. Even when they had been talking to Izzy outside, she had warned them not to push him too hard, but even she didn't know what was bothering him.

He opened his eyes, blinking a few times. "Sorry. Lost in thought, that's all." He pretended to sweep some dust off his desk, giving him a few seconds to compose his thoughts. "So, essentially what you're saying is that the tour is selling well, yes?"

Bill and Christina nodded.

"Very well." He stroked his beard thoughtfully for a few seconds. He had just had a brainwave.

"Is there anything proposed for pre-show entertainment?" he asked cautiously. He had had a well-known stand-up comedian for his last tour that had gone down very well with tour sales.

Christina frowned and looked at Bill. He shrugged back at her.

Sir Andrew, noticing this, flashed a brief smile. "Don't worry, I'm not picking faults. I was just curious, that's all."

"Did you have something in mind?" Christina asked.

"Not really. It only occurred to me a few moments ago," Sir Andrew admitted. "You know how much I love listening to jazz?"

His guests both nodded. They had regularly heard his stereo from outside his office.

"How about a jazz musician of some kind? I've always wondered if music can have an impact on moods and emotions. Well, I'm positive it does, I just haven't done any positive scientific research on it as yet. I could do with investigating that a bit further..." he tailed off, making a note on the pad in front of him.

"Does it have to be jazz, sir?" Christina asked.

Sir Andrew considered this for a few moments. "Not necessarily, but I'd like it to be. For me, jazz music can be upbeat and uplifting and then in the next moment doleful, mournful and bleak. The range of emotion covered is quite astonishing and that's what I want to try and tap into."

Christina and Bill shared a quick glance. Christina reached into her bag, pulling her tablet out. She turned it around and gave it to Sir Andrew after a few seconds of pressing and tapping.

"Have a look at this and let me know what you think, sir."

A video began playing, starting with the theme from Talent UK. It wasn't something that Sir Andrew normally watched, so he wasn't really prepared for the next few minutes.

When the video had finished and offered him the chance to replay the video, he did so without hesitating.

"Wow," he said a few moments later. "Just... Wow."

Both Bill and Christina were struggling to keep a straight face.

"Who on earth was that?" Sir Andrew asked them excitedly. "That was truly wonderful. Exactly what I had in mind."

"His name's Tim Pointer, sir. He only lives about five miles from here, in Huntingham," Christina replied. "He's made it all the way to the final of Talent UK, and he's certainly had very good write-ups in the press.

Everybody seems taken with him."

"Does he have representation? If so, I want them in here as soon as possible."

"I don't actually know, but I can certainly find out."

"Fine, make that a top priority, Christina. I want him on my tour."

With that, Christina and Bill thanked Sir Andrew for his time and headed out of his study. He had a quick look on his online calendar to see what else the afternoon had in store for him. He had a few minutes before his next appointment.

He sat back in his chair again, gazing into the far corner of his office, thinking about the impact of a musical warm-up act on the tour. Was it possible that music could trigger some sort chemical reaction in the brain? Could this then be harnessed to tackle depression? Or was it more likely that it was purely psychological? He pondered these questions for a few moments, before another knock at the door interrupted him.

Izzy once again popped her head round the door. "It's your three o'clock appointment. Dad's here, sir."

"Very well, Izzy, send him in."

Hayden Smart was a long-time friend of Sir Andrew's. They had lived next door to each other at college, Hayden studying law on the way to becoming a solicitor, while Andrew had gone down the medicine route. Hayden had been a source of great entertainment in the time they had spent together at college and Sir Andrew often wondered how his friend had made his way to the top of his profession. However, they had been great friends since their late teens, with Hayden providing Sir Andrew with legal advice, while Sir Andrew had helped him deal with the emotional impact of a messy divorce in return. Their relationship had also been strengthened by the fact Hayden's only child was Sir Andrew's personal assistant, helping him build his empire to be as successful as it was today. Izzy was the perfect go-between for the both of them and it meant they always knew what was going on in the other's life.

Hayden strode into Sir Andrew's office, immaculately dressed as always in his tailored suit, his coiffured black hair waving behind him. He laid his briefcase on his best friend's desk, making himself comfortable in one of the guest chairs.

"Andy, it's been a while," Hayden said, flashing a brilliant white smile.

Sir Andrew gave a reserved smile back. Hayden was the only person he knew who called him 'Andy'. Even Izzy, who had grown up around him, insisted on calling him 'Andrew', or 'sir', around other people.

"So, I see the next tour has been announced. Sales going well?"

"Fairly well, yes. Some dates are sold out already."

"Any extra dates required?"

"Possibly, but I always like to do a few gigs first, before committing to any more. Depends on how those first few are received."

Hayden nodded sagely. "Sensible enough strategy. No point in over-committing."

"Absolutely. At least the tours keep me busy. Keeps the mind sharp."

"Not as if you've got anybody to leave behind either, makes it easier to be away from home for a few months."

Sir Andrew gave Hayden a hard glare across the desk. The solicitor raised his hands defensively.

"Alright, alright. Touchy subject, I know. Not my fault you and Dorothy, God bless her soul, couldn't have children. How long's it been now since she passed away?"

"Eighteen years next week," Sir Andrew responded defensively, giving his friend a stern look to drop the subject.

"Of course. Terrible, terrible... Seems just like yesterday..." Hayden tailed off, distracting himself by sifting through some paperwork in his briefcase. "Anyway, the real reason I'm here is to go through your will that one of my adoring, faithful pet paralegals has drawn up for you."

Sir Andrew shook his head slowly. "Honestly, Hay, 'pet paralegals'? Really?"

Hayden grinned back at him, handing over the documents he'd found.

Sir Andrew scanned through the pages Hayden had given him. There was only one thing nagging away at him, even more so when he'd read the part about leaving his estate to a national depression charity for which he was a president.

Hayden noticed a frown cross his friend's face. "What?"

"What, what?" Sir Andrew responded.

"You frowned."

"I'm not allowed to frown now?"

"No, it's just you only usually frown when something's bothering you. Is it something wrong with the paperwork?"

Sir Andrew hesitated a moment before responding. "It's the part about next of kin."

"How do you mean?" It was Hayden's turn to frown.

"Well, how accurate do these things have to be?"

"As accurate as possible, ideally. You don't want people coming out of the woodwork to lay claim to your vast fortune and exquisite estate."

Sir Andrew looked up at the ceiling and puffed his cheeks out. "So the more specific I am now, would, in theory, present fewer problems further down the line?"

"Yeah, you could kind of say that," Hayden replied, looking puzzled.

"Right, I see," Sir Andrew said quietly. He stroked his chin pensively, brushing the bristles with his fingers.

"Come on, Andy, there's something bothering you, spit it out. We've been friends for nigh on forty years. If you've been harbouring a secret for that long I'm dying to know what it is."

Sir Andrew was trying to spin a story quickly in his head that could explain his behaviour, when Hayden's words sparked an idea. "There is the possibility I have a brother," he said, trying to hide any signs of relief he'd found a suitable yarn.

Hayden stared at him for a few long moments, his eyes scanning Sir Andrew's face for any sign that he was being dishonest.

Sir Andrew knew it was a useless exercise; he took great pride in being a closed book. There had been a few times in college where Hayden had tried to read into what was going on in his head but had failed miserably. His best friend had learned that it was futile. But there was still that niggle in his gut that made him wonder if Hayden thought there was more to the story.

"Right, a brother. I see…" Hayden said, sounding sceptical. "Well, I can have a look, do some family history, if you like?"

Sir Andrew pretended to think about it for a few seconds, knowing that Hayden would come up empty from any such search. "You personally? Or your 'pet paralegals'?" he said, cracking a smile.

Hayden clapped him on the arm. "Do I look like the sort of solicitor that would spend hours and hours rooting through your family history?" He faked a yawn. "Er, no. I pay my pets well. I'm sure one of them will earn the right to dig up your family tree."

Sir Andrew shook his head slowly, trying to hold back a laugh. "I'll give you some details that will help you, sorry, your pets, with their search. A place to start if you will."

"Right you are, Andy. Talk about it over dinner?"

Sir Andrew looked at his watch. "Sure, why not. I'll hunt out some documents for you. I'll ask Izzy to see if the Golden Bell has a table. You don't mind if I ask her along?"

"Of course not. Say six-ish?"

"I'll see what I can do. Keep that smart phone thing you have on, I'll send you a message. Right, is it time to go back and check your pets haven't wrecked your incredibly plush office?"

As he was leaving the room, it was Hayden's turn to give a slow shake of the head. "Honestly…" he muttered under his breath.

CHAPTER FOUR

Saturday 7th April, early evening
Beans and Banter

Joel was sat at his table at the back of the shop, nursing a cup of decaf coffee. The day had turned into being quite busy in the shop. There had been an unprecedented lunchtime rush and this was the first chance Joel had had to have a break. When he was done, everything would then need setting up for the evening regulars. Most came in for somewhere warm and comfy to chat or read. Joel's favourite time of day was dusk at Beans and Banter. The shop wasn't full, but was quiet enough to allow him to sometimes practise his guitar or to do some college work.

He looked up as his mum came and sat down with him, a cup of tea in hand.

"Everything alright, Ma?"

"Can't complain," she said, smiling. "That's certainly the busiest Saturday afternoon we've had in a long while."

"I know. I couldn't quite believe where the time had gone when I looked at the clock earlier."

"You did a great job, Joel. You always do. Hard workers like you are absolute stars. On that note, though, there were a couple of things I wanted to discuss with you."

"Sure, Ma, what's up?"

"Well, we're hoping to get even busier in the next few weeks, and we feel that we could take on another member of staff, especially to help out on Friday evenings and at the weekends. They are our particularly busy periods, when your dad ran the figures."

Joel just looked at his mother, wondering where this was going.

"I just wanted to give you a heads up. We're not looking to replace you or anything like that."

Joel, still feeling a bit puzzled, looked back at his mother. "So why do you think we'll be getting busier?"

"A couple of reasons. You know that your Dad and I are good friends of Tim's parents?"

Joel nodded.

"In light of Tim's recent success, we asked them if he would be prepared to do some gigs to try and help promote the place. A minor celebrity like Tim, well, could really help us out and bring in some new customers."

Joel felt a little twinge of jealousy. He had really enjoyed his chance to shine on the little stage in the back room. Once again, Tim would somehow manage to take that away from him.

He thought back to the time a couple of years ago when he, Alan and Tim had all been put in the same music class and had quickly discovered they had musical tastes in common. When their teacher formed them into a group, they had surprised even themselves with how well they had fitted together and got on. Alan played the keyboards, Joel played acoustic or electric guitar and Tim obviously played the saxophone. Joel and Tim could also sing, although Tim at that time was much happier leaving it to Joel. Within a term, the music teacher had them doing a set at the end of term school concert, which they had enjoyed, and then Tim entered the group into a local music competition.

Entering in the 'small modern music group' category, they had certainly surprised a few people with their raw talent and boyish enthusiasm, but when faced with deciding which song to perform in the final, Tim and Joel had ended up scrapping backstage. The short of it was, Tim had insisted on singing the song that he had written, with a fantastic saxophone solo in it, and a strong lead vocal line for himself, whereas Joel was relegated to simple chords and backing vocals. Tim's parents had stepped in, trying to make the decision diplomatically, and with Joel's parents nowhere to be seen, the group ended up choosing a completely different song, though still one that showcased Tim's talents above Joel's. The song wasn't a great success, though they had never expected to win, but Joel was always left wondering what might have been.

Since that day, the trio had only played together sporadically, often on a whim, but Tim had always wanted to progress as a musician in his own right. Joel couldn't help feeling a little jealous that a schoolboy fight could have prevented the group being as stellar as Tim was, especially with his current television exploits.

Alyssa was waiting patiently when Joel looked at her again. She had been made well aware of the scrap that occurred between him and Tim; Joel had never let her live it down. Due to their commitments at Beans and Banter, neither of them had been able to make it to the concert. "Joel, look, I know things with you and Tim haven't been the same for a while now, but I really hope you can put that aside. Our business could soar using the publicity if Tim does decide to help out."

Joel shrugged back at his mother. "Ma, I know Tim and I haven't always got on, but if he's going to help the shop become bigger and better, then that's great."

"How about if I asked if he'd be interested in getting the old trio back together? Would you be willing?"

The last thing Joel wanted to do was open up old wounds. There wasn't a future in music for him and although he had enjoyed the couple of shows he'd done for his parents it wasn't something he wanted to do professionally. He hesitated, weighing all of these things up.

Alyssa looked at the indecision on his face and frowned. "I'll take that as a no then."

Joel sighed. "See what he says. If he wants to, then that's great, it can't hurt. And I'll know I'll be a backing singer. He'll unquestionably be the star this time."

His mother smiled at him, patting him on the arm. "Great. It can't hurt to ask, and if he says no then that's his choice.

"If he does say no, can Alan and I do some performing together?"

"I don't see why not. Looks like this will be your chance to ask him, I'll leave you to it."

As Alyssa slipped away, his best friend replaced her, carrying his laptop under his arm.

"Evening, matey, what's happening?"

"Evening. How do you fancy joining me to become a duo to then feature on the list of acts to perform on the back room stage?"

Alan's eyes widened. "Seriously?"

"Yeah. Ma said that'd be fine."

"Crikey. You bet. That'd be amazing experience."

Joel smiled, not wanting to talk about the Tim idea.

"Did your mum mention about any other acts, or is it just us at this stage?"

Joel looked sternly at his friend. "Like who?"

"Like Tim?" Alan asked innocently.

Joel gave Alan a very hard stare. "That sounds like it was your idea." It was a statement, rather than a question.

Alan suddenly looked awkward. "Well, you know, I just thought..." he said, trailing off.

Joel's face darkened. "Dude, I can't believe you did that! After all the issues with that music festival nonsense; seriously, what were you thinking?"

Alan took a deep breath. "Joel, come on, he's a national star now. Imagine the punters in here if he played, that's some serious money. And who better to be his band? Two college mates. The story writes itself." He noticed Joel was still looking nonplussed. "We haven't got any plans yet for the summer. If it works out for us, we could be touring the country with him. People always want to know who the other members in a band are. And I can't believe you've still got a grudge about that music festival debacle after this much time. Seriously, you need to get over that. Water under the bridge now."

Joel just looked at his best friend, not knowing what to say. He was still annoyed Alan had gone behind his back.

"Listen, we don't even know if he'll have us. But it wouldn't hurt to ask. Imagine touring with him. Imagine the venues, all that attention from girls."

It was at that point that Amie and Hannah appeared at the table.

"What attention from girls?" Amie asked innocently, looking between the two boys.

"Joel and I might have the faintest possibility of touring with Tim this summer," Alan said proudly.

Joel just shot him an irked look. It was bad enough discussing it with Alan, let alone involving other people. Having recalled the music festival incident made him feel bad enough already; he didn't then want to involve other people in pointless speculation.

"And how will that get you attention from girls?" Hannah asked quietly.

"Yeah, how much more attention do you need?" Amie said with a laugh. She pulled her sister towards her. "We're all the attention you can handle," she added, giving Joel a smouldering look.

Joel and Alan shared a glance, neither of them expecting that kind of reaction. Were the girls jealous?

"Oh come on, it's completely different. We'd be famous! Who wouldn't want a piece of us?" Alan remarked.

"Well, if that's how you feel..." Hannah muttered.

Amie meanwhile was busy twirling a finger through her hair, playfully thrusting her chest in Joel's direction. "Well, I'm a little bit offended, Han. I can't believe they want to go around the country, getting off with teenagers in whatever city they're in. Sounds like they don't know how good they have it at home."

Joel and Alan were really baffled at this point. Joel knew that they both got on well with the twins, but he'd never imagined there was anything more than friendship. Did the twins fancy them?

"Oh you two, you should see your faces!" Amie squealed.

Both boys visibly relaxed, Joel breathing a huge sigh of relief.

Deciding to change the subject, Hannah pulled a book out of her bag and laid it on the table.

Joel noticed it immediately. "What's that, Han?"

"It's the latest book from Sir Andrew Anderson," she said, without looking up.

Joel felt a little shiver run down his spine. Why was Sir Andrew Anderson suddenly everywhere?

"Ah yes, it's a bestseller isn't it? Any good?" Alan asked.

Hannah opened the book, leafing through a few pages. "Yeah, I've quite enjoyed reading it to be honest. I'm only halfway through, but he's got some very interesting ideas and views on 'positive readjustment' as he calls it. It's been a good follow-up to the counselling I had after my incident."

"Is there any information on him in that book? Like a biography or anything?" Joel asked.

Hannah gave him a strange look. "There're a few details I suppose. He starts by explaining his passion towards tackling depression and it now being viewed as a global medical issue, rather than just people being miserable. Then he always uses the example of how he couldn't conceive with his wife, and then how she passed away a few months later, leaving him with no family. He was an only child, so he was quite literally on his own growing up. Now he has no children, no wife, nobody. It's enough to make anybody feel a bit glum, to be honest."

"So what's with reading it then, Han?" Alan asked.

"Well, it's been a bestseller, and I saw a news story with him where he spoke about it. The presenters were saying how interesting it was, how it had made an impact on them, so I thought I had nothing to lose by reading it. I've found it to have a few little techniques in it that are quite easy to remember and do actually work."

Joel, meanwhile, was trying to process asking the twins if they were interested in the extra hours available in the shop. He didn't want to cause any awkwardness or competition between the two of them, but then he knew if he didn't ask them they would be offended. Amie, in particular, he knew had asked if there were any hours going previously.

"So my ma was talking earlier about us possibly being busier on Friday evenings and weekends in the next few weeks. She wants to take on another member of staff, and I wondered if either of you would be interested in applying?" Joel looked inquisitively at the two girls, with Alan trying to catch his eye. His best friend was looking at him with a bemused expression. Joel quickly imitated playing the piano, which made Alan understand why Joel wasn't asking him.

Joel noticed both girls' faces light up and they shared one of their looks where they could tell they knew what the other was thinking.

"Look, I can see you're both interested. Have a word with her; she'd be pleased to hear from you. I mean you live just over the road, you pretty much know your way around inside, plus we all know what you're like."

Joel and Alan watched them both head off to find Alyssa in the kitchen.

"Which of them do you reckon will get the nod?" Alan asked.

"If I had to put a few pence on it, then Amie. It's not that I think Hannah would do a lousy job, but Amie would at least put a smile on people's faces." Joel noticed Alan prickle a bit at his comment. "What? Sticking up for Hannah now are we?"

Alan's cheeks reddened. "I just think she deserves a break, you know?

She's clearly having a tough time of it at the minute, what with Tim being away. She used to be quite close to him. Who knows what's going on there. None of us have seen him or heard from him. It must be ten times worse if you're close to him." He paused, looking Joel straight in the eye. "Plus we all know you fancy Amie anyway, so it makes total sense you'd want her to work here."

It was Joel's turn to prickle. "You what?"

"Oh come on! She wants a bit of you too. Did you not see all that boob-thrusting malarkey she was doing earlier?"

Joel looked bewildered. "Boob-thrusting malarkey? What on earth are you blabbering on about?"

"You know, when we were discussing that fantasy tour idea, supporting Tim. Do you reckon Amie was being jealous? Or just pretending?"

Joel thought about it for a few moments. "I didn't notice that much to be honest. I know she can be a bit flirty, but that's just Amie… right?"

Alan gave him another hard look. "Let's just say she isn't like that when she's talking to me."

Joel remained quiet. Could it be true? He'd always liked Amie. But she was a year older than him. It just wasn't the done thing for girls to date younger guys. It hadn't occurred to him that she could like him too.

He looked up again as the girls returned. Both looked reasonably cheerful, which he hadn't expected.

"And?" he asked.

"Meet your new co-workers!" they chorused.

"We start tomorrow evening, just as a trial," Amie added.

Joel was very aware of Alan trying hard to catch his eye. "Wow, that's great, you two. Guess I'll be seeing even more of you than I do already."

"Yeah, and who knows where that's going to lead," Alan muttered under his breath, to no one in particular.

CHAPTER FIVE

Sunday 8th April, morning
Great Bournestone Manor

Sir Andrew opened his office door to welcome in the two people sat outside.

"Hello to you both, and a Happy Easter. I trust Izzy has offered you refreshment?"

They both nodded meekly, showing him their cups, still bewildered as to what they were doing in the office, and at the home, of a well renowned businessman and author such as Sir Andrew Anderson on Easter Sunday.

"Wonderful, wonderful. Right – lets get down to business shall we? Please, have a seat," he said, gesturing at the chairs in front of his desk.

Sir Andrew took a deep breath and sat down as well, leaning back in his chair, hands steepled beneath his chin.

"Mr and Mrs Pointer, I want to offer your son, Timothy, the chance to perform as the opening act on my upcoming tour."

He tried to keep a straight face while they processed the news he had just given them.

"Oh my word, that's… so… unexpected!" Mrs Pointer exclaimed.

Mr Pointer, a little more reserved Sir Andrew noted, was smiling pleasantly, clearly trying to keep his cool in front of a person of Sir Andrew's standing. He gave Sir Andrew an apologetic look while his wife was practically on the verge of tears.

"Hold it together, Olivia darling," Mr Pointer whispered, glancing over at Sir Andrew, who was brushing down his suit, trying not to intrude in their moment. "We're keeping this busy man occupied."

"Yes, Sam, OK," Olivia Pointer sniffed. "Sorry," she said towards Sir Andrew.

"Not at all, I can understand what you must be feeling. Is this the first engagement that your son has been offered?"

He noticed them look a little uncomfortable and waited patiently for an answer.

"He's had an offer from friends of ours to play in their coffee shop on a regular basis, but this is the first tour as such," Olivia proffered eventually.

"Hmmm… That does surprise me. I'd have thought somebody would have snapped him up by now. He quite obviously has some talent."

"I imagine people would wait to see the outcome of the final tonight before making any offers. A Talent UK winner would be more attractive than a Talent UK finalist," Sam Pointer pointed out. "He may have got to the final, but we don't know if he stands a chance of actually winning."

"We're trying to not get our hopes up too much," Olivia added.

"Understandably so. In which case I'm glad I'm first in the queue, as it were. I just wanted to explain a little bit about my vision for this tour, so you can be assured what I'm planning on doing will fit in with your own vision for Timothy."

He waited for them to nod before he continued. "As I said, I would like him to open for me. It's about thirty minutes he would need to play for, every evening. I have a list of tour dates here," he said, passing them a list. "I don't really want him to have to play anything specific. The pieces I've heard so far would be perfect in my eyes. The soulful, purposefully mournful tracks and the uplifting, awe-inspiring tracks are the ones I'm after. I don't know whether you know what my tours are about?"

Olivia was looking at him, as if she was fit to burst. "You're the depression mogul! I actually have your latest book here in my bag." She bent down, scrabbling at her feet.

Sam looked helplessly at Sir Andrew, whose blue eyes twinkled back at him. Sir Andrew was reminded of the times that Dorothy had met other famous writers whose books she carried about with her wherever she went, with that awkward moment where he was left looking at the author, whilst his wife was rummaging in her bag.

Olivia proceeded to offer him a slightly tatty, well-thumbed version of his latest book. She was still wittering about it being such a wonderful book that had reached into her soul and made her see things from a completely different perspective, prompting helpless looks from her husband, and a wry smile from himself.

She's just excited; don't be callous, he told himself sternly.

Picking up the book, he opened the front cover. "Is there anything you would like in here specifically, Mrs Pointer?"

"Well, n-no, not r-really," she said with a stammer. "Just something nice."

Smiling, Sir Andrew picked up his fountain pen. After writing his message and signing the inside of the cover with his usual flourish, he scratched at his beard.

"So, we've established that I'm the 'depression mogul', as you put it, Mrs Pointer. Do you know how the tours work?" He handed the book back and looked at the Pointers to see them shake their heads. "Well, they're more like a workshop to be honest, but due to their popularity, my team and I have moved out into theatres now. We're talking audiences of five hundred to a thousand possibly at the larger end. The last tour worked in that sort of format, so if it isn't broken, I don't see why I should fix it."

He paused, checking that they were still with him.

"I want Tim to be the precursor to the whole experience. I want his music to flow through everybody there, to touch every corner of their souls, to find parts of themselves that they never knew they had. I believe he does this quite naturally, but from what I understand, he has certainly gripped the Saturday evening television watching public with his melodies. As far as I'm concerned, they're the demographic I'm trying to reach with my books: Joe Public and family. Having Tim there would set everybody up for having an enlightened emotional experience. Thoughts?"

Sam was the first to respond after several moments of deep thought. "It's certainly a generous offer, sir. We only have Tim's best interests at heart. The exposure for him to be part of such an amazing opportunity would certainly do wonders for him as a musician. All we believe that he's wanted, ever since he first picked up a saxophone, was to be an artist with his album in people's homes. This could certainly be great for him and get his name known in the world."

Sir Andrew frowned and fixed Tim's father with a piercing stare. He reminded himself that Izzy referred to the stare as if he was switching his headlights on so he tried not to give Sam full beam just yet. "I sense some hesitancy on your part, though, Sam."

Olivia put a hand on her husband's knee. "We'd just like to run this by Tim. It seems a bit unfair making all these decisions on his behalf. We haven't seen him for a few weeks with all of his rehearsing. We only occasionally get to speak to him on the phone. We don't exactly know if he's got anything planned for the next couple of months. He might be expected to tour with the show or something." She shrugged. "I hope you understand."

"Of course, of course. This wasn't an ultimatum. It was merely an offer. I just feel Tim could make a real difference to my tour." He patted his desk and stood up. "Please, my phone is on my desk, feel free to give him a call. I'll wait outside. If you need anything, please just press the 'page' button on the phone and Izzy will answer. Now can I get you refills?"

They both nodded and told him their preferences. Sir Andrew picked up their cups and left his office.

Izzy looked up from her computer screen as he shut the door quietly behind him.

"Problem?"

"No, just discussing. I think they're on board."

"Excellent. Do you think it'll happen?" She went back to looking at her computer screen and began typing.

"I hope so, I really do. Tim Pointer could certainly give this tour something… I don't know. Extra?"

"I totally agree, sir. He's not bad looking either, if I'm allowed to say."

Sir Andrew looked surprised. "Isabella? Is that you in there?"

She frowned back at him. "Yes, sir, it is."

"I see. I'm just not used to hearing you express opinions about the opposite sex, I suppose."

"I don't have opinions very often, sir."

"It's fine by me, Izzy. I'm not complaining."

"Lets just say I'll be looking forward to meeting him."

"I'm optimistic you will. And all being well you'll have the tour to get to know him better. I'm now beginning to wonder if I can include him and his music in my actual workshop."

"I understand, sir, I do," Izzy replied, tapping away now on her keyboard. "What other self-help workshop oligarch would have a national television icon as part of his act? It's that sort of thinking that's kept you on top all these years."

Sir Andrew smiled to himself. Izzy wasn't wrong; he had been at the top for a long time. There was still work to do, however. Tim hadn't signed up to anything yet.

CHAPTER SIX

"Hi, Tim," the backstage helper said cheerily. She was a short, stout girl in her late teens with a big heart and a big personality. Her name badge introduced her as Beatrice Smith.

Tim was sat on a packing box, staring into the middle distance, trying to concentrate on his performance later. He was tapping away on his saxophone case, lost in the moment, until Beatrice had woken him out of his reverie.

He smiled awkwardly at her for a few moments, not having a clue what to say. In the end, he gave a helpless shrug and turned his gaze to the floor. Beatrice, who he had seen a lot over the past few weeks, shrugged back at him and headed off down the corridor. Tim wondered if she had developed a soft spot for him over the past few weeks, but their conversations never went very far.

He had always found it difficult to step out of his comfort zone. He wasn't one for approaching people. He wasn't even one for being approached. He had mostly got through school so far by pretending he was invisible, barely speaking to anybody, except when he was spoken to. It had dawned on him recently that he preferred to let his music to do the talking. Sure, he had his small group of friends, but he often wondered what on earth they saw in him. Even Hannah, who he had kept in touch with a lot via text when he was in Huntingham, hadn't messaged him in a while. He'd been so busy trying to write and arrange his own music in his room at the Talent UK headquarters, he barely had time to start a conversation with the other contestants let alone anyone else. He spoke to his parents only occasionally.

Even when he was sat in Beans and Banter, he was often staring into space, listening to the songs playing in the background and imagining how he could form them into saxophone pieces. Indeed, it was one of those evenings when the topic of Talent UK came up and the first seeds were sown. And how he had ended up sat on the packing box.

He let out a sigh. Even when a fairly attractive girl like Beatrice wandered his way he could only smile awkwardly. What kind of girl would ever want to be around him? It never crossed his mind to think that Hannah could be that girl. She had always been a friend to him, nothing more.

Looking up at the ceiling and shaking his head regretfully, he pondered his song choices for the final. He had been required to choose an interpretation of a well-known performance and then a free choice. He'd gone with Queen's 'Bohemian Rhapsody' as his interpretation piece. It was a song close to his heart, being one of the first songs that he could remember as a child. His parents were both huge Queen fans. It had been the only choice from the moment the show's producer announced the categories for the final. His dad had helped him with choosing the date of the well-known performance. Sam and Olivia Pointer had been at one of the July concerts at Wembley Stadium in 1986, where they had actually met, and they had often recalled seeing Freddie doing press ups on stage after the final notes. Being an only child and having since watched the DVD of the concert, he wanted to pay tribute to his parents in some way. He couldn't think of any greater acknowledgement than his own interpretation of one of the greatest songs of all time.

His free choice was his own interpretation of Gerry Rafferty's 'Baker Street'; a song already well known due to its infectious saxophone riff. He had kept faithful to the original, but had replaced the vocal line with his own musical style, giving him full freedom to express himself. It had proved a winner with the judges early on in the competition, and after coming off stage that night, Tim felt it was the first time they had really taken him seriously as a competitor. It was a no-brainer to use the song as his free choice.

Deep down, Tim knew he had what it took to win the competition outright. He had continued to improve week on week, winning the continuing praise of the judges, whilst remaining there or thereabouts in the public votes. He'd never been in the bottom three throughout the previous five weeks, but consequently hadn't ever topped the public vote. In some ways, he felt that was probably a good thing. He wasn't an outright favourite, and therefore, in his eyes, he was under no pressure to win.

He'd already surpassed his expectations in many ways. Getting to the final in itself was fantastic, in terms of life experience and performance experience; the emotional ups and downs along the way perhaps not so.

***

"Tim Pointer?" called one of the floor managers, who had appeared from the rehearsal studio looking rather flustered.

"Here," the boy replied, grabbing his case.

"Tim, great to see you, how's things?" the manager asked when Tim reached the studio doors, not really caring for an answer.

Tim shrugged. "Fine, I guess. Few butterflies more than anything."

The manager mumbled something disinterestedly; he didn't want to get involved too much with these pampered pop stars. Although Tim had always been polite to him, he had to admit. The previous group, the outright favourites, an electrical string group called Zing, were the fussiest, most stuck-up wannabe celebrities he'd ever met. They had even started making dressing room requests in the last couple of weeks, which, of course, had to be his responsibility to sort out. Dressing room requests! A few weeks of fame, winning several hundred thousand votes in the process and suddenly they could swan about like they were royalty. It put a bitter taste in his mouth. Ordinary folk like Tim he could stomach. All the lad wanted to do was play his saxophone to people who wanted to listen. His wife at home was a big fan of Tim's, always wanting to know if he'd bumped into the teenager and what he was like backstage.

Once Tim was in the studio and had assembled his saxophone, the manager took a deep breath and gave him a pat on the back. Tim turned around in surprise.

"If I don't see you before, all the best for the final, mate. My wife, Jenny, she's rooting for you."

The boy looked like he had no idea what to say, possibly taken aback by the kindness a virtual stranger was showing him.

"Thanks…" he tailed off, looking for the manager's name badge, "…Cliff. That means a lot to me. I won't let her down." He gave Cliff a broken smile.

"Good lad," Cliff mumbled under his breath. "I hope the rest of the country is rooting for you too."

***

"Tim, come over here, my favourite saxophonist. How's this fine Sunday treating you?" asked the woman stood next to the piano. She was dressed more casually than Tim was used to, just in jeans and a brightly coloured top, though still showing more cleavage than was strictly necessary. A trademark of hers, Tim realised. Her long black hair was tied back in a loose ponytail, and she had barely any make up on. Tim had rarely seen her looking so ordinary. Fast forward a few hours, and her entire appearance would be transformed, Tim was sure of that.

This was one of the judges and the brains behind the show, Topaz Carminati. Tim was a little surprised to see her, as she had never been seen at any of his previous rehearsals. Having said that, this was the last practice before the final, and he supposed she had to guarantee outstanding performances. It was Easter Sunday; millions of people would be watching.

Tim didn't get the opportunity to reply before she was talking again.

"I'm sure you're thinking what on earth I'm doing here. Well, I'm only checking up on all the acts to make sure everybody is in tip top form for tonight." She flashed a beaming smile.

Tim nodded.

"How's your preparation been? Any issues?" she asked, looking concerned.

Tim waited a few seconds before replying, just to see if she jumped in again. "No, not really. Just a few nerves."

"Ah, nerves. Our faithful friend. A blessing and a curse."

Tim shrugged.

"So, what delightful pieces are you going to be amazing the world with tonight, Tim?"

Tim mentioned the two songs he'd chosen, causing the pianist to smile; they had enjoyed working together on the original performance of 'Baker Street'.

Topaz gave the pianist a stern look before she turned her attention back to Tim. "Well, you've made some great choices. Think you can pull them off?"

"No problem." Tim almost surprised himself with the confident response. It had come from a place deep within. The same place that was telling him he could win tonight.

"That's great, Tim. Shall we run through them now? I'm just letting you know I've got some ambience wired up, just to give you a feel for the background noise tonight. Just so you're not too shocked. It's always louder than you think."

"OK, can we start with 'Bohemian Rhapsody'?" A nod came from the pianist. Tim fiddled with the mouthpiece on his saxophone, composing himself. He closed his eyes, trying to imagine standing on stage, preparing to play his pieces. The country would be watching his every movement. He swallowed. His heart felt like it was trying to escape his chest. His nerves sure felt more like a curse than a blessing right now. Topaz then switched the ambience on, which made his heart beat a little faster. He took a deep breath, and began.

He was into the first few bars of the song when he felt the buzz of his mobile phone in his pocket. Frowning, he fished it out, not used to getting calls during the day or recognising the number. Had something happened to his parents? He held up a hand of apology to Topaz, who looked less than amused. Tim rushed out into the corridor, confusion and worry clouding his face.

"Hello?"

"Hello? Tim?"

"Dad? What's up?" he hissed. "I'm in rehearsal." He looked awkwardly over his shoulder, thankful that the doors were firmly shut.

"We figured that, but something urgent has come up, otherwise we wouldn't have bothered calling."

"Where are you guys? This isn't your regular number. Is Mum OK?"

"She's fine. It's Sir Andrew Anderson's number. He's asked if you'd join his tour as a warm up act."

Tim fell silent. That had been a bit unexpected.

"Tim? You still there?"

"Yes, I'm still here," Tim responded quietly.

"Well, will you do it?"

Tim sighed. He felt honoured to be asked to do a tour already, without the competition even being concluded yet. So why was he hesitating? His parents had let him know about doing the small gigs in Beans and Banter, which were fine, but a whole tour?

"Can I fit it all in?" he asked.

There was a rustle at the other end. "I've got the tour dates here. It doesn't start for a couple of months, and it's only a short slot. Thirty minutes or so. The venues look like town theatres mostly, not arenas or anything like you'd be playing tonight. But Sir Andrew says there's usually a minimum of five hundred people. It'd be a bit more intimate than the sort of thing you're doing at the minute."

"OK, well, if you guys think that this would be good for me, then I don't see why not?"

There was a pause on the line.

"Dad? Did you get that?"

"Yes, son, we just hadn't really discussed if we thought it would be good for you. Is it something you want to do? Did you want a music career for example? If so, this would be unbelievable experience for you."

Tim was silent for a few moments. It was true that his saxophone had been his passion for as long as he could remember. He had often told his parents of his dream of having an album on people's coffee tables. But so far, he didn't have any plans for the summer and if it meant he got to travel the country and play his saxophone at the same time, then that would be fantastic. But then, he hadn't enjoyed being on his own quite so much during the last few weeks. He had wondered if the loneliness was starting to play on his mind a bit and he was beginning to retreat further and further into his self-created virtual shell. Could he handle a whole summer of it?

"Sorry, son, I know you're processing, or whatever you call it. Do you need some more time to think about it?"

"No, Dad, I've got nothing to lose. Sign me up. I know you've got my best interests at heart. If you think this is a good move for me, I trust your judgement."

"Thanks, son. I'll let you know some details as soon as we have them. Right, you get back to your rehearsal. Speak to you later."

"Bye, Dad." His phone then bleeped to say the call had ended.

He didn't really have time to process it all. Not without knowing a few more facts. He had a final to rehearse for.

He headed back into the studio, coming face to face with an angry-looking Topaz.

"And what was so important that you had to waste precious minutes of my time?" she asked, a furious glare etched across her face. "There's a reason, you know, why we put a blackout on outside communication while you're a participant on this show. It's to stop moments like this from happening."

There was something about her demeanour that made Tim not want to mention that he'd been offered the opportunity to do a tour. "Sorry, I thought something had happened to my parents. They would be the only people who would ring like that," he replied, not looking directly at her.

Her look darkened further. "Well, if they need to speak to you again before the end of this rehearsal, then you can let them go through to your answerphone. Clear?"

Tim nodded and put his saxophone to his mouth, his mind wandering towards standing on a small stage somewhere, doing the only thing that made him feel truly alive.

CHAPTER SEVEN

Sunday 8th April, early evening
Beans and Banter

With the final of Talent UK being on, the coffee shop was busier than normal for a Sunday evening, meaning the twins were both kept busy clearing cups and plates from tables, and providing an *ad hoc* waitressing service, due to everyone's attention being glued to the big screen. It was the perfect experience for them to see what working in a busy coffee shop would be like.

Both were being given a few shifts to see how they did, with a view to only taking one of them on. Joel had an inkling that Amie would take to it better than Hannah would, Amie being the social butterfly that she was. He noticed that particularly the older male customers were talking to her a lot of the time while she was on the shop floor, whereas Hannah was just flitting in and out of the tables, barely being noticed. However, it did mean that Hannah got more work done, clearing tables with a minimum of fuss. It was a toss up between the two, and Joel was, secretly, quite glad that he wouldn't have to make a decision.

Joel found he was based in the kitchen that evening, in charge of the oven and the sink. The group had even had to give up on their regular table, such was the crowd in there. It meant Alan found himself in the kitchen too, sat looking out of the kitchen hatch at the giant screen, engrossed by the Talent UK final.

Joel's parents were being kept busy behind the counter, quietly pleased at how popular the venue was proving, bearing in mind it was Easter Sunday, no less. The big screen television was definitely the main source of interest, though.

When it was time for Tim's first performance, a great cheer went up in the shop, quickly turning to silence, punctuated by the hum of the oven. Joel put his tea towel down and went to join Alan at the kitchen hatch. He hated to admit it, but he wanted Tim to put in a good performance, and wished he'd had that feeling earlier so he could have messaged him.

A few minutes later, with Tim looking rather relieved and more relaxed than when he started, the judges and the crowd in the studio were all cheering him. There were even a few punters in the shop standing on their feet and applauding him, which bemused Joel. It had been a brilliant performance with Tim's trademark heart-wrenching melody accompanied by the famous 'Baker Street' riff. The comments he received from the judges were also extremely positive and Tim left the stage, waving to the audience and a beaming smile across his face.

All the hype in the media, though, had been about the string quartet, Zing. They were next on after Tim, and another hush fell over the crowd in Beans and Banter following the introduction on the screen.

The image on the big screen went dark, and a deep rumble came through the speakers, which Joel realised after a few seconds was the lowest note on the cello. With that auspicious start, suddenly there were bright flashes and coloured lights everywhere as Zing burst into their rendition of 'Hall of the Mountain King'. It was a totally jaw-dropping performance, and Joel felt a little light-headed when it came to an end. Alan next to him looked similarly stunned.

Amie and Hannah then popped their heads through the hatch.

"Hey, you two," Amie said. "What did you two musicians make of *that*?"

"Tim better up his game for his next song," Joel said once he'd recovered. "I mean, Tim was great, but Zing were just… they were something else. They're going to be hard to beat."

"Totally… Wow. They were unbelievable!" Alan responded, his eyes wide in disbelief.

"I thought Tim showed a lot of potential, though," Amie said, to which Hannah nodded. "I mean, he's shown his versatility throughout the whole show, he just doesn't have the set to have the same sort of effect Zing did."

"I see what you mean," Joel replied. "He's got far more individual skill than the four of them in Zing put together."

"It's just whether the public see that or if they get blown away by all the special effects with Zing," Alan added.

"Totally. But think of it this way, whose album would you rather have at home?" Amie asked.

"Tim's," both boys said unanimously.

"I agree," Hannah added quietly. "But this isn't a competition to see who can get an album in people's homes. It's a competition to win Talent UK. And Zing's performance is just a step above Tim's at the moment."

They all fell silent at that. Tim would probably last longer in the music business overall, but they couldn't argue with Hannah's logic.

Alyssa Wright then appeared in the kitchen carrying several packets of bacon, looking a little flustered. "Right then, boys and girls, wash your hands, if you haven't already, and prepare to get busy. Amie and Hannah, can you go and wait on the tables again please? Joel, can you get this bacon grilled please? I'll start buttering rolls."

"Bacon rolls, Ma?"

"You bet. Pass me those rolls please, Alan; they're right by you."

Alan duly obliged and even offered to help out, which Alyssa was extremely grateful for.

"Joel, when the bacon is ready, start stuffing them in these rolls, a couple of slices in each please. Alan, you keep buttering. I'll go and wash some plates up. I want the girls to go around the tables and sell them at a pound per roll."

Joel's dad now had a queue at the counter, furiously trying to manage the till and coffee machine at the same time. Joel was pleased that they were so busy, and was also glad the girls happened to be there too. Their trial shifts couldn't have started on a better day.

For the next half an hour or so, they were all working furiously, until everybody had their refills, and most of the bacon rolls had been snapped up too. Joel, dripping with sweat, having been working next to the oven, was relieved to have a rest. Alyssa thanked Alan for his help too, slipping him a twenty-pound note from the till. A lull fell on the shop again, as the crowd settled down to watch Tim's second performance.

Amie and Hannah joined the boys again in the kitchen. Joel noticed how closely Hannah was watching Tim on the screen. They were showing the highlights of his time on the show, and kept cutting to where he was standing now, looking increasingly nervous. There must still be some sort of feelings for him, Joel thought. He saw her then mutter something under her breath.

"What was that, Han?" he asked, causing everybody in the kitchen to look around at her.

Hannah looked a bit startled. "Nothing. Nothing at all," she replied hurriedly.

Amie frowned at her sister. She had been getting increasingly frustrated with Hannah recently, who had been saying quite a bit under her breath at home when she was asked a question. Then, when probed about it, she refused to reveal what she had said. It served to wind Amie up even further.

"Han," she snapped, "why do you do this? Just tell us what you said!"

Joel and Alan looked at each other, sensing a French sister stand-off. It all became irrelevant a few moments later when a loud gasp went up in the shop, and confusion reigned. Joel realised everybody was looking at the screen.

The show's host was about to interview Tim, in the wings of the Talent UK studio, but Tim just didn't seem to be there. Every time a question was asked, he stared at the host blankly, seemingly unable to reply. He appeared to be rigid, frozen like a statue. His saxophone hung limply around his neck, his arms by his side.

"Guys, look at Tim. Something's wrong," Joel said, pointing at the screen.

They all watched as the host put a hand on Tim's shoulder with an expression that turned to horror as the teenager crumpled to the floor at his feet.

The camera cut to the host looking rather panicked and even Topaz in the background of the shot was looking concerned. The show then cut to adverts.

Amie, who had been glaring angrily at her sister, seized the initiative and headed out of the kitchen, grabbing her note pad on the way out. Hannah's only reaction was to stare at her feet.

Alan was the first to break the silence, putting a hand on Hannah's shoulder. "Hey."

Hannah reached up and grabbed his hand, but continued to look at the floor.

It was only then that Joel noticed the tears making tracks down Hannah's face. Not wanting to get in the way, he went to help his parents behind the counter.

"Hannah, come on, it's not that bad," said Alan, trying to be reassuring, but looking increasingly nervous.

At that point, Hannah did then turn to face him. "How do you know?" she whispered, her tone angry. "How can you stand there and tell me it's not that bad? You can't possibly know whether it's bad or not!"

"It's true. I don't. But these things have a way of sorting them out. I've experienced it myself."

Hannah snorted. "You have no idea what I'm going through."

Alan looked at her imploringly. "So tell me. Tell Amie. Tell *someone*."

Hannah took a deep breath. "But… but it's so… silly! I've got no need to feel like this, or act like this."

"Come on, Han, there must be something deep down that's causing you to be like this. Not just a fight with your sister."

Hannah's hands were clenched into fists. "I just feel like I should be able to handle this on my own. I've had so much counselling after my suicide attempt last year, but things still get to me. I hate it. I absolutely hate it!" She slammed her fists on the counter top making a loud bang.

This caused Hannah to break down even more, and she turned around to press her face into Alan's chest. Alan naturally put his arms around her, and rested his chin on her shoulder, while she tried to get her sobs under control.

Joel meanwhile, was stood behind the counter, working the coffee machine, trying to keep an eye on Amie as she went round. The encounter with her sister didn't seem to have affected her; she was smiling at and joking with the customers as she took orders. Joel noticed her frequently pointing at the screen and shrugging.

"Hey, son, keep an eye on what you're doing."

Joel realised he'd spilt coffee grounds on the floor, which his father had spotted.

"Sorry, Pops," Joel mumbled.

"Got your mind on the girl, hey?" Joel turned to face his dad who was trying to hide a smile.

"No… I was just thinking about Tim. I wonder what's happened. Amie couldn't figure it out either, but I think she thinks that Hannah knows something."

"Wish I hadn't asked," his dad said, with a chuckle. "Any ideas what could have happened to Tim?"

"None. He just didn't look right before he ended up on the floor. It's really strange."

"You're right, son. That's not the Tim we know. It's like his mind wasn't connected to his body."

There was a hush again in the shop as the TV returned to the Talent UK studio. Topaz was stood in the middle of the stage alongside the host, who looked a bit annoyed at not being the centre of attention.

"Apologies for the unexpected ad break to all you television viewers. Just to give you a bit of an update, Tim Pointer has been taken to hospital, due to falling ill, so he will no longer be able to perform his second track. However, we will still be counting his votes. If any viewers have been affected by the scenes you've seen this evening, please make note of the telephone number across the bottom of the screen."

Joel snorted. "We could all see he had fallen ill; we just don't know what's wrong with him."

"Well at least he's not been disqualified or anything. We can still vote for him," Amie said, having appeared at the counter.

"We wish Tim a speedy recovery, he's in the best medical hands now and we look forward to having him back on the show when he's better," Topaz continued from the screen. "And now, can I make it my greatest pleasure to introduce…"

Joel turned away from the screen, and noticed Alan and Hannah had been watching from the hatch. "None the wiser really, are we?"

Alan shook his head, while Hannah, who was looking a bit calmer, just shrugged.

They were all feeling a bit helpless and wondering if they could have been better friends to Tim, even from a distance, while he had been with Talent UK.

CHAPTER EIGHT

Monday 9th April, mid-morning
Southwick Park Hospital

Tim was aware that he could hear voices. He thought it sounded like his parents, but he wasn't sure how that could have happened. He realised there were a few unexplained things happening. There was a regular bleeping noise and the smell of chemicals; was he in a hospital? His eyes took a few seconds to focus and the worried face of his mother greeted him.

"Tim? Tim! Are you alright?" She reached out and grabbed his arm, squeezing it until he winced.

He nodded. He tried to speak, but realised his throat was dry and scratchy, so could only make a hoarse 'wha' sound.

"It's alright, Tim, you relax," his mother reassured him, stroking his face. "You've been under an awful lot of stress recently and the doctors have said your brain was in some sort of stupor state."

Tim pulled a confused expression. He really had no idea what was going on and hoped his face was conveying that, particularly as his voice couldn't.

"You've been here for about twelve hours or so," Olivia Pointer said reluctantly, noticing her son's eyes widen in shock. She looked helplessly at Sam, who shrugged.

"I'll go and tell someone he's awake," Tim's dad muttered, leaving the room.

Tim noticed his mother looking at him, her eyes swimming with tears. He slowly reached out his arm and grabbed his mother's hand. Tim gave it the biggest squeeze he could, trying to convey that he appreciated her being there.

Olivia Pointer sniffed and offered a weak smile. "It's alright, Timmy, I'm just glad to see you're still with us. We've been very worried about you."

Tim reached out his arms and his mother gingerly gave him a hug. She had called him 'Timmy' a lot when he was a baby, and she usually called him that when she was at her most emotional.

Tim's dad then returned, a strapping young Indian doctor in tow, who seemed to have a permanent toothy grin. It made Tim feel slightly uncomfortable bearing in mind his current state.

"Hello, Tim. Nice to meet you, I'm Dr Sanjay," the doctor said, with a strong Cockney accent, which Tim hadn't expected. "You were admitted Sunday evening at about eight thirty." The doctor paused for a few seconds, waiting to see if Tim gave a reaction.

Tim nodded, this being nothing new. He just wanted to know what had happened to him.

"You've been in what appears to be a stupor state since yesterday evening," Dr Sanjay continued. "What's caused this hasn't been established as yet; we're running tests to see if we can find out any details. We may also need to refer you to a psychiatrist as you don't go into a stupor for no reason."

Tim, still feeling completely bewildered, just stared back at the doctor, who flashed a brilliant white smile back at him.

"Try not to worry, I understand you're a bit confused as to what's going on. We've got you well monitored, your vitals appear normal, and we'll see if we can get to the bottom of what caused this."

Tim nodded.

"I just need to ask you a few questions to build a complete picture. Your parents have filled in a lot of the details for me, age, profession, et cetera," Dr Sanjay added, unclipping the clipboard from the bottom of Tim's bed. "Can you tell me what date New Year's Day is?"

"1st January," Tim replied automatically, not recognising his own voice.

"Good, good. How about Bonfire Night?"

Tim had to think a bit harder about that one, before it popped into his brain. "5th November," he said with relief.

"OK, now for the difficult one. Can you tell me the last thing that you remember?"

Tim tried to get his mind to recall what he'd been doing yesterday evening. His head felt like it had been stuffed with cotton wool. He was sure he had a memory, but it was just on the fringes of his mind; it was like looking into a muddy pond and struggling to see his reflection.

"Don't worry if you can't tell me, I can see you're thinking about it," Dr Sanjay said, writing on the clipboard.

Tim tried to get the memory to focus, but his mind just wasn't clearing at all. He shook his head, trying to stem the sense of panic that was growing in his stomach.

"No? Not to worry, Tim, it'll all come clear in good time. Now, the important thing is to rest. Sleep is a wonderful healer."

As the doctor left the room, Tim's father followed him out, which served to confuse Tim; what else was there that his father could possibly ask? Why couldn't it have been said in front of him?

"It's good to have you back, son," Olivia Pointer said, giving Tim another hug, a bit stronger this time.

"Thanks…" Tim replied gruffly, his voice still sounding different to normal. Not sounding like he was used to was starting to unsettle him.

Olivia sensed he wasn't quite up to talking much. "Don't worry, Tim, just listen."

Tim nodded.

"We'll get to the bottom of this. You've been under an enormous amount of stress in the past few weeks. We are all only speculating as to what happened at the minute. The doctor said they are running tests, to see if there's anything showing up that shouldn't be." She reached out and grabbed his hand. "If there's anything going on, please tell someone. It doesn't even have to be your dad or me. But you don't go through an episode like you did yesterday without something being wrong somewhere. Can you think of anything?"

Tim gave her a puzzled look and was about to say something when his father came back into the room and handed him a plastic cup of water.

"Here," he said, offering the cup to Tim. "I thought this might help your throat."

Tim took a gulp of water, swilling it around his mouth before swallowing. It refreshed him and his throat did feel a little better.

"What did I miss?" Sam asked.

"I was telling Tim he needed to tell someone if something was wrong and then you came back in, dear," Olivia said, frowning. "He was just about to say something as well."

They both turned towards Tim, who took another gulp of water before he spoke. "I was just going to ask if you could tell me what happened."

"You really have no idea, do you," Sam stated.

"No," Tim said, still sounding hoarse, but feeling less scratchy now. "I feel like I have the ability to remember. I just can't put it into words. Does that make sense?"

Sam Pointer put his hand on Tim's shoulder, and gave him a strained smile. "Not really, son, no."

Tim could feel something inside him begin to tense. "You don't believe me?"

Sam looked away. "I didn't mean it like that, Tim, I just don't really understand what's going on. I… *We* want you to be alright. You're special to us, incredibly special, and it's killing us to see you like this."

Olivia had been sitting on the chair by Tim's bed, watching the exchange between father and son play out. She could sense Tim becoming frustrated. She and Sam had agreed to not say anything about the Talent UK final, unless Tim brought it up. Seeing how irate he was getting, not knowing what had happened or why he was here, she decided to be proactive.

"Timmy, honey, relax. It's hard because we don't have any answers. All we do know is that you were taken ill backstage at the Talent UK final." She paused a few seconds to see how he took it.

Tim's mind suddenly flooded itself with memories. He could remember being on stage at Talent UK and even being backstage. But it still didn't explain to him how he had ended up in hospital.

"Did that help, son?" Olivia asked.

Tim's face told her that something had been shaken loose. It didn't really prepare her for his next question, however.

"Did I win?" Tim asked, his voice coming over all scratchy again.

He could tell from the reaction of his parents that he hadn't. Both of their shoulders had slumped.

"Was it close?"

His mother spoke up first. "We didn't know if the public were voting for you out of pity or whether they liked you…"

"But Zing won overall. By about four hundred votes," his father continued.

"It was the closest competition in years, apparently," Olivia added.

Tim sighed. Like that was any consolation. "I only remember playing 'Baker Street'; did I not get to perform 'Bohemian Rhapsody'?"

"No, son," Olivia said sadly. "You were taken ill before you got on stage. They were trying to interview you and you just didn't respond."

Tim frowned. "What do you mean I didn't respond?"

"Well, you were being interviewed, but you didn't answer any questions, you just weren't there in spirit."

Tim tried to rack his brain to see if he could remember that, but he was coming up blank. He then realised something. "You mean that got shown on TV?"

His parents looked uncomfortable again.

"Great. So what happened then?"

"We were watching the show at home with your sister, so we went to Mrs Arnold next door to see if she could have Alice to stay, and then got straight in the car and headed down here," Olivia said.

"Your mother had a call from the show while we were in the car to let us know you were at Southwick Park," Sam continued. "We've been here since then, waiting for you to wake up."

Tim was now feeling awash with emotions and wondered if he would have been better off not knowing what had happened to him. He then saw his parents share a look and knew they were going to let him know something with him that they, so far, had been withholding. He waited a few seconds, but was being kept waiting. He was starting to feel anger bubbling in his stomach, to add to the maelstrom of other emotions already flooding his system.

"Mum, Dad, please. Just say it, whatever it is. I've had enough revelations today to last a lifetime."

His dad took a deep breath. "Well, having spoken about this at length," he said, holding up his hands in surrender, "we both feel that this tour that you wanted to go on might be best put on a back burner."

Tim could feel his heart pounding in his chest. It felt like the walls were closing in. The bubbling in his stomach began to get more towards boiling point. "No…" he whispered.

"Tim, after all you've been through, all the pressure you've been under for the show, this then happens. How can you expect us to be happy for you to tour the country?" Olivia responded.

"Mum, it's a different sort of pressure I'll be under! I'll be able to enjoy myself on the tour."

"You mean you hadn't been enjoying the show?"

Tim paused to think about it. "No," he said carefully. "There was the pressure of winning. There were all the hours I had to put in practising. There was being cut off from the outside world. There was losing contact with my friends. No, I didn't enjoy doing the show."

"Why didn't you tell us?"

"Because I thought you'd be disappointed in me! I wanted to prove to you that I could do it, and prove how good I am at playing the saxophone." Tim looked at both of his parents, who were looking rather awkward. "I just wanted to make you proud." He stared defiantly at them both.

"Oh, Tim," his mother sighed. "We are so very proud of you. When you told us you were applying for Talent UK we were a little bit taken aback as you'd never done anything on a wider scale than Huntingham before. But then you made it through to the finals and we could see how much belief you had in your playing and how other people reacted to it. Don't ever think we aren't proud of you, because we are."

"And I think I've earned the right to perform on this tour. The only real happiness I've felt in the last few months was when I was playing and seeing the crowd responding to me. I'd never felt more alive." Tim folded his arms across his chest in determined fashion. He could see his parents were both reconsidering their stance.

"OK, Tim, we'll think about it some more. We don't need to make any snap decisions now. Lets get you better, see if anything can be done to make sure this doesn't happen again and make a decision then," Sam said.

Olivia nodded her agreement. "We'll give Sir Andrew a call today and let him know how you're doing. You never know, he might not want you to do the tour if he thinks you're not up to it."

Tim gave his mother the sternest glare he could muster, trying to make her feel a stab of guilt again.

"I didn't mean that he won't want you, but if he thinks the tour would do more damage than good, he's hardly going to agree to it," Olivia added hastily. "He's a doctor after all. And a psychology specialist."

"Right…" Tim said slowly. "But if he thinks it's fine then I can go?"

His parents shared a look. "We'd like some assurances from him, but yes. There would be no reason why we wouldn't let you pursue your dream," Sam said.

Tim was feeling a bit calmer now and realised he was exhausted. The last few minutes had made him realise how fragile he actually was and he leant back on the bed and drifted off as the tiredness hit him like a wave.

CHAPTER NINE

Joel passed his mother on the way down the stairs at the back of the shop.

"Morning, sunshine. What time do you call this?"

Joel looked a bit sheepishly at his mum. "I've not been asleep all this time, Ma. I've been doing some reading," he said, pointing at his laptop tucked under his arm.

"College work?"

"Mostly. Been catching up on the events with Tim too. Reports are saying he's being released today."

"That's good. Are you going to meet up with him when he's back, do you reckon?"

Joel thought about it for a few seconds. "I don't see why not. I'm presuming you'll still want him to do some gigs here?"

"Of course, providing he's alright and he feels up to it."

"Well, I'm sure he'll be in here as soon as he feels up to it. Can catch up with him then," Joel mumbled, still not one hundred per cent comfortable talking about Tim. He went and sat down at the regular table in the shop and opened up his laptop again, a little frustrated with his mother.

He had been reading the latest news online with regards to Tim's progress before deciding he'd best have some breakfast. As his laptop awoke from its slumber, he was a little surprised to see Hannah sit down opposite him at the table.

"Hey."

"Hey yourself," Joel replied. "What's bringing you around this early?"

"Joel, it's nearly eleven. This isn't early." She gave him a trademark Hannah frown.

"Alright, alright, calm down," Joel replied, raising his hands in mock defence. "I've been busy reading about Tim online. He should be home today." He gathered by the look on Hannah's face that this wasn't news.

"I'm here for another shift. Your dad said I'd be working with you today. Hope that's OK."

Joel looked surprised. "Of course, no problem at all."

Joel returned to look at his laptop, and clicked on another article. This one discussed whether the pressure of winning reality TV shows was a good thing to exert on the public, citing Susan Boyle and Tim as examples of where it could go wrong.

After a few moments of mildly engaging reading, Joel decided to break the silence, peering over the top of his laptop. "Any plans to see Tim when he's back?"

Hannah looked up from her mobile phone. "I don't know. I still can't contact him."

"Oh right. I keep forgetting he wasn't allowed outside contact or anything while he was on the show."

Hannah gave him a forced smile.

"Have you seen this article?" Joel asked, spinning his laptop around to face her. He watched her closely while she read the first few lines of the article.

"No, that's a new one to me. Basically, blaming what happened to Tim because he couldn't handle the pressure of winning. Yeah right." She looked up at Joel. "Wouldn't you agree?"

Joel shrugged. "I guess only Tim will know what actually happened. The rest of it is all speculation."

Hannah snorted, trying to cover it up with a cough, but didn't say anything further. Joel was reminded of when she had predicted something happening to Tim during the Talent UK Final and wondered what she could possibly know. Or why she didn't want to say anything about it.

"Come on, Han, you know something about this. Stop being so cryptic." Joel felt the full heat of Hannah's glare and could feel his own frustration begin to bubble. "Really? I mean you fancied the guy for ages, and he ends up disappearing, and yet you can predict something happening just by watching him on TV? But you won't tell me or even your own sister what you think is wrong with him? I'm sorry, Han, but that's just... stupid."

Judging by the look on Hannah's face, Joel wondered if he'd gone too far. She looked as if she'd just been slapped. Joel felt his frustration fizzle out and he ended up feeling a little guilty.

After a few seconds of stunned silence, Hannah's gaze took on a far away look. "Do you reckon Tim ever fancied me?" she asked quietly.

Joel looked at her, confusion etched on his face. "What's that got to do with anything?"

"That doesn't answer my question."

Joel conceded that point to her and gave the question some thought. He hadn't really taken that much notice of Hannah and Tim together, trying to work an angle on Amie himself. They'd all hung around in a big group most of the time. Hannah had always been near or next to Tim, but he couldn't say that he'd ever shown any interest in Hannah. If anything he knew more about Alan's intentions towards Hannah.

"I honestly couldn't say, Han, I really don't know."

"Did he ever talk to you about me?"

Joel shook his head. "Look, me and him haven't been the best of friends for a while, but he never said anything to me about how he felt about you."

Hannah looked disappointed and Joel felt a bit sorry for her in that moment. "Have you ever talked to him about it, Han? Does he know you like him in that way?"

She shook her head. "I never got the chance. I'd thought about it, but then he went on Talent UK."

"And with his contact blackout he couldn't tell you he was going and then you couldn't contact him anyway," Joel confirmed, making sense of the situation. "So you just got left in limbo this whole time?"

"Yes. I thought I'd scared him away."

"You're joking! How could you scare him away?"

Hannah looked up at Joel, her eyes brimming with tears and Joel's heart went out to her. He clambered out of his chair and went to sit next to Hannah, putting an arm around her shoulders. She rested her head on his shoulder. "Because I'm me," Joel heard her say.

Joel heard a cough behind him. Turning around, he saw Alan stood there and quickly took his arm away from comforting Hannah, causing her to turn around as well. Alan's glare was firmly fixed on Joel.

Hannah awkwardly looked at her watch, and pushed her way past Joel, mumbling something about starting her shift. Alan took the opportunity to sit down next to Joel and confront him.

"What was all that about?" Alan asked, somewhat aggressively.

"What was what all about?"

"That," Alan said, jabbing a finger to where Hannah had been sitting.

Joel looked at his best friend squarely in the eye. "She needed a friend, Al. That's all. She's taken all this Tim stuff hard."

"And you thought sticking an arm around her was the best way to show what a great friend you are?"

Joel could tell Alan was still hot under the collar. "Don't get me wrong, I like Hannah, but I haven't any feelings in *that* way for her."

Alan visibly relaxed. "Alright, buddy, I get it. I just don't know how to tell her. Can't even get her on her own at the moment."

Joel clapped him on the shoulder. "It's tough, Al, I know it is. Girls hang around in groups, and the fact they're twins makes it even harder. Amie and Hannah are inseparable."

"True that, Joelly. Any ideas?"

"How about a date? There are plenty of restaurants in town. Should always be room for four."

"But we always hang out together? How would it be any different to what we do already?" Alan pointed out.

"True. We could always try going separately? Or one of us could go somewhere else?"

They both considered Joel's suggestion for a few moments, before Alan broke the silence. "I'm not sure how Hannah would react to an actual date. Could I see about coffee here or something? Then you could go out, somewhere fancy."

"Seems a bit daft that. Why shouldn't you treat her somewhere? Being wined and dined might be perfect for her. Show her you really mean business?"

"I can see that, but I don't even know if she likes me. You haven't got that worry with Amie. She's into you."

"You think?"

"Well, you're into her, right?"

"Sure. She's amazing."

"Does she know how you feel?"

Joel realised his silence spoke louder than words.

"I reckon Amie feels the same about you. Think about it: she's always sitting next to you, playing with her hair, laughing hysterically at your *jokes*…" Alan had stopped to do the quotation marks in the air. "How you two aren't together by now is scary."

"Alright, alright, I'll ask her out on a date. But only if you promise to do the same for Hannah. She could use someone in her life now that she can depend on and bring a smile to her face."

"Deal," Alan said, offering his hand.

When they had shaken hands, something occurred to Joel. "What are you going to do about Hannah's feelings about Tim? Is that going to be an issue?"

"I'm sort of hoping that won't be an issue any more. He left her, Joel. He left. I know if someone left me suddenly, with no explanation, then I certainly wouldn't have feelings for them any more."

"Yeah, but that's you, Al. No offence, but Hannah is a very different person. And she's a girl. Girls have different agendas when it comes to this sort of thing."

"And you became the world expert in girls overnight?"

Joel shot him a frustrated look. "I'm not saying that, I just want to make sure you know what you're getting yourself into."

"What do you mean?"

"I'm thinking about her depression and the fact she fancied Tim for ages, Al. What makes you think she's over him? She was asking if he'd ever let on if he felt the same way, before you arrived."

This caused Alan to raise his eyebrows.

"She's got some sort of connection to him," Joel continued. "That incident last weekend during the Talent UK final was weird. It's like she knew what was going to happen to him. I even asked her about it earlier, but she went all defensive on me. To me, that's not the act of someone who doesn't have a crush any more. Has she moved on? I'm not so sure."

"Do you reckon it's mutual?" Alan asked, sounding a little nervous.

"Whether it's two-way, I don't know. As I told her, he's not said anything to me about it; Tim isn't really on my list of people to talk to these days."

Alan ran a hand over his head, ruffling his hair. "Are your folks around? I'd like to ask them a favour. Just had an idea."

"Sure, Pops is usually in the kitchen at this time."

Alan left the table leaving Joel sat there wondering what his best friend could possibly be asking.

Alan headed past the counter, trying hard not to stop and look at Hannah, who was warming up some milk with the coffee machine. He knocked on the kitchen door, seeing Joel's dad there, buttering rolls.

"Hi, Mr Wright. Busy getting ready for lunchtime?"

"Oh, hi, Alan," came the reply. "Can I help you?"

"I hope so, I was just wondering if I could use the back table this afternoon? I've got some coursework to do, and I'm hoping a different venue will help me get it sorted."

"Sure, don't see why not, Alan. Though I expect to see you working hard, not distracting the staff, or I'll have to ask you to leave."

"That's great, Mr Wright, thanks," Alan said, turning to leave.

"Though, Alan," Ted Wright called, causing Alan to turn back again. "If it gets busy, I'd have to ask you to go upstairs to Joel's room or something. We would need the table space."

"No problem. Will do."

Joel looked up again as Alan returned to the table. "Your dad said I could do my college assignments here for the afternoon. I just need to go and grab my laptop."

"Oh right, I see. Trying to catch a word with Hannah?"

"Got it in one. Though your dad did say I wasn't allowed to distract the staff. And I really do have work to get done."

Joel sighed. "Yeah, that sounds like Pops. I'd better go and get dressed, I start in a few minutes."

CHAPTER TEN

Sunday 15th April, mid-morning
Great Bournestone Manor

Tim looked out of the back window of his parents' family hatchback as it cruised up the drive towards Great Bournestone Manor. He was impressed as soon as they had reached the gates of the place, smoothly opening when their car had approached. The drive was lined with white birch, almost skeletal looking with its white bark. Sunlight sparkled off a pond or a lake in the distance. Tim couldn't tell which it was from the car.

As the manor house grew bigger he was even more dumbstruck. His parents had lived in their three-bedroom semi-detached house on the outskirts of Huntingham since before he was born; rarely had he seen evidence of such wealth.

"Enjoying yourself back there?" Sam Pointer asked, looking at him in the rear view mirror.

"It's impressive, Dad. Can't believe places like this exist. Can only dream of having a place like this to live."

"Well, keep working hard, and you never know, son. The world is your oyster, and all that."

Alice, Tim's sister, was sat next to him in the back of the car. On hearing what their dad had said to Tim, she left out a derisive snort.

Tim turned to her, looking annoyed. "What was that for?"

"What was what?" came the retort.

"You snorted."

"Yeah. And?"

"Do you not think I could own a place like this?"

Alice glared at her older brother. "No. You'd be lucky if you could afford a brick."

Tim turned away to look out the window again, his insides boiling with frustration. He generally got on well with his sister, but since he had been getting a lot of attention following the Talent UK final, she had become very bitchy.

"Now, now you two," came the warning from the front of the car.

Everyone fell silent again until the car stopped in front of the manor.

"Do we just go and ring the doorbell?" Tim asked.

Alice snorted again. "No, you dingbat, there'll be someone watching on the cameras, they'll come out and meet us."

"Oh, right," Tim mumbled, climbing out of the car. "Didn't realise you were such an expert in rich people and their houses."

After hearing his sister mutter something about 'Keeping Up With Somebody-or-other', Tim noticed that a woman had appeared at the door and was waving at them.

"Hi again, Mr and Mrs Pointer," Izzy said shaking hands with Tim's parents. "And hello, Tim," she said, in a way that made Tim blush. "It's great to meet you. I'm a big fan of yours, you were brilliant on Talent UK."

Tim was aware of Alice rolling her eyes and becoming very interested in an app on her phone.

"Thanks," he said hoarsely, giving an awkward smile. Izzy had turned on the charm for him, so much so it felt like his head was spinning. Her dark chocolate hair was tied up in a way that he found very appealing.

He had been kept away from the fans most of the time on the show. Sometimes it had felt like he'd been kept in a box, and that the show hadn't been real. Throughout the week he had spent in hospital, the comments he had read on the clips of him on YouTube had amazed and surprised him. They had come from all around the world. He had even found a few spoof accounts set up of him on Facebook and Twitter. Quite why anyone would pretend to be him, he had no idea, but it had made him realise that he had reached all the corners of the globe with his music.

Not all the comments he'd read had been positive, though. He'd tried not to let the negativity break his spirit, and for every derogatory comment there had been easily three encouraging ones.

Returning to the present, a gentle breeze had blown a lock of Izzy's hair over her face, which she proceeded to tuck behind her ear, having to readjust her white designer frames as she did so. To Tim, it was if it had happened all in slow motion and after everything that had happened to him in the last week, it was one of the most amazing sights in the world.

His dad ended up giving him a nudge to knock him out of his reverie.

"I'm Izzy, by the way, Sir Andrew's PA," she said, once Tim was focused back on her. "If you'd like to follow me, I'll take you through to Sir Andrew's study."

They all followed her inside, Tim marvelling at the sweeping staircase and the expensive-looking art lining the walls. He gazed in wonder at what Sir Andrew had spent his fortune on, wondering if he would ever be able to afford even one of the paintings on the wall. Alice was torn away from reading what her friends were doing to have a look at the artwork.

Having seen all this the previous week, Sam and Olivia shared a helpless look with Izzy, who shook her head gently and flashed them a smile.

"Come on, kids," Olivia said. "Let's not keep Sir Andrew waiting."

Reluctantly walking on, Tim's head kept swivelling from side to side as he tried to take it all in.

Sir Andrew's door was open, so Izzy led them all straight in. Sir Andrew's gaze was focused out of the window, and Tim immediately noticed the quiet burble of what he thought was Bob Berg's saxophone coming from the hidden speakers in the study.

As the small crowd entered, Sir Andrew turned towards them and sat down behind his desk.

"Good morning to you all. Sam, Olivia, welcome back, lovely to see you again. Timothy, great to see you, and… who might you be?" Sir Andrew asked the youngest member of the Pointer family.

"Alice," she mumbled.

It was Tim's turn to snort, prompting a glare from his sister. He'd not seen Alice be shy in front of anybody before.

"Alice, wonderful. Well, it's a pleasure to meet you, young lady. Please, have a seat." Sir Andrew gestured towards a chair in front of his desk. "In fact, how rude of me. Everyone, please, pull up a pew. A big welcome to Great Bournestone. I trust Izzy will get you some refreshment?"

Izzy took their orders and left the room. Tim was itching to ask Sir Andrew about who was still playing in the background.

Almost as if he sensed Tim's urgency, Sir Andrew cast his piercing look on him. "Now then, Timothy, what a great pleasure of mine this is."

Tim nodded.

"I trust you recognise Bob Berg coming through the speakers?" Sir Andrew continued. "Taken from us far too soon, rest his soul. Terrible way to go, in a car crash…" Sir Andrew tailed off, as his eyes clouded over. "He was a regular at 7th Avenue South in New York City, got to see him a few times there when I was in the States in the early eighties. His tenor saxophone playing was some of the most passionate and soulful saxophone I can remember at that time."

He paused and closed his eyes for a few seconds before reaching for the remote control and switching the music off. "Anyway, I didn't ask you to come in to listen to a lecture on Bob Berg. I'm here to talk about you, Timothy Pointer. It's great to see you on your feet. How are things with you? And do you prefer Timothy or Tim?"

"Everyone calls me 'Tim'," he replied, looking Sir Andrew square in the eye. "I'm generally alright, just needing to rest and not do anything too stressful." He was perched on the edge of his chair, feeling his heart thudding in his chest and he suddenly realised he was nervous. Was Sir Andrew going to say he wasn't up to it?

"I see," Sir Andrew said, looking up as Izzy brought the drinks in. "Well, I know it's been a week since your parents were here agreeing to sign you up to opening for me on my tour and a fair bit has happened in that time. The tour is due to start in July, it's selling quite well and I just wanted an update and to see how you feel about it all."

Tim thought about it for a few seconds, aware that everyone was looking at him. "For me, playing the saxophone has been all I've wanted to do since I've started playing. I've written some of my own pieces and I've adapted some of my favourite popular songs for saxophone. I just feel complete when I'm playing, like nothing can hurt me. It almost transports me to another place. A special place, where everything feels right with the world. I can't quite describe it any better than that to be honest." Tim realised he was rambling and came to a halt.

Sir Andrew's face wasn't giving anything away, but he sat and stared at Tim for a few moments. "Playing the saxophone isn't just a hobby for you then?" he asked eventually.

"No, sir, it most definitely isn't," Tim replied. He was doing his best to keep his gaze focused on Sir Andrew, whose piercing blue eyes felt like they were searching his soul.

"I see. What would your ultimate dream be with regards to your saxophone-playing?"

The question took Tim aback and it took him a few moments to muster a response. "I don't really know. I want to go as far as I can before I no longer enjoy playing the saxophone."

"It was your dad, if I recall correctly, who was sat in that spot last week and said he believed you wanted your album in people's homes." Sir Andrew stopped to glance at Sam Pointer, who responded with a look of surprise. "So, my question to you, Tim, is, where's the sky?" Sir Andrew continued. "If the sky is your limit, where's the sky?"

The question flustered Tim somewhat. He had no real idea what his aims were. The saxophone was something he played, mostly for pleasure. It wasn't a competition for him, he had no desire to do grades, and he hadn't even been having lessons the last couple of years, having found them too constrictive and binding. Being on Talent UK had given him a flavour for performing for people, which he had thoroughly enjoyed. All he really wanted to do was play the saxophone, however. Whether that was in front of people, or in a studio, he didn't mind.

Tim sighed. Would that be enough for Sir Andrew? "I don't know how high the sky is, if I'm honest with you, sir."

Sir Andrew gave him a smile. "Not to worry, Tim, I'm not testing you. I'm just trying to get a feel for what you want to get from the tour."

"For me, the tour is my opportunity to go to some far flung corners of the country and play my saxophone." Tim then had a thought that struck him. "With that in mind, could I use that sort of travelling to sell an album? I could then bring the albums to the public, rather than it having to go to shops. I mean do you have your books for sale as merchandise? A CD could be made available next to it."

Sir Andrew's face remained blank. "It's certainly an interesting idea, Tim. You've caught me on the hop here, I'll need to talk to my tour management team," he said, writing on the pad in front of him.

"That's OK, I just thought I would ask. It's not that I've got an album or any recordings, but if it was possible, it would be a great opportunity to record one for the start of July."

"I see. It would see you through the next few months. Do you not have exams or anything like that to work on?"

Tim looked a bit awkward. "Not this year. With going on the show, I had to get special permission from the college to leave. After how the show went, I'm not really sure I want to go back to college now."

"That's a big decision to make now. Have you spoken to your parents about all this?" Sir Andrew asked, glancing towards Tim's parents. They both shook their heads.

Tim shrugged. "I'll need to talk it all through with them I think, but if the tour is going well, then A Levels can wait, as far as I'm concerned."

"Fair enough. That's a conversation you need to have with them. Now, talking about the tour going well, I take it that's something you're wishing to pursue, judging by what you've said already this morning."

It wasn't a question, Tim realised. He nodded.

"Excellent," Sir Andrew said with a smile.

He proceeded to explain to Tim what the tours were about, what he hoped to achieve and what he wanted from Tim's performances, having run through it with Tim's parents the week before.

His talent with speaking had even torn Alice away from her phone and she was listening intently.

"Now then, Tim, this is a question I've been avoiding, but I'm afraid I really must ask. Is there any explanation as to what happened last week? I've read an awful lot of speculation in the press about stress and burnout. I'm no stranger to such things but in my professional opinion, there appears to be more than meets the eye?"

This time, it was a question.

Tim shrugged, and rubbed the back of his head awkwardly. "I don't really remember much about it to be honest, and I've seen the video footage of it this week, and still can't explain it. I wasn't particularly stressed and the doctors didn't say much about burnout."

"Is there any chance it's psychological?" Sir Andrew asked.

Tim looked at him blankly. "I've heard that mentioned, but I don't think so. Mum, Dad, do you know any more?"

Sam Pointer cleared his throat. "We've heard lots of theories over the last week, most of which have been disproven through the tests they've run.

He's been allowed home on the condition that he takes it easy."

"Interesting. Well, I take it he's been referred back to the local hospital? You won't be having to take trips to London for the next few months?"

Tim's parents shook their heads.

"Well, that's something at least. So, if you're having to take it easy, you've got no exams or anything to do, what are you going to do with your time?"

"I've got lots of music I can be trying. I've got my own compositions I want to work on and I'll try to rewrite some of my favourite songs with a view to getting an album laid down at some point, if it's not before the tour. There's a coffee shop in town that have asked me to join their list of artists and that would mean perfect low-key performances for me."

"Well, it sounds like you'll be very busy. I really hope I get the chance to use all the music you'll be working on."

"Thanks," Tim said, with a smile. "I hope so too."

"Well, unless there's anything else you wanted to ask, that concludes everything I've wanted to say for today," Sir Andrew said, looking at them all.

"If I may," Alice piped up, "Sorry, excuse me, but I just wondered, like, just how rich are you?"

Tim turned around to frown at his sister. He couldn't quite believe she'd just asked a man of Sir Andrew's stature such a question. To his surprise, Sir Andrew threw his head back and let out a large laugh that went on for several seconds. Tim spotted there were tears in his eyes.

"Oh, Alice, that's the hardest I've laughed in a good long while."

Alice didn't look impressed at his reaction. "Yeah? And?"

Sir Andrew's eyes were twinkling with mischief. "My personal finances aren't something I'd reveal to anybody. But lets just say I'm hoping to feature in the Sunday Times Rich List somewhere. You can have a look in a couple of weeks." He was amused to see the teenage girl's eyes widen with that response and she immediately reached for her phone.

Sir Andrew merely smiled as they all stood up to leave. "Well, thank you all for your visit this morning. Please stay in touch and, Tim, I hope your recovery continues well."

***

Sir Andrew watched them make their way up the drive from his office window, deep in thought.

"So, it all seemed to go well," Izzy said, making Sir Andrew jump.

"Yes," Sir Andrew sighed. "I just really hope Tim's able to join the tour. There's something more going on than meets the eye with him. I can't quite put my finger on it though."

"Frustrating when that happens, isn't it?" Izzy asked rhetorically.

"Well, Tim certainly took a liking to you, Isabella. I caught him staring at you when you weren't looking earlier," Sir Andrew said, a knowing look on his face.

"And what makes you think I wasn't looking?" Izzy replied innocently. "He's at least a minor celebrity at the moment. He's very shy and quite humble with it, which I find quite attractive. Plus you've seen the videos of him performing as well; he's a proper star in the making. I couldn't take my eyes off him."

Sir Andrew chuckled. "Poor lad won't know where to look next time if you're around."

"You're anticipating there being a next time?"

"I'm wondering if his parents being here meant he couldn't be as honest as he could have been."

"So, what, invite him for private counselling sessions?"

"To me, from the footage you've shown me, I think he was in a stupor state when he had that incident on the show. That indicates something psychological, possibly depression."

"What would he have to be depressed about, though?"

"You've met his family now. What did you make of Alice?"

"She's like a polar opposite of him but just seems like how I was at her age. He finds her irritating perhaps, but I can't see it being anything more."

"Exactly. She's just like you were, with your precocious attitude at that age. And his parents? What did you think of them?"

"They seem like nice, ordinary people."

"Did they appear over-protective? That might not be the right word. How about demanding? Do they seem like the type to be too demanding and pressuring?"

"Not at all. The two times I've met them they just want the best for him. They seem supportive if anything."

"To me that says there's something internal that could be bothering him. I can't see it being someone causing him to be depressed. I can't sense physical abuse or anything like that. Although it wouldn't be the first time I've missed something like that," Sir Andrew said, trailing off.

"The one-to-one sessions would be a win-win for you though, if you think about it."

"I have thought about it Izzy, I've thought long and hard about it. Would I be overstepping the mark? Can I really take a boy like that away from his parents to try and fix something I don't even know he's got?"

"Andrew, look at me," Izzy said, grabbing his arm. "You want Tim for this tour, correct?"

"Correct."

"Then you have to speak to him. On his own. Satisfy your own curiosity about him. Your gut feelings aren't usually wrong, they've usually been right down the years. If he's so important to the success of this tour, then you've got to do everything you can to ensure he's ready for it."

Sir Andrew sighed. "You're absolutely right, Izzy. I want to give him a chance first, though. I won't go in with all guns blazing and demand that he attends any one-to-ones. I'll leave that as a last resort. I'll add his parents to my list of calls I need to do, say, in a couple of weeks. I'd like their permission before I even contemplate such sessions." He looked down at his list and saw what he'd written earlier. "Izzy, do you know of any recording studios in the local area? Say, within a thirty mile radius?"

"Follow me, I'll have a look on the Internet," Izzy said, beckoning him to her desk outside his office. "No, the closest would be Nottingham," she confirmed, on completing the search. "That's thirty-five miles away. Doesn't appear to be anything closer."

"Interesting," he said, scratching his beard. "Also, it's just occurred to me, is Tim on social media at all? Try Facebook first."

Izzy pulled up Facebook on a web page and found an artist page with Tim's name on. There were several on there but she chose the one with the most likes as being the most likely to be the actual Tim.

"Is there any way you can keep track of him on there?" Sir Andrew asked.

"Of course. I'll just follow the page. Do you want me to find him on other social media too?"

"If he's on there, Izzy, then yes."

Izzy easily located him on Twitter, YouTube and Instagram as well.

"Excellent. Keep a track on him, Izzy. Let me know if there's anything unusual that crops up."

"Will do, sir. I'm certainly not going to complain at keeping tabs on him."

"That sounds like I don't give you enough work to do," Sir Andrew said wryly. "If that's the case I've got a project I'd like you to work on."

"Oh goody, another one of your hare-brained projects for my beloved daughter."

Izzy and Sir Andrew both looked up as Hayden appeared in the doorway.

"Hello you two," Hayden said, flashing them both a toothy smile. "So, Andy, what have you got up your ridiculously large sleeves for Izzy to slave over?"

Sir Andrew outlined his plan to them both, which led to Izzy sitting down behind her desk for some more Internet-searching.

The two men headed into Sir Andrew's study, Hayden closing the door behind him.

"I presume this is in reference to the search for my brother?"

"It is, I've got a couple of my finest paralegals working on it. Miranda Strawson and Phil Hollis, you've met them both before. Been with me for a few years. Class of 2005, I think. Slaving away, making calls, visiting registry offices. Just wanted to update you really."

"Well, thanks for coming all this way to tell me that. Have they been able to find out anything?"

"I could use a few more details about your parents and their families. Just so I can ensure there's enough research going on. I did ask you in the Golden Bell last week if you could hunt some family details out."

"I've got a box of family stuff here that I've found. I've made some notes on what I think I can remember about what I heard as well," Sir Andrew said, pointing to a box in the corner of his study.

"Well, that'll just be the ramblings of a senile old man," Hayden joked. "Why would anybody in their right mind want to run through all that?"

Sir Andrew merely sniffed at that comment. "I hope you're paying them? The idea of someone volunteering for this at your firm is a little concerning. Although I wouldn't put it past you to pass this off on the work experience student."

"Of course, they earn a pretty penny at Smart Solicitors. Right, lets get this box downstairs to my carriage and I'll be out of your hair. Or what's left of it," Hayden said, running a hand through his own hair.

"That hair transplant you had has made you very insouciant towards your flowing locks. I advise you to rein it in a little," Sir Andrew responded with a strong glare at his friend, who merely replied with another toothy smile.

CHAPTER ELEVEN

Monday 16th April, early evening
The Pointer House

"That alright for you, son?"

"Yes thanks, Mum," Tim said, as his mother cleared the table.

"Any plans for the evening?" Olivia Pointer enquired casually.

"No, nothing special."

His mother looked at him, reluctance showing on her face. "We need to talk about something that came up yesterday."

Tim looked at her blankly.

His mother laid her tea towel on the dining table and rested both arms on it, sitting down to face him. "What do you want to do in the future?" she asked.

Tim sighed. It wasn't something he had particularly thought much about. He had spent the day so far choosing and arranging songs that he wanted to take on the tour with him. His future plans didn't extend past July. "I don't know, Mum. Find a girlfriend, settle down, have a family and get a nine-to-five job in an office somewhere?"

His mother snorted, but then looked embarrassed as she realised she wasn't sure if he had been joking. "Really?" she asked, covering her mouth.

Tim gave her a derisive look. "Sure, that would be great and all. By the time I'm forty." He watched his mother closely as her eyes widened, but she didn't say anything for a few moments.

"It is a serious question, Tim. I am genuinely asking out of interest," Olivia said, her tone firm.

Tim's shoulders dropped. "I know, Mum. The answer is I just don't really know. I'm really enjoying my music and until that runs out then I don't know what else I can do with my life."

"OK, son. But think about it, please? At least while you've got all this free time for a couple of months."

Tim sensed his mother was beginning to fret. "OK, alright, Mum," he said reassuringly. "I can have a think this week and maybe see what I could do with the GCSEs I got last year. But only as a back up plan. Music is my main focus at the moment."

Olivia looked relieved. "Thanks. Now, have you got some music to work on this evening?"

"I've got some more music I want to look at but I haven't got anything planned," Tim said, narrowing his eyes at his mother. "Why?"

"If that's the case would you mind giving Alice a hand with her revision? Your dad has been delayed at the office again and she wants some help with her maths."

Tim tried to convey a look of frustration to his mother; helping his sister was the last thing he wanted to do. On seeing that she was standing her ground he sighed. "Sure, no problem. She's in her room I take it," he said, sounding resigned.

"Yes, whilst she's revising she has her meals in her room."

Tim gave his mother a look of surprise. "Well I never knew that. You always made me eat down here, regardless of what I had planned."

His mother looked frustrated. "To be honest, Tim, you've not been here for the last few months and as you've probably been able to tell, Alice has been rather difficult to tolerate recently. She's a teenage girl. Your dad and I felt letting her have her own way once in a while wasn't the worst thing in the world. We had just let you go for Talent UK, and because we said yes to you, we could hardly tell her no."

Tim noticed his mother shrug awkwardly, which usually meant the conversation was over. As he headed up the stairs he realised Alice wasn't the easiest person to live with, so it made sense to try and keep the peace. He hadn't missed her at the dinner table, as tetchy and unpleasant as she had been over the last few days. If she'd been like that since he'd left, he could understand why his parents had given in.

He tapped on her door. "Alice!" he called. "It's me. Mum said you wanted some help with your revision?"

He heard some scuffling and what sounded like giggling, which confused him slightly. Sighing, he opened her door. What he didn't expect was the reaction. What greeted him was an indignant shriek and the door slammed closed again.

"Go away!"

Tim, by now, was thoroughly puzzled. "Ally, do you need help or not?"

There was a pause. "Yes," came the reluctant reply. "Can you give me a few minutes?"

"Why? What are you up to?" he asked, though he'd already decided he was going to barge his way in this time.

He found himself confronted by a room covered in notes and textbooks. The bed and desk weren't anywhere to be seen and even standing space on the floor was limited.

"Oi, get out! You can't just barge in here? I could have been naked or something."

Tim then realised the giggling he'd heard came from the computer.

"Hi, Tim," chorused a pair of Alice's school friends. He ignored them for the moment.

"So, you're revising by video-conference now? Is that how this works?" It came out more accusatory than he'd meant.

Alice didn't even look guilty. "Yeah. Beats having to drag all my stuff around to their houses, I can spread out here. And don't be so rude, say hello. Chloe and Jessica are big fans of yours, no idea why." Alice pointed to the two girls as she said their names. Chloe had jet-black hair, with a shaven patch above her left temple and big-lensed glasses framing sly-looking hazel eyes. It gave her an elfish look, which Tim found a bit creepy. Jessica, on the other hand, looked as innocent as a baby, her face was almost perfectly round, punctuated by wide blue eyes that appeared as big as saucers and her short blond hair styled into a pixie cut of which Tim had seen a lot of down in London.

"Hi," he said tentatively, waving at the computer monitor on Alice's desk.

"Hey," they both replied, looking a little bit awestruck. Tim brushed it off, he'd realised it was going to happen more and more these days.

"He's actually really cute," he heard one of them mutter, which sent all three girls into fits of giggles.

"Hold it right there, Chloe," Alice said sternly, which for some reason set them all off again.

Tim rolled his eyes and took a seat in his sister's desk chair, waiting for the laughter to stop. He waited for a few moments until everybody regained their composure.

"So, Tim, tell us. What was it really like being on Talent UK?" asked Chloe, twirling a finger in her hair.

"Yeah, was it really cool? Did you meet lots of famous people?" Jessica added, her excitement almost palpable.

"It was amazing, overall," Tim admitted. "There were lots of people about, but I was expected to rehearse all hours of the day, so didn't really get to meet them as such."

"What was, like, your favourite bit?" Jessica asked.

"To be honest, it was just having the opportunity to play my saxophone. I never expected to get as far as I did, and all that was just an added bonus."

"What's Topaz like behind closed doors?" Chloe asked, continuing the interrogation.

Tim gave a bemused smile. "She's lovely, but is incredibly driven. I can't really say much more than that. You've seen what she's like every week on the show."

There then fell an awkward silence. Tim was conscious Alice had never asked him about Talent UK but he had never felt obliged to tell her about it. He felt if she had wanted to know what it was like she would have asked him. On the other hand, getting the attention from Alice's friends was quite refreshing. He hadn't really had the chance to talk about it all in the past week, having been on his own a lot of the time in the hospital, sleeping for most of it, looking on the Internet for the rest of it. Actual conversation was a pleasant change.

"So, do you want some help with your revision?" Tim asked, deciding that it would probably be best to try and ignore the two girls staring at him and focus on his sister, who was now sat cross-legged on her bed, fiddling with her nails.

"Yeah, whatever. It's on the floor somewhere. The teacher was next to useless but he was very dreamy. You get lost in his eyes…" Alice trailed off, her eyes taking on a far away glaze.

"He's extremely fit," came the confirmation from the computer.

"Great," Tim said sarcastically. "Come on then, I've got thirty minutes I can spare you now, what do you want me to help you with?" He didn't have a timeframe on his plans, but he was damned if he was going to spend more than half an hour with three fifteen year olds talking about how dreamy their maths teacher was.

Once Alice had rummaged through her various piles of paperwork to find a previous exam paper, she thrust it in Tim's direction. "Here. This question," she said, pointing at the bit of paper with lots of stars drawn on it. "None of us can agree on the answer. You got a B at Maths, so this should be bread and butter for you."

Tim held his tongue, trying not to react to the latest jibe. He read through the question, trying to get the maths cogs in his brain working again. He asked for a pen, had one thrown at him by his sister, and made some notes on the question paper.

"Have you thought about it like this?" he asked, referring to the notes he'd written.

Alice peered at his notes, muttering something about scruffy handwriting. "I just don't get it, how do you get that from reading that question? It just makes no sense to me."

There was a general noise of agreement from the computer. Alice snatched the pen from Tim's hand and proceeded to scribble next to where he had written.

"So, would you have gotten that as the answer," she asked, tapping the paper impatiently.

Tim had a scan through her working out and nodded. "That makes sense to me."

"Finally. Right, girlies, this is what Tim did and what I got as the answer underneath." Alice was holding up the mock exam paper to the webcam, which led to some noises of puzzlement and then understanding when it dawned on them what Alice had done.

"Why doesn't it say that in the question?" Jessica asked, ruffling her hair in frustration.

"Yeah," Chloe said, "It's stupid. How were we supposed to get that?"

"Well, glad I could help. Was there anything else?" Tim asked innocently, hoping there wouldn't be.

"We're good, thanks," Alice said firmly and Tim thought he detected a sense of disappointment on the screen.

"Right, well I'll leave you to it. Do you want me to take your dishes downstairs?"

Alice merely responded by thrusting the dinner plate in his direction. He decided there was no point in telling her to have a bit of class, so he shrugged at her and left her room.

When he reached downstairs he found his mother cleaning the kitchen.

"Everything alright up there?" she asked.

"Sure, messy room, hostile attitude, but all-in-all she's fine."

"Did you get her maths issue sorted?"

Tim nodded.

"Great. I'll message your dad and let him know," his mother said, reaching for her phone.

Tim took that as his cue to leave and automatically headed upstairs. Once he was back on the landing, he saw into his room and had a twinge in his stomach. He had spent most of the day trying to put something down using a music-writing programme on his computer, but hadn't really achieved anything he'd hoped for. He had been in there all day and he really wanted a change of scenery. Something had been nagging at him since he'd arrived home and he wanted to fix it.

Reaching for his phone, he swiped down through his contact list on his messaging app until he found Hannah's face.

Hey, he messaged. He sat and stared at his phone for a few minutes, but all he could see was the fact they'd last messaged each other over three months ago. That hurt him a bit more than he thought it should have.

He glanced at the status bar at the top, telling him if the other person was online or offline. *Hannah French – offline.* Deciding that either she was busy or she didn't want to talk to him, he put his phone away.

He pushed his door fully open, and sighed. The house where he had had many happy memories as a child had lost its sparkle since he'd returned home. It wasn't the same and he wasn't quite sure why. He was wondering if it was because he'd had a taste of a different life, he was loath to say a better life, and it had changed him. He'd become somebody. When he'd left he was nobody.

He couldn't complain about the facilities in the house for Talent UK. It was a step up from the tired home he'd left behind. But now he was home, it was back to the same old furnishings, the same four walls of his bedroom and the same old view from his window. Tim shook his head. They were arguably the things he missed most when he had been away. Now he was struggling to be around them.

He had a seat on the swivel chair in front of his desk, relaxing back into it, staring up at the ceiling. He was considering messaging one of the other members of the group, just so he wouldn't have to sit in all evening.

He reached down to switch his computer on when he felt his phone buzz in his pocket. He was so excited he nearly threw his phone across his room trying to get it out of his pocket. He was bitterly disappointed when he saw it was marketing text message. What was PPI anyway? Sighing, he put his phone away again, only to feel it buzz almost straight away.

This time, it was a message from an actual person, the symbol of a little phone inside a circle appearing in his status bar at the top of his phone screen. When he unlocked his phone it was the message he'd been waiting for.

Tim? was the reply from Hannah. He noticed she was still online as well, and he couldn't type his reply quickly enough.

Yeah, it's me. How are you?

I'm fine. How do I know it's you?

Tim wasn't quite sure how to answer that. He figured she was just being cautious, checking his phone hadn't been stolen or something.

Could always ask me a question? One I'll only know the answer to was his eventual reply.

OK. Where was our first kiss?

Tim eyes grew very wide and he could feel his heart start to thump in his chest. He'd never kissed Hannah. That he could remember. He immediately wished he hadn't just thought that. Had he lost some memories in the wake of the Talent UK incident?

His phone buzzed again. *Only joking. What's my favourite song?*

'Relieved' wasn't a strong enough word for how Tim felt.

That was a bit mean. Thought I was losing my mind. 'To Be With You' - Mr. Big.

Sorry. So what's up?

I'm bored. Are you busy?

No...

Tim gave it a few seconds to make sure he was doing the right thing. In the end he just decided to go for it.

Fancy a coffee?

Sure. I'm revising right now, so give me an hour?

Tim gave a celebratory fist pump to Hannah's response.

Beans and Banter in an hour? was his reply.

Great. See you then.

She'd even added a smiley face. Tim couldn't help but mirror it, a big beaming grin spreading across his face.

CHAPTER TWELVE

Monday 16th April, early evening
The French House

Amie looked over at her sister sat on the other end of the sofa. Hannah was staring at her phone, a smile creeping across her face. All revision had been abandoned; Hannah's notes were ignored as soon as her phone had buzzed.

It was rare for Amie to spot a smile, particularly recently, with Hannah having been looking so miserable. She was also curious as to what could have appeared on Hannah's phone to brighten her day in such a way.

"What are you smiling at?"

Hannah visibly jumped.

Amie frowned, worried about her sister now. "Are you alright, Han?"

Hannah flashed her sister a fleeting smile. "I'm fine. You caught me by surprise. That was Tim asking if I wanted to go for a drink."

Amie looked surprised. "Really? The actual Tim? I didn't think he would have the stones to message you after all this time."

"Well maybe he does have some stones," Hannah said, with a frown. "Don't try and take this away from me. I don't want to lose this opportunity with him."

Amie sighed. She didn't want her sister to go through all the pain of the last few months again. "What's Alan going to say?"

"Alan? What's he got to do with anything?"

"Did you not see him on Saturday when you were working? He really wanted to talk to you. Plus, he's been acting a bit weird around you for a few weeks now. If I had to put money on it, I would say he fancies you."

Hannah looked taken aback. "Really? But, when… How? I've never noticed anything like that."

"You know when I had to drop your tablets in, because you'd left them here. He was sat at the back table, pretending to do something on his laptop. Every time you walked past him, he was watching you."

"That's a bit creepy," Hannah said, with a wince.

Amie rolled her eyes. "Er, yeah."

"Why didn't he say anything? We've hung out a lot recently; he always ends up sitting next to me somehow. He's had lots of opportunities to ask me out."

"Who knows, Han? I'd have thought he would have said something to you by now."

"Maybe he's scared? Doesn't want to ruin a friendship?" Hannah looked at her sister imploringly.

"Maybe. But if he's serious, he's going to have to tell you sometime."

"So, what do I do? You could be way off the mark here. I don't want to look like an idiot, accusing someone of fancying me."

"You're asking my advice about how to treat a guy? You've never asked me anything like that before," Amie said with a scoff.

Hannah frowned again. "You don't have to be such a bitch about it, I was just asking for your help."

Amie looked surprised. "Did you just call me a bitch?"

"I did. It was justified."

Further surprised by Hannah's defiance, Amie thought it best to back down. "Fair enough. Sorry, Han."

"So what do I do?" Hannah repeated.

Amie looked into her sister's eyes, searching to see if it was a genuine question. "OK, look, I can't give you the answers. I don't have the power to do that."

"What do you mean?" Hannah replied, looking confused.

"All I can do is ask you some questions. Just answer them as fast as you can. It'll tell you what your gut reaction is."

"Alright, like what?"

"Let's try a test one first. What do you prefer: coffee or tea? Remember, answer as fast as possible."

"Coffee. I don't get it. You know I don't like tea."

"OK. How about... bath or shower?" Amie was trying to test her sister with that one, knowing that Hannah didn't really mind either way.

"Shower," Hannah responded immediately, then giving a look of surprise.

"See? Gut reaction. You didn't know you liked showers more than baths did you?"

Hannah shook her head. "Not really. I guess they're just more convenient."

"Great. So, let's see. A question about the boys... So, between Tim and Alan, who do you find most attractive?"

"Alan," came the instant response.

This time it was Amie's turn to look surprised. "Really?"

"Yeah. Tim's got the better personality. We've got some history and I think we're quite similar in many ways. Don't get me wrong, though, Alan is kind and has a funny sense of humour but, out of the two of them, Alan is better to look at."

Amie was secretly enjoying the discussion with her sister. Since Hannah had been diagnosed with her depression last year, times like this had been few and far between. Hannah was now taking Prozac for her depression and Amie was starting to wonder if her sister was now coming out of her shell that had been established long before her diagnosis and which her previous Cymbalta medication hadn't helped to eradicate. Perhaps there was a breakthrough coming.

"OK, fair enough. I can't disagree with you, to be honest. Neither of them comes close to Joel though, he's a good all-rounder. Just what I look for in a guy." Amie clapped a hand over her mouth; she hadn't intended to share that with Hannah.

Hannah gave her sister a piercing stare. "I always suspected… It's true? You fancy Joel?"

Amie hated feeling vulnerable, particularly where her sister was involved. She'd been trying to be the strong twin, trying to protect Hannah as much as possible. Having to admit to having feelings was something that made her feel very open and exposed.

"Yes, Han, it's true. All that pretend flirting wasn't pretend at all. I really think I fancy him."

"Well, that's great! He clearly has a thing for you, so why aren't you together?"

Amie realised that was a good question. Why wasn't she already with Joel? Was she scared of admitting her feelings? Was she trying to protect her sister in some weird, messed-up way?

"I don't know. I guess I've felt like this for a while without wanting to admit it. I'm here for you, Han, and I've never really wanted boys to get in the way. I don't want you to feel like there's nobody for you to turn to. I'll always be here for you." Amie had made her way up the sofa and put an arm around her twin sister's shoulders.

"Thanks, sis," Hannah whispered, resting her head on Amie's shoulder. A tear rolled down her cheek, touched by Amie's sudden outburst.

After a few moments, Hannah sat up, tear tracks scarring her face. "What I'm struggling to get my head around is why you'd sacrifice yourself for me. I don't get it."

Amie looked puzzled. "I've not sacrificed anything."

"You have, you're still single, when you could have been with Joel. I can look after myself."

"Look, I'm your sister. Your twin sister. I'm duty bound to look after you. I've struggled to understand why you're depressed when I don't feel like that but I've tried to come to terms with it. I meant what I said, Han, I want to help you through this."

"Do you think I can be fixed?"

"That makes it sound like you're broken," Amie replied.

"It's how I feel a lot of the time, like there's something wrong with me," Hannah said quietly.

"How do you mean? I don't understand."

Hannah paused. "It's hard to explain," she said eventually. "I just don't feel happy. Not like you always are. I want to be like that."

Amie then felt a pang of guilt. She couldn't help the way she was. She had always had the point of view of living life to the fullest and making the most of what life had given her. She had always been that way. Growing up, she had always been closer to their dad and Hannah had been closer to their mum and it was something that their dad had seemingly instilled in her; she remembered school athletics with him giving her some last minute words of encouragement, telling her to just go out and enjoy it before she made her way to the blocks at the start of her race.

Even when they had both come home from school and their mother, eyes red raw, met them at the door to give them the news that their dad wasn't going to be living there any more, it hadn't really affected her. She had carried on living life to the fullest while her sister had taken it hard and had eventually attempted to take her own life.

The shock after that event had been hard to take but it had made her even more determined to enjoy her life. She loved her bright colours and in taking up art had, deep down, hoped some of it would eventually rub off on her sister.

"Look, Han, ever since Dad left, Mum hasn't been here for us, and I've been wondering if that's contributed to it in some way. I'm not blaming Mum, she's had it tough too, bringing us up on her own. She works every hour at work that she can get to try and support us."

"What are you trying to say?"

"I'm just saying I get that you have depression. You took it pretty hard when Dad left. You've been broken-hearted for the last few weeks too. Even if Mum isn't here for you, I want you to know you'll always have me. For anything."

"It's true, I guess, about Dad. And thanks, sis, I love you, I always will."

"Don't mention it, just don't feel like you have nobody to turn to. And I love you too."

"Thanks, Amz, I know," Hannah said and she reached over and gave her sister another hug.

Amie broke the hug when she heard scuffling coming from the front door and glanced at the clock on the wall. "Is that Mum coming back from work now? She's later than normal."

There was the jangle of keys being put on the table next to the front door, which closed with a bang and Christine French popped her head into the front room. She was quite obviously the reason for the twins' red hair, tied back in a loose ponytail, similar to Hannah. Big bags under her eyes highlighted how tired she was along with deep frown lines connected to the hand life had dealt her in recent months.

"Hello, kids," she said, with a sigh.

"Hi, Mum," they both replied and went over to give her a big hug.

"Just to warn you, girlies, it's not been the best shift ever. I'm very tired, I just want a glass of wine and a bath and I'll be off to bed. I thought that shift would never end."

"Don't worry, Mum," Amie said. "There's a bottle of Prosecco in the fridge. I put it in at teatime, so it should be fairly chilled now."

Christine smiled at the twins. "I need to make the most of this, I'll be on my own when you two decide to move out."

"Oh, Mum, don't worry about stuff like that, make the most of us now," Amie said. "Anyway, there's some good news; Hannah's got a date."

Christine put her bags down on the floor, looking at them both in disbelief. "Really?"

Hannah nodded.

"Well, that's great news! Congratulations!" Hannah got pulled in for another hug, this one lasting a little longer than the last.

It took a few seconds for the hug to break and it was only then that Hannah noticed her mum's eyes swimming with tears.

"Who is it with?" Christine asked, looking concerned.

"It's alright, Mum. It's somebody you know. It's Tim. And it's not a proper date. I'm only going for a coffee in a few minutes."

Christine was relieved and concerned at the same time. "Tim? Really? After all this time?"

"Yes, and I've been through all this with Amie already. It's just a drink."

"Well, even so, darling, that's wonderful. What time are you meeting him? Have I got time to straighten your hair for you?"

Hannah's eyes widened in surprise. She turned to Amie, who gave her a look that suggested to go with it; it was unlike their mum to make an effort like that after work.

"Come on then, love," Christine said, reaching for Hannah's hand to lead her upstairs. "Have you got an outfit sorted?"

Amie watched them go up the stairs, feeling guilty for feeling jealous of her sister. Their mother had never offered to do Amie's hair, nor discussed what outfit to wear for a date.

Then it occurred to her that maybe she wasn't the only one who was offering support to Hannah after all. That could only be a good thing.

CHAPTER THIRTEEN

Hannah grabbed a jacket off the hooks by the front door, making sure she had got her keys. She turned to have a quick look in the mirror, to admire how straight her hair was. She didn't usually bother with her appearance that much. She didn't even own a set of hair straighteners, so to have it done felt a little bit alien. It had been a good bonding experience with her mum, though. Her mum had wanted to know as much as possible about Tim, which had been difficult to answer as Hannah herself wasn't totally sure how she felt. But she couldn't complain. She had never talked to her mum about boys. She had never had to, to be fair. She was more appreciative of the fact that her mum had taken some time out of her routine to make time for her. That had meant a lot.

Amie had then surprised her further by offering to do her make-up. Hannah had insisted on any eye shadow being kept fairly neutral, vehemently refusing any of her twin's flamboyant colours. A touch of blusher, a dash of mascara and a few minutes later, here she was, admiring her reflection in the mirror downstairs. Amie had insisted of taking a photo of her and Hannah had wondered if she should use it as her Facebook profile picture, she liked how she looked that much.

As she left the house she took a deep breath, trying in vain to spot Tim through the windows of Beans and Banter across the road. She was feeling both excited and nervous.

Her sister had confused her a bit by throwing Alan into the mix. The last few months had been hard since Tim had disappeared and there had been a lot of hurt. Was it time to move on? The feelings were still there for Tim, though. She realised that she just needed to know how he felt about her. Once she knew that she could decide whether there was something to fight for or whether she would have to get over him.

She pushed the door open, an elderly couple letting her through. As she stepped over the threshold she became aware of the familiar smell of coffee beans and the acoustic rock soundtrack playing on the sound system; she wasn't a massive fan, it was more Amie's thing. It was something she was becoming more accustomed to while Amie had playlists upon playlists of coffee shop music.

"Hi, Hannah," came the cheery greeting from Joel's mother, who was clearing a table near the door. "You're looking beautiful tonight, very pretty. Your hair looks wonderful. Coming in for a drink?"

"Hey, Mrs Wright, yes, I'm meeting somebody," Hannah replied, trying her hardest not to blush. She then wondered why she hadn't said she was meeting Tim. And why was Alan now starting to nag away at her brain? She looked across at their usual table to see if he was sat there and she felt a twinge of disappointment when she saw it was empty.

Alyssa Wright gave Hannah a searching look and then shrugged. "Can I get you your usual?"

"Yes please, that'd be great," Hannah replied, relieved to have some breathing space. She had scanned the shop but couldn't see Tim sat anywhere either.

She settled at a table near the window, butterflies in her stomach as she tapped the tabletop nervously. Joel's mum returned a few moments later with a large hazelnut latte for her.

"There you go, pet. You look like you need one of these."

"Thanks," Hannah replied, taking a sip of the whipped cream from the top of the mug. She gave a weak smile, trying to be polite.

"Is there anything I can help with, Hannah? You seem tense."

Hannah looked up into the warm, friendly eyes of Alyssa Wright and felt desperate to open up to her. She just didn't know what to say. It didn't seem fair to dump a whole maelstrom of conflicting emotion and what ifs on a parent of one of her friends. And her employer, she then realised.

Perhaps sensing the teenager's turmoil Alyssa put a reassuring hand on Hannah's arm. "Doesn't matter, pet, you know where we are. See you on your next shift."

Hannah took another sip of her latte when a figure walking past the window caught her attention. She was suddenly conscious of her heart thumping in her chest.

Tim pushed open the door to Beans and Banter, looking around as he did so. He was wearing his hood up, which Hannah found strange, something he never usually did. Even so, she could tell it was Tim, with his build and the way he walked; with his head naturally bowed and shoulders rounded.

She let him look around a bit before she waved at him.

"Hey," Tim said, as he pulled up the chair opposite her. He still had his hood up, and he kept looking over his shoulders every few seconds.

Hannah couldn't tell if he'd noticed the effort she'd put in, so she kept it casual. "Hey."

They both looked at each other a little awkwardly for a few moments.

"Does anything look different about me?" Hannah asked, trying to break the silence.

Tim gave her a thorough once-over with his eyes. "Well now you mention it…"

"What do you think?"

"You look amazing, Han, you really do."

Hannah rewarded him with a rare smile.

"So, when did you start wearing make-up?"

"Erm, it's a recent thing. Since I've started working here, really." Hannah found herself loath to say she had only put it on tonight; she didn't want to come across as being desperate or having made a special effort for him.

Tim raised an eyebrow, scarcely visible under his fringe. "When did you start working here?"

"About a week ago. Amie and I are just doing a few shifts here and there. They're hoping to become busier soon. I was working the night of the final. They had it on in here. Quite a crowd."

"Wow, I'm not sure what the biggest revelation was there," Tim said, looking unsure. "It's great that there were lots of folks in here for the show, but also that you guys are working here too. Were you rushed off your feet?"

"It *was* busy, don't get me wrong. But it was manageable. A lot of people were sat there cheering you on."

"Wow," Tim repeated, a dreamy look in his eyes.

Hannah meanwhile was trying her hardest not to look at a group of girls sat on a table behind Tim, who were busy whispering and pointing in her general direction. Were they pointing at her? She couldn't be absolutely sure but she still felt a bit uncomfortable.

Tim noticed Hannah looking uneasy. "Why are you frowning?"

Hannah gave him an awkward look. "It's the girls on that table. I don't like being pointed at. Had enough of being pointed at and laughed at in my life."

Tim glanced at the table behind him. He smiled but didn't say anything, which only served to frustrate Hannah further.

"Hey, don't look so smug! It's not a good look for you."

Tim tried really hard to wipe the smile off his face. "I think they're looking at me, Han, not you."

Hannah sighed with relief. "Of course. That would make much more sense."

"They followed me here. They were on the corner near my house. I think they thought it was me but they weren't too sure. I don't mind signing autographs or having pictures taken but I needed to meet you first."

"Is that why you had your hoody up? And you were looking over your shoulder?"

Tim nodded, still trying his hardest not to let his face burst into a grin.

Hannah paused. She'd presumed it was because he didn't want to be there and was ashamed to be seen with her. "All that attention. That must be hard to deal with." She was trying really hard to not mention the comment about meeting her first.

"It sort of is. Believe me, it's nice to be recognised. But trying to keep a low profile when you don't want to be seen is difficult. In some ways, whatever happened on the show has made me more high-profile now."

"Really? How come?"

"It gave a different news spin on the whole thing. My mum has asked the phone company to change our home number now. There have been media requests from all over the country. Newspapers, TV channels, websites – it's all been rather crazy."

"Will you ever do an interview?"

"Maybe. I know I'll get asked a lot about my health and I haven't got any answers."

"Even now?"

"I can't explain what really happened. I just remember getting my saxophone out of the dressing room and heading towards the backstage area. Next thing I remember is waking up in hospital. It's not really much of a story."

Hannah looked surprised. She debated whether to tell him her theory and decided to leave it for now. If he asked, she could always tell him. She decided to change the subject. "Do you want a drink? I've got to go and pay for mine, so I can always order one."

"Yeah, I'd like that."

"Still drinking americano?"

"Sure, how did you remember?" he asked, looking surprised.

"I just remember these things, that's all."

With that, Hannah left the table quickly before Tim could say anything else. When she reached the counter, she sneaked a look over her shoulder to see what he was doing but he was only looking out of the window.

"Hi, Mr Wright," Hannah said to Joel's dad behind the counter. He was busy reading something and frowning. Through the hatch, Hannah noticed Mrs Wright busy washing up in the kitchen.

"Oh hello, Hannah, didn't see you there, love. What can I get you?"

"White americano please. And I need to pay for a large hazelnut latte."

Mrs Wright rushed out of the kitchen. "Don't worry about the latte, Ted, that was my treat. So, Hannah, who's your friend?"

Hannah hesitated, not sure whether she should give Tim up or not. "It's Tim," she said finally. "But please can I talk to him for a few minutes? He doesn't want to be recognised in public just yet."

"That's fine, Hannah, not a problem. Just tell him we'd like to speak to him when he's finished?"

Hannah agreed and headed back to the table with Tim's coffee. He was still sat there, staring out of the window, looking rather absent-minded.

"Alyssa and Ted want to talk to you at some point. I said I wanted to talk to you first."

"Ah right, that'll be about the gigs here, I think."

Hannah looked taken aback. "Really? Like performing live? In here?"

"Yes, there's a few things to be worked out, but I'd really like to do some performing here. It's a place close to my heart, I've got a few memories of some of the times we've had in here and, well, it just makes a lot of sense. I'd get some performing experience and Joel's parents were saying how much of a boost it would give their business."

"Oh, Tim, that's great. You'll pack the place out."

"Well, there's only one thing putting me off at the minute," Tim said, fiddling awkwardly with his cup.

"What's that?"

"Joel's parents asked me if I wanted a band made up of Alan and Joel."

"And what's wrong with that?"

"Well, you know Joel and I had that, shall we say, disagreement, at the music festival a while ago? We've always been a bit frosty since then. I'm surprised they asked. I'd have thought that was the last thing he would have wanted."

Hannah pondered this for a few moments. "Maybe you need to talk to those two. I seem to remember them being excited about the idea of being in a band. They were joking about touring the country with you only a week or so ago."

Tim sighed. "You're right, Han, I'll have to talk to them. I mean, playing in a band would be great, I just don't want the past to get in the way."

The conversation lapsed into silence as they both smiled awkwardly at each other before taking a sip of their drinks. Hannah was trying desperately to think of how to address the shyness between them. How could you ask someone how he felt about you when you weren't even sure yourself how you felt about him?

Hannah decided to try and be proactive. She was determined to find out how Tim felt about her before letting any of her feelings show. Having seen him talk about performing in Beans and Banter she could feel some feelings stirring; old feelings that she hadn't felt for a few months. Just being around him and seeing him again was having an effect on her insides.

"How have you been since the show ended?" she asked Tim, trying to sound as innocent as humanly possible.

"It's been a bit strange. I've been on my own a lot," Tim admitted.

Hannah was really trying hard to contain her feelings now. Could she be the one to stop him from feeling lonely? But thinking about it, did she really want to be? Why did Alan keep appearing in her mind?

"How about you? It's been ages since I've seen you," Tim went on.

"Wonder why that was," Hannah said, sullenly. She watched that one sting him a bit.

"Bit harsh. I had the chance of a lifetime. It meant I had to leave my friends behind and go and pursue it. I never dreamt I would get as far as I did. If you were in my position, would you not have gone?" he asked, looking straight at Hannah.

"I get that, Tim, I really do. I just wish you could have told me. I wouldn't have told anybody."

"Look, Hannah, I really wish I could have done. It's just they scare you into accepting all these rules and if you're found to break any of them, that's it; they'll just throw you off the show."

Hannah bit her tongue. "I'm sorry. I didn't realise the show meant that much to you. I thought that I had meant more to you."

Tim gave her a scared look over the rim of his cup. "Yeah, well, maybe you do mean something to me," he mumbled.

Hannah thought that was what he had said but wasn't one hundred per cent sure. She ended up giving him a confused look, trying to work out exactly what her ears had heard.

"So, enough about me. I think you know what I've been up to these past couple of months. What's been going on in Hannah's world?" Tim asked, changing the subject.

Hannah, once again, had reached an impasse. Did Tim really want to know what she had been up to? Or was it just polite chitchat that he was after? She decided that there was only one way to find out: lay it on him and see how he reacted. If he wanted to stay and listen then that would show he may still have feelings for her. If he looked disinterested or left then she would know she could move on.

"Well, it's been fairly busy. Exams. Working here. Trying to deal with all that and depression hasn't been fun." She was watching him carefully to see how he reacted.

"How's the depression been going?" Tim asked, taking a sip of his coffee.

"OK, I guess. I've changed my medication. I'm on Prozac now instead of the Cymbalta I was put on originally."

"Any changes?"

"I've noticed some mood swings, which are difficult to handle, but it's better than that numb, emotionless existence I felt under the Cymbalta."

"Wow. Well, that's great news. You feeling a little bit more... human?"

Hannah ran her fingers through her straightened hair and the image of herself in the mirror before she left the house flashed up in her mind's eye.

"Yes, it's taken a few weeks to come out of the funk, but I'm hoping there's some more progress to be made. I'd love to be in a place where I don't need the pills any more."

"How are you dealing with the dips?" Tim asked.

Hannah swallowed. There had been a few incidents where she had experienced sudden 'dips' in the past. These were usually isolated incidents where her mood plummeted, mostly leading to tears and Tim had been there for a few of them.

"I haven't had a major dip like those ones since the new pills kicked in," she said. She refrained from telling him that the last one she had experienced was after realising he had left.

"Well, that's great!"

Hannah smiled briefly. "Yeah, I guess so. I've also been reading this book."

She bent down to drag Sir Andrew Anderson's book out of her bag.

Tim's eyes widened but he didn't say anything.

"What?" Hannah asked, noticing his reaction.

Tim looked about nervously. "I'm not sure I'm supposed to tell anyone. Promise me you'll keep this under wraps. You can't even tell Amie?"

"Are you not bound by any confidentiality agreement or anything this time?" Hannah asked, a little sarcastically.

Tim just gave her a look. "Just promise me, that's all. I don't want to be accused of leaking anything before it's been formally announced."

Hannah nodded her agreement, wondering what on earth Sir Andrew Anderson's book and Tim could be connected by.

"I'm in talks with Sir Andrew about being the warm-up act for his tour. It starts in July."

Hannah didn't know what to say and ended up imitating a goldfish for a few moments. "Really?" she squeaked.

"Hannah, I really wouldn't lie to you about stuff like this. This is great for me to be able to talk to someone about it. My parents support me but they're always busy and Alice doesn't really care."

Hannah's heart reached out to him in that moment. She remembered what Amie had said to her earlier that evening. It felt like Tim needed someone in the same way as she did. Could she be that person? But if she was going to be that person for Tim, then why did Alan keep appearing? It then occurred to her that she knew exactly what she had to say.

"Listen, Tim, I was talking to Amie earlier and she said something that I want to say to you."

Tim didn't reply so Hannah carried on.

"I want you to know you'll always have me. For anything." It had felt quite easy to say it. It was how Amie had said it to her. And she really wanted to be there for him. But did she mean it? The fact that she kept thinking about Alan suggested not. Or at least not completely.

Almost as if he sensed Hannah's turmoil, he looked deep into her eyes again from under his fringe. "Hannah, listen," he whispered. "I want us to try and get back on the road we were on before I left."

Hannah was very aware of her heart thumping a samba beat in her chest. This wasn't her making the decision. This was her insecurity and her need to feel loved letting Tim decide that she had chosen him. But she didn't have the heart to hold him off or even to try telling him that she fancied Alan too. She didn't even know how to put that into words. Nothing made sense any more.

Tim continued, "I've spent a lot of time on my own recently and one of the things that I realised was that I'd never done that before. There was always someone here. It was usually you. I always want it to be you."

Tim had left his seat and was practically kneeling on the floor next to Hannah. He gently rested his hand on her knee. She felt frozen to the seat and didn't dare move.

"Sure," she said hoarsely and Tim threw his hands around her shoulders and pulled her in for a hug that lasted several seconds.

Hannah, her chin resting on Tim's shoulder, briefly closed her eyes. She really hoped she was doing the right thing. When she opened them the first thing she saw was a figure looking at them through the window. It was dark, but she could tell they were wearing glasses. It was only when she noticed a look that appeared to be fury cross their face it dawned on her who it had been.

The figure then disappeared before she could confirm but she was fairly sure it had been Alan. And suddenly, things seemed a lot more complicated.

CHAPTER FOURTEEN

Joel was conscious of his mobile phone buzzing on his bedside cabinet. He was also conscious that he was comfortable under the covers. It was still dark in his room, which he found very odd. Normally, he was a sound sleeper, going to bed in the dark and waking when it was light. It must have been the middle of the night, he realised.

Reluctantly, he leaned over to see what was causing his phone to be vibrating so much. Unlocking the screen, his phone reliably informed him it was only a few minutes past twelve, so it wasn't as late as he'd thought. He was surprised to find he had five text messages and three missed calls, all from Alan.

He decided to start with the messages in chronological order.

Hey buddy, you up?

All fairly normal, Joel thought. He read on.

Joel, come on, dude, be awake.

Still no clue as to what was so urgent.

I need to talk to you.

Still nothing as to what this was about. Joel noticed the fourth message had come a few minutes later.

Seriously dude, WAKE UP!!! You could sleep through an earthquake.

Another few minutes then passed before Alan had sent him the final message.

OK, I get it, you're gone until the morning, sorry. Just call me when you get this.

Thoroughly mystified, Joel checked what times the calls had come in. Alan had tried twice before he sent the texts. It must have been the final call that woke him, a few minutes ago.

Slightly hesitant, Joel hit the call button on his phone. It didn't even ring once before Alan answered.

"Joel, where have you been!"

"Al, what on earth has happened?"

"It's Hannah, mate, she still loves Tim."

It wasn't quite what Joel had been expecting to hear. In the pause that ensued while he was trying to react, he realised he could hear background noise.

"Al, where are you? Why is there loud music? What have you done?" Joel asked, more confused than he was before he started the call.

"I'm in a club in town," came the reply that Joel didn't want to hear and he then realised that Alan was slurring his words.

Joel swore under his breath. "Alright, which one? I'll walk and meet you. *Outside* the club. I'm not going to even try and get in."

"Diablos. On King Street."

"Right, gotcha. Give me fifteen minutes."

Hanging up, Joel reached out and switched on his light on the bedside table, so he could find his clothes. He rescued his jeans out of his washing pile and found a t-shirt on the floor. Was it clean? Joel realised he didn't care. As far as he was concerned, the middle of the night was for sleeping, not worrying about what he was wearing.

King Street was right in the centre of Huntingham, and featured a number of clubs and bars. Diablos was a fairly new club, and had a bit of a reputation at college for being rather lenient with its age restrictions. Joel knew that Alan had been in there before, so wasn't overly surprised to hear he'd been in there again.

He could hear the floorboards creaking from the room next door and he knew one of his parents was now awake. Sure enough, a few moments later, a knock came at the door.

"Joel, you alright, son?" came the whisper through the door. Joel couldn't tell which parent it was.

With a sigh he opened his door to find his dad on the landing. Joel wore a guilty look on his face. It was unusual for him to wake his parents in the night. In fact, he could only think of a handful of occasions he'd been the reason why one of them had to come in and find out what he was up to. He was renowned for being a solid sleeper.

His dad looked him up and down, giving Joel a puzzled look in return.

"Hey, is everything OK? I could hear you scrabbling about," Ted said in a low voice.

"Did I wake you up?" Joel asked, desperately hoping he hadn't.

Ted gave a quiet laugh. "No, don't panic. I was reading something on my Kindle. So what's up?"

"Alan rang. He sounds drunk and he's in a club in town," Joel replied, matching his dad's volume.

Ted closed his eyes and took a deep breath. "Come on then," he said, turning around and walking towards the stairs.

Joel didn't understand. "Pops? Where are you going?"

"You mean 'where are *we* going'."

"Do I?"

Ted stopped at the top of the stairs and sighed. "Come on, son. If he's out in town then anything could happen."

Joel wasn't quite sure how to respond to that, so silently followed his dad downstairs and into the yard behind the coffee shop where their car was parked.

"Right," Ted said when they had both climbed in to the family's pale blue Honda Jazz, "Where am I heading?"

"Diablos," Joel replied, checking his phone to see if there had been any further communication from Alan. There hadn't.

"Is that the fairly new place on King Street? Behind Waitrose?"

"I think so."

"OK, no problem," Ted mumbled, putting the car into first gear and pulling off.

"Mind if I put some music on?" Joel asked after a few moments of silence.

"Be my guest," Ted replied, keeping his eyes focused on the road.

"Any preferences?"

"No, you choose, son."

"Thanks," Joel said, rooting through the CDs in the glove compartment. "Didn't know you liked Einaudi," he added, when he sat up holding the Italian composer's 'Islands' album. "Is this Ma's?"

"I think I got it for her for Christmas. I quite like it too. Lovely melodies. Would love to have a piano night in the shop. I've got the sheet music for some older Einaudi stuff at home, quite fancy performing it."

"Wouldn't we need a better piano? The battered old thing at home wouldn't sound great on the stage."

Ted looked a little hurt. "That piano has been through a lot with me. I was ever so proud when you first banged your little fists on it as a nipper. Still proud seeing you play it these days too."

"I didn't know that, Pops? I didn't even know you could play the piano."

"Guess that's something you've learnt about me tonight then," Ted replied, a twinkle in his eye.

Joel thought about it for a few seconds. He'd never really connected with his dad on any sort of personal level. Finding out he'd played the piano was a bit of a surprise. "It's true. It's that thing that the twins always talk about, where you realise your parents are people, who have lives and interests; they're not just your parents."

"I remember that with my own folks," Ted admitted. "My dad was a violent drunk who drank himself into an early grave. Mum always used to say he'd been working, but he always came home late and smelling of booze. He used to beat Mum up a bit, though he never touched my sister or me. I don't even think they knew we knew. He used to hate the piano. It was Mum's you see. She loved her music; she had played all the way through college and saved like mad when she was a nurse so she could buy her own piano. He used to come home and find her playing it and get really angry. Don't know why it wound him up. I've played it since I was at school. When Mum passed away, I inherited it. Your Aunt Hilda ended up with the house and I got Mum's piano."

"I'd never twigged I never knew what happened to your parents, Pops. Or that you even had parents."

Ted gave a wry smile. "Mum died of cancer about a year before you were born. I was still a teenager when Dad's liver gave up. It was a blessing in disguise. It's why you've never met them. Since you were little, your mum's parents were the only grandparents you had. You just grew up with it like that. You'd never seemed interested so I never said anything."

"Was that a dig at me?" Joel asked, unsure.

Ted shook his head. "Not at all. Was just trying to make the point that I'd never told you because you'd never asked."

"Makes me wonder what else I should have asked over the years," Joel added.

"Well, if you think of anything, just ask. I'm quite happy to tell you. You're grown up enough now to understand some of the harsher things in life. Having an alcoholic dad though, is something I hope you never have to experience. Having to hide under your bed hearing your dad beat up your mum is one of those things that children should *never* have to go through."

"Seems to happen a fair bit these days, according to the news. Even the parents taking it out on the kids too."

"That's right, there's some shocking stories out there, son. Alcohol or drugs are usually involved. It was one of the reasons why your mother and I wanted to set up a coffee shop that would be open in the evenings; prior to Beans and Banter there were only pubs, bars or clubs in Huntingham – all of which sell alcohol. Plus you hear about domestic violence more these days than you ever did when I was young." Ted paused for a few seconds, a sad, dreamy look on his face. "Anyway, on the subject of alcohol, we're on King Street. Give Alan a ring, see where he is."

Joel duly obliged, although there was no answer. Frowning, he typed out a quick message.

Dude, my dad brought the car. Where are you?

Ted quickly pulled into a recently vacated parking space, a few yards down from the front doors of Diablos. He turned to look at Joel, who was still frowning. "What's up?"

Joel looked up from his phone. "I'm just a bit worried. He answered his phone straight away in the club…" Joel trailed off as he spotted a person in a bright blue jacket tumble out of the front door of Diablos, followed by two angry-looking bouncers, who were waving their arms furiously.

Ted saw Joel react and grabbed his arm. "Wait, is that Alan?"

"Looks like it," Joel mumbled, straining his neck to see over the car in front.

The bundle in the blue jacket splayed on the street, looked very still. Seemingly satisfied, the bouncers tossed something at the bundle and returned inside the club.

Ted was almost amused. "Why are we still sat here? If that's him, we can't leave him on the path like that. Anything could happen to him."

With that, they both climbed out. As they approached, it was obvious that it was Alan, minus his glasses and his hair looking rather ruffled. Joel spotted Alan's glasses on the pavement a few feet away and went to retrieve them. He guessed they were what the bouncers had thrown at his best friend. "Al, are you alright?" Joel then asked, bending down to put a hand on Alan's back. He was concerned, as he still hadn't seen Alan move.

Alan then stirred, which Joel presumed was a good sign. "Should we roll him over, Pops?"

Ted nodded and reached down to help Alan over. There were a few scratches on Alan's face, including a cut lip, which showed something had definitely happened to him.

"Well, he's breathing, so that's always a good sign," Ted said. "He doesn't half reek of alcohol though."

"His t-shirt and jacket are all damp," Joel said, pointing at the stain. "I'm beginning to wonder if he's had a drink thrown over him."

"That would make sense," Ted said, grabbing Alan under the armpits and lifting him to a seating position. "Grab his feet, will you? We can lie him across the back seat." They half dragged, half carried Alan to the car.

Once Alan was lying in the back seat, Ted grabbed a bottle of water out of the boot of the car and flicked a few drops of water on to Alan's face, causing him to flinch and screw his face up.

"Al, can you hear me?" Joel asked, shaking his best friend gently by the shoulder. "It's Joel."

Alan let out a low groan as a response but his eyes were still firmly closed. Joel and Ted shared a look.

"OK, you can hear me. Do you know what day it is?"

A frown appeared on Alan's face. "Mhombay," came his reply, sounding like his mouth was full of cotton wool. It made Joel wonder if Alan had bitten his tongue.

"Right, well it's now Tuesday but at least you know what day it was before this all started. What have you had to drink?"

"Warper."

Another look was shared between father and son, Joel shaking his head in disbelief; even in a slightly battered and inebriated state, Alan still managed to find humour in the situation. "Now, now Al, you've had more than water, haven't you," Joel said sternly.

At this point, Alan's eyes flickered open, taking a few seconds to focus. "Well, dhere was wops of ice. Dhap's warper?"

Not wanting to argue whether drinking ice counted as water or not, Joel asked his next question. "So, how do you feel?"

Alan thought about it for a few seconds before a forlorn expression crossed his face. "Bip wuff."

"I bet you're feeling rough. Your face is in a bit of a state, you've cut your lip, you smell like someone tried to drown you in Malibu and I'm presuming you've bitten your tongue, which is why you sound like you're talking with a pair of socks in your mouth. Plus it looked like you were thrown out of Diablos. Overall, yeah, bet you do feel rough." Joel realised he was practically shouting at Alan now. He felt his dad's hand on his shoulder and knew he should stop.

Alan had a very sorry-looking expression on his face and gave a weak shrug.

"Come on, dude. What's this all about? You said on the phone Hannah still loves Tim? What happened?"

Alan sighed. "Anna mep Dim lasf nipe anb I faw dem ugging."

Joel couldn't believe it. "They were hugging? I thought you meant you'd caught them behind the bins or something."

A look of horror flashed across Alan's face but he said nothing more.

Ted cleared his throat. "What Alan says is true. Hannah came in to the shop last night and met Tim. They had a coffee together, hugged each other at the end and then they both left separately. Nothing else happened. That I saw anyway."

"And that's a good enough reason to go on a bender, get yourself in this state and wake me up in the middle of the night," Joel said, his anger rising. "And my dad," he added hastily, when he'd caught Ted's eye.

"I'm sowwy," Alan said, humbly. "Ip was unexpeckeb." Alan's apologetic expression did nothing to dampen Joel's fury.

"Unexpected? Have you even spoken to Hannah about it? What makes you think that they're anything more than friends?" Joel noticed tears start to well up in Alan's eyes, which took him by surprise. "Alright," he said, with a sigh. "Come on, let's get you home to bed. We'll discuss this in the morning."

Ted took his cue and climbed into the driver's seat. Joel sat in the back with Alan, who had shut his eyes and appeared to be sleeping. Joel decided it was pointless pursuing it any further. Trying to understand Alan was hard enough, without him getting emotional. He ended up looking out of the window, and felt his eyelids getting heavy.

They didn't say another word, letting the sound of Einaudi wash over them, until they turned into the marketplace where the Beans and Banter shop front was situated.

"What the…" Ted muttered in the front, causing Joel to look up. His father appeared to be looking at an ambulance parked further down the street, with people crowded around it.

"Is that outside the French house?" Joel asked, although he was fairly sure he already knew the answer.

"Looks like it. Surely not… No… It can't be. Is that one of the girls?" Ted asked, straining his neck to try and see who was on the stretcher being wheeled into the ambulance.

As they drove past, Joel's face was pressed against the window of the car desperately hoping it wasn't Amie on the stretcher. He then felt a pang of guilt; he didn't particularly want it to be Hannah either. But still, he definitely didn't want it to be Amie. Due to it being dark, and slightly glared by the lights from ambulance, he couldn't even tell who was standing watching.

"Could you see who it was?" Ted asked, concern etched in his voice.

"No, it was too dark."

"Is Alan sleeping?"

Joel quickly checked. "Yep, looks like he's gone."

"Right, you jump out here and find out what's going on. I'll get the car put away and make up a bed for Al but I'll need your help getting him upstairs. I'll come and find you. Quick, go!"

The car came to a stop and Joel leapt out, his heart thudding in his chest. Please, don't let something terrible have happened, he thought. Please.

CHAPTER FIFTEEN

Hannah was standing on the pavement watching the stretcher be transferred into the ambulance, when Joel came running over. There was a small crowd of neighbours present; most looking like the ambulance being there had awakened them from their beds, such was the display of nightwear on show.

"Hey," he said, rather breathless. "What on earth happened? Are you alright?" He looked at her as a tear rolled down her cheek and he wondered for how long she had been trying to hold it all together.

She looked back at him, wiping the tear away, smudging her mascara, creating a black smudge on the back of her hand. In a croaky voice she said, "It's Mum, she fell down the stairs."

Joel, slightly thrown by how pretty Hannah looked, with her hair straightened and her face made up, was shocked but breathed a sigh of relief. "Crikey, that's terrible. I hope she's alright. How's Amie?" Out of the corner of his eye he noticed his own mother making her way over to them.

"Amie's about somewhere," Hannah said vaguely, her gaze fully focused on her mum in the back of the ambulance.

Joel decided he would be unlikely to get much more out of Hannah, so left her to it. She was hugging herself tightly and Joel wasn't sure if it was just because it was cold outside. Making a mental note to make sure she was alright later, Joel turned to face his mother.

"Hi, Ma," he said, trying to sound casual.

She regarded him with an amused expression. "I hope you've got a good explanation for why you weren't asleep in your room, young man."

"A very good one. I'll explain in a bit but Pops was with me the whole time. I just want to make sure if Amie's OK, if that's alright with you?" He said it as innocently as he could.

Alyssa Wright gave him a knowing smile. "I'll be waiting with Hannah."

Without saying anything else, Joel ran inside the French house. He thought he had spotted Amie on the phone through the front window, so made his way into the lounge first.

She was sat on the sofa, looking despondently at her mobile phone.

"Hey," Joel said gently, causing her to jump.

"Sneaking up on a girl like that, horrible thing to do," she replied, mock-scolding him.

"I just wanted to see if you were OK."

She gave him a tired look and shrugged. "Yeah, I'll be OK, when I know Mum's alright." Her face belied what she had just said.

"Ah right, that's good to know," Joel said, looking awkwardly at his hands, wondering if he should ask whom she was calling. "I hope your Mum's OK too."

"Hope so, the paramedics were really quick to get here," Amie said, glancing out of the window.

"When we got home and saw the ambulance outside, I was worried. I thought something had happened to you or Hannah."

"Oh, Joel, that's really sweet of you," Amie said but was then distracted by looking out of the window. Something had caught her attention and she climbed to her feet.

"It was nothing," he mumbled as she barged past him. He reluctantly followed her to the door and felt really helpless as he saw her nod at one of the paramedics and then disappear inside the back of the ambulance. It promptly drove off.

He couldn't quite explain the empty feeling he had. He had wanted to hug Amie, to make sure she was alright and find out why she looked upset being on the phone. Seeing her brush past him annoyed him slightly but he tried to reason with himself that she was worried about her mum. It then struck him; what had happened to Hannah? He went and stood in the doorway and could see his own mother still comforting the remaining twin in the street.

Now the ambulance had gone, the few people wrapped in their dressing gowns returned to their own homes, some patting Hannah on the arm and offering words of encouragement.

Joel felt like a bit of an outsider, watching everything unfold from within a glass box, until Hannah and Alyssa made their way up the garden path, knocking him from his reverie. It was only then that Joel realised a tall, dark-haired young man in a police officer's uniform was accompanying them.

Joel stood back to let everybody in, his mother giving him a curious look on her way past him and the police officer giving him a polite nod.

Hannah went and sat in the same spot Joel had found Amie in, while everyone else took a seat. The police officer took a seat in a chair underneath the window, where he took a notebook and a pen out of his pocket and gave a brief smile to everyone else in the room.

"Thank you everyone, I'm Police Constable Shaw. I appreciate it's late but I just need to ensure I've covered everything. So, Miss French, I just need to confirm a few details with you, if that's alright and you're feeling up to it?"

Hannah nodded and Joel's mum, who already had her arm around Hannah's shoulders, gave her a squeeze.

"Can you just outline, again for me, what happened here this evening?" PC Shaw asked.

"Well," Hannah began quietly, "I was just coming in the door and I saw Mum at the top of the stairs. She asked how my evening had been and everything, she wasn't quite on the top step at this point." She stopped and fanned her face for a few seconds, tears welling up in her eyes. "And then, she turned around to go upstairs and she slipped!" Her voice cracked with emotion as she whipped around and buried her face in Alyssa's shoulder, clearly sobbing.

Joel sat there, looking on wide-eyed, trying to imagine how he'd react if he'd seen his mum fall down the stairs. He struggled to picture it; it was too horrific to imagine willingly.

PC Shaw looked slightly uncomfortable and was paying a lot of attention to his notebook. Hannah regained her composure after a few minutes and turned to face the police officer again, her eye make-up smudged quite badly now.

"Sorry," she mumbled.

"Not at all, don't worry," PC Shaw replied, flashing a very fake smile.

Joel got the impression this was one aspect of his job PC Shaw didn't particularly enjoy.

"Do you know if your mother had been drinking this evening?" the officer asked.

Hannah nodded. "She usually does have a glass of wine or two during the week."

"It's a regular occurrence then. OK." More scribbling went into the notebook. "How much would you say she drinks on average?"

Hannah looked a little awkward. "It's hard to say. She has a stressful job, and it's her crutch really. She does the Aldi shop every week and gets herself a few bottles."

"So, a bottle a night perhaps?"

Hannah looked shocked. "No, not that much. Say half a bottle on average."

"Had anything, lets say, bad or unfortunate happen to her recently?"

"No. If anything tonight was the happiest I'd seen her in a while."

PC Shaw just looked at her, clearly expecting her to continue.

Hannah sighed. "I had a date."

Joel was surprised to hear her use the word 'date'. From what he'd gathered earlier, Hannah had just met Tim in the shop for a coffee. A 'date' had connotations.

"And was that where you were returning from?"

"She'd been at my coffee shop across the road, Beans and Banter," Alyssa replied, jumping in.

PC Shaw gave her a withering look but said nothing, deciding to scribble in his notebook instead. Joel presumed he had wanted Hannah to reply unaided. He noticed his mother stare back at the police officer without even batting an eyelid. She didn't appear to be intimidated by the attitude on display.

"And, *Miss French*," PC Shaw continued, making it very obvious who he wanted to answer, "where was your sister this evening?"

"As far as I know, she was here the whole time. I went out to Beans and Banter and came home around eleven thirty."

Joel noticed a frown cross his mother's face at that point, and made a mental note to ask her what that was about later.

"And where was she at the time your mother was on the stairs?" PC Shaw asked.

Hannah had to think about it for a few seconds. "Upstairs. She was upstairs in her room. She came running out when she heard my screams."

PC Shaw raised an eyebrow but once again, said nothing. A quick glance at Alyssa Wright's stony expression caused him to return to his notebook. He jotted a few more notes down and stood up to leave. "Well, thank you for your time this evening. Time to get some rest I think. Best wishes to your mother, Miss French."

He sounded relatively humble when he said that, Joel noted.

Alyssa saw him out and returned to the front room. She looked out of the window to watch the police car drive off and tutted. Joel could tell she hadn't been impressed. She turned around, glancing at both Hannah and Joel. "To think, in my day, police officers were supposed to be model citizens. They respected you and in turn, you respected them. It felt like, at one point, Hannah, he was going to accuse you and Amie of pushing your poor mother down the stairs!"

Hannah shrugged. "I only answered his questions. He was just doing his job."

"I agree with Ma, though. There was something a bit opinionated about him. You don't need to go into people's homes with that sort of attitude," Joel said.

"Well, Hannah, if you have to speak to him again, don't let him intimidate you. There's no need for it," Alyssa added. She turned towards Joel. "And you, young man," she said, looking quizzically at him, "we need to get to bed but before that, you need to explain to me why you weren't in yours earlier."

Joel looked a little awkwardly at Hannah, who mistook his glance to mean he wanted to ask something. Joel realised that, in effect, she was the indirect reason for him being awake in the middle of the night. He wasn't quite sure how he could get that across to his mother without upsetting Hannah in some way.

To his surprise, Hannah stood up and offered to put the kettle on. Alyssa shook her head but Joel asked for a cup of tea, just so she would have to leave the room. Hannah left quickly and once Joel heard her rattle about in the kitchen, he visibly relaxed.

Alyssa noticed Joel's change in demeanour immediately, swooping in like a bird of prey. "So, it had something to do with Hannah then?" she asked innocently.

"Yes," he whispered. "I was rescuing Alan. Pops heard me getting ready and took me in the car."

"Where?"

"Alan was in a club in town."

"Doing what?"

"Getting drunk, I think. I hope that's all it was."

"And where is he now?"

"Pops had him in the car. That's a good point actually, Pops wanted my help getting him upstairs at home." Joel started to get up.

Alyssa looked down her nose right at Joel. "Stay right where you are. You're not escaping that easily."

Joel sighed and remembered his mother frowning earlier. "So, why did you frown when Hannah said what time she had got home?"

His mother looked confused for a few moments, but then said, "I was surprised at that. She left the shop at about ten o'clock."

That made Joel frown too. "So where had she been?"

"No idea. But that police officer didn't want to hear my story, so I didn't bother offering that information."

They both sat in silence for a few moments, the noise of the kettle in the kitchen now audible.

"I just don't get it, Joel. I don't understand why you being out of bed has got anything to do with Hannah?" his mother said suddenly.

Joel felt a bit frustrated. Was it not obvious? "Alan saw Hannah meeting Tim in the shop earlier," he said, with a glare.

"And?"

"Well, I don't think he was expecting her to be in there with Tim. She'd gone to a lot of effort; I've never seen her look like that before. She's wearing make-up and everything. Her hair even looks nice. He got a bit of a shock, I think, which is why he went out to drown his sorrows."

Alyssa frowned. "I feel like I'm missing something."

Joel sighed with exasperation. "Don't you get it? Alan fancies Hannah!"

Joel heard a gasp, followed by a crash and looked up to see Hannah stood in the doorway. She was looking at the floor, where the cup she had been holding was now in pieces. She turned around and fled the scene, taking the stairs two at a time.

CHAPTER SIXTEEN

Alyssa and Joel looked at each other, both unsure what to do. Joel was annoyed with himself for revealing Alan's feelings for Hannah but also frustrated with Hannah for appearing at that exact moment.

"I'll go and have a look for something to mop up the mess," Alyssa said, trying her best to sound practical, leaving Joel sat there trying to figure out how he should react.

His mother returned with a cloth a few moments later, noticing him still sat there. "Thanks for all of your help, son," she said sarcastically.

Joel looked at her and shook his head. "Sorry, Ma. I don't know what to do. Should I go after her?"

Alyssa gave him a sympathetic smile. "If I know anything about teenage girls, then you would be best to give her some space for a bit."

Joel gave his mother a confused look. "But she shouldn't have heard that. Alan will kill me. I need to explain how he was going to tell her himself. I owe him that much."

"Really? The guy who went and, by all accounts, got wasted on seeing Hannah with someone else. Do you owe him anything?"

His mother's reaction was a surprise to Joel. "Where's this come from, Ma? You're usually one of Alan's biggest fans."

"Joel, look, son, you're growing up now. You'll be leaving college next year and starting your adult life properly. Alan's instant reaction to anything going badly is to drink his sorrows away. Is that really the sort of person you want to be friends with?"

"Ma, this really isn't the time or the place to have such a conversation and I'm struggling to believe what you've just said. Friendship isn't about fearing what a person will turn into; it's a celebration of all those great times and unbelievable experiences you've been through already. Alan and me, well, we've been through a lot together. I'm not going to give up on him just like that." Joel glared at his mother to make the point he really wasn't impressed with her.

Alyssa Wright regarded her son with a stern expression. "Your dad texted me earlier. He said he'd told you about his dad and that you might ask some questions. Did he tell you what happened to his dad?"

Joel looked up at the ceiling and shook his head. "Yeah, he was a violent drunk who went to an early grave."

"Precisely. Years of alcohol abuse it was. Your dad was a frightened, timid man when I met him. What about Christine tonight? She'd had a bottle of wine, Hannah said. No good comes of alcohol, Joel. It's fine in small doses. Sure, it can lead to some great nights. But there's a darker side to it, if you come to depend on it. People want that great night every night or they use it as a crutch to numb the pain of every day life and then never want to feel the pain again."

Joel was really starting to struggle to believe what he was hearing now. "You're saying that what happened here tonight was because Amie and Hannah's mum had been drinking? Really? Like it's her own fault that she slipped?"

"Yes. I am. And I'll stick by that. We've known Christine for a good few years now, and after all she's been through, I can understand why she gets through the amount of booze she does. She's done everything she can to provide a decent home for the twins. It's her crutch. I'm beginning to wonder if she'd been celebrating getting Hannah to the point where she was going to go out with someone. You saw how much effort Hannah had put into her appearance tonight. I'm fairly certain that Hannah wouldn't have done that herself. It looks like Christine maybe overdid it a bit and was going up to bed when Hannah walked in. It's a horrible thing to happen but perhaps, she had it coming."

Joel looked incredulously at his mother. "I can't believe this, Ma, I love you and all but this is ridiculous!"

"Fine, we agree to disagree, but promise me two things before we leave. One, you'll message Hannah and say we're going and if she needs anything we're across the street. Two, you'll have a word with Alan when he's back with us and tell him he can't go on like this."

Joel glared at his mother but rather sulkily agreed. "Fine. I'll message Hannah now." He fished his phone out of his pocket and typed a message. "And I'll talk to Alan. In the morning, though. Can we please go home and get to bed?"

"Sure. Guess we'll see what your dad has done with Alan."

As they left the French household, Joel felt a little guilty that he hadn't been back to see his dad since being dropped off an hour ago.

Heading around the back of the shop to where their car was parked, they found Ted mopping up in the back of the car. Alan was still flat out on the back seat, audibly snoring.

"Oh, hi, you two. Nice to see you both," Ted said, a little sarcastically.

"What on earth happened?" Alyssa asked, her eyes scanning the back seat of the car with disdain.

"Oh this? Well, Alan decided to throw up, so I'm just cleaning it up."

Joel could feel his mother's eyes burning into the side of his head.

Refusing to look at her, and feeling guiltier by the second, he put a hand on his dad's shoulder. "Pops, Alan's my responsibility. Lets get him upstairs and I'll clean this up afterwards. Don't think I'll be getting much sleep tonight anyway."

Ted delightedly put down the towel and the can of cleaning foam and grabbed one of Alan's legs, pulling him out of the car so they could grab his shoulders.

"I put a mattress in your room, son. Can we make it up there in one trip?"

"Guess we'll soon see. Right, lift him on three?"

Having successfully carried Alan up the stairs between them without any mishap, Joel returned downstairs to carry on cleaning the back seat of the car. His parents had bid him goodnight again, with his mother giving him some stern looks, clearly trying to remind him to talk to Alan in the morning. Joel brushed it off. It wasn't a conversation he particularly wanted to have; how were you supposed to tell your best friend that they had a drinking problem?

Spraying the foam on another patch of vomit, his thoughts drifted towards Amie. He realised he had been preoccupied with worrying about Hannah and her reaction to what he'd said about Alan, he hadn't even messaged Amie to ask how things were. Slipping his phone out his pocket, he opened up his messaging app. To his surprise, she was showing as having been online a few minutes ago; he might even get a reply from her.

Keeping it simple, he typed: *Hey. Just me. Still awake. How's your mum doing?*

He carried on cleaning up, for what felt like several minutes, hoping she would reply. He felt a buzz in his pocket a few moments later and all thoughts about cleaning went out of the window.

Joelly! Great to hear from you. Sorry I rushed off. Hannah and I had agreed I'd go to hospital with Mum. Hannah has a thing about hospitals as you can guess. Mum isn't great but she is stable.

Joel didn't really get what Amie meant. *What does that mean? Is she alright?*

There's a lot of swelling, so the doctors don't really want to say much at the minute. She's been for an x-ray so just waiting to see what's going on with that. She's still wearing a neck brace just as a precaution I think.

Fair enough, Joel thought. He typed back: *How are you holding up?*

I'm OK. Tired.

Yeah I bet you are.

How's Hannah doing?

Joel paused, not entirely sure what to say. In the end he replied with: *She's doing alright. She had the police ask lots of questions. Have you heard from her?*

No I haven't. Let me message her now.

It took a few minutes before Joel noticed she was typing again. *So, where were you coming from earlier? Unlike you to be out at that time of night? I saw you jumping out of your car* was the message he received.

Joel stared at his phone. He was in a complete quandary; should he tell her exactly what happened? He put his phone down on the seat next to him for a few seconds, realising how damp the seat was beneath his hand. He looked down at the can of foam and the cloth, where he had left them on the seat, and, in that moment, made the decision that if this was the consequence of helping his best friend then Alan had whatever was coming to him.

He wrote: *It's complicated.* He left it at that. If she really wanted to know, now was the time for her to say.

It took several moments before he had a reply. *Joel, you still there?*

Feeling guilty, he then realised that Amie probably needed to know anyway. She had always been Hannah's main pillar of support; he was slightly puzzled that Hannah hadn't messaged her about it. He thought Amie would have been the first person to contact.

Yep, I'm here.

Any advance on 'it's complicated'?

OK. I was rescuing Alan from a club in town.

He decided to draw it out as long as possible rather than blurt it all out in one go. That way when he told Alan the next morning he would at least have a very small scrap of defence to work with.

What? Why was he in a club? How did he even get in?

He had some bad news and took it badly. Getting drunk in a club is his way of dealing with things when they get too tough for him. I've had to go out to him before. I don't know how he does it without needing ID or anything. Scary. Tonight, though, he got thrown out of Diablos. Dad and me got there and saw the bouncers chucking him out.

That's crazy. Any idea what the bad news was?

Joel sighed. Of course he knew, but he still couldn't make up his mind whether to say it was because of Hannah.

Sort of. He was hoping something would happen and it didn't.

Oh right. Where is he now?

Joel was slightly relieved; she hadn't pushed on him that hard at all. *He's upstairs on my floor. He threw up in the car so I have to clean it up.*

Yay. Sounds fun.

Where are you? What's happening where you are?

I'm in a noisy ward. Mum's still unconscious but she's hooked up to all sorts of machines busy bleeping away. There's a woman in the bed next to me snoring quite loudly and a man opposite who keeps shouting. Not sure how much sleep I'll get.

Oh, Amz, that sounds horrible. And you still don't really know if your Mum's alright yet?

Joel's heart melted when she replied with the sad face emoticon. He felt so helpless sat in the car. All he wanted, in that moment, was to be at

Amie's side and give her a hug.

Amz, I really wish I was there. Don't think my parents will appreciate being woken up a second time tonight though to give me a lift. Isn't there anyone else you can call on?

I tried my dad. That was who I was on the phone to when you surprised me earlier. I knew Mum still had a number for him in the drawer downstairs. Don't think Hannah knows that. Just thought he might come.

And? What did he say?

He just laughed. Said something about her being a silly bitch and hung up.

Joel couldn't believe what he had just read. What kind of father would say that to a child about their mother?

Amz, that's awful, you'd have thought he would have at least tried to comfort you or something.

I thought so too. Obviously not.

Is that the first time you've spoken to him? Like since he left?

Yes. Won't be trying him again. You know how you want your dad there for those special events in life? Graduation, wedding, maybe even your birthdays?

Sure.

Well he won't be at any of mine or Hannah's. That's for certain. I'll make sure of it.

Joel wasn't quite sure how to respond so decided to change the subject. *Have you heard from Han yet?*

No, I haven't actually. Was she upset when you saw her?

Joel, once again, realised he knew the answer straight away. The last time he'd seen Hannah was the sight of her legs running up the stairs. She hadn't seemed particularly happy.

Not really upset. Perhaps a bit stressed out by it all.

Did you know she'd been on a date tonight?

Kind of. She told the police that was where she'd been. Didn't say who it was with though.

She hadn't needed to, of course; Joel already knew.

Would it shock you if I said it was with Tim?

Not really. Perhaps a bit surprising after he disappeared. I know she was hurting a lot after that.

I wasn't keen. I'm not even sure how it went. I think she got in, surprised Mum and then Mum turned and slipped down the stairs.

That was how Hannah described it. Makes me wonder if she's feeling responsible.

That's Han. She'd feel responsible even if she hadn't been there.

One thing I can't work out though: Ma said she left about 10:00 but she didn't get in until 11:30? Where did she go?

That's interesting. It was definitely 11:30 when she got in. I'll ask her.

The conversation came to a halt for a few moments before Joel received another message from Amie.

Right. I've messaged her again. Thanks for being here, Joel. It means a lot. I wish you were here in person. This is all so scary.

Don't worry about it, Amz. I wish I was there too.

I don't want to cut our conversation short but I need to try and get some sleep. Thank you for being so great. I'll speak to you tomorrow.

Sure. Goodnight xx

He hadn't meant to type the kisses. He was a little nervous as to how Amie would respond. He felt his phone vibrate and looked warily at the screen.

Night xxxxx

Having received more kisses than he sent, Joel felt very satisfied. He noticed his big, beaming smile in the rear-view mirror. Maybe that unintentional slip hadn't been a bad thing after all.

He finished cleaning up the car and headed inside to bed, feeling like the luckiest guy in the world.

CHAPTER SEVENTEEN

Tuesday 17th April, morning
The Wright House

Joel awoke to the sound of Radio 1 coming through his radio alarm. Still feeling drained from the events of the night before, he rolled over and hoped that his radio would just switch itself off. After listening his way through a whole song, Joel heard a shuffling from the floor and he remembered Alan was there. Leaning out of his bed, he patted Alan on the shoulder. "Hey buddy. Come on, it's time to get up."

Alan merely responded with a groan.

Joel climbed over him and prodded him with a big toe. "Dude, after all that's happened, you need to get up. There's a lot you need to know."

Alan, once again, made a noise suggesting he was going to do anything but spring off the mattress at that exact moment. Joel managed to silence the radio and gave Alan one more try.

"Al, it's time to get up and face the consequences of what you started last night." Joel then gave his best friend a hard jab in the ribs.

Alan winced and opened one eye. "Bloody hell, I've got a right cracker of a headache."

Alan's voice still sounded a bit thick, so Joel presumed his tongue hadn't completely returned to normal size yet, but at least he was easier to understand than in the middle of the night.

"I bet you do buddy; you were quite the adventurer last night."

Massaging his forehead, Alan turned and looked at Joel. "Did we go out drinking?"

Joel looked amused. "*We* didn't. You did."

Alan screwed up his face. "Oh great. What was I reacting to?"

Joel pretended to think about it for a few seconds. "Let me see… Was it… No, it wasn't that. Well, it could have been that. But it wasn't."

"Dude, seriously," Alan said imploringly.

Joel shrugged. "Fair enough," he said, looking Alan dead in the eyes. "I'll say one word. Hannah."

Alan looked a little stunned for a moment and then he clearly began to piece together the fragments of memory from the night before. Joel still found himself amused, watching the expressions on Alan's face as it all fell into place.

"So, you up to speed yet?" Joel asked innocently.

Alan looked a little guiltily at him. "I remember going into Diablos but how I ended up here… I don't know."

"Right, I'm glad you're up to about ten o'clock last night, but there's a lot I still need to tell you. Fancy some breakfast?"

"Sure, if your mum's cooking?"

"She probably will be with the breakfast rush, but I'll see what's happening. First you'd better get yourself cleaned up. You're still in your vomit covered clothes from the night before."

Alan wrinkled his nose. "I wondered what the smell was."

"I'm sure Ma washed the set of clothes you left here when you last stayed so I'll find those and let you have them."

Joel stuck his head out of his door to check if anybody was in the bathroom. "It's all clear, dude."

"Cheers, Joelly. Seriously, dude, thanks. You're a legend."

Joel shrugged. "You'd do the same for me. Now go on, get yourself sorted and I'll see what's happening downstairs."

Alan made his way across the landing to the bathroom, pausing at the top of the stairs before continuing. "Something wondrous is definitely cooking down there," he said over his shoulder.

Joel padded downstairs, ruffling his own hair in the mirror on the wall as he went. He agreed with Alan about whatever was cooking as he followed the scent of frying meat to the main kitchen. Even at this time of the morning his parents would have been serving coffees and breakfast rolls for an hour. With the train station located around the corner, and with Huntingham being on a direct train link to London, they had discovered that hot food and drink at that time of the morning was turning out to be quite popular with the business commuters.

"Morning, Ma," he said as he pushed the kitchen door open.

Alyssa looked up from the griddle pan and smiled, although she didn't look too impressed. "I hate it when you say that. It means I've been up for a couple of hours. And after the night we had, all I want to do is go back to sleep."

"Pleased to see you too, Ma," Joel replied, brushing off his mum's comments; she was definitely crabby following the night before. "Can I nab anything for breakfast?"

"Is your booze-addled pal awake too? Hope he's got a rotten hangover."

"Ma, you need some more coffee, stop being such a grump. Al's up, he's having a shower. Do you know where his clothes are from the last time he was here?"

"Ah, the last time he got wasted," Alyssa commented, her expression turning sour. "They should be in your wardrobe somewhere, they were washed."

"Thanks," Joel said, looking at what was in the deep-fat fryer. "Any hash browns left?"

"Sure, should be in there."

"Great, we'll be down shortly. Save some bacon for us too."

Joel could hear his mother tut with exasperation as he headed back upstairs. He was fairly certain, as grumpy as she was in the morning, she would leave a plate out for them both.

Both teenagers reappeared a few minutes later, with towel-dried hair and glowing from a hot shower. Joel nipped back into the kitchen and found the plates his mum had duly left out on the counter nearest the door. He looked at her bent over the sink and thought he should make the effort, despite her bad mood.

"Thanks, Ma," he said, putting an arm around her and giving her a kiss on the cheek. "You're fantastic."

Muttering something about not wanting her only son to go hungry, she carried on rinsing the crockery, her cheeks taking on a pink tinge.

Collecting breakfast, he slipped into the regular spot beside Alan. "There you go, buddy," he said, putting the plates down.

"Thanks, dude," Alan said, helping himself to a slice of bacon. "So, what have I missed?"

Much like his tomato ketchup, Joel decided to lay it on thick. "Well, after Pops and I rescued you from being chucked out of Diablos, we got home to find an ambulance outside the French house."

That stopped Alan in his tracks. "Wha?" he said, around a mouthful of bacon.

"Don't worry, the twins are both alright, as far as I know. Their mum had fallen down the stairs."

Alan swallowed very loudly. "Is she alright?"

"I was messaging Amie in the middle of the night and all she knew was that she was stable."

"That doesn't really say anything; just means her vitals and all that are fine. No idea of the damage?"

"Not at that time. Too much swelling or something."

Alan chewed pensively on another slice of bacon. "How are the twins holding up?" he asked, after a few moments.

"Amie's strong. She's holding up quite well, determined to not let anything defeat her. She seemed a bit shaken when I saw her, but she's a trooper; she'll always find some inner strength and fight through all this."

"Alright, alright. I know you can wax lyrical all day about how amazing Amie is. How's Hannah?"

"Well, she got a bit of a grilling at one point from a police officer. Ma thought she was being accused of pushing her mum down the stairs although I thought he was just asking questions."

"Seems harsh. So then what happened?"

Joel scratched his chin, trying to decide how he should tell Alan what he had let slip in the middle of the night. There just didn't seem to be any way he could soften the blow. "I may have told Hannah you fancy her," he blurted.

Alan's eyes widened considerably.

"It sort of slipped out," Joel added, hoping he could explain himself so Alan didn't take it too badly. "I hadn't meant for her to hear it. Ma just couldn't understand why you'd taken yourself into town, so I was trying to explain it to her. Hannah was making a cup of tea and she came back quicker than anticipated."

Alan's face didn't exactly look pleased but he carried on chewing his breakfast.

"Please say something," Joel pleaded. "This silence is killing me."

The response, when it came, was with a much darker tone than Joel had been anticipating.

"Do you know what you might have just done?" Alan's voice was quiet but brimming with anger.

This time it was Joel's turn to look wide-eyed. "No…" he said slowly.

"Have you heard from her since?" Alan asked, his eyes boring into Joel's.

"No…" Joel repeated.

Alan finished his plate and stood up to leave. "Listen, Joel, I really hope I'm wrong. Keep your phone on though. I might need your help."

Joel looked confused. "Where are you going?" he asked as Alan made for the door.

"Where do you think? To see Hannah!" came the frustrated reply.

Joel sat back in the seat and put his hands behind his head, his ears picking up one of his favourite acoustic rock anthems playing on the shop's sound system. He listened to the rest of it for a few minutes, his mind trying to work out what had just happened. He really hadn't expected that response; he'd thought Alan would just brush it off and be fine with it. He checked his phone to make sure he had 'vibrate' switched on and slipped it back into his pocket.

Finishing his breakfast, Joel then took both plates back to the kitchen, where Alyssa was now sat reading a newspaper and drinking a cup of coffee.

"Thanks, Ma," he said, putting the plates in the sink.

"No problem," his mother replied, not looking up. "Where did Alan dash off to?"

Joel sighed. It was extremely rare for anything to get past her. "To check on Hannah."

Alyssa was struggling to keep a smile from crossing her face. "Ah, I see. So you told him."

Joel nodded.

"Well, it's the best thing. Better for you to tell him than for him to find out from Hannah."

Joel wasn't impressed. "Ma, you can be so blunt," he said angrily. "I just don't know what to say to him now. I've totally broken his trust."

It was Alyssa's turn to sigh and she put her newspaper down. "You do nothing, son. There's nothing you can do. It's up to Alan. If he decides that you've overstepped with what you told Hannah then that's it; your friendship will be over. But if your friendship is strong enough, it'll ride this storm. If it isn't, it'll sink. What does that meerkat say on those adverts? Simples?"

Joel, reeling slightly from his mother using 'simples' to finish a sentence, didn't know what else to say.

"Listen, if you're worried, have you seen who are sat at the counter?"

Joel peeked through the serving hatch and noticed Alan's dad, Duncan, and Alan's older brother, Simon, sat there.

"Talk to them. Maybe they can help. What you don't want is for Alan to have another of last night's adventures. Then he definitely won't be entitled to breakfast," Alyssa said with a glare.

"Fair enough, Ma. I'll see what they say." Joel left the kitchen and climbed on a stool at the counter next to Simon.

Duncan Proctor, Alan's dad, worked in London for an accountancy firm and usually stopped in at Beans and Banter for a coffee before catching his train. More recently, Simon had joined him, having been offered a graduate position in the legal department of Duncan's firm. This morning, they were both sat on the stools in front of the counter, dressed in their work suits, chatting away to Ted about the pros and cons of the Chancellor's recent budget announcement.

"Joel! Good morning, young man, how the devil are you?" Duncan asked, pumping Joel's hand in a firm shake, as was his custom. Simon, who was more reserved, just smiled in greeting.

"I'm good, thanks," Joel replied, always slightly amused by Duncan Proctor's larger than life attitude.

"Heard the news about Christine French. Terrible that. Just makes you think that it could be one of us next, though," Duncan commented.

Joel nodded. "Amie said she was stable last night. Haven't heard from her yet this morning though."

"Well, do send our regards," Duncan said solemnly. "Anyway, you look like you came over to ask a question. I'm sure you're not that fussed about politics. What can we do you for?" He then took a sip of his coffee.

"Well," Joel began, but then hesitating when he realised he didn't know if his family knew about Alan's antics. "I've had a bit of a falling out with Alan. I said something to someone else that I probably shouldn't have that may make things difficult for Al and I'm worried as to how he'll react." He received only puzzled looks. "I think I know how he'll react now, but I just wondered if there was someone to look out for him."

Duncan looked thoughtful. "I'm presuming that's why he ran out of here like the world was ending?"

Joel nodded.

Duncan turned to Simon. "Si, you probably know this side of him better than me; what do you think?"

Simon looked surprised at being asked. Joel got the impression that Simon Proctor, with his reserved character, didn't normally say much. "Are you referring to my little bro's annoying ability to be able to get in to clubs in town?"

Joel, with much relief, nodded again. "I just wasn't sure if you knew."

Simon laughed. "We've been there a few times with him. I take it you've been to the rescue as well?"

"Most recently as of last night, yes. Pops and I went out to get him from Diablos."

Duncan looked over at Ted who, although busy frothing milk, nodded his confirmation. "And then you came home to find out about the twins' mum? Quite a night for you," Duncan said with an appraising look.

"So, will someone keep an eye out for him?" Joel asked, brushing off Duncan's comment. "I'm just worried if he goes out two nights in a row he'll get himself into trouble. And I don't know if he'll contact me tonight."

Both Proctors agreed to keep an eye on Alan when they got back from work that evening. Then, looking at the clock on the wall, they said their goodbyes and headed off to the station to catch their train.

CHAPTER EIGHTEEN

Tuesday 17th April, morning
Outside Beans and Banter

Alan stormed out of Beans and Banter, rage etched across his face. He just couldn't believe that Joel had told Hannah how he felt about her. He didn't care either that it was a mistake. As far as he was concerned it was a gross breach of trust. Joel shouldn't even have been talking about it to anyone. What business did Joel's mother have knowing whom he fancied? It made no sense. He had a good mind to ring Amie and tell her how Joel felt about her and see how Joel liked it.

It should have been him to tell Hannah. He'd been working on the perfect date for her, ever since he'd made that agreement with Joel on Saturday. That realisation just wound him up even further.

He winced as he came to a stop before crossing the road; it was bad enough having to do all this as it was, but the hangover was an extra inconvenience. His main concern, however, was Hannah.

He had always been worried about her depression and he feared that the events of the last twelve hours might be too much for her. He had tried so hard to erase parts of his memory from last year but they kept resurfacing.

***

24th June 2011

Alan turned up at Beans and Banter only to find out Joel was still at school. They were both in the middle of their GCSEs and Joel must have been sitting an exam in a different subject to him. He had been particularly concerned with his Chemistry exam that was approaching and as it was a subject Hannah was studying at A Level at the moment, a few weeks ago she had offered him some help. With all the other exams he had on, it had proved tricky to fit in any time so he found himself knocking on her front door to see if she was in. He thought he heard a crash coming from inside the house when he knocked, which confused him. He tried peering through the letterbox, which proved fruitless.

"Hello!" he called, listening keenly for a response. There was none.

Making his mind up he decided to take a look around the back of the house to see if he could see anything or anyone. In all fairness, Amie and Hannah were probably both still at college and their mum would be working. It still didn't explain the crash he had heard. He could see that a drawer was open in the kitchen, which he found odd; the French house was normally immaculate.

He tried the back door, which, to his surprise, sprang open.

"Hello!" he called again. "It's Alan, is anybody home?"

Still just silence. However, he thought he could hear some music coming from somewhere. This was getting spooky now.

He began to climb the stairs. "Hello?" he called, sounding less sure of himself. He wasn't sure if he wanted a response or not.

He kept following the music, which he then identified as being some sort of jazz. Was somebody having a bath?

He listened carefully outside the bathroom door but couldn't hear anything coming from inside. It was definitely coming from one of the bedrooms.

All of the bedroom doors were open except one. It appeared that this room was where the reedy saxophone sound was playing.

Alan knocked gently on the door. "Hello? Anybody in?"

Still no response. He looked up at the ceiling, trying to make his mind up whether to go in or not. Anything could be happening in the room; things he didn't wish to know about, for example.

He tried one more time. "Hello? It's Alan. I've been calling for a few minutes and I've not heard anything, so I'm coming in."

Giving it a few more seconds before he opened the door, nothing could have prepared him for what he saw on the other side.

Hannah was hanging by her neck from the skylight, from what he presumed was a belt. Her dressing table chair was lying on the floor and he realised that could have been the crash he heard. Hannah's face had a purple tinge to it and her eyes were closed. He saw a bottle of vodka on her bed and an empty box of paracetamol next to it; all the capsule pods appeared to be open.

He found his feet wouldn't move fast enough. He was in a state of shock. He didn't know what to do first; should he get Hannah down or ring an ambulance? His mind was also tumbling with so many questions. Was she trying to commit suicide? He knew her dad had left a few weeks ago; was it something to do with that? How long had she been up there?

Rather than standing there trying to do several things at once and getting nowhere he decided that action was required. He stood the chair back up again and positioned it under Hannah's feet to give her some support and so the belt then became slack.

She looked very limp. Her head was now flopped forward and she still had her eyes closed. He took her weight on his shoulder so he could reach around and undo the noose she had made. He found his hands trembling, which was making undoing the belt rather tricky. It struck him that they were in a weird kind of hug. He pushed that thought aside so he could focus on trying to loosen the knot.

When he finally got her down, he then laid her on her bed. It then occurred to him to check for a pulse. He really hoped there was one. He wasn't sure how he would feel if it turned out he had just been holding a dead body.

He reached for her wrist but wasn't sure if what he was feeling was his own blood pounding through him. His heart was thudding and he realised he was sweating profusely. He thought he could see her chest rising and falling but it was quite sporadic. It was then he realised he should probably call an ambulance. He saw Hannah's mobile phone on her bedside table and quickly grabbed it.

"Emergency. Which service do you require?" came the response once Alan had dialled 999.

"Ambulance, please."

He was then connected to the ambulance service and was put through to a young-sounding female voice. He was taken through the initial queries such as his telephone number and current location, which he found slightly irritating; didn't she realise something serious had happened?

"What's the problem?" he was eventually asked.

Alan couldn't find the words for a few seconds. "Well, I think my friend has tried to commit suicide," he spluttered out.

"OK. How old is the patient?"

"She's seventeen."

"OK. Is the patient breathing?"

"I think so. It's very ragged. She has a pulse too."

"OK. Is anyone else there with you?"

"No," Alan replied. "I've just found her in her bedroom. There's a half empty bottle of vodka up here and I think she's taken some paracetamol too." He took a deep breath, trying to calm his racing heartbeat. It was very difficult trying to put it all into words. It had been hard enough seeing it let alone trying to describe it.

"OK, stay with me. Can you check on the patient's breathing again please? Try putting your ear to her face. Can you feel any breath on your cheek? Can you hear her breathing?"

Alan could feel a slight tickle of air on his cheek and felt slightly relieved. "Yes, yes I can."

"OK, you're doing great, Alan. Just a few more minutes and the paramedics will be there."

110

"Thanks."

"Do you know if she's taken any vodka? Can you smell it on her breath, for example?"

Alan didn't even need to sniff now he was crouched over her. "Oh yes, she's definitely drunk some."

"OK. What's the best way of getting into the property?"

"Back door. Gate and door are open."

"Thank you. I'll pass that information on. Please stay on the line."

There were a few moments of peace and Alan could hear the general hubbub of the call centre in the background.

"OK, Alan, are you still there?"

"Yes, I'm here."

"Is the patient still breathing?"

He leaned over Hannah again. "Yes."

"OK. You're doing great. How does she feel? Is she warm? Is she cold?"

Alan grabbed one of Hannah's hands. "Her hands are cold."

"OK. Can you feel her forehead? Is she cool to touch?"

"She's quite cool. Do I need to cover her with something?"

"Ideally, yes."

Alan saw a blanket on the end of her bed and grabbed that.

"OK, Alan, the paramedics are coming up the street. Stay with the patient until they get there. Make sure you have a drink of water as well. I'm sure this has been stressful for you."

"Thank you, you've been very helpful," Alan replied.

"OK. You take care now. And I hope your friend is alright."

Alan was very tempted to reply 'OK', but decided against it. "Thanks," was all he said.

He then heard knocking coming from downstairs and a voice shouted, "Hello! Is Alan here?"

"Yes, I'm upstairs, you'll see me from the landing!" Alan called. He could hear heavy footsteps on the stairs and then a tall, balding man in a green uniform appeared.

"Hi, Alan, who is the patient?"

"Her name's Hannah."

"Right you are. I'm Dave. I have a colleague outside called Sandra…"

***

After that point, his memory was a bit blurry. Hannah was taken out on a stretcher that Sandra brought in and then taken to hospital. Alan decided to go with her in the ambulance, but he wasn't sure he wanted to be there when her family turned up. He didn't want anybody to know she had made a very serious attempt to end things. He was scared about her being sectioned or told she was crazy.

He had made the decision to try and clear up any evidence of the attempt before he left the house. He had put Hannah's chair back and had hid the belt, vodka bottle and paracetamol box in his own bag. He had also made sure he shut the kitchen drawer, where it looked like she'd got the paracetamol from, on his way out.

At the hospital Hannah had her stomach pumped and was conscious again within a few hours. Alan had waited until he knew she would make a recovery and she wasn't in any immediate danger. He gave a receptionist the contact details he had for Amie and their mum but he had then slipped away and caught a bus home before Amie and Christine even knew he had been there.

It had been put down as a failed suicide attempt, which had eventually led to Hannah's depression diagnosis. But Alan had always wondered what would have happened had he not turned up at the French house that day. Would Hannah still be here? He didn't want to think about that question too much.

He didn't know if anybody knew he had saved her, apart from the ambulance operator and the staff at the hospital. The group ended up presuming that she had called 999 herself before stepping off her chair and it was just a cry for help rather than a proper attempt to end her life. Alan didn't even know if she knew what she'd done. Somehow he had never got around to talking about it with her. Hannah had started on anti-depressants and had begun to receive some support and it just never felt like the right time to talk about it. He didn't want to remind her about a very dark moment in her life. Nobody should ever feel like they should have to die, as far as he was concerned.

As he knocked on the front door, all he was telling himself was that Hannah wouldn't be hanging from the skylight. She wouldn't. She was a stronger person now. Things had improved so much for her since that fateful day last year. Even Tim leaving hadn't appeared to shake her too much, in the sense that she hadn't had another incident.

But, and, in his mind it was a big 'but', how would she have reacted to being told he fancied her? He felt like they had been in the 'Friend Zone' for some time. He really couldn't predict what stepping outside of that zone would do to her. Combine that with her mum falling down the stairs and being in a critical state in hospital and it seemed like a perfect cocktail for suicide.

He knocked on the front door of the French house.

"Hannah?" he called. "It's me, Alan. Hello?"

He stood there for a few moments, waiting as patiently as he could, desperately hoping there would be an answer this time.

CHAPTER NINETEEN

Tuesday 17th April, morning
Izzy's flat at Great Bournestone Manor

Izzy's mobile phone alarm woke her from a peaceful sleep. Reaching out, she switched it off and rolled over.

Today was going to be a good day; she could feel it. She had her latest project in mind and she had a clear plan.

As part of being Sir Andrew's personal assistant and right-hand woman, she was entitled to stay in an outhouse at the manor. It meant she didn't have to travel far to reach her office. It was a two bedroom converted barn that Sir Andrew was planning on renting out one day. It was her father, Hayden, who had suggested Sir Andrew could do it up and have it for Izzy when she turned eighteen and left school. Sir Andrew had agreed and she had left home and gone to work for her father's best friend.

She had decided when she was a teenager that university wasn't really for her. Her father had had grand plans for her to become the next hotshot solicitor to take over the family firm, but she had seen the stress levels and long hours that he had put in and had refused to do as he wished. She could still remember her father's face when she told him that she had no interest in a legal profession and just wanted to work in an office somewhere. It had taken her mother to have a quiet word in his ear to calm him down. Even then, he had still interfered and gone to Andrew to ask if he'd take his daughter on. Looking back on it now it had been worth it, though. She had earned enough money to afford a top-of-the-range car, some wonderful tanzanite and diamond jewellery, her prized silver watch and she was allowed to live in the lovely outhouse building that she had made her own.

Now, a decade on from leaving school, she had started wondering about settling down and starting a family. Most of her friends, who had gone off to university, had now settled down with partners. Every week it seemed like there was another pregnancy announced on Facebook and she had felt like she was losing touch with the girls. In the last ten years, she had been all over the world, travelling a lot with Sir Andrew and as a result hadn't found a 'special someone' (as her best friend, Tamara, called it). Sure, there had been men here and there but nothing that had ever lasted more than a few weeks. Her father had always pointed her in the direction of 'the next big thing' at his office but she had found them very career-driven and she found that boring.

It was meeting Tim that had made her recently question her choices in men. The attention she had received from him was something different to the attention she was used to. Normally, she was the person with the higher social status and also the link to a better job. 'If I can win over the daughter, I'll be quids in with Mr Smart and he'll have to make me a partner in the firm' was one of the things she had been told one evening over dinner. Tim, having been on Talent UK, meant he was a superstar in her eyes. He wasn't interested in her to become the next partner at Smart Solicitors. He had genuinely looked at her as a woman. And that had made her feel butterflies in her stomach – something she hadn't felt in a long time.

It was crazy, though. She was over ten years his senior; he was still a teenager for crying out loud! There was no way she would ever end up going out with Tim.

But there was a small voice in her brain that kept popping up with awkward little thoughts. Why couldn't you end up with Tim? He obviously likes you. He's going to be eighteen soon; he'd be old enough to make his own decisions. It's a crazy world we live in; age is much less a taboo thing now. Who says you can't end up with him?

But still. She would never act on it. It had just been nice to be looked at again and it gave her some hope that maybe, just maybe, a marriage and a family might be around the corner.

However, when she sat down and looked at her options, they were limited. Tamara had told her about online dating, which seemed like the best option available to her. At least she could be honest about herself and then see if anybody would match up with her.

She headed into her bathroom and looked at herself in the mirror. She looked sternly into her caramel-coloured eyes, trying to reinforce the point that Tim just wouldn't happen. However, she still didn't look convinced. And if she couldn't convince herself...

Jumping in the shower, she turned the water up to scalding hot; just the way she liked it. She let the heat soak through her, trying to forget thinking about Tim. Glowing red when she exited, she checked herself out in the large mirror on the wall. She had had long dark hair for as long as she could remember, reaching down to the middle of her back when it was brushed straight. She had never dyed it; she'd never seen the point. Her mother had always encouraged her to brush it a hundred times a day when she was little, a ritual she had continued since then. Her hairbrush was never far away. She wrapped her towel back around her and headed back to her bedroom.

She tied her hair up into a loose ponytail, and got herself ready for her morning exercise routine. She kept herself relatively fit by running. The manor grounds were perfect for that. Sir Andrew didn't mind and as part of her morning routine when she was on a fitness drive was for him to wave at her as she finished with a sprint down the drive. He had even opened his office window on her nineteenth birthday and played 'Chariots of Fire' through his speakers, which had been a slightly surreal moment, suddenly turning a casual jog into what she imagined was a sprint for Olympic gold. Every time she had run down the drive towards the manor since, she set her mp3 player to play that song.

Once she had dressed herself ready to go into the office she headed towards the back of the manor house. She usually started her day in the manor kitchen with some fresh fruit or porridge. The housekeeping team had shrunk a bit compared to when she had first started. Mr and Mrs Connolly, a vibrant elderly couple whose infectious enthusiasm had revitalised the remaining housekeepers at the manor, led the current team.

The Connollys were also residents at the manor and over the last few years Izzy had spent several evenings in their company. They had three grown-up sons whom Izzy had met at Christmas parties held for the manor staff but the couple had always made her feel like an adopted daughter.

Mr Connolly was in charge of most of the cooking, splitting his time between the manor and an acclaimed restaurant in Huntingham called Signature, where he was the head chef. Mrs Connolly managed the housekeeping team of which there were three regular women, plus two extras Izzy had seen come in for the large events.

She pushed open the large door that led into the main kitchen. Mr Connolly was busy at the stove, while Mrs Connolly was sat at the wooden table nursing a cup of coffee.

"Morning," Izzy said with a smile.

Mrs Connolly looked up and returned the smile. She was a stout woman, with rosy cheeks and shoulder length greying hair. Her bright-green eyes always lit up when she saw Izzy, which made Izzy feel rather special.

"Good morning! How are we today?" came Mrs Connolly's usual greeting in her broad Bristolian accent.

"I'm... fine," Izzy replied, hesitating slightly, which Mrs Connolly seized on immediately.

"Only fine?"

Izzy sighed. She hadn't wanted to burden anybody with her thoughts about Tim, but it appeared her voice did. "Yeah, I'm just getting older and I would love to have a family at some point. I realised that this morning and I'm trying to come to terms with it."

Mr Connolly, a giant of a man who had clearly enjoyed his own cooking over the years, turned around and shook his head. "Honestly, the plight of these gorgeous young women these days," he said, also with a lilting West Country accent. "Look at you, girl. You're stunning. A knock out. Any man should be honoured to have a woman like you on his arm."

Izzy blushed. She had never considered herself to be that good-looking, which made her wonder if that was why she was still single. She tried to look after the way she looked, hence the running, but she didn't have a face or body for modelling, for example. She sat down at the table next to Mrs Connolly, who reached out and patted her on the arm.

"Bob's right, honey. Your body clock just appears to be ticking. It's perfectly natural. It's nothing to get concerned about though. If you want these things to happen, then they will, because you'll want it to happen so hard, you'll be subconsciously working towards it."

"I just worry. I'm seeing my friends all announcing weddings and babies and I just wonder when my turn will come. I've not even got a boyfriend."

"Well, why not?"

Izzy looked surprised. "What do you mean?"

"Why don't you have a boyfriend? You must have plenty of opportunity?"

Izzy was taken aback. Was it really that simple? "I guess. I just haven't found anybody I really like." She tried very hard not to let the little voice in her head mention Tim.

"Are your standards too high? Or unrealistic, perhaps? Or is it even confidence in yourself? Do you not like the way you look? There must be some reason."

"I've been on dates and things, my dad is always trying to set me up, but I just find them boring, or too career focused. And I don't have a problem with the way I look. I know I'm not a supermodel, but I'm not the back end of a bus or anything."

Mrs Connolly looked surprised. "And when was the last time you went on a date you arranged yourself?"

Izzy shrugged. "I can't actually remember."

Mrs Connolly watched the realisation sink in. "So, bearing that in mind, are you into this online dating that seems very popular these days? Our Richard found his girlfriend through one of those sites."

"It's something I'm going to have to look into more, I think. I just feel like I should be able to go out and meet somebody."

"That's quite difficult to do if you never go out," Mrs Connolly remarked. "We see your light on in your flat most evenings and your car is always parked next to it."

Izzy couldn't argue. How did she expect to meet someone if she enjoyed her own company at home all the time? There was silence as she processed this. "You're right, I need to do more," she said after a few moments. "I can't sit and expect a family to drop into my lap."

"That's my girl," Mr Connolly said, looking over his shoulder.

Mrs Connolly beamed at her. "That's great, honey. You'll find someone,

I know you will."

Izzy was trying to shake the image of Tim from her mind's eye. Why did he keep appearing?

"So, Izzy darling, what have you got planned for today? Something exciting with the tour coming up?" Mrs Connolly asked.

Izzy grinned. "Nothing to do with the tour, but it's top secret. Sir Andrew is keeping it very close to his chest at the minute."

Both Mr and Mrs Connolly looked surprised but said nothing. They'd been employees long enough to know that whatever Sir Andrew had up his sleeve was usually worth waiting for. They had both been a little sceptical about his first UK tour, but he had invited them along to the opening night and were both giving him a standing ovation at the close.

"So, is there any breakfast available?" Izzy asked. "I've got a long day ahead of me and I want to get cracking."

Laughing, Mrs Connolly pointed to the fridge. She returned to her newspaper while Izzy polished off the fruit salad they had saved for her.

Izzy usually had breakfast in silence, watching with amusement as Mr Connolly pretended to sound interested in whatever news stories his wife shared with him. This morning was no different as Mrs Connolly tried to engage her husband in a debate about fracking and also the rise in cyber-warfare. At one point, when her head was buried in the newspaper as she was reading the article on fracking out loud, Mr Connolly managed to quickly turn around to Izzy and mime shooting himself, which nearly made her choke on her breakfast.

Once everything was cleared away and Izzy had finished a glass of orange juice, she said her goodbyes to the Connollys and headed back to her flat to plan out her day ahead.

She fired up her laptop on her desk and found an online map of Huntingham. It was the closest town to Great Bournestone and was the first on her hit list. She made a note of certain shops to visit and looked up some places to eat, just in case. She then climbed into her car and with her mp3 player plugged in, headed out along the country roads towards Huntingham.

CHAPTER TWENTY

Tuesday 17th April, morning
The French House

Alan could hear footsteps gradually getting louder, which was encouraging. He was peering through one of the obscured glass panels on the front door and he could see someone with red hair coming towards him. It had to be Hannah. It had to be. Amie was at hospital looking after their mother and he didn't know that any other red-haired family existed.

Relief washed over him as Hannah opened the door, looking a little stressed. He let out a big sigh and engulfed her in a big bear hug, wrapping his arms around her so tightly he could feel her ribs. To his surprise, she rested her head gently on his shoulder for a few seconds. It felt... nice. No, it felt better than that. It felt... right? Was a hug like that supposed to feel right?

"Hey," Alan said, once the hug had broken apart.

"Hey," came Hannah's reply as she looked up into his eyes.

He looked down at her, scanning her face, trying to read her expression. "How are you holding up?"

She turned away from him but beckoned him in. "I'm alright," she said as he walked past her.

"That doesn't mean anything. Come on, tell me how you're really holding up," Alan said with concern.

Hannah sighed and gave him a frustrated look. "It's hard, Alan, I won't lie to you. I'm here, Amie's at hospital and the whole time I'm wondering how my mum is."

"Any news on her this morning? Joel told me that she was stable. He'd been messaging Amie overnight."

"Amie's last message just said she was still waiting for a doctor to come and see Mum this morning. She's in a coma at the moment, so there's not much that can be done really. I'm just trying to get on with everyday stuff so I can try and take my mind off worrying."

"Fair enough," Alan said, not knowing what else to say. He couldn't remember the last time he had seen her so frustrated. But, he realised, it was better than finding her hanging from her skylight. And he realised he hadn't seen her show this much emotion and wondered if it had anything to do with her change in medication.

There was silence between them for a few moments while Hannah finished packing her and Amie's bags. Alan could hear her muttering under her breath something about how disorganised her sister was and she disappeared for a few moments, returning with a file that was then unceremoniously shoved into Amie's rucksack.

Alan spent this time looking around the kitchen. He noticed a calendar on the wall, divided into three; each of them had a column with various notes added in.

"Is your mum down to be working today?" Alan asked.

Hannah cursed and strode over to where Alan was standing. "Damn you and your inquisitive mind," she said, half-joking. She looked at her watch. "I'd better call them and let them know. I hope she'll still get paid."

Alan frowned. "Won't she get sick pay or something?"

"I hope so, but she's been working so many extra shifts lately, I doubt she'll get the equivalent," Hannah said looking worried.

"OK, don't panic. Do you want me to ring them instead? I don't mind. If they'll speak to me that is."

Hannah looked at him pleadingly, her eyes brimming with tears. "Please," she said quietly.

"Do you have a number to ring?"

Hannah fished her mobile phone out of her pocket and read out a number that Alan dialled on the home phone. It rang a few times before somebody answered.

"Hello? Fosters House Care Home, Angie speaking." The woman sounded very flustered.

"Ermmm, hi," Alan started nervously, "I'm ringing on behalf of the French family." He looked across at Hannah, who had sat herself at the kitchen table, and was resting her head on her hand, looking at the floor. He really felt for her in that moment and wanted to just drop the phone and give her another hug.

"How can I help?" Angie was sounding a bit calmer now.

Alan proceeded to explain what he knew about the events of the night before, glancing at Hannah every so often to make sure she was alright.

"Well, thanks for letting me know," Angie said when Alan had finished. "Can you tell the family I'll notify Gill and we all hope she gets better soon."

"Thanks. I'll pass the message on," Alan replied politely, presuming that Gill was someone senior to Angie.

Hanging up, Alan looked over at Hannah again, who now had tears running down her face. "Han, what's wrong?" he asked gently.

"I just feel so helpless, Al. I'm stuck here in this house, trying to do

119

normal things like get my and my sister's bag ready for a trip to the college library and all I can think about is my mum lying in a hospital bed in a coma. I don't know what to do with myself."

"Hannah French, look at me," Alan said, determined to make sure she wasn't going to think too negatively. He took her face in his hands and she looked up at him, a flash of fear in her eyes. "You are doing amazingly well, don't put yourself down," he said gently.

Hannah swallowed nervously but didn't say anything.

Taking Hannah's silence to mean he needed to continue, Alan went on. "Look, I think it's remarkable you're even contemplating going to college when your mum is in hospital. I know it's only a study day and it won't be lectures or anything, but I don't think I'd even want to leave the house."

Hannah whispered, "What did you expect?"

"Honestly?" Alan asked, reluctant to say what he was thinking. He was still having difficulty shaking the image of her hanging from her skylight from his mind.

"Were you worried about me?" she asked, looking up at him, her eyes wide.

Alan was slightly stumped by the question. "Well, yes, I suppose I was," he said eventually.

"Why?"

Alan hesitated. "I guess it's because of your attempted suicide last year. I didn't want to find you hanging from your skylight." He nearly added 'again' but held his tongue. He still wasn't sure if she knew he had been involved in her still being here.

Hannah looked at him strangely and he wondered if he'd given it away that he had been the one who had given her a second chance. "That's an odd choice of phrase," she said.

"I don't understand," he replied as innocently as he dared. All the time he could feel her eyes scanning him. It was like she was looking around inside his head.

"Remember my 'incident' last year?"

Alan nodded.

"Well, that was how, you know, I'd planned on..."

"Yeah, I understand. How you wanted to end it all," Alan finished.

Hannah looked slightly ashamed. "That's right."

"So, what happened? I didn't know that had been your chosen method. We've never really discussed it," Alan said, sliding into the chair opposite her at the kitchen table. He was intrigued to see if she had known he'd been there or not.

Hannah looked surprised but didn't complain. "I've mentioned it before at the coffee shop," she pointed out.

"That you had tried. Not *how* you had gone about it."

Alan watched as Hannah accepted that one. Nobody in the group had ever asked for the details. They knew that she had tried to hang herself but he couldn't remember ever hear her saying how she had tried, and, ultimately, failed.

"Fair enough. It's not really something you talk about with other people, is it? It just freaked me out a bit, what you said, because that was how I'd planned on doing it," she said quietly. "I found the biggest belt I could and learned how to make a noose online. I'd tried to cover all bases and I'd dosed myself up with paracetamol and a bottle of cheap vodka I'd been given as a birthday present."

Alan nodded. He was trying to keep Hannah opening up to him; he'd never experienced this before and it felt like she was letting him in. Normally she was so quiet and reserved, listening to everyone else and their life events. This had been a big part of her life, albeit a very dark part, but in getting her to talk to him about it – well, it felt special. He realised, in that moment, that he was actually enjoying hearing Hannah talk about herself. It was new and he liked it.

"I remember putting the belt around my neck and I nearly didn't do it because I was so woozy. I almost fell off the chair while I was climbing up and I thought it was a sign. But then the sun went behind a cloud outside and the room became darker and it was like it took over me. I can't really remember much after that. I just remember wondering who would find me and if anybody would miss me. One of my last thoughts was that I'd not even written a note or anything. I'd tried. I just didn't know what to write. Then the next thing I know is I'm wretching my guts up in hospital."

Alan looked at her sheepishly. "Do you even know how you ended up in hospital?"

"No. Not really. All they could tell me was that the paramedics found me in my room. It was just a bit weird, that's all."

"How so?"

"I must have rung them myself. There was a 999 call on my phone. I just can't remember making the call."

Alan shrugged. "There must have been a part of you that wanted to carry on living."

Hannah nodded. "There must have been," she agreed, but she was fixing him with a hard stare again. "There's just one thing about the whole incident I can't figure out." She took a deep breath. "How did one of your pens end up in my room?"

Alan was trying really hard to stop a guilty look crossing his face. It was definitely possible he'd left a pen. He always had them in one of the front pockets in his bag and one could have easily fallen out; those pockets were usually open.

"Mum said that nobody had been in my room until I came home. She'd shut the door and left it as it was," Hannah continued. "Which means that either you were in my room before or after and nobody knew. That's a bit strange."

Alan remained silent, hoping that she'd somehow talk herself around to thinking he couldn't have been there. It could have been anybody's pen; how did she know it was his?

"And also, I know it was your pen. I'd got you those ones with your name on the previous Christmas."

He couldn't really deny it; the evidence was pretty damning.

"So," Hannah continued, "what do you have to tell me?" She fixed him with a stern glare and she had folded her arms by this point.

"I don't understand, Han. Why haven't you mentioned this before?" he asked, weakly trying to turn the spotlight back on her.

"That doesn't really answer my question," she replied, icy glare still fixed on him. "But I'll tell you. I was waiting for someone to talk to me about it, just so I could ask them about why there was a pen in my room. I figured that whoever spoke to me first about it would know a bit more. If nobody had mentioned it, I would have just chalked it up to one of those great life mysteries."

He puffed his cheeks and let the air out slowly. "I guess it's pointless me keeping quiet about it," he said quietly. "Yes, I was in your room."

"When?"

He winced. "You were hanging from your skylight when I was there."

Her eyes widened. "So it was you? You were the one who got me down?"

He nodded, still unsure if she was annoyed. She was so difficult to read at times. All he could tell was that she was now trying to fit the missing pieces of the puzzle in.

"Was it you who rang the ambulance then? Off my phone?"

He nodded again.

"Why? Why did you get me down?" she demanded, folding her arms. "I just can't figure that out."

Alan held his hands up as if she was threatening him. "Nobody should die because they're miserable. That's just my opinion."

She looked puzzled. "I don't get it. I have a right to die if I want to."

"Then why are you still here? Why haven't you tried again since?"

She didn't answer.

"Listen, Han, I was coming round to see you for some help with my Chemistry. You'd offered a few weeks before. I didn't expect to find you trying to top yourself. I couldn't leave you there. So I got you down, called an ambulance and once I was sure you were alright, I left the hospital."

"And you've said nothing about it since then? Why?"

Alan hesitated. "I don't know. I guess I was hoping you would think there was some sort of guardian angel or something watching over you. You never really spoke about it and I never wanted to talk about it. How on earth do you start a conversation like that?"

Hannah was looking slightly bemusedly at him. "You know what this means?"

He shook his head, racking his brain as to what it could possibly mean; was she mad with him for letting her live?

CHAPTER TWENTY-ONE

Hannah flung her arms around Alan, this time taking him by surprise. She held on to him for a few long moments, until he rested his hands gently on her back.

"Oh Alan," she said, her voice muffled by his shoulder. "Thank you. Just... Thank you."

Alan looked confused, but said nothing while the embrace continued, his arms holding her a bit tighter now.

"You're not saying anything," Hannah said, looking up at him.

He smiled down at her. "I was just enjoying the hug."

She carried on looking up at him, his smile beaming down at her, making her feel like she was basking in the glow of a spotlight. Time felt like it stood still, and Hannah had no idea how long they stood there in that moment. It was like nothing she'd felt before. She almost snorted when she thought that if Alan hadn't found her when he had, she wouldn't be here now hugging him.

The realisation that Alan was in fact the one who had saved her from ending it all at the blackest of one of her darkest moments made her see him completely differently. Would Tim have found her? Would he have kept it a secret for this long? They were questions she could find the answers to later. Right now, she wanted to stay in Alan's arms for as long as she could and hold on to this blissful sensation. Everything suddenly seemed right in the world.

When the hug did eventually break apart, Hannah felt breathless. Her heart felt like it was beating a samba against her ribs and butterflies were dancing in her stomach. She was a little confused; she had never felt like this when she was with Tim. Sure, she knew she fancied him, but this... Well, *this* was a whole new level.

"I still can't believe it was you," she whispered.

Alan gave her another heart-warming smile. "You say that like it's a bad thing."

"I don't mean it like that. I've just been convinced for so long that I'd somehow rung an ambulance; I just didn't remember calling them. I did wonder if the alcohol and paracetamol had affected my memory."

"Hey, that was a logical conclusion. I think, deep down, that's what I'd wanted you to believe. That you had changed your mind."

"Well, I'm glad you did."

She cuddled into him again and they stood there for a few minutes in the middle of her kitchen. Her mind began to race and she could picture herself standing at various landmarks snuggled into Alan's chest; at the top of the Eiffel Tower, looking over Paris; on top of Sugarloaf Mountain, at the foot of Christ the Redeemer; at Niagara Falls, feeling the spray on her face as they watched the ebb and flow of the waterfall. She wanted to experience all of these things, and more, with Alan. It was new to her, wishing for a future, and she had never felt so alive.

"Hannah?"

Alan's voice shook her out of her reverie. She looked up at his face and gave him a lingering smile.

"You looked like you were dreaming there. You alright?" Alan asked sounding concerned.

"I'm great," she replied. "No, I really am!" she added when she saw him frown.

"OK. Well, in that case, I really want to take you out on a date. Not like to Beans and Banter; a proper date."

Hannah was a little shocked. "Do I need to wear a dress?" she asked, her voice a mix of nervous and excited.

"What, like a long flowing dress?" he replied, looking confused.

"We're not getting married, silly," Hannah giggled, and then immediately looked scared. "I didn't mean to mention marriage, I'm sorry!"

"Hey, it's OK. There's plenty of time for all that," he said, looking relaxed. "The perfect date is one that's outside, but I do have a wet-weather option too. I'm thinking you probably won't want a dress for either date. Just normal clothes."

"OK," she said, her mind racing. What sort of dates didn't need a dress? Where would he take her? What time of day would it be? Did she need to take anything? Had she just panicked him by mentioning the 'M' word? Would Amie be able to do her hair for her this time?

"So, how's Friday for you?" he asked, seemingly unaffected by Hannah's mention of becoming a husband.

"Well, I'm free in the afternoon? Any good?" Hannah said, watching him closely for any sign that he was going to run away screaming about commitment issues.

"All you'll need will be yourself. I'll cover the rest."

Hannah's face could barely contain her excitement. "This is so cool!" she squealed.

Alan looked surprised at her outburst. "Have you never been on a date before?" he asked.

Hannah suddenly went back into her shell. "No," she replied. "Sure, I met Tim at the coffee shop but that wasn't like a proper organised date. He just asked me to come for a coffee for a catch up." She noticed that at the mention of Tim, Alan's emotional shields went up.

"No, don't do that," she said quickly, reaching out for his hand. "I'm not good at this, I'm sorry."

Alan visibly relaxed. "Sorry, I just can't understand the whole Tim thing. After how he treated you, just disappearing like that. Well, it annoys me. You deserve better."

Hannah shrugged. "I think we're over it now. But I don't want to talk about Tim. That's all in the past."

Alan looked relieved. "Great. It's just… Well, when I saw you hugging him the other night, you guys looked… happy? I honestly thought I wouldn't have a chance at asking you out."

Hannah's insides squirmed. It had been Alan at the window.

"And then Joel told me this morning that you'd overheard him telling his mum that I fancied you," he continued. "I've been trying to tell you for a while, but something has always come up."

Hannah fought to suppress a smile. "Yeah, I did hear what Joel said."

"I could have killed him when he told me that. I really could."

"He didn't mean it. He thought I was in the kitchen," Hannah said, trying to stick up for Joel.

"Even so, I've no idea why he was talking to his mum about it," Alan growled. "I'm still mad at him about it."

"Come on, it was late, everyone was shocked and tired, and where were you while all this was going on?"

Alan looked sheepish. "In the back of a car, lying in my own vomit."

"You were what? Why were you doing that?" Hannah said sounding confused.

"After I saw you and Tim, I had one of my drinking sessions," Alan admitted. "I was trying to numb the pain."

Hannah frowned. "Great, so you're a really sensitive alcoholic?"

"Maybe a stress-induced one," he said, rubbing the back of his head awkwardly. "It's not the first time.'

Hannah tutted. "So how did you end up in a car?"

Alan looked irritated. "Joel came and got me," he said begrudgingly.

Hannah's expression was one of mock surprise. "Ah right, I see. So while you're busy complaining about Joel being a rubbish friend for letting a not-very-secret secret slip, he gets up in the middle of the night to fetch you from a binge-drinking session. And then he realised he'd made a mistake and owned up to it. That's pretty noble. Where on earth would you be without him?" Hannah asked, looking stern, both hands on her hips.

"Look, I'm grateful, I'm not denying he's a great friend. But I just want him to keep stuff like that to himself. As far as I'm aware girls like spontaneity. I wanted to surprise you; ask you out on a date out of the blue. I'd been trying to find the right moment to ask you. He ruined that for me."

"So is that why you were sat stalking me in Beans and Banter that weekend?"

He looked a bit awkward. "You saw that?"

"It was actually Amie that pointed it out. She always thought you had a thing for me. I'm going to have to tell her she's right, which isn't particularly enjoyable." She frowned as she realised something. "And, bearing in mind everything we've discovered this morning, if Joel hadn't let it slip, do you think I would have said yes?"

Alan looked puzzled. "You mean you only said yes because you already knew I liked you?"

"Kind of," Hannah admitted. "It helped if anything."

"Are you only saying this so I forgive Joel?"

Hannah was becoming frustrated. "No. Stop bringing Joel into this. I'm saying it because you're being an idiot and thinking what happened was a bad thing. Maybe, if it hadn't happened, we wouldn't be here right now. I was taught a lot about perspective and how to counteract negative thinking in the counselling I had after my incident."

Alan made an 'oh' shape with his mouth and the conversation lapsed into an awkward silence, broken only by Hannah's phone buzzing in her bag. Fishing it out, she saw it was Amie trying to ring her. She showed Alan the screen and answered.

"Hi, Amz. What's up?"

"Han, thank heavens. Where on earth are you?"

"I'm at home. Why?"

"Will you make it to college before the library opens? You know how busy it gets if we can't get our favourite spot."

"Doubt it. Sorry, Amz," Hannah said ruefully. "How's Mum?"

Amie sighed. "No change. I wanted to get to college to take my mind off it all and try and get some studying done."

"OK, well, I am sorry. If it's any consolation, something really great happened this morning. There's a lot to tell you," she said, looking across at Alan and giving him another lingering smile.

"Great. I need some good news right now," Amie said huffily.

"I'll tell you more about it when I see you, Amz. Right now, I need to catch the bus."

After saying their goodbyes, Hannah then hung up. Looking up at Alan, she said, "Come on, Al, we need to get a move on. We might just catch the quarter-past bus if we're lucky."

Alan grabbed Amie's bag and waited patiently while Hannah locked up. They wandered outside towards the bus stop around the corner. Hannah was really tempted to reach for Alan's hand while they were walking, but thought better of it; she wanted Alan to make a move like that. Weren't boys supposed to initiate the romance? Perhaps Friday would tell her more about Alan and his romantic intentions.

They didn't say another word to each other until they were on the bus; Hannah was feeling quite comfortable with the silence. It was nice just to have him there. There wasn't the awkwardness that she sometimes felt with Tim. Alan was tall and quite striking to look at – just as his brothers were – and she remembered the question that Amie had asked her the night before. She realised, in effect, that had been only a few hours ago. It felt a lot longer with all the events of the early hours.

They took a seat together towards the back of the bus. Hannah watched Alan for a few moments as he seemed more interested in his phone, but he then spent a while staring out of the window. Hannah wondered if he was thinking about the situation with Joel.

Her phone buzzed again and she saw it was a message from Joel.

Hey. Is Alan with you?

She smiled. Trust Joel to still worry about his best friend, even if Alan was annoyed with him.

He is. We're just on the bus to college.

Great. Thanks. How is he?

She glanced over at Alan before replying. *He's fine. Seems to be over whatever you guys fought about. Are you at college already?*

That's good then. Yes, I'm in the library. Can you tell him that's where I am?

Sure, will do. See you later.

Hannah tucked her phone back into her bag.

"Everything alright?" Alan asked. Hannah hadn't spotted he wasn't looking out of the window any more.

"It was Joel seeing if you were with me."

"Ah right," Alan mumbled. "What did you tell him?"

"I said we were on the bus together. He wants me to tell you he's in the library. The usual spot."

Alan nodded but said nothing for a few moments.

Hannah studied him closely, trying to read his thoughts. She couldn't really tell if he was still irritated by what Joel had inadvertently told her or not, though she suspected he had mellowed slightly from when she'd opened the door to him earlier.

"I've just been trying to replay how I got here. You know, where you imagine yourself going back in time to where it all began, seeing the steps you took to get to a certain point? I've realised I never truly understood that quote by Soren Kierkegaard we were taught in Philosophy; the one about you have to live life forwards but understand it backwards. Something like that."

Hannah shook her head in puzzlement.

Alan sighed, as if he realised he wasn't getting his point across very well. "Joel and I were talking about you a few days ago and if someone explained to me then that I'd be here now, having asked you out, I really don't think I'd have believed them. I honestly never thought I'd have a chance to get round to asking you out. I've been trying to think of a way to get into a position where I could ask and you'd say yes for ages. I guess he just accelerated things along a bit."

"I still don't get why that annoys you," Hannah commented.

"It's just the whole pursuit of you has been taken away now. I was sort of looking forward to that. But, as you've said, if he hadn't done what he did then this might not be happening."

"But you're still annoyed by it?" Hannah asked.

Alan nodded. "Absolutely. It's just so irritating for someone else to come along and make something I'd been planning for ages just look and seem so easy."

Hannah looked at him incredulously. "Is this what guys are like, generally speaking? Getting frustrated over stuff that works out well for you?"

"Pretty much, yeah," Alan said meekly.

Hannah snorted. "Well, I think that's just stupid. It doesn't even make sense. Even when you get what you wanted, you want for it not to have happened because it didn't happen in the way you wanted?"

Alan considered it for a few seconds. "Well it doesn't sound great when you put it like that…" he trailed off, scratching his jaw.

"Hopefully it might help you understand where I'm coming from. Come on, Al, it is ridiculous." She paused for a few seconds. "Having said all this, I really do think we should try and get Joel and Amie to go on a date together."

Alan puffed his cheeks out in frustration. "Right," he said, his tone still sounding annoyed.

"Now, now; don't sound so irritable. He did you a massive favour, remember? I think one good turn deserves another."

Alan sighed. "OK, I'll try," he said sulkily.

"How mad would you say Joel is about Amie?"

"Loads. It's why it's so frustrating that he's not asked her out or made any sort of effort to."

Hannah nodded. "Amie admitted she has feelings for him last night. That's the first time I've ever heard her say she fancies him."

Alan raised a quizzical eyebrow. "That's interesting. I didn't realise she knew herself that she did. *Why* aren't they together?"

"Because you haven't set them up yet?" Hannah asked, her eyes sparkling with humour.

Alan sighed at her. "Very funny," he said sarcastically.

"What do you say then? Think we can get them to go on a date together?"

"Probably. You mean like a surprise date?"

"Absolutely. Amie's pretty much got her marriage proposal and wedding plotted out in her head, so I'm sure I know what she likes."

Alan's eyes widened. "Why has she got her proposal and wedding planned out?"

"Do you not know many girls, Al? It's like a right of passage to becoming a woman, dreaming and planning events like that."

Alan looked blankly at her. "It is?"

"Oh, Alan Proctor. You have a lot to learn," Hannah said with a laugh.

"Does that mean you've got all this stuff planned out too?" Alan said, sounding a little scared.

"Of course," Hannah said, a big smile on her face. "You'll just have to get to know me a little better to find out stuff like that."

"Great," Alan mumbled. "Can't wait."

"Oh don't be like that. There's plenty of time. I don't plan on being married before I'm thirty," Hannah continued, watching him carefully again to see if marriage talk was putting him off; it certainly didn't appear to be. "So you'll help me plan this date?" she asked hopefully.

Alan pretended to think about it for a few seconds. "Well… Sure. Of course I will."

"Good. Amie deserves a bit of a break, she deserves to be happy and she's really into Joel. Hey, Al, we could be the ones who start something amazing. How cool would that be?"

"Pretty cool," Alan agreed, just as the bus turned into the college road. "What do you need me to do?"

"I've got no idea what you've got planned for us on Friday, but do you think Amie and Joel would be able to join in?"

Alan considered this for a few seconds. "Yeah, it could work."

"It's not going out for a meal or anything like that, is it?"

He shook his head. "Well, there is a catering option, but for both dates we're not doing anything like sitting down as a quartet. We do that enough as a group at Beans and Banter."

"I'm fairly sure I'd be able to get Amie to come with me, to like, drop me off or something. Do you think you could get Joel there?"

Alan smiled. "I don't think I'll have too much of a problem. I'll just say I need some help setting some stuff up."

Hannah frowned at him. "I can't even imagine what you've got planned."

Alan looked smug. "That's a good thing. I really want this to be a surprise."

CHAPTER TWENTY-TWO

Parking her car in the middle of Huntingham, Izzy made her way to the first music shop that was on her list. Abraham's Classical Emporium was apparently owned by David Abraham and had been in business over thirty years.

It was a small, dreary shop, in desperate need of a lick of paint, but appeared to be well stocked in music books and instruments when Izzy looked in the window.

A bell tinkled as she pushed the door open, causing the tall, bearded man behind the counter to look up suddenly. He had thinning grey hair pulled back into a ponytail and slightly wild-looking grey eyes. Izzy presumed he didn't usually have many customers first thing in a morning.

"Hi," she said casually.

"Good morning, love. What can I help you with today?"

He had a broad Yorkshire accent and a big smile that instantly made Izzy feel welcome. She noticed he wore a name badge that had 'David' written on it, so she presumed he was the owner. "I'm after some information about the music scene in the local area and I was wondering if you could help," she said. "I'm assuming you're Mr Abraham?"

"That's right, love. People round here call me Dave," he said, gently stroking his beard. "Information you say. Well, depends what sort you're after really. That could mean anything."

Izzy smiled politely. "What sort of demographic do you cater for, Dave?"

"Mostly school children, love. I only really stock your classical orchestral instruments. There's other shops in town that deal with electric guitars and drum kits, that sort of thing."

"Not really your kind of thing?"

"When I was a youngster, perhaps," he replied, stroking his beard again. "Now, I'm looking forward to drawing my pension to go travelling around the world, watching the world's most famous orchestras."

Izzy seemed surprised. "That's quite a dream to have. Do you get to travel much now?"

Dave shook his head. "Not really, this shop is my life. Christmas and Easter I get a couple of days off."

"Do you ever get asked about recording studios?"

Dave looked thoughtful for a few moments. "Occasionally, I suppose, love. I thought the schools did that sort of thing, if needed."

Izzy nodded and reached for her phone; schools were another line of attack that she needed to add to her list.

"So, I presume you're one of these project managers, love?" Dave asked while she tapped on her phone.

Izzy looked up and smiled. "I'm just doing some research into what the local facilities are like. I haven't found much on the Internet. Nottingham seems to be the nearest place with a studio, and it seems quite expensive."

"Not wrong there, love. Those places charge an absolute fortune. I guess they must have an awful amount of hi-tech equipment in them," Dave added sagely.

"Well, I was wondering if you knew whether your clients would benefit from having a recording studio in town."

Dave looked surprised. "Seriously, love? Is that what you're looking to set up: recording studio facilities?"

Izzy nodded.

"Wow. That would make a real difference to this town. Where are you getting the funding from, if I'm allowed to ask?"

"I have a private investor, but he's asking for some research to be done to see if it's worth his investment," Izzy replied, not giving anything away. "Hence why I'm here."

"That's fair enough, love. Well, please keep me updated if it goes through. I'd be interested in having the details on file in case there's any queries."

"Thanks, Dave, I appreciate that. I'll be in touch, all being well," Izzy said, and offered a business card to him.

Dave studied it and smiled. "Any relation to that solicitor in town, love?"

Izzy couldn't believe someone had made the connection; her dad must have been even better connected than she thought. "He's my dad. But he's not my investor, in case you were wondering."

Dave shrugged. "Can't blame a guy for asking. Hayden's a good man, given me some sound advice over the years. Always talked about his daughter, but I'd never met her until now. Give him my regards, love."

Izzy smiled and offered her hand out to Dave. She received a firm shake in return. She then headed out of the shop, pulled out her phone and looked at her organiser. She found her next destination and realised it was only a couple of streets away.

She turned up at the door of Destiny Music, which was a lot more modern. Her research had told her that there were some teaching rooms upstairs in the shop too, which Izzy thought was a good idea.

She was quite surprised when she opened the door to the shop to hear how much noise was going on inside. It was impressive how the shop front had been soundproofed, as she hadn't heard anything while she was walking up the street. Destiny Music focused on having instruments on display and letting people try them. Izzy spotted a group of youngsters playing around with electric guitars, a middle-aged woman looking like she was fighting with a drum kit and a frustrated-looking dad letting his toddler bash the keys of an electric piano.

The counter was conveniently placed next to the door, saving Izzy from having to traipse across the shop floor. She approached the two teenagers stood there and gave her line about looking for information about the music scene. She noticed the two boys share a look and one picked up a phone and asked for Eric to come down.

Izzy waited patiently, scanning the shop to take in more of what was going on. It was considerably busier than Abraham's Classical Emporium, though Izzy wasn't sure how many people were actually planning on buying anything.

'Eric' turned out to be a diminutive, jovial woman in her early thirties, with bright blue hair tied back into a ponytail. Izzy wondered if she was actually above five foot in height, as even she towered over the shop owner.

Once Eric had established who had caused her to come downstairs, she turned to Izzy and invited her into the office upstairs. She introduced herself as Erica Cameron, otherwise known as Eric. She explained she came from a musical family and wanted children to have some of the musical opportunities available to her as a child. The shop actually hired out the instruments, customers paying for how long they played, which Izzy thought was quite an impressive business idea. There was even a room in the shop where gamers could play 'Guitar Hero' or 'Rock Band', with the hope that being surrounded by the actual instruments would inspire them to pick one up. The whole ethos of the shop was geared towards getting people into music.

She was very enthusiastic when Izzy explained about the recording studio idea. She reeled off three artists who had come in recently asking about recording facilities, so she was sure that there would be demand. Izzy, once again, left a business card and headed back out into the street, feeling satisfied that there was at least some interest.

She looked at the next location on her list and realised she'd need to go back to her car to get there with it being on an industrial site on the outskirts of Huntingham. She realised it was nearly eleven o'clock – time for a drink. Checking her other list of places to eat, the closest one was a coffee shop called Beans and Banter. Their website was advertising for local musicians as well for special performance nights, so she planned on being able to do some research there too.

Izzy was impressed with the cosy atmosphere in Beans and Banter the moment she walked in. There was soft, acoustic rock music playing in the background and there were lots of comfy chairs. She noticed a newspaper clipping framed on the wall which talked about the conversion from the Red Lion Inn and how the shop would aim to compete with the pub culture in the town with its late opening hours. Once again, it was a business idea that she couldn't help but admire.

She made her way up to the counter, where the tall, thin, middle-aged man behind it was whistling along to the music whilst frothing milk. He looked up as she approached.

"Good morning, haven't seen you in here before. What can I get you?"

Izzy was slightly taken aback. "Do you know everyone who comes in here then?" she asked.

"We have our regulars and I like to try and keep tabs on everyone who comes in. Good customer service and all that. My name's Ted by the way. I run this place with my wife, Alyssa."

Izzy was slightly amused to see Alyssa pop her head out of the kitchen hatch and smile. Behind Ted's back she gave Izzy a helpless shrug. Izzy stifled a giggle. "Hi, nice to meet you both. I'm Izzy." She then noticed Ted looking expectantly at her. "Please could I order... a... do you do those iced juices? I'd really like a mango one if you do."

Ted was trying to hold back on a smile. "I think I can rustle up one of those; drink in or take away? And what size would you like?"

Izzy confirmed she was staying in, asked for a small sized one and handed over the required money. Ted confirmed she could have a seat and he'd bring it over, so Izzy headed over to find a comfy chair in a corner.

She settled into a well-padded armchair and leaned back to stare at the ceiling. She thought about her visits this morning and realised she was feeling encouraged. There was definitely some interest but it dawned on her that she would have to speak to some artists about whether they would find it useful. She reached for her phone and added 'artists' to her list of people to contact.

Ted then appeared with her drink, in a tall glass, accompanied with a slice of orange, which Izzy thought was a nice touch. "There we go, Izzy. Enjoy your drink and I hope we see you back soon."

"Thanks, Ted, that's very nice of you," Izzy said with a smile. "Actually, I was hoping to speak to you about your music nights you have here, if you have a few minutes?"

"Let me just check Alyssa's alright to stay behind the counter and I should be able to spare you a few minutes; it's relatively quiet at the moment."

He duly returned a few moments later and lowered himself into the armchair opposite her. "So, what can I help you with?" he asked, crossing his legs in the way that only men can do.

"Well, I'm currently doing some research into setting up a recording studio nearby and was wondering what the local music scene was like; what sort of artists do you have playing here, for example?"

"Right," Ted said slowly. "We have only recently started our showcase nights here. Our son, Joel, plays guitar and he has a few friends who have played here too. We're actually in talks with Tim Pointer, you know, the lad from Talent UK? He's a local lad and he's in Joel's social circle so he's said he'd be interested. We'd be really lucky to have him; the place would be packed. We showed the Talent UK Final the night it was on and the place was heaving. It was the busiest I've ever seen it in here."

Izzy looked at him very wide-eyed. She was a little shocked at how small the world appeared in that moment. The very mention of Tim made her cheeks flush as she remembered what she had been thinking earlier that morning.

"I see," she said, a little hoarsely. Clearing her throat, she continued, "Have you had many bands play here yet?"

Ted shook his head. "Not many, only a couple, if I recall correctly. I've been contacting the local agents and we've got a few possibilities but there's nothing confirmed yet."

Izzy then asked if she could have the numbers for the agents, to which Ted agreed and fetched a ring binder for her. She added the contact details for three agents into her phone; it would save her having to research it all later and at least she had some names rather than having to make appointments through receptionists or secretaries.

Ted then excused himself and headed back to the counter, ring binder in hand.

Izzy put her phone back in her pocket and drank some of her drink; it was wonderfully refreshing and she made a mental note to mention the shop to her friends.

She was about to get ready to leave when her ears caught some of the conversation from the table next to hers. A quick turn revealed it to be coming from two elderly ladies sat there with drinks.

"...young lad who works here, the one who looks like that 'Smile' bloke, Elsie. What's his name again?"

"Sir Andrew Anderson, Margaret. I've got his latest book here; it's quite a good read."

"I know what his sodding name is, Elsie, I used to work for the man."

Izzy remained in her seat, sipping her drink and pretending to be looking at her phone. She had her back to the two women, and was straining her ears without trying to make it obvious she was eavesdropping.

"I know you did, dear. I was just letting you know I've read his latest book. You should read it."

"Anyway, that young waiter, barista… whatever you call them these days. He's got the same eyes as Andrew. Those piercing blue eyes are something you never forget."

"I'm not quite sure what you're trying to get at, Margaret. Are you accusing Sir Andrew of fathering a child?"

Izzy frowned; Sir Andrew seemed like the unlikeliest person to cover something up that huge. She was fervently hoping nobody interrupted the two women; she really wanted to know more details.

"I'm not accusing anybody of anything, Elsie, I'm just pointing out that there were a few strange goings-on when I worked for the man. It could be pure coincidence but I wasn't born yesterday. Now I've seen this boy, I smell a rat."

"Like what, Margaret? What sort of goings-on?"

"There were always rumours that something happened on New Year's Eve in 1993. Sir Andrew had drunk a considerable amount and retired to bed quite early for him and the daughter of the chief housekeeper had disappeared. She then turned out to be pregnant and was strangely looked after by Sir Andrew. She had a special room in the basement I found out."

Izzy couldn't believe what she was hearing.

"Then, when she was about due, she strangely disappeared and then Miranda and Derek, the chief housekeeper and her husband, both retired shortly after to go and live on some obscure Scottish island. It was most strange."

"Even so, Margaret, it's all a bit, well, circumstantial."

Izzy agreed it was rather circumstantial, but she wondered if her father knew anything more about the events of that New Years Eve. She finished her drink and got up to leave, reaching for her phone as she did so.

CHAPTER TWENTY-THREE

Tuesday 17th April, morning
Huntingham College Library

Joel was sat in a remote part of the college library, trying to get his head around some college work that he should have done. He was finding it difficult to concentrate after the events of the night before. His brain was wondering how the twins' mum was one minute and then if Alan had calmed down the next. Even after messaging Hannah and finding out he seemed alright didn't really put his mind at ease. The fact that Alan was coming to college with Hannah must mean that things with those two were alright. He was just concerned that his own relationship with Alan might have been broken beyond repair.

Joel then thought about Amie. Every so often she would just pop into his head, and do a crazy dance, or pull a funny face at him, then disappear. The last time he'd seen her in the flesh, she'd been climbing into an ambulance. He then pulled his phone out to read the conversation they had had during the night. Even though she wasn't writing it out to him there and then, just reading that she had wanted him there made him feel like he meant something to her. He realised that he hadn't messaged her this morning and typed out a quick message: *Hey. Just thinking about you. Hope you and your mum are OK.*

He sat and looked at his phone for a few moments before trying to get his head back into his studying. It was several minutes before he felt his phone vibrate.

Joellyyyyyyy. Morning sunshine. I'm all the better for hearing from you.

Joel wasn't quite sure how to reply, so kept it brief.

You seem in a good mood - has there been some good news?

No. Nothing from the hospital yet. It's why I'm on my way to college.

Joel was surprised by that. He really didn't expect Amie to be in any sort of mental state to think about college.

Wow. Didn't expect you to be in college.

If there weren't exams coming up, I certainly wouldn't be.

Ah right. Forgot about them. Anyway, be great to see you. I'm in the library until eleven if you're free.

Thanks. I'll try and find you. You in our usual spot?
Sure am. Be great to see you.
You too. See you later xxxx

Joel tried to get his head back on to his work, but his mind kept drifting. He was chuffed at getting another four kisses in a message.

Returning to his work, he stared intently at his notes but the words just kept swimming in front of him. A deep frown crossed his face as he realised he'd turned a page but couldn't remember a thing he'd just read. Still trying to concentrate, he wasn't aware that Alan was sat across the desk from him, until he felt someone kick him under the desk.

"Ow!" Joel exclaimed, his fists clenched until he realised who it was. "How long have you been sat there?"

"Hey," Alan said, a wide smile on his face. "You were frowning for a long time looking at that."

"Thanks," Joel muttered, looking back down at his notes. "It's not been the best twenty-four hours in the world."

"Yeah, I've heard all about it now," Alan said sympathetically. "I just wanted to say how sorry I am about how I reacted this morning. If I was to be brutally honest, you may have done me a massive favour. Like, *totally* massive."

Joel looked up at him, noticing the smile was even wider than the last time, if at all possible. "You mean…"

"That's right."

"You asked Hannah out?"

"Yep."

"What did she say?"

"What do you think she said?"

Joel shook his head. "All that rubbish you gave me this morning, and then this happens. Dude, that's amazing!" he exclaimed.

Two girls sat at the next table turned around and gave Joel evil looks. He held up a hand in apology.

Alan grinned. "It's great," he said, lowering his voice. "I owe a lot to you, in many ways. Hannah made me see that I'd been a bit of an idiot."

Joel snorted but said nothing.

"Well, yeah, I get that *now*," Alan went on. "At the time I was a bit put out, but maybe it was the catalyst for this. You just sped things up a bit."

"Is that all the credit I'm going to get?"

"To be fair, it wasn't as if you meant to do it. It just sort of happened for you."

Joel conceded that point. "Fair enough. So, when and where are you going?"

"The date is on Friday afternoon. I've got a few ideas. It might be weather pending, though; what I really want to do might not be any fun in the rain."

Joel couldn't even begin to guess what Alan had in mind.

"So, what are you doing on Friday afternoon?" Alan asked.

"Hearing about how amazingly well your date went?" Joel replied, a little facetiously.

"Apart from that," Alan said, smiling.

"Nothing planned as yet, apart from coursework. And possibly revision. Why?"

"I might need your help with something," Alan said, trying his best to keep a straight face.

Joel looked at him for a few moments, trying to work out what on earth Alan was up to but came up with nothing. "Is it to do with your date?" he asked tentatively.

"Not exactly. I can't really say much more than that," Alan replied, unhelpfully. "Is there any news on the twins' mum by the way? I hope she's going to be alright."

"Yeah, me too. I've not heard anything new this morning. All the waiting… it's awful. I'd hate to be in the twins' position. And they haven't even got their dad to help. It's just them. I know I couldn't survive more than a weekend on my own without either Ma or Pops being there."

"No, you're quite right," Alan said after a few moments thought.

"Anyway, moving on. How's Hannah this morning?"

Alan smiled.

"Dude, seriously, you've got to stop doing that. It's getting annoying already. You look like the Cheshire Cat."

"Sorry. I've got a girlfriend before you have. Just to rub it in." He looked at Joel's face and reverted back to topic. "She's doing alright. Better than I expected her to be."

"How did you expect her to be?"

"Hanging from her skylight," Alan said bluntly.

Joel looked shocked. "You thought she would attempt to commit suicide again? But she's been doing so well!"

"I know."

"Hang on, did you discuss this with her?"

"I did."

Joel couldn't believe what he was hearing. "Was the mention of suicide before or after you asked her out?"

"Before."

"And she still agreed to going out on a date with you?"

"That's right."

Joel shook his head in disbelief. "I've no idea how you've managed that. I thought I understood girls to a certain extent, but I wouldn't have brought up something like suicide and then get that girl to go out with me. You must be a smooth talker."

Alan looked amused, but didn't say anything.

Joel then caught sight of a flash of red hair over Alan's shoulder and waved. Amie and Hannah wandered over and both boys stood up to hug their respective twin. Hannah and Alan held on to each other for a little longer than usual and it became what Joel considered to be a cuddle. He coughed loudly, which caused them to separate and look a bit awkward.

"I take it you've heard about your sister and my best friend," Joel said to Amie, when their own hug had broken apart.

"She's taken great pleasure in telling me how she's got a boyfriend before me," Amie replied, flashing a smile at her twin.

"Oh really," Joel added, looking pointedly at Alan, who responded with a grin.

"Yes. About time, though, I must say," Amie commented, which caused Hannah's eyes to narrow.

"Hey, I've already admitted you were right about Alan, give it a rest," Hannah said and Amie held up her hand to say sorry.

Amie's phone then rang and she headed out into the stairwell to answer it. The other three shared suspicious looks with each other. Joel started packing his bag; he had seen her expression when she saw who was ringing on her phone screen and she had looked scared. He assumed it was from the hospital. She returned a few moments later, looking very pale.

"Amie? What's up?" Joel asked, worried about her.

"That was the hospital," Amie said faintly. "They've asked for me to come back in."

"Is that not a good thing, Amz?" Alan said, a bit confused. "Could she not have woken up?"

Amie shook her head and buried her face in her hands.

"Did you ask them why?" Hannah asked, putting her arms around her sister.

Amie glanced up at them all, her eyes glistening and her bottom lip trembling. "It's code isn't it? That's the code for 'your mum has died, come and collect her stuff'. The nurse on the phone was fighting back tears, I could hear it in her voice."

Joel took charge of the situation. Grabbing his bag off the table, he then put an arm around Amie and she snuggled into his chest, her tears running into the fabric of his t-shirt. Alan put his arms around Hannah as well, as she had taken on her sister's pale complexion. The two boys led the twins out into the stairwell, where they could talk a bit louder, and they couldn't disturb anybody trying to work.

Joel tried to be realistic. "Amz, let's deal with the facts. You don't know for certain that your mum has gone. You've based it on a tone of voice, from someone who rang you."

Amie pushed him away from her, her face flushed with anger. "Don't be an idiot, Joel, you think I don't know that tone of voice? My mum works in a care home. There were a number of shifts she came home and told us that a resident had died. You can't just ring up someone's family and tell them 'Hi, how's things? Oh yeah, by the way, come and collect your mum's things, she's partying in the clouds now'. Mum had to make those sorts of calls where you ask the family to come in, it's urgent. And you can't say it sounding hopeful, so they get their hopes up that the resident has somehow made a miraculous recovery. So don't tell me that I don't know for certain. I do know." She buried her face in his chest again, her body jerking as she sobbed.

Joel was taken aback. He didn't have a clue what to say. All he could think of to do was to keep hugging her, and let her cry herself out.

Alan then spoke up. "Listen, as much as I hate to say it, we can't stay here all day with life on pause. If it has happened, then we need to get to the hospital, so you girls can say your goodbyes. And if you get there and find that your mum is still with us, then that'll be a nice surprise for you both. But, either way, we need to move."

Amie wiped both eyes with the back of her hands. "Al, what you say makes a lot of sense, but I'm just really scared." With that, she threw her arms around her sister.

Hannah then took Amie by the hand and beckoned the boys to follow them. Joel looked at Alan, who shrugged, and they both set off after the twins.

They ended up standing at the college bus stop, where it took a few minutes of waiting before the next bus for the hospital arrived.

It was a journey that the four of them spent in silence, each of them lost in their own thoughts. Joel realised it was the waiting that was the worst bit of all this; whatever had happened had already happened. They just had to wait to find out what it was. Even though it wasn't his own family member that they were heading towards, he still felt nervous. He was very aware of his basic human functions – breathing, blinking and a pounding heart rate to name a few – and he just couldn't take his mind off thinking what he would say if the worst had happened. What do you say to somebody who had possibly lost their mother in the way that the twins had? He had no idea. He just hoped his brain would think of something appropriate if the time came.

The bus pulled up and they traipsed off into the body of Huntingham's hospital. Strangely, Amie looked very reluctant, whereas Hannah had a steely gaze in her eyes. Joel would normally have expected it to be the other way around. He realised Alan next to him was taking big gulps of air, seemingly nervous too. Joel put an arm around Alan's shoulders for a few seconds before it was brushed away. He was a little comforted to know he wasn't the only one feeling anxious.

Amie knew the way, having been there only a few hours previously. Joel had no idea how far they walked, down the wide corridors that were dimly lit but painted pastel colours to try and add some light. The air smelled faintly of bleach and of the alcohol hand wash that could be found at the entrance of every ward they passed. Joel noticed many of the people wandering the corridors were stern-faced, possibly visiting an ill friend or relative, or having to come to terms with news from their own appointment. There were people smiling as they passed the maternity unit, and people in tears outside the critical illness wards; the hospital was awash with a range of emotions – unbelievable highs, gut-wrenching lows and everything in between.

It took a few minutes before they arrived outside the Washby Ward where Christine French had been admitted last night. Pressing the buzzer, a voice answered and asked who was there. Amie replied, introducing them all, and the doors opened automatically. They headed to the reception desk a few yards ahead of them. The woman behind the desk politely explained that Joel and Alan would have to wait in the sitting room in the ward, as they could only permit family members at bedsides at that time.

All four of them headed to the sitting room where the girls gave both boys a hug each. Nothing was said again; nobody seemed to know what to say. The two girls held the other's hand and returned to the desk to find out what had been so urgent only three quarters of an hour ago.

CHAPTER TWENTY-FOUR

Hayden was sat in his office at Smart Solicitors based in the middle of Huntingham. He was looking through emails on his touch screen computer, tutting as he deleted junk mail that had got past his spam filter.

He had decided today was a good day to get organised. After the Easter weekend, work was starting to pick up again and the eight hundred or so emails sat in his inbox needed dealing with. Melissa, his receptionist, had informed him that he didn't have any appointments until one o'clock so he'd made best use of an empty morning.

His father had founded the office in 1961 on Church Street and it had been there ever since. It was a tall, Victorian building, covering four floors, including a basement. Hayden's father, Alec, had passed away quite suddenly shortly after Izzy had been born in 1984 but was immortalised in a large portrait in the reception area. At times when there were difficult cases or moral issues that arose, Hayden would often find himself standing alone, in the office after hours, in front of the painting asking for guidance.

Hayden's top floor office at Smart Solicitors had been refurbished over Christmas the previous year and had been given much-needed modernisation. His office now contained a six-metre fish tank built into one wall and he took great pleasure at looking at the collection of cold-water fish he had collected over the years. His favourites were the longfin barbs, which he had been initially disappointed with when he'd bought them. He had been sold several drab-looking fish, on the promise that they would soon show their colours. 'Soon' had turned out to be a few months down the line, but they had added some wonderful colours to his tank once their dorsal fins had developed. He also kept white-cloud mountain minnows and leopard danios and found he did a lot of thought processing while watching them zip around the tank. A cold-water fish tank had been a feature of every office that a Smart had sat in at the Church Street premises since his father had first opened for business fifty-one years ago.

The opposite wall to the fish tank was lined with books, mostly legal textbooks but he did have a section including signed copies of Sir Andrew's works. Hayden had found that having his friend's books had been a talking point for some clients over the years and he took great pleasure in fetching them off the shelf to tell a tale of the message that had been scrawled inside the front cover. The rest of that wall was filing cabinets and then a large printer in the corner. There were some comfortable chairs for clients opposite his large desk, which was by the window. He had made a point over the years of looking out of the window as clients came into the room, pretending to be lost deep in thought. He had picked up from his father to try and judge clients by using other senses before looking at them. How a client smelt and sounded had told him a lot about them before turning around to greet them; it often affected his attitude towards them. The clients that were audibly crying obviously had to be dealt with differently to the aftershave-doused playboys that came through the door.

That little nugget of knowledge he passed on to his paralegals every year was usually met with scepticism, but he always encouraged them to try it. He often received grovelling apologies a few months down the line. His senses were so finely tuned, he could often tell which of his staff was talking to him before they had even said anything, without him having to look up from his desk.

Any available surface was usually covered in paperwork, and his graduate trainees were often baffled by his ability to find something they needed at a moment's notice. He wasn't generally an untidy person, but since his divorce from Irene a few years ago, that Sir Andrew had helped him through with some useful mental techniques and several bottles of the finest Scotch whisky, he had let standards slip. They had met at an office party when he had been training to be a solicitor straight after college in 1977. His father had just appointed her as a secretary and Hayden and Irene had hit it off straight away. They married in 1980 and Izzy was born four years later. However, once Izzy had grown up and refused to take on the family business, a divide occurred in his relationship with his wife. Irene accused him of blocking her out because she hadn't borne him a son who would have wanted to continue the family business, which he flatly denied to her face. Deep down, though, he had been very put out by Izzy's choice and as she wasn't there any more, Irene had taken the brunt of his frustration. That was until one day he came to the office, found a letter of resignation on his desk, along with a set of divorce papers and a short message in a card informing him she had emigrated to Spain to live with her sister, that she had had enough of the long evenings in the house on her own while he was at work, and that although they had had many happy years together, since Izzy had moved out, they had drifted apart and she couldn't see a future together. He hadn't heard from her since. He knew Izzy kept in touch with her via the Internet but he had never wanted to go down that route. The emotional turmoil he had lived in, having to deal with living in a family home to what then became a bachelor pad, had formed some deep scars. It was a part of his life he wanted to leave behind.

His first call on finding Irene's note had been to Andrew, who had been in the early stages of his first tour in 2003. Hayden cancelled his appointments for a week and had driven all the way to Devon to tag along with his best friend. He'd sat in the audience while Andrew talked to people in Torquay and Plymouth and at one of the talks had been questioned at one point as to how he was feeling. He couldn't believe his best friend had asked him in front of a room full of strangers; Andrew had well and truly ambushed him and Hayden had had to fight back tears in admitting that his wife of twenty-three years had just upped and left him one day and his whole world had fallen apart. That evening, Andrew had hired a boat and taken them both out into the English Channel, with a cool box filled with bottles of Hayden's favourite ale on board. They had travelled several miles out to sea so they couldn't even see the lights from Brixham, where they had been staying. Andrew had killed the engine, so that all they could hear was the water lapping at the sides of the boat, and by the glow of the moon and the pinpricks of light provided by the stars, Hayden was encouraged to talk.

The ale had loosened his tongue and Hayden had admitted to blaming Irene for not providing him with anything other than a daughter. He and Irene had tried before and after Izzy was born; their dream had been to have at least three children. However, for whatever reason it hadn't happened, and although he loved Izzy to bits, he had always felt like the final piece of his perfect life had been lost. He didn't know if Izzy knew that was how he felt, but having seen the woman she had matured into, he was grateful she hadn't obviously blamed him for her mother leaving.

Andrew had been very sympathetic, having had his own issues with not fathering children, and just asked the odd question here and there to keep Hayden talking. They ended up chatting most of the night, returning the boat as the first fingers of dawn were creeping over the horizon. A friendship that had lasted thirty-three years at that point was further solidified that night.

Hayden heard a knock at his office door and heard the buzz from the rest of the building as the door opened. He never took his eyes off the screen in front of him until the person was right in front of his desk. Still keeping his eyes on his screen and casually deleting the odd email, his senses told him it was Phil Hollis, one of his paralegals working on Sir Andrew's family research.

"Morning, Hollis. What can I do you for?"

Phil Hollis had been one of those trainees who had been a 'senses sceptic', as Hayden liked to call them, and still found Hayden's ability to know who was there without looking irritating. He was tall and wiry, with close-cropped hair, failing to hide the fact his hairline was receding.

"Morning, boss," Phil said, which made Hayden flinch; he hated being referred to as that, something of which Phil was well aware. Hayden knew he did it to get revenge for identifying him without sight. "How are you this morning, boss? Mel said you were in early but you had no appointments."

"I'm wonderful, thanks. How's the family?" Hayden asked politely. Phil's wife had recently given birth to twin boys, so Phil had been looking rather tired at the office since they had arrived.

"Well, it was a better night, thanks for asking. So, what's going on?"

Hayden closed his eyes and turned towards his longest serving member of staff before opening them again. "I'm just sorting through some emails, Hollis. What's with the questions? Struggling for something to do?"

"No, boss, not at all. I just wondered if you had a few moments to spare about Sir Andrew's family research."

"I see. Well, now's as good a time as any. What is there to report?"

"That's sort of the problem. Randy and I are still struggling to make any progress." Miranda 'Randy' Strawson was the other paralegal at Smart Solicitors that was working on Sir Andrew's case.

Hayden tried hard not to smile at Phil's last sentence, but a slight grin crossed his face, making Phil realise what he'd said.

"Oh come on, boss, there's no need for that. I'm happily married, remember?" Phil said, twiddling his wedding ring awkwardly.

Hayden spotted it but didn't mention it. "Sorry, it just tickled me. Randy's not your type anyway."

"How do you know I'm not hers?" Phil asked, a little defensively.

"Really, Hollis? I don't think Randy's particularly selective. You're too much of a family man to get tempted by that seductress," Hayden said, looking directly at the paralegal. He became concerned when Phil turned a bright shade of crimson.

"Hollis... no, surely not! When?" Hayden exclaimed, gesturing Phil to have a seat.

"A couple of nights ago," Phil muttered, angry for letting himself be caught. "Sally's not really been up to it. She's so busy with the twins, she's exhausted and I just haven't had a look in." He eased himself into the chair. "Is this going to be a problem?" he asked, looking worried.

"I don't know, you tell me. What's happened between you and Randy since? Have you seen her?"

"Only in the office and you know what she's like in the office," came the muttered reply.

"The ultimate professional, I know. I was a little surprised to find about her other side. But that doesn't answer my question. There was a reason I put you two together and that was because of your experience and your research capabilities, not your flourishing sexual chemistry. Will you two still be able to work together?" Hayden asked, looking at Phil sternly.

"I think so. She knows I'm married and I'm not planning on leaving Sally. It's just been a tough few months, that's all. She caught me at a weak moment."

"It takes two to tango, Hollis, that's all I'll say. What did you tell Sally?"

Phil looked a bit awkward. "I told her I was working late. That there was an overnight project we had to work on."

"Ah, the old classic. Does she suspect anything?"

"I don't think so," Phil said, looking nervous.

"Don't be stupid, Hollis, women always know," Hayden said, sounding harsher than he had intended. Phil's face dropped and Hayden did feel sorry for him in that moment. "Listen, Phil," he said, which caused Phil's head to shoot up; Hayden only used his first name on very rare occasions. "What you've said between these walls will stay between these walls. But I don't want this to affect your work. As soon as that happens then we'll have a problem. Is that clear?"

Phil nodded, looking relieved.

"Good," Hayden said, seeing the door open over Phil's shoulder. "Randy, good morning. Come and pull up a chair," he said, beckoning her over. "What a coincidence; were your ears burning?" Hayden tried to keep a bemused expression from crossing his face.

Randy looked at him carefully, before turning to Phil. "I see you told him," she said, not unkindly.

"It was written all over his face," Hayden said, before Phil had opened his mouth. "Ah well, he's joined the club at least."

Phil's face was an image of confusion slowly merging with horror. Randy just smiled sweetly, tucking her blond curls behind her ears.

"Now you know why she's called Randy," Hayden commented. "I called her Strawson for about a month before I fell under her spell. She's been 'Randy' ever since, if you pardon the pun."

Phil was staring blankly in disbelief, while Randy just smiled.

"Anyway, I wasn't wanting to speak to you about your personal lives. How's the research coming along?" Hayden asked, looking between them both.

Phil glanced over at Randy who took the lead. "It's been unproductive, to be honest. The box of stuff you gave us last week hasn't turned up anything at all."

Hayden looked pensive. "So, what are your guts telling you? Where has Andy got this notion from that there's a mystery long-lost brother out there somewhere?"

They both shrugged.

"No, I don't know either," Hayden said, scratching his jaw. "For me that means he could be trying to hide something that he doesn't want us to find."

"Like what?" Phil asked.

"If he's lying then it's something he wants to keep a secret, which means it's something pretty big," Randy said.

"I agree. I hate to admit it, but I'd have thought you would have found something if there was anything to find. I've known Andy more than forty years and this is the first time I've ever heard mention of a possible brother. With him being a person in the media spotlight, a brother would surely have been easy to find." Hayden stopped as a thought struck him. "He was reading his will and the brother only came up when he read the bit about next of kin…"

"So, is he covering something up? A long lost relation?" Randy mused.

"Possibly, possibly. Or even something closer," Hayden added, frowning as he racked his brain for any nuggets of information.

"Well, we've contacted all available family members. His mother is in a retirement home on the Isle of Wight and appears to have dementia. She didn't even remember you, Hayden," Phil said, looking through his notes he'd brought in with him.

"His father passed away years ago now. There were a couple of uncles that we spoke to who didn't have a clue, insisting Sid was a stand up guy and was so proud of his only son," Randy added.

Hayden's face was impassive. "I'm just suspicious; what are we missing, guys?" His phone then buzzed. He pressed a button and said, "Yes, Mel, what's up?"

"Izzy's here to see you, and she says it's urgent? I had replied to her text she sent to say you didn't have any appointments until one, hope that's OK."

"Not a problem, Mel, send her in," Hayden said.

Izzy duly appeared a few moments later, once she'd made her way from the ground floor. Phil and Randy had packed up their things and passed Izzy in the corridor outside.

"Izzy darling, what a pleasant surprise," Hayden said, stepping out from behind his desk to give her a kiss on the cheek. "What's so urgent?"

Izzy then explained what she had overheard in the coffee shop. Hayden's eyes widened when his daughter explained about Miranda and Derek Forbes disappearing at about the same time as their daughter's due date.

"Blimey, Iz, I think you've stumbled on to something massive here. I remember the New Years Eve you're talking about. Your mum and I were there. There was a bit of commotion when Laura disappeared, but she turned up fine and well the next morning. And I do remember Miranda and Des leaving very suddenly in September-time; Andy was gutted when they left, but they'd given him so many years of great service he couldn't exactly refuse. They retired to some obscure Scottish island, if I remember rightly."

"So, what do you reckon, Dad? Could it be true?"

"I don't know, Izzy. I'll have to do some further investigating before I can make my mind up. But even so, following the meeting I was having just before you arrived, you've sorted a workload out for Randy and Hollis." Smiling from ear to ear, Hayden picked up the phone on his desk and dialled an extension number. "Randy? Get yourself and Hollis back in here. We've found something that I want you both to investigate. Oh, and be prepared to pack a suitcase – I might need you to go to Scotland."

CHAPTER TWENTY-FIVE

Tuesday 17th April
Huntingham Hospital

Leaving the boys behind in the waiting room, the twins trudged back to the reception desk, walking as if their shoes were filled with concrete.

"Amz, wait," Hannah said, pulling her sister by the arm.

"What, Han?" Amie replied, a little frustrated.

"I don't know. I just want to know if everything will be OK."

Amie nearly blew up at her sister, but took a deep breath before replying. "I can't say, sis. All I know is things might be a bit different for a while. Things aren't going to ever be the same again."

"OK, Amz, I'm sorry. I'm just scared."

"What does your magic book say about dealing with this sort of situation?"

Hannah's eyes narrowed. "You mean Sir Andrew's book?"

"That's the one."

Hannah sighed. "If I remember correctly, it says to smile."

"Smile?"

"That's the one," Hannah replied facetiously.

"That's it?"

Hannah nodded.

Amie considered this for a few moments. "So, basically, if we smiled at each other for a bit, it can make this whole situation better?"

Hannah shrugged. "It doesn't even have to be at each other; it can be in a mirror even."

"Fancy trying it?"

Hannah nodded her agreement and the two sisters ended up facing each other, looking a little awkward.

"So, who starts? I just don't feel like smiling," Hannah said.

Amie rolled her eyes. "Oh go on then," she said, giving Hannah the biggest grin she could muster.

Hannah returned the smile and Amie immediately felt a little brighter inside.

"You know what, Han. I do actually feel a little better," she said.

"Me too," Hannah replied, sounding reluctant. "Not being quite so scathing about my 'magic' book now, are you?"

Amie held her hands up. "Sorry. So what do we now?"

"Fancy a hug?"

"A hug?"

"Yeah. I'd like one."

Amie stretched her arms out and Hannah embraced her and they held each other tightly for a few moments.

"That's better," Hannah said, her voice muffled by Amie's shoulder.

"So I guess this is it, Han, we just need to find out if Mum has gone."

Hannah gave her sister a strange look. "What do you mean 'if'? You were adamant earlier."

"I know I was, but maybe Joel was right. Maybe I was jumping the gun a little. And maybe I was in a dark place. Your smile gave me some hope."

Hannah didn't look as if she knew what to say, her mouth opening and closing for a few seconds.

"Look, Han, I just want this over and done with. Our family has had enough drama in the last couple of years, I just want to find out what's happened with Mum and then move on with our lives."

"Fair enough. Shall we get this done?" Hannah said, pushing Amie in the direction of the reception desk, now manned by a stout, black woman with scraped-back, braided hair, dressed in a standard royal blue uniform.

"Hi," Amie said to the nurse when they got there. "Can we see Christine French now, please?" The words almost got stuck in her throat. Amie was forcing herself to be strong, not just for herself, but for her sister too, although she, too, was very scared about what they would discover. Hannah was holding her arm tightly. Amie was sure she would have bruises later; her twin was holding on to her that firmly.

"Sure, follow me," the nurse said with a strong South African accent, offering a half-smile as she climbed down from the chair. Her name badge showed her name to be Wendy. Amie and Hannah shared a look; neither of them could read what Wendy's expression meant.

The twins followed the nurse down the corridor, in the opposite direction to the waiting room.

Amie noticed Hannah's expression had returned to a frown. "It's going to be OK, Han. Don't worry. I can smile at you again if you need me to. You'll still have me, no matter what," Amie whispered in her sister's ear.

Hannah replied with a weak smile, her expression then returning to a frown. Amie realised that was probably the best she would get.

They walked past various rooms, each containing patients looking more and more ill the further they went. Amie hadn't picked up on it earlier as it had been dark when she had arrived, and when she'd been leaving she had just wanted to get out. The whole time she was walking she was desperately hoping that their mother was still with them. Her mind was so clouded she just couldn't read what her gut was saying any more. She realised her hands were clammy and she could feel a bead of sweat running down her back. Her tummy also felt like it had twisted itself into knots. She hated feeling this nervous.

As they approached their mum's bed, the first thing that Amie noticed was that there were still machines bleeping; surely that was a good sign. Amie looked at Hannah, who appeared to have picked up on the noises as well and was looking hopefully back at her.

Wendy parted the curtain that was surrounding the bed to let the girls in. She picked up the notes clipped to the end of the hospital bed and gave them a quick scan, scratching her braids, causing them to ruffle. She casually smoothed them down, before checking the time on the watch clipped to her uniform.

"Well, the specialist has been to see your mum this morning, girls. He's a very nice man, and he was very sad to hear about your mum," Wendy said.

Amie shared another look with Hannah, who was looking impatient.

"Sorry, excuse me, but is Mum OK?" Amie asked.

Wendy looked confused. "I don't understand."

"I was rung by someone who asked me and Hannah to come in; it sounded urgent."

"I see," Wendy replied, sounding as if she didn't see at all. She referred back to the clipboard again and both girls saw a look of realisation dawn on Wendy's face.

"What?" Amie demanded.

"I'll need to fetch a colleague," Wendy muttered and hurried away before either Hannah or Amie could say anything further.

Amie, eyebrows knitted together, gestured for Hannah to sit down in the chair at their mum's bedside. Amie had spent several hours in that chair and didn't really want to sit in it again.

Hannah nodded and sat down, leaning forward, her elbows resting on her knees as she held her face in her hands. She was staring blankly into space.

"So, Amz, what's going on?"

"I have absolutely no idea, Han, this is really weird."

"But these machines are still bleeping, right? Tell me that means she's still with us?"

Amie nodded. "As far as I can tell. This looks like the heart rate monitor, and she's got a steady heart rate of fifty-five beats per minute. It's pretty constant. Blood pressure appears to be normal as well. That's what I'd refer to as 'vital'."

"What have they said to you about her? Like, will she ever be alright again?"

Amie sighed. "They said that they didn't know. They ran some tests late last night and were waiting on the results this morning. Maybe that's why we've been called in."

Hannah made an 'oh' shape with her mouth, but didn't say anything and they lapsed into silence again.

"She's very still, isn't she," Amie commented a few moments later. "Having said that, she's wearing a neck brace, and her left arm is in a cast. There could be other bits held in place; maybe not a massive surprise to see her being still after all."

Hannah nodded. "It makes me wonder if she's there or not. Does she even know we're here?" She reached out and grabbed their mum's limp hand and held it tightly.

Amie was stood at the end of the bed, trying to make sense of the notes on the clipboard. "I've got no idea what all this means. It could be anything. I can only just about make out her name."

The conversation lulled again. Amie was stood on her feet, a bundle of nervous energy, whereas Hannah was still sat on the chair, having barely moved position from when she first sat down.

"I tell you what, Han," Amie began, "it's the waiting that's horrible. All the time I'm just constantly thinking of what could be wrong with Mum. It ranges from whiplash to a broken neck."

"Oh don't say that, Amz, that's awful," Hannah replied, looking shocked.

"It's true though. She's still got that brace on, and we have no idea what's under it."

At that moment, an elderly male doctor appeared at the curtain. He had the look of a crazy scientist, with glasses and a tuft of hair above each ear. Amie and Hannah shared a look with each other that said they knew what the other was thinking.

"Miss French," the doctor said to Amie, before double taking when he noticed Hannah. "And Miss French?"

Hannah merely nodded.

"I see. Sorry, I had no idea there were two of you," the doctor said, scratching his jaw. "Anyway, would you like to follow me?"

The twins, slightly baffled, followed the doctor down the corridor to a small, dimly-lit room that contained a desk and some standard office chairs.

"Have a seat please, girls," the doctor said, gesturing towards the chairs. He settled in to the chair on the other side of the desk.

"Right," he said, slapping his knees. "I should probably introduce myself. I'm Doctor Morris and I'm an orthopaedic surgeon on the Washby Ward."

"I'm Amie and this is Hannah," Amie said, making the introductions.

"Identical twins?" Doctor Morris enquired.

They both nodded.

"I see. Rare." He paused a moment while he spotted a bottle of the alcohol solution and proceeded to rub some into his hands. "Sorry about that. Old habit," he said, when he noticed the two girls staring at him. "Anyway, your mum was admitted to our ward late last night. Her notes said that she had fallen down the stairs. Her blood tests have come back and there was a large amount of alcohol in her system. Can I ask if your mother was an alcoholic?"

Amie winced. "I wouldn't have said she was an alcoholic, as such. She enjoyed a bottle of wine now and again, but it was just her way of dealing with everything. She had drunk a bottle of wine last night though, she'd had some good news for the first time in a while."

"I see. Had a hard time of it recently?"

Amie nodded. "Our dad left us last year and she's worked every hour she can to try and keep a roof over our heads. She's been stressed, depressed, angry, tired... You name it, she's had to deal with it."

"I see," Doctor Morris said, rubbing his jaw with a large hand. "To give you an update on her situation – there's still quite a bit we can't tell at the moment as there is a large amount of swelling. However, it appears that she may have some internal bleeding, possibly down to broken ribs. There does appear to be some damage to her spine as well, possibly nerve damage, which would be expected with a fall such as hers. The paramedics gave her stitches on her scalp, as she took a nasty bump there too. The neck brace is precautionary at this stage, mind you. She's also dislocated her left shoulder and broken her left ulna," he finished, pointing to the underside of his arm.

"So, what does this all mean?" Amie asked.

"Well, I need to speak to a neurologist to see if there's anything else we can do. At the moment she's comfortable. She's been unconscious since she arrived. She had also stopped breathing on the way to the hospital, the paramedics informed me. We've put her on a breathing machine just to try and keep her stable."

Hannah's eyes widened and Amie, too, was a little shocked.

"I had no idea about that. The paramedics were all very calm in that ambulance."

Doctor Morris smiled. "They're very good at what they do."

"Yeah, damn right they are. And I just thought all the machines and things she was plugged in to were routine things. It sounds like Mum's been through a right battle."

"There's no easy way to say it, girls, but your mother is very ill. She's in a coma, possibly down to an impact injury to her head. We won't know how much she'll be affected until she comes out of the coma. There's a nine-point scale for comas, one being the lightest coma. Your mother is currently at seven."

"Does all that mean she has brain damage?" Amie asked, a frown showing on her face as she tried to connect the information strands together.

Doctor Morris nodded. "It would certainly appear so. But, as we can't say exactly how long her brain was starved of oxygen, it's extremely difficult to be able to say exactly how it may affect her."

"Where do we go from here?" Amie asked, sounding very hoarse; she felt like her throat had dried up completely.

"We'll need to try and get her into surgery as soon as possible to see what the cause is of the internal bleeding. That's the first step. We can then also see if there's a way of reducing the fluid around her spine and brain."

"Will we get our Mum back?" Hannah asked quietly.

Doctor Morris hesitated and puffed his cheeks out. To Amie, it felt like the world stopped for a few seconds and in that moment she knew that life for her and Hannah would definitely change.

"It depends what you mean by 'back', Miss French," he said, eventually. "Will she return to the same person she was before she fell down the stairs? Possibly, maybe a few years down the line. At the moment, we don't know enough to be able to tell how much damage has been sustained; time will tell on that one." He glanced at the watch on his wrist. "Right, if you can excuse me, I have to prepare myself for surgery. Your mum's will hopefully be the one after this."

The doctor stood up to leave and gestured the two girls outside. He then swiftly departed down the corridor, leaving them stood there, minds swirling, trying to process what they had just been told.

"I guess we should find the boys," Hannah said, not quite sure what else to say.

"Sure, I just want to go and see Mum again," Amie replied. "A lot of what happened last night is blurry. I just don't remember it all. I messaged Joel for a bit, but I then fell asleep in the chair. I guess I was fortunate that everyone came here to Mum instead of her having to be transported around. I just want to see her and tell her things will be alright."

They made the short walk back to their mother's bedside, where they found Wendy busy writing on their mum's clipboard.

"Is everything alright?" Amie asked, surprised to see the nurse there.

Wendy looked up at her. "Just one of her vitals had dropped suddenly, but it's corrected itself. Bit strange, but when she's had the amount of trauma she's had, then perhaps not surprising. She's going to be prepped for surgery in a few moments – did Doctor Morris go through it with you?"

The twins nodded.

"Good. He's a great surgeon. One of the best I've ever seen. He'll do his very best to fix your mum up."

The two girls said their thanks to Wendy, who promptly disappeared with a swish of the curtain. The two girls separated and went to stand on opposite sides of the bed; Amie to their mum's left and Hannah to the right.

Amie stroked her mum's arm, careful not to press too hard on the cast and Hannah clasped her mum's hand in both of hers.

"Mum," Amie began, catching her breath as she felt the tears begin to roll. "I really don't know what to say. The doctor said that you've suffered quite a lot and that you're in a coma, so I don't know if you can even hear us." She turned to look at the heart rate monitor, but it persisted with its regular bleep. She had hoped that her mum's heart rate would have increased or for something to have changed. "OK, well I'm going to talk anyway; it makes me feel better."

Amie looked up into Hannah's eyes, and noticed that they were beginning to well up too.

"We've not been told a lot about what's wrong with you; the doctors don't seem to know at the minute. They're going to have to operate on you as they're concerned about internal bleeding." Amie paused and took a few deep breaths, trying to maintain her composure. "You look pretty beat up, Mum. It's horrible to see you like this. I just hope you're still in there. We miss you." Amie leaned over and gave her mother a kiss on the cheek and Hannah took the opportunity to do the same. It was as close as they could get; the breathing apparatus didn't allow them any nearer.

"Is there anything you wanted to say, Han?" Amie asked, a little pointedly.

Hannah thought about it for a few seconds before looking a little resigned. "There's a few things I need to tell you, Mum. I kind of feel responsible for all this, but I know you'd be annoyed with me if I tried to blame myself for just a horrible, unfortunate accident."

Hannah took a deep breath before continuing.

"I'd been at my happiest that I could ever remember for a few hours last night. Everything I'd ever wanted appeared to be coming together. Tim said he wanted to see me. You were so thrilled to see me going on a date but it didn't go that well, in all fairness. I ended up telling Tim I wanted to be there for him, but I've been getting closer to Alan in recent weeks. I got a bit trapped in the moment. At one point, I gave Tim a hug and I saw Alan look in through the window and I realised I had a decision to make. When the shop closed I didn't come straight into the house. I went to sit behind the garden shed and looked up at the sky. I just sat there thinking for a while and wondered about life and where I wanted to go with it and who I wanted to spend it with.

"There was a bit of me that wanted to see how things would go with Tim; he wanted to carry on where we had left off but he hurt me more than

I cared to admit. Amie made me realise that last night that I was actually attracted to Alan. I hadn't realised that before."

Amie looked across at her sister with a shocked look on her face. She had wondered how Hannah had been feeling about everything and even what had happened to her sister between Beans and Banter closing and when she had actually arrived home. She couldn't quite believe what she'd heard.

"I had reached a decision last night that I was going to try and pluck up some courage and ask Alan out. I was coming in the house to tell you all, if you were up. There were still lights on, so I knew one of you would be there. I just think I caught you by surprise, Mum. I don't know if you were worried about me, or anything, but as the door opened you turned and lost your footing and you tumbled down the stairs. All those happy feelings I had were gone." Hannah's face then cracked as tears began to make tracks down her cheeks.

Amie's expression had barely changed. She had never heard her sister talk for this long nor had she even known how Hannah had been feeling about Alan and Tim.

"In the midst of being interrogated by a police officer trying to see if either of us had pushed you down the stairs," Hannah continued, "I overheard Joel telling his mum that Alan had fancied me and I had a little bit of hope again. I went to bed feeling optimistic and hoping you were alright and going to pull through.

"I got up this morning as normal, and discovered Alan was knocking at the door. He looked really worried and I couldn't figure out why. He had apparently been out drinking the night before because he thought I had chosen Tim over him and Joel and his dad had been out to rescue him."

Amie was still shocked. Hearing everything that had happened to her sister in the last few hours had put her own boring evening into perspective. After Hannah had gone out, she had done some college work for a bit and then watched some DVDs in her room before hearing her mum scream and she had run out of her room to find out what had happened.

Hannah was still talking to their mum. "He came in and asked me out. I said yes. I'd never imagined telling you I had a boyfriend under these circumstances. I just hope you pull through so you can see how happy I am.

"But there's something else, Mum," Hannah said, looking at Amie for the first time. "I've no idea if you knew, but when I tried to hang myself, it was Alan who found me and called the emergency services. I only found out this morning. I didn't fail. If he hadn't found me then I probably wouldn't be here. He gave me another shot at life, particularly when I didn't think there was a life to be lived. That was why he'd been so worried when he came round; he thought I'd topped myself."

Amie stared wide-eyed at her sister, who was looking a bit guilty. That was something she hadn't been told earlier. She had always presumed Hannah had rung the emergency services herself and she had never intended to go through with it properly; it had just been a cry for help. After all that she'd just heard she was beginning to wonder if she knew her sister at all.

"So yeah, that's what's new with us," Hannah went on. "Love you, Mum. Hope you feel better soon." Hannah gave their mum another kiss on the cheek and Amie followed suit.

Wendy then popped her head around the curtain. "Sorry, girls, we're going to have to get your mum ready for surgery now."

With her head spinning from all of the revelations that she'd just heard, Amie took Hannah's hand and gave it a tug; they couldn't stay any longer.

The twins said their goodbyes and headed back to the waiting room to sit with the two boys and wait for news on their mother.

CHAPTER TWENTY-SIX

"Timmy?" came a muffled voice from outside his room.

"What, sis?" Tim called.

"Can I come in?"

"Why? You usually just barge in anyway."

"Mum sent me. And you've wedged your door shut again."

Tim sighed and pushed himself away from his desk to remove the doorstop from under his door. "Fine, come in."

Alice burst into the room and went to sit cross-legged on Tim's bed.

"So, Timmy, what have you been doing?" Alice asked, her voice as innocent as a toddler's, as she fluttered her eyelashes at him.

Tim narrowed his eyes at his sister. "I don't get this; what's the catch?"

"Come on," she said, really drawing it out. "Can't a little sister come and ask her amazing big brother what he's busy doing?"

Tim made a face at her. "Yeah right, come on. I'm not an idiot. What do you want?"

It was Alice's turn to sigh. "OK, alright. Mum said if I talk to you for ten minutes then I'm allowed over to Chloe's house later."

Tim pretended to look interested but slowly turned himself back towards his desk.

"Oh come on, bro! Do you want your ickle sister to lose all her friends?"

Tim continued to ignore her.

"Seriously, Timmy, come on. I just need to talk to you for ten minutes and I promise I'll be nice to you for a few days."

Tim thought about if for a few seconds before shaking his head and concentrating on his computer screen.

"Fine, Mr Tough Guy. I'll be nice to you for a week."

Tim was intrigued now. Why was his sister trying so hard? He span around to face his sister. "Three months. I'll then be on tour and won't see you for a while." It was actually a bit less than three months but he wanted to give himself some room to negotiate with.

"Ten days."

"Two months and thirty days."

"Two weeks."

"Two months and four weeks."

"Oh come on Timmy, I can't be nice to you for that long! It'll kill me."

"Two months and a week is my final offer. I'll be on tour and you'll be shot of me for another six months. I'll be home for Christmas."

A deep frown crossed his sister's face. "So I have to be nice to you for, like, seventy days and then I'll not have to see you until Christmas?"

Tim nodded. "That means you'll need to be pleasant, no snide remarks and no making fun of me. And I'll do the same for you. Deal?"

It looked like she was disgusted with the offer; the thought of having to be 'nice' to Tim for that long was horrifying but she agreed. "Deal. But it starts tomorrow. I've still got another few minutes to spend in here. Mum's downstairs with a stopwatch."

Tim turned back to his computer again, trying really hard to prevent a smile showing on his face.

"So, what are you actually up to?" Alice asked, without faking it to be nice this time.

Tim sighed. Just a few minutes, he told himself. "Listen to this," he said, pressing the play button on his screen.

"Wow," Alice said sarcastically, after the music stopped. "What on earth was that rubbish? It sounded like someone was trying to drive me completely insane."

"It's a track I've written, Alice. I'm aiming to try and record an album."

"Is that all you've written?"

Tim could begin to feel his blood boiling, but knew this was always the risk if he chose to engage his sister like he just had. "That's just part of one of the songs I've written recently, thank you," he said, through gritted teeth.

"Well, it's… average. I certainly don't like it. I don't think you can really write music. I'd leave it to a professional, personally."

Tim decided it was the complete lack of emotion showing on Alice's face that was the most irritating thing while she talked to him. She knew it irked him something rotten, but she was an absolute master of it. He really hadn't missed it while he was with Talent UK. He'd much prefer to talk to an annoyed, stressed-out Topaz than have to spend more than ten minutes with his sister.

"So, have you done your minutes yet?" Tim asked, more out of hope than anything else.

Alice looked at the time on her phone. "You know what?" she said, a wicked smile on her face. "I might just stay for a few more."

"Fine," he said. "Your choice. I thought you'd much rather spend the time with your friends, who actually like you and think you're a worthwhile human being." He sneaked a look over his shoulder to check that one had landed. He saw her flinch a little, which made him feel better.

"You know, you actually talk a lot of sense for a poor, knuckle-headed musician, who's going to be living with his parents for the rest of his life."

"I'm sorry, sis, but that didn't even hurt a little. You're losing your magic. You'd better go before you make it any worse and I start laughing at you. And remember our deal; it starts now!"

Tail definitely between her legs, she left his room, but not before giving him a vicious glare over her shoulder. She had sufficiently riled him, though. He slumped back in his desk chair, wondering what the point of writing his own music was if he couldn't even get his own sister to say it was good.

Deciding to make himself feel a bit better, he logged on to Facebook. He had been working on his artist page and recently posted a few videos of him playing his saxophone in his room, experimenting with his solos and riffs. He'd put a couple up at the weekend and hadn't logged on since, feeling like he should be spending any spare minute on his music.

Skipping over his homepage, he clicked straight on his artist page. He was pleasantly surprised to see he'd reached several hundred people, who had all been liking his page since Saturday. He'd also received nearly double that in notifications and almost a hundred messages.

He decided to type a message to say thank you. *Hi everyone! Thanks for liking this page; it'll be the best place to catch new updates about me and my music. I'll soon be announcing my plans for the summer. In the meantime, keep looking out for videos of me I'll post from time to time. And, as always, keep your comments and stories coming in. I'll reply to as many as time lets me.*

Within a few seconds of hitting 'post' he already had seven likes. He found it amazing that people were reading what he was writing during the day.

Recalling all the reading he did from when he was in hospital, he settled down into his chair to have a look at what people had been writing to him. Many of the messages were along the lines of: *Hey Tim, I saw you on TV on the Talent UK Final, you were amazing. Would love to hear from you. xxx*

He just didn't quite know how to take people like that. Were they genuine? He decided he would never know unless he reached out to someone; fair enough, he might get his fingers burned, but he was determined to be somebody who interacted with his fans. He chose a person at random, by scrolling through the messages and stopping the cursor on someone. Nadine Fredrickson was the girl he chose. Her message was simply: *Hi. You're the best saxophone player I've ever heard. Is there any chance you would play at my school? My friends would never believe it if you showed up in our music class. N xx*

He chuckled to himself. It would be a bit bizarre to see someone who had been on television appear in a random music class. He clicked on Nadine's profile to see where she went to school. It turned out, with a little bit of Internet searching, that her school was in Ipswich. He gave it some consideration but decided that maybe that was a bit far to travel on a whim. Instead, he had a quick look at Sir Andrew's proposed tour dates to check if they were going anywhere near Ipswich. He then replied: *Hi Nadine. Sorry I won't be able to make it to your school before you break up, but there's a good chance you might be able to see me in Ipswich during the summer. Keep a close eye on this page for more details as and when I have them. Tim x*

He then clicked on another random post. This was from Gemma Hughes who merely said: *Hey Tim, I'm a huge fan of yours and I've followed you since the early days of Talent UK. Everyone in the pub in my village was supporting you for the final. Please could you wish my daughter, Mathilda, a happy birthday? She's eleven today and it would be totally amazing to have someone like you send her wishes. Gem xx*

Tim considered this request for a few minutes. Rather than typing a reply, he switched his webcam on and picked up his saxophone. He stood across the other side of his room, facing the camera. "Hi, Mathilda. I had a message from your mother saying that you're eleven today. I just wanted to play something special for you."

He then proceeded to play 'Happy Birthday' with a small, flashy solo at the end. Letting the saxophone go slack around his neck, he stared into the camera, smiled and said: "Happy eleventh birthday, Mathilda. I hope it's wonderful."

Tim returned to his desk, switched the camera off and edited the video, removing the beginning and end when he was getting into position. He uploaded it as a reply to Gemma's post and smiled. He wasn't sure who would be more excited – Gemma or Mathilda.

He then scrolled through some more posts trying to see if there was anybody who he recognised. He didn't have to scroll very far to see a message that made him smile.

Hey Tim, it's Beatrice. I was a backstage helper on Talent UK. Do you remember me? Hope you're OK and it's fantastic to see you still playing. Can't wait for an album! Be great to hear from you xxx

Tim was surprised to hear from her but was equally thrilled to finally have the chance to try and talk to her. She had always been friendly towards him. He realised talking to someone online was a lot easier than in person as he typed a response.

Hi Beatrice. Great to hear from you! Thanks for always being so nice to me on the show. I never really knew what to say to you but you were always so lovely. I'll be hopefully releasing an album in due course. Stay in touch. Tim x

Feeling more positive than he had when he logged on originally, he clicked the home button on Facebook and immediately his mood dissipated.

He sat and stared at the top item for a few moments, not quite sure how to process what he'd read. *Alan and Hannah are in a relationship.* It just didn't make sense. He couldn't fathom how that situation would have even arisen. He felt like he'd been punched really hard in the stomach. He just hadn't seen it coming, particularly as he'd felt like Hannah was very much in his camp after their meeting in Beans and Banter. Yesterday, it had only been yesterday. What on earth had happened in less than twenty-four hours?

He didn't remember the meeting with Hannah going badly. In fact, he recalled it being quite positive. He knew he'd hurt her when he left suddenly; she'd told him as much. But hadn't she said that she wanted to be there for him? How could she do that if she was dating somebody else?

He finally plucked up the courage to scroll down a bit to read something else but then landed on a post from Amie. *Sat in hospital, desperately hoping Mum is alright. Come on Mum, you can pull through this. You've had it tough these last few months but me and Hannah are sending every ounce of strength we can. We love you xxxxxxxxxxx*

He clicked on Amie's profile, but that was the only post she had put up in the last twenty-four hours.

He leaned back in his chair and looked up at the ceiling, letting out a big puff of air. His mind was whirling trying to figure out what had gone on since he last looked online; Alan and Hannah were dating and the twins' mum was in hospital. He had a quick look through the rest of the stories on his news feed, but there didn't appear to be anything else new or out of the ordinary.

In that moment, he suddenly felt disconnected from the world and from his friends. None of them had messaged him to let him know what was going on; why couldn't they have told him? Was he no longer part of the gang? Had they moved on without him? Thinking about it, in some ways he supposed they had; Amie and Joel were sure to end up with each other some day and now Alan and Hannah were going out with each other. Where did that leave him?

He realised he didn't actually know. And that scared him.

In a split-second decision he realised he had to get out of the house. Switching off his computer and grabbing his hoody off the back of his chair, he agonised over whether to take his saxophone with him. In the end, he decided to pack it up and take it with him. He still wasn't one hundred per cent sure where he was going, but he knew he just had to leave his room for a while.

"I'm going out, Mum!" he called when he reached the bottom of the stairs.

"OK, tea's at six, be back before then!" came the call back.

Tim was slightly surprised that she didn't ask where he was off to. Since he'd been home from hospital she had wanted to know exactly where he was every single minute of the day. He decided to pop into the kitchen.

"OK, will do. I'm just going for a walk; I need to clear my head," he said.

"Thanks, Tim, I trust you. You're quite capable of going out on your own," his mother said from her position at the kitchen table, turning around to give him a smile. "Your sister... Well, she needs to earn that trust."

It was a windy day, and he could see the clouds racing across the sky. The wind chill made him shiver, so he zipped his hoody closed and pulled up his hood. He decided to head towards town and strapped his saxophone over his shoulder, the heavy case bumping into his back as he walked. Even with his hoody done up, he could still feel the wind rustling his fringe. The cool air was actually quite refreshing, but he could still feel the anger inside him.

His head naturally bowed, he always watched where his feet were going. He found himself going past several of his pavement landmarks; these were little things in the pavement like potholes and manhole covers that marked his route into town. He was pacing furiously, feeling more annoyed at his friends with every step he took. He referred to them as friends, but he was beginning to seriously wonder if they thought of him as one.

Tim wandered across Huntingham, past Beans and Banter, through the marketplace, before ending up at the door of Destiny Music. He'd decided to see if they had a room available where he could just play his saxophone. It had taken him about thirty minutes to get there and his fingers were itching to play. He was slightly intrigued to see whether his anger would show up in his music, and if he could somehow channel that into his writing. Playing the saxophone, he hoped, would soothe his tortured mind and transport him to another world where everybody was his friend and nobody was forgotten.

He noticed Eric behind the desk and made his way over to her.

"Hi," he said. "Are there any playing rooms available? I just need a room to play in for an hour or so, please."

"Tim Pointer? Well, this an honour," Eric said, giving him a wide smile. "I didn't think we'd ever see you in here again, what with your new-found fame and all."

"How could I not be in here? This is where I mostly learnt to play."

"How are things, young man? I hope you're feeling better."

Tim didn't really want to talk about what had happened with his health, so just held up his saxophone case. "Please, Eric, I really just need to get some playing done."

Perhaps sensing his urgency, she turned to the computer. "Room 5 is free until two p.m.," she said, keeping her voice neutral. "Oh, Tim," she called, as he made his way across the shop floor.

He turned back, out of politeness more than anything. "Yes?" he said impatiently.

"Do you know anybody called Isabella Smart?"

He shook his head. "I don't think so. Why?"

"She came in here earlier asking about recording studios. She asked if there were any artists that were interested, to let her know."

Tim was a bit suspicious now; the name sounded familiar. "Did she have long dark hair and glasses?" he asked, slightly confused as to why he could feel his heart beating against his ribs.

Eric nodded. "Sure did. Do you know her?"

"Yeah, sort of," he said hoarsely. "I've met her." Not for the first time today, he was stunned. Why was Izzy coming to music shops to ask about recording studios? Did it have something to do with his request to sell an album at Sir Andrew's gigs?

"Well, she left a business card. Take her number and get in touch with her if you want more details," Eric said, handing over Izzy's card.

Tim wiped his forehead with a sleeve. "OK, thanks," he muttered, pulling his phone out of his pocket and recording her number in his contacts.

He then managed to escape from Eric and headed to the stairs in the shop to find Room 5. He flicked the little sign on the outside to say 'Occupied', shut the door and propped his saxophone case up against it; he didn't want anybody to interrupt him.

He felt a little strange about getting Izzy's number, without her even being there. He'd been in awe of her the day he'd visited Great Bournestone Manor and was taken by how nice she had been to him. On a day when he felt like his friends had abandoned him, a voice inside his head was telling him to give Izzy a call.

He thought about it for a few seconds. In the end he decided that he should just do it. The worst that could happen was that she didn't answer. If that was the case, he couldn't feel any worse than he already did.

He shrugged and pushed the call button on his phone.

CHAPTER TWENTY-SEVEN

Tuesday 17th April
Huntingham Hospital, Washby Ward

Both boys looked up as the door of the waiting room opened.

"Hey," Alan said. "What's the news?"

The twins explained the news about their mother which left both boys looking glum.

"It doesn't sound great, does it," Joel commented.

Amie shook her head and sighed. "Not really, no. But she's still fighting and we'll know more after the surgery."

"So, what's the plan?" Alan asked.

"Mum's heading for surgery now and I'm presuming it'll be a few hours, judging by what needs doing. She's only in prep at the moment, though."

"Do you know where the surgery is taking place?" Joel asked.

"No. I'll ask at the desk on the way out," Amie replied. "Why?"

"I thought you'd want to wait outside so you know what's happened as soon as the surgery has finished, that's all," Joel said, looking between the two girls.

"Joelly, that's really sweet of you. I'll definitely ask on the way out. What do you guys want to do in the meantime?"

Joel and Alan shared a look before they both shrugged.

"Anywhere but here, to be honest," Joel said.

"Great, that's helpful, guys," Amie said, struggling to hold back a smile, as both looked a bit awkward.

"Shall we get some lunch or something?" Hannah suggested.

"Top idea that, Han. Let's go," Alan said, jumping out of his chair.

"Yeah, there's got to be a restaurant or a cafe somewhere," Joel said.

"You two suddenly seem eager to get out of here," Amie commented, a quizzical eyebrow raised.

"It's been a long hour and a half. We've been reading a book on Alan's phone; there's really not much else to do in here," Joel said, looking around the room.

There were no magazines, televisions or anything else to occupy the mind, the girls noticed. The room contained eight chairs and a two-seater sofa. There was a window looking out over Huntingham, but another wing of the hospital slightly restricted the view.

"We couldn't quite see where Beans and Banter is, but we spotted your house," Joel added.

"Yeah, so we've just been sat on the sofa reading. Thankfully you're allowed to use phones in hospitals these days," Alan said, pointing over his shoulder to the sofa.

The image of Joel cuddling up to Alan to read his phone made both girls giggle.

Both Alan and Joel looked confused. "What are you giggling at?" Alan asked, rather baffled.

"Never mind," Amie said. "You've just made us both smile, that's all you need to know."

"Shall we get going then?" Alan asked, offering his arm to Hannah.

The four of them left the waiting room and headed towards the ward exit, Amie pausing at the desk to enquire about the location of their mum's surgery.

"Got the details?" Joel asked when Amie returned.

"Sure do. It's a bit of a trek, but we've got to go that way to get to the restaurant anyway," Amie replied.

They all set off, Amie and Joel walking in front of Alan and Hannah who still had their arms linked.

"How are you holding up?" Alan quietly asked Hannah as they walked.

"Yeah, not too bad," Hannah replied, stroking the hair out of her face and tucking the strands behind her ear. "It's just still difficult to know what to do or how to react at the minute; everything's so subject to change."

"How do you mean?"

"Well, the surgery will probably go one of two ways: Mum will recover, or it'll bring to light something we don't know and possibly make things worse."

"Oh, right. I see what you're saying; you can't move on because you don't know what you're moving on from."

"Hopefully, we'll know a bit more this afternoon. I just want to know if Mum's going to pull through, what we're going to need to sort out for her. Will we need to adapt the house? Will one of us have to be there to look after her? But then, if she doesn't make it, because she is still very poorly, then what will we need to sort out?"

Alan unlinked his arm from hers and put it around her shoulders. "Look Han, if there's anything I can do…"

"I know, I know. I get it. I just want some facts to deal with, not this whole uncertainty."

Amie sneaked a glance over her shoulder, hearing the quiet tones that Alan and Hannah were talking in and she smiled. It was nice hearing

Hannah chatter, even if the circumstances weren't particularly great. She too had been concerned how Hannah was going to react to everything, and she was thrilled that Hannah hadn't reacted too negatively; sure, she appeared to be upset, but there hadn't been any signs of her tablets not being able to cope with it.

The group followed the signs to the hospital restaurant. With it being lunchtime, it seemed quite full and there was a little bit of a wait, which Alan wasn't particularly impressed with. Joel found this slightly amusing; of all the places to have to wait in a hospital, the restaurant was probably one of the lowest priorities. He was fairly sure if patients and visitors were given the choice of having to wait for results or appointments, or waiting in a queue for some food, they would choose food every time.

"Calm down, dude," Joel said, putting a hand on Alan's shoulder. "Our time will come. Use the time to choose what you want to eat."

Alan turned to face Joel, looking irritated. "Seriously, where do you get rubbish like that from?"

"I work in a coffee shop. You hear things," Joel said simply.

Alan looked back at his best friend, his annoyance dissipating into a grin. "Well played, Mr Wright. Well played."

The boys ended up being served first, as the girls were being indecisive about what they wanted. Joel and Alan then went to find a table and ended up at a four-seater table that had just been vacated in the middle of the restaurant. Joel found it interesting watching the behaviour of the restaurant staff; his parents were particularly strict about having tables cleaned as soon as customers left, whereas it didn't look like anybody had cleaned their table for a while. He supposed that was down to people being expected to tidy their own plates away in the restaurant. He felt like asking for some cleaner and a cloth from the counter, it frustrated him that much.

Alan spotted Joel looking disgustedly at the table. "Grimy tables getting you down?" he asked.

Joel nodded.

"Makes you appreciate your folks' place more and more I guess," Alan added.

"You could say that. I don't get out much," Joel replied, causing Alan to laugh.

The girls came and sat opposite them and they all ate in silence, each of them lost in their own thoughts, and wanting to eat as quickly as possible to get out of the restaurant as soon as they could.

When they had all finished and tidied their table away to Joel's satisfaction, they headed out of the restaurant to find the surgery wing. They stopped in front of a hospital map conveniently located on the wall. Amie pointed out the surgery wing and they set off in that direction, resuming their formation – Amie and Joel walking in front of Alan and

Hannah. Amie took the opportunity to link her arm through Joel's this time, which made him smile.

They reached the reception point, explained whom they were waiting for and were informed that the surgery was due to take place at any minute. Amie asked if there was anywhere for them to sit and wait, and they were directed to a foyer with some chairs in.

It was a foyer where there wasn't a lot to be spirited about; the four teenagers found themselves thrust into the middle of other people's lives, all of whom were waiting for news on a loved one's operation.

Having established where they would find the two girls, Joel and Alan excused themselves for a while as they realised they would be faced with more waiting around. They headed back towards the main part of the hospital, where they had found the restaurant. Alan had seen a shop there earlier and wanted to have a look to see what was on offer.

"What sort of puzzle books do you like, mate?" Alan asked, gesturing at the books on the shelf.

Joel regarded them with disdain for a few seconds. "I don't really know, not something I've ever looked at."

"Really? What on earth do you do in the back of the car on long journeys? Or on the train?"

Joel frowned. "I haven't really been on a long journey in the car where I could do puzzles or anything. And I don't think I've ever been on a train."

Alan considered this. "Because of Beans and Banter?"

Joel nodded. "Sort of. I haven't been on a car journey that lasted more than an hour for at least ten years. My parents were both doing catering when I was younger, so the hours could always be a bit unpredictable. They decided they wanted to work their own hours and that's when Beans and Banter was born."

"Do you not have grandparents or aunts and uncles to visit?" Alan asked, surprise registering on his face.

Joel shook his head. "Not really, no."

"How much extended family do you have?"

"There's my dad's sister, Hilda, who I think I've only met a handful of times in my life. She ended up inheriting the family home when Pops' parents died. He ended up with his mum's piano and I think that's always been a bone of contention between them. She's been a spinster all her life. From what Pops told me about his upbringing, that's not massively surprising."

"And on your mum's side?" Alan enquired, without looking up from a crossword book.

"She's an only child, like me. Her parents are still alive, but they retired to Canada a few years ago and I can't remember the last time I saw them. There's a picture somewhere of me as a baby with them, but nothing recent."

Alan pondered all this information for a few moments. "See, I find it really weird. I'm trying to imagine what life would be like without an extended family. I've got seven sets of aunts and uncles and twenty cousins. I just can't imagine being the only person of my generation."

"I'm just used to it. I don't know any different, so how can I compare?" Joel said, picking up a guitar magazine and having a casual flick through it.

"True," Alan agreed. "So, do you want anything? My treat. I get the feeling we might be sat there for a while."

"Yeah, this guitar mag, if that's alright with you," Joel said, holding it out to show his best friend.

Alan pulled a face, trying to pretend it was too expensive. "Yeah, sure," he said, with a straight face a moment later, snatching it out of Joel's hand and heading over to the kiosk. Alan was carrying one of the puzzle books he had been looking at.

"Thank you!" Joel called after him, smiling widely but shaking his head. He was pleased that there didn't appear to be any issues following what had happened that morning.

After Alan had paid for everything, they slowly made the walk back to the foyer.

"So, you and Hannah then," Joel commented, hoping Alan would expand on what had happened.

"Yeah," Alan said dreamily, smiling the cheesy smile he'd discovered earlier. "She's great. I never thought I would ever be able to call her my girlfriend."

"Me neither. Particularly after what you said last night about her date with Tim."

Alan winced. "She explained that to me. It's fine."

"Does Tim even know?"

"If he checks Facebook he might, but I certainly haven't told him."

"You've made it official already?"

Alan gave his cheesy smile again. "Of course."

"How are you going to handle Tim, though? He's not going to be happy about it. I always thought he and Hannah would end up together one day."

Alan stopped walking and turned to face Joel. "To be perfectly honest, buddy, I don't really care. He's just going to have to deal with it. I'm sure the fame he's experienced has meant he's got girls throwing themselves at him. He'll have no end of choice. He's had years to make a move on Hannah. I know how much pain she felt when he disappeared. She's got over that and now she can move forward with her life." He turned away and carried on walking.

Sensing Alan was getting tetchy, Joel decided to leave it. If it had been him, he would have probably sent a message or at least tried to get in touch with Tim. However, Alan was very strong-minded and often didn't care about whom he upset with his actions.

They walked the rest of the distance to the foyer where the girls were sat. To their surprise, both girls were chatting with the people sat next to them, but they stopped and looked up when they saw the boys return.

"Hey," Alan said, immediately sitting down next to Hannah and putting an arm around her.

"You guys have been a while; everything alright?" Amie asked.

"Yeah, fine. Just wanted to get something to read," Joel replied, holding up his magazine.

Amie's eyes sparkled with mischief. "Oh I see. Didn't fancy cuddling up to Alan again?"

Joel pulled a face at her. "No, not really. No offence, Al," he said, holding his hand up.

Alan pretended to look hurt, but then cracked a smile. "None taken."

Alan had ended up sat between the two girls so Joel had to sit elsewhere. He ended up sitting next to a man, who Joel guessed was a similar age to his dad. The man for the most part was leant forwards, head resting on his fists, elbows pressed into his knees. There was a glum expression on his face. For the first twenty minutes of Joel sitting there, this man appeared to be on his own, until a young girl, who couldn't have been more than ten, came and sat next to him, accompanied by, presumably, the child's grandmother.

Joel had been reading his magazine in earnest for half an hour or so, when the locked door opened and a nurse appeared. "Mr Francis?" she called, and the man next to Joel sat up.

"Yes?" he said.

"Would you like to come with me, your wife is in recovery."

"Can I bring my daughter?" he asked, sounding hopeful.

"I just need to speak to you first, please," the nurse replied, her tone suggesting that he should do as he was told.

The man looked disappointed, but kissed his little girl before following the nurse. Joel noticed Alan and the girls were watching Mr Francis as he disappeared behind the door. Joel was wondering what that little exchange meant; was it a positive outcome? It sure didn't sound like one if the daughter wasn't allowed with him. He headed over to Alan, Amie and Hannah and crouched in front of them. "So, when do you reckon you'll have news on your mum?"

"No idea. That guy had been sat here the whole time, and he's the first person we've seen being summoned. Didn't sound great, though, did it? Surely the daughter should be allowed through if his wife was alright," Amie said, to which the group nodded.

The foyer returned to its low hubbub, with people glancing every so often at the locked door that Mr Francis had disappeared through. It was another half hour before he appeared and ushered his family through. Joel could read nothing on Mr Francis' face, and so the fate of Mrs Francis remained unknown.

Joel returned to his seat and focused back on his magazine, reading the articles that he'd wanted to read first and then starting at the beginning and reading through the entire publication cover to cover. He was so engrossed he hadn't even noticed Amie had come over to sit next to him, until she jabbed him in the ribs.

"Hey you," she said quietly.

"Ow!" Joel exclaimed, over-exaggerating slightly and rubbing his ribs. Amie just looked innocently at the ceiling, knowing she hadn't hurt him and Joel swiftly stopped being dramatic.

"Funny," she said sarcastically. "So, lets play a game. Who do you reckon is sat here? Like, who are they and who are they waiting for?"

Joel turned and looked at her, puzzlement written on his face. "Say what?"

"Have you never played that game? You choose a person, and then take it in turns to invent details about them: give them a name, where they were born, how many brothers and sisters they have, what pets they have, what they do for a living and even things like what age they'll die at and where they'll be buried. If not, we're going to have some fun at work."

Joel still looked at her. "I don't get it; how are we ever going to know if we're right?"

Amie looked frustrated. "It's not about being right; it's about using your imagination and convincing me that it could be true."

Joel frowned. "Where's the fun in that?"

Amie made a face at him. "Well, if you don't try you'll never find out," she said with a pout.

Joel realised this was her way of trying to pass the time and take her mind off things, so he decided he had nothing to lose. "OK, go on. Who's our first victim?"

Amie looked around the foyer, assessing who would be suitable for their game. "How about him," she whispered, pointing discreetly to a man, with his greying hair tied back into a ponytail, sat in the far corner of the foyer staring at his phone.

Joel sneaked a peek at him. "So, what do I have to do?" he whispered back.

"Tell me his name."

Joel just said the first name that came into his head. "Fred."

"Fred what?"

"Frederick Harold Barker."

Amie smiled. "Harold?"

"Yes. It was a family name that his mum insisted on him having."

Raising her hands defensively, Amie considered her next move. "OK… Fred is looking good for his age, he's recently turned fifty, but he's always been a big fan of rock music since he was a youngster, hence him keeping his hair long."

"He's self employed as a gas boiler engineer, running his own company 'FHB Plumbing and Heating'," Joel added, warming to his task.

They traded information about 'Fred', establishing, among other things, that he was waiting for news of the surgery on his wife, Annie, who was a rock chick in her late forties. They lived in a three bedroom semi-detached house with a hot tub in their back garden and had never had any children because he had been impotent since he had suffered a motorcycle accident in his early twenties.

When it was Fred's turn to be called through the locked door, it turned out his real name was James Wright, which caused Joel to look horrified and Amie to giggle; neither of them had anticipated him having the same surname as Joel. Alan and Hannah looked over at them, confused as to what could be causing that reaction. Amie ended up having to message Hannah to explain and Joel took great pleasure in watching Alan's reaction when Hannah relayed the information to him.

In the end, the two couples spent the next few hours playing the game, creating all kinds of weird and wonderful back stories as people came and went, some through the locked door and others disappeared down the corridor, presumably to find another part of the hospital to wait in.

The next time the locked door opened, to Amie and Hannah's surprise, Doctor Morris appeared. They hadn't seen another doctor appear from behind that door all afternoon.

He scanned the room for a few moments before spotting the twins, and gestured them over. The girls hugged both boys again. They all realised that this was the moment the girls had been waiting for all day.

"Best of luck. Hope it's good news," Joel whispered to Amie. She gave him a weak smile and hugged him again, holding him for a few long seconds.

When both girls were ready, they looked at each other, took a deep breath and, holding hands, they headed towards the door to discover what their and their mother's destiny was.

CHAPTER TWENTY-EIGHT

The corridor the twins entered was brighter than the foyer they had just left, which caused them both to squint until their eyes adjusted. They followed Doctor Morris; Amie trying to put on a defiant expression, Hannah a more neutral one, preparing to face whatever life was going to throw at them.

They had both tried to scan Doctor Morris' face for information, but had drawn blanks; a silent look between them both confirmed as much. They really couldn't tell if the operation had been a success or not; the wait had to go on.

Doctor Morris led them down the corridor that had small rooms either side with clear glass windows, albeit blinds on some of them. Amie noticed James 'Fred' Wright in one of these rooms with a formidable-looking woman she didn't recognise. However, it took her a few seconds to realise that James was crying. Amie squeezed Hannah's hand and pointed towards the room, which made Hannah look and subsequently lose a little of the colour in her face. It turned out to be a sad footnote to their afternoon of playing games about the people sat in the foyer.

Doctor Morris continued to trudge on, seemingly aware that the girls were following him, although he never turned around. Eventually he turned right and entered a room that contained an empty bed on one side and another bed currently surrounded by curtains.

Amie cast her mind back to earlier when they had been visiting their mum in the Washby Ward, remembering how relieved she had been on hearing the bleep of the machines as they approached. She was dearly hoping there would be a similar sort of relief this time around.

Hannah was the first to notice how silent it was, her hand going straight up to cover her mouth. Amie, confused by Hannah's reaction, then caught on a few seconds later. They then only had to look at Doctor Morris' face to confirm what had happened.

"No..." Hannah whispered, tears making tracks down her cheeks. "No..." she repeated, a little louder. Her lips began to tremble and her shoulders began to shake with sobs. "No!" Hannah yelled, her face buried in her hands.

Amie put her arms around her sister and pulled her in close, trying her hardest to remain as strong as she possibly could. It was impossible to stop the flow of tears, though; she could feel them pouring down her face. She tried to open her mouth to say something comforting but didn't know what to say. What could be said in a moment like this? She pulled Hannah in closer trying to stop the shudders her sister was experiencing.

"I'm afraid so," he said, looking between both girls. "There was nothing we could do. The broken ribs had caused more damage than first thought, and it turned out that the aorta had been nicked. We just couldn't stem the bleeding in time. The post-mortem will tell us more, as I'm also not sure if she would ever have come out of the coma; the injuries sustained to the skull looked rather severe…" he trailed off, appearing to not know what more he could say.

Amie still had hold of her sister while trying to fight back the floods of tears herself that she really wanted to let out. A few strays were running down her face, which she angrily wiped away with the sleeve of the top she was wearing. Hannah had at least stopped shuddering, but her face was still pressed into Amie's chest, unable to stop the tears flowing.

Doctor Morris just stood there, twitching the curtain, looking a little awkward.

"Can we see her?" Amie plucked up the courage to ask, her voice faint and croaky.

"Of course, she's right here," Doctor Morris said, pulling the curtain to one side.

Hannah reluctantly stood up and they both shuffled forward, neither of them wanting to be the first to see their mum's body. Amie was chewing her lip nervously, almost not wanting to look. Hannah still had her hands in front of her face, but had spread her fingers at least.

Doctor Morris cleared his throat. "I'll have to leave you to it now, girls," he said. "A colleague of mine from Bereavement Services will be with you in a few minutes. She'll be able to explain what happens next." With a swish of the curtain, he disappeared, his footsteps growing fainter as he departed.

Amie thought that was an incredibly bizarre phrase to use at that moment in time. Who cared what was going to happen next? What could possibly be required to be run through in the minutes after their mother had passed away?

Taking a deep breath, Amie forced herself to look at their mum. The first thing she noticed was how peaceful she looked. With no machines surrounding her and no tubes running across her body, she also looked frail and small in the hospital bed. She didn't look to be in pain; her eyelids weren't tightly closed, they were just closed. Amie had read somewhere that dead bodies could sometimes look like they were sleeping. Perhaps it was after the surgery, but it wasn't the case here. Amie wasn't expecting her mum to blink or twitch. The only way Amie could describe it was that there was no life force in their mum any more.

Amie stroked her mum's arm again, as she had done a few hours earlier, the cast still on, although it seemed irrelevant now. "Hi, Mum," she began, but she had to stop as she squeezed her eyes closed as tightly as possible to try and stop the tears from escaping. Taking a deep breath through her nose to try and stop her face from quivering, she soldiered on, determined to say what would be one of the final things she would ever get to say to her mother. "I know you're not in there any more but I hope you can somehow hear me, if you're in the clouds or between the atoms or somewhere." She took another long breath in through her nose. "I love you. You were the best mum that anybody could ever have wished for and there won't be a day that goes by where I won't think of you in some way." She glanced across at Hannah, who nodded. "We both will. You'll forever be in our thoughts and our hearts. You gave us a great start in life and we'll do our very best to make you proud of us."

Hannah held up a hand, letting Amie know she wanted to say something. "I just can't believe that you're gone," she began, her face all shiny with moisture. "I don't get it. It's so unfair. You never put any evil into the world, you were always so kind to everybody you met. You were well loved at Fosters House; everybody we met there always said how much you smiled and brightened up their day. All the residents were pleased when you were on shift. You had arranged their Christmas carol concert there for over twenty years, getting a makeshift choir together of the carers' families. You always used to tell us how much joy you brought to the residents' faces when you took your two red-haired daughters in for that concert. How can someone who makes that much of a difference to people be taken away? It's not right. It just isn't."

Amie stood there for a few moments, looking at her sister, trying to judge if she was alright. Hannah's face was streaked with tears and she had to keep wiping fresh ones away every few seconds. Amie noticed her sister's bottom lip kept trembling, stubbornly refusing to stop no matter how much Hannah tried to bite it.

They lapsed into silence for a bit. Amie had actually forgotten her mum had organised those concerts for that long and immediately felt guilty for not remembering something like that.

"Han?"

Hannah looked up at her sister.

"I'd forgotten about those concerts," Amie mumbled, burying her face in her hands.

Hannah got up and put her arm around Amie's shoulders, which Amie found ironic; surely she should the strong one trying to comfort her sister?

"Don't worry. You'll remember things that I'll have forgotten," Hannah said softly.

Amie took her face away from her hands, revealing some red-rimmed eyes. "Like what?"

"I don't know, but I'm sure there are some. How about holiday memories?"

Amie cast her mind back to the first holiday she could remember. "Do you remember going to Scotland? We had a few holidays there over the years."

"Mum got us out of bed in the middle of the night and put us in the car," Hannah said, her eyes focusing in the middle distance as she tried to remember. "Where did we end up having breakfast?"

"Washington services, wasn't it? Just outside Newcastle?"

"Yeah, that's right. And we still didn't reach the cottage until nearly tea time."

Both girls smiled and swapped their memories of adventures on beaches and in rock pools, of ice creams and milkshakes, and playgrounds and castles. They were interrupted when they heard a swish of the curtain and turned around to see the formidable-looking woman, who had been in the room with 'Fred' earlier, stood there holding a white clipboard.

"Hello, girls. I'm Anita from Bereavement Services," she said kindly, her voice soft and gentle in stark contrast to her appearance. She had eyebrows angled downwards, making it appear she had a permanent frown. Her hair was tied back severely into a bun and she wore thin glasses perched on the end of her beak of a nose. She was also over six foot tall and incredibly thin. She made the girls feel like they were looking at a strict headmistress as opposed to someone who would help them find out what was going to happen to them next. Her voice, though, sounded like it came from a sweet, loving grandmother who enjoyed preparing home-cooked meals and knitting next to the fire. It was a complete contrast and it meant the twins stared at her for a few seconds.

Amie then made the introductions which Anita noted on her clipboard.

"I know you want to say as much as possible to your mother, however, I do need to run through some paperwork with you both." Anita held back the curtain, indicating that the twins should follow her.

They nodded, and not for the first time that day, ended up walking hand in hand behind a member of the hospital staff.

They entered an empty room from the corridor they had walked down earlier, once again containing a desk and chairs. "Have a seat please, girls," Anita said gesturing towards two chairs. Once they were all seated, Anita looked down at them, appearing to glare over the top of her glasses at them. "OK, so I'm just going to run through some paperwork with you. It's all fairly standard, I just have to let you know what to do and where to take these bits of paper."

She said it in a way that sounded so gentle and caring; it just threw Amie because her facial expression didn't appear to match the tone.

"I just need to check, that you are Christine French's next of kin?"

"That's right," Amie replied.

"Presumably daughters," Anita continued, not asking a question. She glanced between them both. "Identical twins?"

The twins nodded and Anita checked off something on her clipboard. Amie frowned at that; could that really be a question on the form?

"Is your father still about?" Anita asked. "Or did your mother have a partner at all?"

Amie frowned again. "Does the clipboard ask that?"

Anita's nose twitched. "No," she said. "I was merely enquiring in case I need to run through this information with someone else."

Amie rolled her eyes. "Dad left last year. As far as we know there's nobody else. Just us." Another scribble on the clipboard made Amie's teeth start to grind.

"If you're expecting a medical certificate, there won't be one at this stage. From what I understand, Doctor Morris has had to refer your mum to the coroner as she died under general anaesthetic during an operation," Anita said.

The twins both nodded again.

"The coroner will do a post-mortem, hopefully in the next couple of days. They're pretty quick here. He'll then send all the paperwork to the registry office if no inquest is required."

"What is the paperwork for?" Amie asked.

"In simple terms, it's so you can book the funeral."

"What are the chances of an inquest being required?" Hannah asked, her voice sounding relatively calm.

Anita seemed surprised. "Ah, she speaks," she muttered, further ruffling Amie's feathers. "Well, your mother suffered some horrific-looking injuries, having seen the notes. If the coroner deems that she died from her injuries, then an inquest may be needed." Anita looked up to see the grim looks on the girls' faces. "It's difficult to say at this stage whether one will be needed or not. Doctor Morris has given his account of what happened. It's up to the coroner."

"So we're now waiting for the coroner to do the post-mortem; is that right?" Amie said, trying to make sense of it all. Her head was spinning and she felt like she wasn't taking much in.

"That's right, yes," Anita confirmed.

"Then what?"

"You'll then need to go to the registry office in town once the coroner has sent the paperwork. If there has to be an inquest, then the findings of the inquest will be disclosed in the register, and you won't need an appointment; the death will just be recorded and the funeral paperwork you need will arrive in the post."

That seemed fair enough to Amie. She didn't really know what to expect from all this, so was hoping there wouldn't be much to do.

"That's the formal stuff done and dusted, girls," Anita said, removing the top form on the clipboard and putting it on the desk next to her. "Next, I need to inform you of the stages of grief." She glanced at both girls in turn. "It's worth keeping an eye on each other over the next few days as well, so listen to these symptoms carefully. I have a list of them here; would you like me to copy them so you can have one each?"

Amie and Hannah glanced at each other then nodded.

"If you give me a moment, I'll just nip to the photocopier," Anita said, standing up and leaving the room.

Amie turned to Hannah. "Oh my word," Amie began.

"I know!"

"How have you managed to stay so calm?" Amie asked her sister.

"With a lot of difficulty. I've been staring out of the window a lot. I've noticed how much she's got under your skin."

"I just can't believe something so serious gets dealt with by such a complete freak," Amie said. "Seriously, I was this close to going for her," she added, showing her finger and thumb about a millimetre apart.

Anita returned at that moment, looking between them both again, a quizzical eyebrow raised. Amie wondered if she'd heard any of the conversation, but certainly wasn't going to ask her.

"Right, so, these are the stages of grief," Anita said, handing them each a sheet of paper. "There are four stages. You can look on the Internet and find more, but our guidance is that these are the four you'll need to keep an eye on."

Amie and Hannah studied the sheet handed to them. The four main headings were: Acceptance, Pain, Adjusting and Moving On.

"Do have a read, but just to let you know they won't necessarily happen in that order or for long or even at all."

Both twins nodded.

"On the back of that sheet there's a list of possible feelings that you may already be experiencing."

Flipping the page over, Amie noticed it mention emotions such as guilt, anger, sadness and feelings such as shock and exhaustion. She had certainly felt most of them already that day.

"You may want to share this information with your loved ones," Anita continued, which made Amie wonder whether Joel came under that category. "Just so they can watch out for you. Do either of you work?"

They both nodded. Amie noticed what she thought a look of surprise cross Anita's face. Hannah just squeezed her sister's hand, sensing Amie's fury level rising again.

SCOTT MCCLAIN

"I'd pass on the information to your employer as well," Anita said, standing up. "That's all I can go through with you today. The department number is on the front of the sheet I've given you. If you need to speak to us at all, just give us a call. It can be about anything: how you're feeling, if you're worried about each other or you want to know what's happening next."

Amie nodded but couldn't think of anything worse than ringing and speaking to Anita.

"Do you have any questions at all?"

"No, not right now. But we've got your number," Amie said, gesturing towards the sheet of paper in her hand. Hannah had shaken her head.

"Excellent," Anita said with a smile that looked more like a grimace.

The twins both gave strained smiles and followed Anita back to the foyer to find Alan and Joel. They both trudged reluctantly down the corridor realising that once they came out of the locked door, their lives would have to move on without their mum being part of it. And in that moment, it felt to Amie like the most impossible thing in the world.

CHAPTER TWENTY-NINE

Tuesday 17th April, afternoon
Huntingham Town Centre

Izzy returned to her car, having been in to visit Sound East Midlands, a shop based on an industrial estate on the edge of Huntingham. The visit had gone along the lines of the two she had done earlier that day and she made a mental note to pick up some more business cards when she reached home.

She checked her silver watch on her left wrist and was surprised to see it was nearly three o'clock. She paused as she reached her car, trying to work out if she had time to squeeze another visit in, albeit with a bit of a drive to the next town. She then realised it wasn't as if she had any plans for the evening. Tamara had been talking for a while about having a catch-up and with it being bargain night at the cinema, she had wondered if it was worth messaging her best friend and asking if she was free. She fished her phone out of her bag and typed out a message to Tamara.

Hey you. Was thinking about the cinema tonight. What say you? X

It took a few moments before she received a reply. *Oh Iz, I can't tonight darling. It's date night for me and Pete. Sorry. Tx*

Izzy felt a bit deflated. She didn't particularly like Pete; he was a very impulsive man who was a keen boxer, and Izzy was fed up of hearing about what he'd had tattooed on him that particular week. However, Tamara was smitten with him and after her last relationship had broken down, leaving her with two children to bring up on her own, Izzy was pleased she was happy. Tamara must have sent the children to their dad's house for the evening, otherwise Izzy was fairly sure she would have been asked to babysit.

She climbed into the car, keeping her phone in her hand. She sat and tapped the steering wheel trying to think whom else she could ask. Had anybody else mentioned that they needed to catch up recently? Izzy couldn't think of anybody who had said that to her.

She sent out a couple of messages to friends who didn't have children, but it was more on the off chance than with any certainty that they would say yes. She was about to put her phone back in her bag but was surprised as it began ringing in her hand. Frowning as she didn't recognise the number, she thought about letting it run through to her voicemail, but then realised it may have been one of the shops she'd left a card with. She pressed the answer button.

"Hello, Isabella Smart speaking."

There was a pause before a voice said, "Izzy? It's Tim."

She wracked her brain, trying to remember if she'd spoken to a Tim today.

"Izzy? Are you there? It's Tim Pointer. Is it not a good time?"

Izzy's heart suddenly felt like it was situated at the back of her mouth. Several thoughts ran through her brain at once. How did he get her number? Why was he calling? Why hadn't she recognised his voice? Did he somehow know what she'd been thinking about him? She paused with that last one; that was ridiculous. How on earth could he know?

Coming back to reality, she remembered that he was still on the line. "Sorry, Tim, hello? Can you hear me?"

"Hi, Izzy. Yes, I'm here."

"Hi. You were breaking up a bit there," she said, proud of herself for giving a reasonable explanation for her silence. "Couldn't hear much at the beginning. Signal can't be very good where I am. Seems to be a bit better now, though."

"Why, where are you?"

"I'm sat in the car park outside Sound East Midlands."

"Ah right, another music shop," he said, sounding curious. "So, is that anything to do with you asking about recording studios?" he asked a few moments later.

"It is," she said coolly. "How did you find out?"

He explained Eric had given him her number and had told him that Izzy was asking about recording studios.

"Well, it's true, I am doing some research into the recording studio scene locally," she commented.

"Why didn't you ask me? I could have told you there wasn't one," Tim said, sounding a little hurt.

"I realised that pretty quickly when all the Internet could tell me was that there's a couple in Nottingham, and nothing really east of there. I needed to visit the shops and performing venues to try and connect with a whole range of artists. If there's no demand for that sort of thing, then there's not much point in supplying those facilities."

"Oh," was all that Tim said in reply.

"However, it was what you said to Sir Andrew that gave him the idea, if that's any consolation."

"Really?" Tim asked, sounding brighter.

"It's true. He then asked me to look into it. A studio might need to be hired if he decides to go with your album idea. The price, his royalties, as well as your own, and how many copies are all variables that he'll need to factor in."

"I'm just amazed that it's being looked at as a realistic idea. I only thought of it at that moment; I don't think I ever thought he'd go for it."

"One of the things I've learnt about Sir Andrew over the years is that he knows lots of things and lots of people; he's an extremely knowledgeable man. He thinks things through; he likes to have every angle covered. However, he does accept that he's human and that he can't possibly know and think of everything. When someone comes up with something he hasn't thought of he gives it a lot of respect. It's one of the things that's made him very successful, not just as a GP in his medical days, but even more recently as a businessman."

"It seems like he's earned his right to go on these tours and own a huge house."

"Definitely. He's not earned it by accident. He knows the right sort of people to make these things happen. How he can tell, I have no idea. He can read into things where there doesn't even appear to be anything going on. It's an amazing skill."

"I see. So it's a good thing?"

"He took you seriously, Tim. Where I'm from, that's big."

The conversation lapsed into silence for a few moments before Izzy had an idea. "Have you got any plans for the evening, Tim?"

"No, nothing planned. I don't really have a busy schedule at the minute," he replied.

Izzy detected a hint of regret in his voice and made a note to ask him about that later. "Do you fancy meeting up for a drink tonight?" she asked.

There was a pause.

"Izzy, I'm not old enough to drink," Tim eventually said. "I barely look seventeen, let alone trying to pass off for being eighteen."

Izzy sighed. "I wasn't suggesting going to a bar. How about a coffee? I know you know of Beans and Banter."

There was another pause.

"I can't think of a reason why not," Tim said, making her cringe slightly. Did he want to meet up with her?

"Great, you know how to make a girl feel special," Izzy replied, hoping he would sense the sarcasm in her voice.

"I didn't mean it like that," he said, sounding defensive.

Izzy chuckled. "I know, I'm just being awkward. Sorry. It'd be great to see you later. Say half-seven?"

"Yeah, I'm looking forward to it."

They said their goodbyes and hung up. Izzy tipped her head back in her car seat, leaning against the headrest. She realised that she was actually looking forwards to that evening now, rather than sitting at home with the bottle of prosecco in her fridge that had otherwise been her next best offer.

She switched on the ignition and pulled out of the car park, heading back towards home. Her mind replayed parts of the conversation. The part where he had said he was looking forwards to tonight had actually sounded like the most genuine thing he had said.

It then struck her. Was Tim lonely? It seemed like a real possibility.

She considered this all the way back to the manor, trying to work out how somebody like Tim could be lonely. Hadn't he been a star of Talent UK? How could somebody who had awed thousands of people not have any friends? She then wondered if she had discovered what Tim's mystery was; Sir Andrew had been convinced that there was more than met the eye with Tim.

***

Tim ended up sitting on the chair in the room at Destiny Music staring at the now blank phone screen. Had that call really just happened? He pinched his arm to make sure he wasn't asleep, wincing when he confirmed that he was definitely awake.

He almost felt ashamed to have been so annoyed with everybody earlier. With a smile on his face, he assembled his saxophone and lost himself in his music.

In the end, Eric had had to knock on the door to get him to stop. Tim had lost complete track of time and was surprised to find the couple of hours had elapsed that quickly. An angry music teacher and bemused student were pleasantly surprised to see Talent UK star Tim Pointer had been practising in their pre-booked room. An autograph on the student's music book had been enough to assuage any negative feelings.

Tim's mood on the journey home was in complete contrast to how he had felt on the way to Destiny Music. He couldn't care less about his friends now. A girl, no, a woman, had agreed to meet up with him in an evening. That had to mean something; he couldn't be undateable for a start.

A frown then crossed his face. Undateable. Did that mean... Was this a date?

His heart suddenly seemed to begin thudding in his chest. Did he need to wear something nice? Should he take flowers? Would she be expecting a kiss?

Thinking about how he was going to approach his 'meeting' with Izzy managed to get him all the way home. However, he still wasn't sure whether it was even a date.

He was trying to work out if his 'meeting' was something he should talk to his mum about. Would she freak out, though? He had been surprised by her not enquiring as to where he was going earlier. Should he be honest and say he was going to meet up with a girl? He realised he'd done it again. Izzy wasn't a girl. She was definitely a woman. Why had she asked him to meet up with her? He didn't even know how old she was, but he knew she was at least five years older, if he had to have a guess. It still struck him as being a bit strange; he was seventeen, due to turn eighteen just before Christmas, and he had never been on a date. An actual, proper date with somebody he wanted to call a girlfriend.

It was something he'd thought a lot about, but he'd only ever imagined going on a date with Hannah. Now that door had apparently closed, he had suddenly discovered Izzy had flown in through a window. But then, did he want Izzy as a girlfriend? Wasn't she so far out of his league it was unreal?

He considered what he actually knew about Izzy. Apart from being Sir Andrew Anderson's assistant, he realised he knew very little about her. She had made out that she had seen him on Talent UK, so she probably knew more about him. He realised he didn't even know what colour eyes she had. He'd just not absorbed details like that about her. He'd never honestly have believed it if someone had told him after he'd first met Izzy that a few days later he would be going on a date with her.

A date. Maybe it was a date. He was more comfortable calling it a date now. A meeting implied they were going to talk about the tour. He was fairly sure that she wouldn't have asked him to go out to a coffee shop in an evening if she'd needed to run through some tour details.

"Tim?" a voice called as he opened the front door.

"Yes, Mum, it's me," he replied, heading into the kitchen. "I'm back." He showed her his saxophone case. "I went to Destiny Music for a bit. Just needed to get out of my room for a while." He sat himself at the worktop in the kitchen.

"You have spent a lot of time in there recently," Tim's mum said sternly from the sink, without looking at him. "Getting out is good for you."

"Would it be alright if I went to Beans and Banter tonight then?" Tim asked, while his mum was seemingly encouraging him to leave the house.

"I don't see why not," his mum replied. "Alice has gone to Chloe's and your dad doesn't want to do much in the evenings at the moment after he gets home from work. You get yourself out and meet up with your friends."

"Thanks, Mum," Tim said, not bothering to correct his mother. His friends were the last thing on his mind.

"So, what's the plan for the rest of the afternoon?" his mother asked.

"I'll probably just be in my room again," Tim said, a little forlornly.

"Writing?"

"Mostly. I've found that people have been discovering my Facebook page. Every time I log on there's another twenty or so people who have followed it. I've had some great feedback. I've also had some strange requests."

"Like playing 'Happy Birthday'?"

"You heard that?" he asked.

His mother turned around with both hands on her hips. "Timothy, we live in a semi-detached house. We don't have any soundproofing. Of course I heard it. I've been listening to what you've been playing up there for the last week or so."

Tim had never thought that his mother could hear him; she'd never mentioned it previously. "And?"

"And what?"

"What did you think?"

"Oh, Tim, you're an amazing saxophone player. I think everything you play is great."

"See, why can't Alice just say something nice like that?" Tim asked, sounding whinier than he'd intended.

"Giving you a hard time, is she?"

"A little. She just seems to take every opportunity she can to get under my skin."

"You know your Uncle Mark?"

Tim nodded. Mark was his mum's older brother.

"Ask him one day what I was like as a fifteen year old. Alice will seem fairly pale in comparison, I can assure you."

Tim wasn't quite sure how to process that. He couldn't picture his mother being obnoxious.

"Just don't feel like you have to hide in your room. Alice is at Chloe's. Your dad is at work. You can come downstairs and write if you like."

"Thanks, Mum, but I've got everything set up upstairs."

His mother shot him a worried look in the way that only mothers can do. "Alright. But the offer's there. Chicken pie is in the oven, it'll be ready about six."

Tim took the opportunity to leave at that point, heading back to his room. He ran his fingers through his hair and wondered if he should wash it. He decided he should make some sort of effort and emerged from the bathroom a while later, hair dripping wet.

He raided his wardrobe, finding the smartest shirt he owned, which was usually saved for musical performances. He debated whether to wear a tie or not, but decided that as he wasn't going to a funeral or a job interview, the ties could remain where they were.

He decided to pass some time on Facebook. He was rather amazed to see that the few requests he'd done earlier had gone down exceptionally well; his fans had reacted in their hundreds and the requests had flooded in. He spent the rest of the afternoon searching through them trying to put some positivity into the world. He hoped, in a roundabout way, that the happiness he was feeling could be reciprocated by fulfilling people's wishes. He recorded a few more performances of 'Happy Birthday' for people, varying from Elise from Liverpool asking for it to be played for her grandmother who had just turned eighty to Frank from Middlesbrough asking for a rendition for his little boy who had turned ten.

When he appeared downstairs for dinner, wearing his hoody over his clean shirt, his mother regarded him with a bemused expression. "Who on earth have you been playing 'Happy Birthday' for all afternoon?"

Tim explained about his Facebook page, which only served to worry his mother further.

"Alright, Tim, well, as long as you're happy with all this attention. You've not had any relapses have you? You can remember where you've been and what you've done?"

"Yes, Mum. I feel fine. I've not blacked out or anything."

"OK," she said, still looking worried. "Just don't work too hard."

"I won't. It's not stressful doing these requests. It's just a bit of fun. I've met some nice people doing it."

His mother smiled at him, although without the normal twinkle in her eye. Tim spotted it and figured she must just be worried about him.

Over dinner Tim ran through some of the plans for his songs, which ones he wanted to cover and the sort of song he wanted to write himself. His mother provided her input, talking about some of her favourite songs, which would appeal to her generation. Tim noted these down on his phone, intending to go and listen to them later.

With it nearing seven o'clock, Tim stood up to leave.

"Would you like a lift?" his mother asked. "But in exchange you'll have to help me with the washing up."

"Yeah, thanks Mum. That'd be great," Tim said, beginning to clear the table.

Fifteen minutes later, once all the cutlery and crockery had been put back in their appropriate drawers and cupboards, Tim and his mother left the house.

"Do you give Alice many lifts, Mum?" Tim asked, as he clipped his seatbelt in.

"Not really," his mother replied. "Why do you ask?"

"You've never offered me a lift before."

A rosy tint coloured Olivia Pointer's cheeks. "You've always been so independent, and you never complained about walking anywhere."

"So, why did you offer tonight?"

His mother considered this for a few seconds. "Well, your dad has been working late a lot, and it meant I didn't have to wash the dishes on my own. Plus, I'm meeting up with my friend Julie, so I thought I could drop you off on the way."

"Oh right," Tim muttered, not having a clue who Julie was. "I wondered if you were being overprotective again."

His mother just frowned at him, saying nothing.

The rest of the journey was made in silence. Tim stared out of the passenger-side window, his arm resting on the door, head resting on his left hand. They drove past a park that Tim had walked through earlier on his way to Destiny Music. Tim frowned as they drove past. There was a group of teenagers stood near the gate and Tim could have sworn he saw Alice and Chloe in the crowd. What concerned him most was that some of the boys looked like they were smoking, but his mum drove past too quickly for him to be absolutely sure.

Frowning, he made a mental note to ask Alice where she had been. He could have been completely wrong, but something was nagging at him. He realised it was what his mother had said to him earlier about her being like Alice at her age.

"Mum, did you ever smoke?"

She glanced at him. "That's an odd question. Have you got something to tell me?"

"No, Mum. I'm not a smoker. I just wondered if you'd ever smoked when you were younger."

Seemingly satisfied, she replied, "I used to. Before I met your dad. He made me quit. And then you came along, and I vowed never to smoke around my children."

"Was it difficult?"

"Not really, no. I just figured your dad meant more to me than lighting up every few hours."

The conversation lulled again, and Tim's thoughts turned towards meeting up with Izzy. She hadn't crossed his mind for a few hours. He wondered if she'd been stressing over what to wear, or whether to have a shower. He nearly snorted. Like she would worry about things like that to meet up with him.

"Here we go," his mother said as the car pulled up opposite Beans and Banter, almost outside the French family house, which gave him a slight twinge of regret. It felt a bit strange going into the shop and not meeting up with Hannah and the rest of the group.

Suddenly, as he climbed out of the car and said goodbye, he realised he was nervous again. No matter how he tried to think about it, he couldn't get over the fact that he was going on a date.

An actual date.

CHAPTER THIRTY

Izzy turned her mp3 player up in the car on the way home, her mood the best it had been for a while. She was sure she had drawn some funny looks from other drivers as she sang along at the top of her voice as she sped down the country roads.

Her car threw up dust as she made her way down the drive on reaching Great Bournestone Manor. She had decided she had to share the news with Mrs Connolly and made her way into the manor house's kitchen. Mr Connolly had usually left to work at Signature by this time and Izzy knew that the chief housekeeper could be found in the kitchen with a cup of tea. Izzy had often gone in for an afternoon chat with her and Mrs Connolly was always very happy to see her, not having any daughters of her own.

"Hello, chicken," Mrs Connolly said as the door opened, not looking up from her magazine.

Izzy smiled, as she always did to that greeting. "I've got some news."

Mrs Connolly looked up, eyes narrowed, as if she wasn't sure yet how she should react. "Go on."

"I'm meeting up with someone tonight," Izzy said, as nonchalantly as she could, pretending to admire her fingernails.

"Seriously?" Mrs Connolly asked, a beaming smile spreading across her face.

Izzy nodded.

"That's wonderful!" Mrs Connolly exclaimed, rushing over to give Izzy a bear hug. Releasing her, she gestured Izzy to sit down at the table with her. "So, who is he? Tell me everything. How did you meet him? Was it online?"

Izzy relayed the conversation that she'd had earlier, without revealing who it was with.

"Well, he sounds like he's into you, if he wanted to meet up with you tonight," Mrs Connolly pointed out. "What's his name?"

"Tim."

"That's a good first name. Tim what?"

Izzy hesitated.

"What? Come on, it can't be that bad. I went out with a gorgeous young man when I was your age whose surname was Pincock. My friends never let me live that down."

Izzy smiled again. "It's nothing to do with his name, Mrs C. It's Tim Pointer. The guy off Talent UK." Izzy watched as Mrs Connolly's jaw dropped, before the housekeeper then regained some composure.

"You certainly aim high, don't you? Well I never. If you'd told me this morning that within a few hours you'd have secured yourself a date tonight, I wouldn't have believed you."

"Thanks, Mrs C," Izzy said. "But you called it a date. It isn't a date."

"Isn't it?"

Izzy felt a bit awkward. "Well, no. I'm just meeting up with him to have a coffee and a chat really. "

"To chat about what?"

"I'm not sure really. I'd love to hear more about his experience on Talent UK for a start."

"So you're going to interview him?"

Izzy pulled a face. "No. I'm not going to write down his answers," she said with a laugh. "It's not like that."

"Where are you meeting him?"

"Beans and Banter in Huntingham."

"Oh, that's lovely. It's a wonderful coffee shop. I know Alyssa and Ted well, both great people."

"I know, I met them earlier. First time I'd been in."

"I am glad. One of those special places that not enough people know about and when they discover it they wonder why they haven't heard of it before." Mrs Connolly looked into the middle distance for a few moments. "OK, returning to whatever it is you're going to tonight. So you're not getting him drunk. It's just a coffee."

Izzy nodded. "Absolutely."

"What were you planning on wearing? That'll go some way to telling yourself if you were thinking of it as a date or not."

"I don't actually know."

"Little black dress?"

"Not really appropriate for a coffee shop is it?" Izzy asked rhetorically.

"Jeans and a polo neck jumper?"

Izzy grimaced. "I'm not going that frumpy."

"Right, so you've ruled out sleeping with him on the first date and also coming across as being frigid. Now, you tell me, what's in between?"

Izzy frowned. "I'm not sure I have much in between, to be honest."

"How about a dress with leggings, chicken? Very popular with the girls these days, my Richard tells me."

"And what does that translate as?"

"You sort of have the best of both worlds. You have the formality of the dress, offset by the casualness of the leggings. Wear some flat shoes too. None of those heels. Then it could go either way. You'll disarm his senses; he won't know what you're thinking."

Izzy felt like a teenager being told off by her mother. "I just don't get it; why are you analysing what I'm going to be wearing?"

"Because that's what he'll be doing, chicken. That's what he'll be doing."

"He's seventeen!"

"And?"

Izzy stopped. "You mean even lads at that age can read into things like that?"

"Ever since that boy became a teenager, he's been counting on having an opportunity like that. He'll have been thinking about getting it on with every girl his age wearing a low cut top to college. I was almost embarrassed to go shopping with my Richard when he was a teenager. He ogled almost every girl in sight."

Izzy looked embarrassed. "I don't think Tim's like that, though."

"Not to your face, perhaps."

"Mrs C, he's seventeen," Izzy reiterated. "He's still a teenager. He's not going to be staring at boobs all day."

"How many teenage boyfriends have you had, Izzy? I'm guessing it can't be many."

"Two," Izzy replied after a moments thought.

"And did you ever catch them staring at your chest?"

Izzy nodded. "I wondered at one point if my eyes were in my bra."

"So why's Tim going to be any different?"

Izzy couldn't answer that one. She was hoping Tim would prove Mrs C wrong. She couldn't remember him looking at anything else other than her face when she'd last met him.

"How many boyfriends have you had in total, then?" Mrs Connolly asked to break the silence.

"Still two. I broke up with Carl in 2003. He was my last actual relationship I've had with anybody."

"Nine years ago? You'd have been nineteen!"

Izzy felt a twinge of embarrassment. "That's right. Carl couldn't cope with my career prospects. Sir Andrew went on his first tour, so I went with him and he couldn't cope with the distance. He began hooking up with my friends. I've been trying to move my career forward as much as possible ever since."

"So this is a big night for you? You're going out to meet somebody you maybe actually want to start calling your boyfriend?"

Izzy considered this. "Yes. I like Tim. I don't know if he likes me or even if he'd want to be my boyfriend."

"As you've already said, chicken, he's seventeen. Is that going to be a problem?"

Izzy looked at her blankly, before realising what she meant. "Is his age going to be a problem? I don't know. He seems quite mature for seventeen. He's had the life experience of being on Talent UK but then he won't have had any experience in paying bills, for example. I've been worrying about how old he is but I'm starting to wonder why. But then, I don't even know if he'd want to go out with someone as old as I am."

"Alright, chicken. You seem to have thought about it at length. I'll give you a break. I hope you enjoy your date and find what you're looking for," Mrs Connolly said with a smile.

"But tonight isn't a date."

"What is it?"

"I don't know. I'm thinking of it more as a meet up. Like a pre-date?"

"So does Tim know it's not a date? It's just a meet up?"

Izzy stalled. "I have no idea. I just sort of said I'd see him at seven thirty."

"Honestly, Izzy, I hate to think what that poor boy has been going through these last few hours," Mrs Connolly said, shaking her head despairingly.

***

Tim made his way into Beans and Banter. He realised it had only been twenty-four hours since he was last in there meeting up with Hannah. It felt longer.

As he stepped over the threshold he automatically looked towards the back corner, as he had always used to do, to see if the group were there. He felt a slight twinge of regret when he saw their normal table was empty. Part of him really wanted to message Hannah and find out where they all were. He stood there for a few moments looking and reminiscing about some of the times he had spent with the other four at that table. The jokes, the stories and the memories all came back to him and he wondered if he would ever be able to make new memories with Amie, Hannah, Joel and Alan again. His gut feeling was telling him that he probably wouldn't; they had moved on without him.

Shivering as a draught ran around him as the door behind him opened he remembered the reason why he was there. Maybe it was time to make some new memories with some new people.

He wandered up to the counter, unzipping his hoody, not recognising the person behind the counter. He wondered where Joel's parents were.

A tall, thin man with a pointed chin was wiping cups with a tea towel. He looked up as Tim approached. "Hello. Before I go any further I just need to let you know there's no fresh food available tonight, only what's left in the cabinet. What can I get for you?"

Tim shrugged. He wasn't there to eat, still being full from his mum's chicken pie. "Ermmm, hi. Can I have a white americano please?"

"Certainly, young man. Coming right up."

Tim watched with bemusement as the new barista swiftly assembled the espresso machine and then set it to pour. It was something he'd seen Ted, Alyssa and Joel do so much over the years it seemed really strange watching someone else do it.

"Was there anything else, young man?"

Tim nearly began humming 'YMCA'. "I just wondered where Ted and Alyssa were this evening."

"There's been a family incident and my partner and I are looking after things for them. That's all I'm allowed to say."

Tim shrugged. He presumed he'd find out on Facebook if it was something with Joel.

The man's eyes narrowed as a look of recognition crossed his face. "Say, are you Tim Pointer?"

Tim nodded.

"Wow, it's a pleasure to meet you," the man said, offering his hand, which Tim shook. "Didn't know you were a punter in here. Don't remember seeing you in here before. My name's Rick and this is my partner Nicky." Rick turned and called for Nicky to come out of the kitchen. A few moments later a short, tubby man with what looked like an orange glow appeared, looking frustrated.

"What?" Nicky said, rather abruptly.

"Meet Tim Pointer," Rick said, gesturing towards Tim.

"Really?" Nicky said incredulously, before he turned and recognised the teenager stood on the other side of the counter. "Hi, Tim. Great to meet you. We were in here watching the final, cheering you on. Big fans, we are. You're going to be a star, even bigger than you are now."

Tim felt slightly embarrassed but was glad they hadn't mentioned his collapse backstage. "Thanks, guys. Always nice to meet my fans."

"Say, could we have a picture with you?" Rick asked, fishing his phone from his pocket.

Tim duly obliged. A customer from a table near the counter offered to take the picture as both men joined Tim in front of the counter.

As Tim picked his drink up off the counter, he was surprised to see Izzy stood there. Before he said anything, he was amazed at how she looked. His eyes ran from her feet all the way up to her hair, which she had let run free. He had only seen it tied up before. She was wearing a brightly patterned dress that came down to the middle of her thighs, but over black leggings, which was a fashion look he hadn't seen before.

"Wow…" he whispered. "You look… You look amazing."

She just flashed him a smile. "Thanks. You scrub up pretty nice too."

Tim almost didn't believe her and felt a little underdressed. He was wearing his concert shirt, but then he realised she would have only seen him in a t-shirt and jeans previously. He wondered if he should have gone for a tie after all.

Rick gave an unsubtle cough. "Perhaps a drink for the lady?"

Tim jumped, causing him to stop staring at Izzy. She just flashed him another smile. Tim noticed for the first time she had slightly uneven front teeth, which made him feel a bit better about himself; she wasn't absolutely perfect, so his untidy hair and scruffy jeans weren't that bad after all.

"Sorry, Izzy. What would you like?"

"A pot of tea would be lovely, please," she replied. "Been a while since anybody bought me a drink," she added with a giggle.

Tim felt his cheeks burn as he turned back to the counter. He thought he noticed Rick trying to keep a smirk from crossing his face. Rick was standing by the coffee machine pouring hot water into a navy blue teapot, which Tim noticed was also the main colour of Izzy's dress. One of the charms of Beans and Banter was their collection of multi-coloured teapots. Tim had never been to a coffee shop or cafe before where there had been anything other than generic white or stainless steel teapots.

With the drinks served and paid for, Tim and Izzy found a table for two in the corner near the front window.

"So, Tim, how's things? I know it's been a few days since I last saw you."

"They're fine," he replied, taking a sip of his coffee. "I've been in my room most of the time."

"Do you not get lonely?" Izzy asked.

He thought carefully about his answer. "Not really," he replied, not wanting to admit that he was. "I have a group of friends who I hung around with all the time before I went on Talent UK. But I've only seen one of them since I came back and that didn't end up going too well."

"What happened? Or am I not allowed to ask?" Izzy asked, pouring herself a cup of tea.

"You can ask; it's OK. I had a crush on the girl for a long time. Her name's Hannah. I always felt we were like kindred spirits and it nearly killed me when I got the news I was going on Talent UK because I couldn't tell her. They make you sign all these confidentiality agreements and I had to leave without telling anyone. I know it hurt her when I left. I really wanted to meet up with her when I got back. I ended up asking her yesterday so I met her in this very coffee shop last night."

"And?"

"I thought it went quite well. But I logged on to Facebook earlier today and she had just started a relationship with another one of my friends. She never mentioned it last night."

Izzy looked at him strangely. "How bizarre. I was telling a friend earlier about what happened with my last relationship. I'd gone with Sir Andrew on his first UK tour. My boyfriend couldn't handle the distance and he started seeing one of my friends. He claimed it was because he'd been so used to having me around, he couldn't cope with me not being there. Either way, he didn't need to start sleeping with my friend. So maybe she missed you so much but because you weren't there she had to move on."

Tim sighed. "Possibly. I guess I should get over it now, but it's hard to just leave your past, and everything you've ever known, behind."

Izzy looked at him with a puzzled expression. "Says the guy who came second on Talent UK? You were away from home for three months! How did you cope then?"

Tim felt a bit uneasy. "Not brilliantly. I'm a bit strange with people I don't know that well face-to-face. I don't really know how to start a conversation. Other people have to break the ice first."

Izzy smiled. "You didn't speak to anyone while you were there?"

"Not really. There was this one girl, Beatrice, who spoke to me, but I never knew what to say to her. Then the rest of the time I just played my saxophone. There was so much practise that I had to do and I could lose myself in my music. I've been doing that a lot since I've been back as well."

Izzy just continued to smile back at him, which was beginning to confuse him.

"Why are you just smiling at me?"

"Because you're talking to me. I feel a bit honoured."

Tim hesitated. She was right – he had been talking to her. He just felt at ease around her. He got the impression that she was interested in Talent UK, but that wasn't the reason she was there; she wanted to know beyond all that. Who he was. What he liked. Where his favourite places were. And then it struck him that he wanted to know those sorts of things about her as well. Was he attracted to Izzy?

"So," Izzy said, breaking the silence, "what's it like being relatively famous?"

Tim shrugged. "It's alright. I'm not going to actively pursue fame as a career. It's amazing, though, logging on to social media every day and seeing that a few more hundred people have gone on to my pages and liked or followed overnight. That sort of attention can give you a real buzz."

"Yeah, I saw your Facebook page went berserk earlier after you had put up that first 'Happy Birthday' video for that little girl."

Tim could feel his cheeks begin to burn. "You saw that?"

"I may have logged on when I got home earlier and had a look at your page," Izzy said innocently, pretending to look out of the window. "I thought it was really sweet."

"Thanks," Tim said, and took another sip of his drink so he didn't have to say anything else.

Izzy was studying him closely. "I see what you mean," she said, causing him to look blankly back at her. "About talking to people."

Tim suddenly felt very vulnerable. "How do you mean?" he half-whispered.

"About you and conversation. And I don't mean it negatively. It's actually quite refreshing for me to be out with someone who isn't a complete, overconfident berk. If they'd have done a video message for a complete stranger I'd have had that stuffed down my throat all evening, with them bragging about how kind and sensitive and adorable they are. You just aren't like that. Don't change, Tim. Even if we go our separate ways tonight and never see each other again, don't change that about yourself. Promise me that."

Tim, a little overwhelmed, nodded dumbly.

That ended the conversation for a while and they both focused on their drinks. Tim felt a bit awkward now that Izzy had mentioned going on other dates. Was this even a date? Should he try and establish whether it was or not this early on when he was having, by all accounts so far, a nice time? Could you have a date over a cup of coffee and a pot of tea? When one of the people present was a teenager and the other was in their mid-twenties? He'd heard people at college going out and getting wasted and counting that as a date. Tim was fairly sure that tonight wasn't going to go down that route but, even so, he wanted to know.

Izzy was looking at him strangely. "Everything alright over there?" she asked.

Tim felt like the spotlight was on him. If he was honest with her, it would have a big impact on the rest of the evening but at least he would then know whether they were on a date or not. If he could somehow keep it together and he could keep Izzy talking then at least he wouldn't be on his own in his room for an evening.

But what was the best thing to do? Take a risk with the possibility of long-term happiness? Or be nice, play it safe, not put himself on the line and go back to his boring life? Was Izzy even meeting up with him just to keep an eye on him, to see how he was after his incident?

This last thought made him shiver and that gave him a shot of courage to take a risk and find out what was going on.

"How old are you, Izzy?" he asked.

She smiled. "Has that been bothering you?"

"A little," he admitted.

"I'll be twenty-nine in January," she said calmly.

Tim looked surprised. "Wow, OK."

He was quiet for a few moments while he thought about her age. Would someone that old ever date a teenager? He hadn't realised she was nearly thirty. Would that be weird? Or did she actually want to date him? He decided the only way he'd ever find out would be to ask. He took a deep breath. "Izzy, I need to ask something and I don't want it to spoil the evening," he said.

Izzy shrugged. "OK, fire away."

He took a deep breath, letting the air out slowly before he replied. He'd been so sure of himself when he walked in but now he was second-guessing.

He just hoped that he'd made the right decision to ask the question.
"Is this a date?"

CHAPTER THIRTY-ONE

Izzy smiled reassuringly at the teenager looking at her. Tim looked half-terrified, half-expectant. She decided to play it cool for a few seconds, just to see if she could figure out what he'd been thinking and how he wanted his question answering.

"What do you think this is?" she asked.

"I really don't know," he said in reply. "It's why I was asking."

Great, she thought. She then remembered what Mrs Connolly had been saying about what outfit to wear. "OK. Let me ask you a question. Does what I'm wearing tell you anything?"

Tim looked her up and down for a bit. "No," he said slowly. "Well, apart from you have an expensive wardrobe."

She sighed and then smiled at him. "Let me rephrase that, then. Does what I'm wearing indicate if this is a date or not?"

He glanced her up and down again and shook his head. "Should it?"

Izzy found this amusing and made a mental note to tell Mrs Connolly later. "Never mind. Just a private joke." She noticed him looking baffled and decided to throw him a line. "One of my friends said that you would be able to tell what my intentions were from what I was wearing."

"I don't understand," Tim replied, frowning at her.

She was finding his naivety quite refreshing. "If I'd arrived wearing a black dress cut down to here," she said, pointing to her diaphragm, "and finishing about here," she added, pointing to an area towards the top of her thighs. "What would that have suggested?"

"You found it to be strangely warm outside?"

Izzy laughed. "Oh, Tim, seriously, you're amazing."

He smiled back at her, but didn't look like he had got it.

"Would you like an insight into the female mind?" she offered.

He nodded.

"The 'little black dress' is one of the most important items of clothing in a girl's wardrobe," she said, pausing to see if he was keeping up, which he appeared to be. "If I had turned up tonight wearing mine, it would have been a sure sign that it was a date, and, more importantly, that you would have gotten lucky at the end of the night."

Tim's eyes widened. "Do you actually own a dress like that?"

"I do. Gutted I'm not wearing it now?" Izzy asked, trying to stop a smile spreading across her face.

Tim said nothing, but his face told her that he was a bit disappointed.

"Well, think of it this way. If I'd turned up in a polo neck jumper and jeans that would have meant the complete opposite of the dress."

"And you're not wearing that…" Tim said, sounding like he was cottoning on.

Izzy smiled. She realised she hadn't strictly answered his original question though, confirmed by what Tim said next.

"I still don't get it though, Izzy. Are we on a date or not?"

Izzy thought about it for a few moments, taking a sip of tea as she did so. She still wasn't sure what Tim wanted. The only clue she had was that he was referring to it as a date. That indicated a preference. She looked over at him, catching his eye. He had the look of an adorable puppy, that sort of adoration and longing that Tamara's Dachshund, Nexus, had when he wanted to go out for a walk. It was a new look to have staring across at her. She had grown accustomed to the looks of lust or disregard she'd experienced on dates. Some men wanted the 'little black dress' experience. Others were there purely to try and gain favour with her dad.

She decided that she couldn't string him along any longer. She had to take the plunge.

"OK, Tim, I'll tell you what I'm feeling," she said, looking across at him. She had his attention now. "I asked you here tonight because I like you. I saw you looking at me the other day when you came to the manor and I haven't had anybody look at me like that for a long time. You've been bouncing around in my mind since then and because I'm a few years older than you, I've thought that it would be… I don't know… weird. Like we wouldn't have anything in common. As we've been talking here tonight, I realise there's more and more about you that I like." She watched as he processed that. "So I guess what I'm trying to say is that I wanted to meet up with you to see if we were compatible. I think you're really cute. You've got a lot about you that I genuinely like and I just wanted to see where this could go. Are we on a date? Perhaps not, but I'd like to be."

"I see…" was Tim's initial response.

"I don't know if age is a big thing for you, I've no idea. It's something that has bothered me since I ever started to think about you but I had an epiphany earlier. You keep bouncing around my head and don't seem to want to go away. I've trusted my instincts enough over the years to know that anything that keeps popping into my head needs to be explored. I've not had a relationship for a while, so it's going to be new and exciting for me. So I really just want to know how you feel. Because if you feel the same way, then I don't see why we can't go out for a few dates and see where that takes us."

She immediately wondered if she'd said too much. However, he hadn't got up to leave. She took that as a good sign, in any walk of life. She left him to it for a few moments and poured herself another cup of tea.

"Thanks, Izzy," he eventually said. "I'd been wondering all afternoon if this was a date. I kept thinking it was, but then I'd convince myself it couldn't be. Then I thought why would you have asked me to go out in an evening to a neutral location like this if it wasn't some sort of date. I just needed to hear you say what it was. Just so I was sure."

Izzy took a deep breath. "Well, now I've sort of broken the ice a bit, can I ask a question?"

Tim nodded.

"Is there any chance at all whatsoever, after what we've said to each other tonight, that you, at some point in the future, could see yourself being my boyfriend?"

"Yes," came the immediate response. "I really want that to happen."

Izzy suddenly became business-like. "OK, in that case we've got some things we need to discuss." She noticed his empty cup. "Would you like a refill? It's my round."

He asked for another americano and Izzy headed up to the counter where she found Rick cleaning the coffee machine.

"Same again?" he asked.

"Please," Izzy said, surprised that he offered. She didn't expect someone new to remember all the drinks that had been sold in the shop in an evening. She looked over her shoulder to see Tim still sitting at their table, looking lost in thought. She wondered what he was thinking about. Hopefully it was about them.

"Penny for your thoughts," Rick said, returning with their drinks. Izzy noticed she had a pink-and-white-striped teapot now.

"They're worth a lot more than that," Izzy replied, smiling. How could she explain that she was in what was effectively relationship negotiations with a television star? It sounded weird thinking of it like that.

Rick laughed. "You're actually the first person not to sell me their thoughts tonight. I've run out of pennies in this till. Even the other regulars have told me their life stories. Well played."

"Are you and Nicky regulars in here then?" Izzy asked.

"You could say that. Ted and Alyssa had to rush off earlier. Nicky and me, well, we're in here a lot. Good food, good coffee and they put on some good events to attract the locals. There's always a good mix of folk in. Nicky used to run a pub in North Yorkshire, so he knows what he's doing. I'm just the pretty face working the till."

Izzy giggled and paid, insisting he keep the change. Tim looked up at her as she returned to the table, smiling at her as she sat down. It was a warm smile; the warmest she had seen him give her so far.

"Everything alright?" she asked.

"Good, thanks," Tim replied. "You?"

"Yeah, I'm fine. Just saw you sat by yourself, deep in thought. Have you got any questions? For example, there are a few things I've thought of that we would probably have to discuss before any kind of relationship could work."

He frowned. "Like what?"

She hesitated. She knew that the age gap was starting to become less of an issue for her but she could bet good money on it not going down well with everybody. "For example, do we tell your parents?"

He froze, looking unsure. Izzy bet he hadn't even considered his parents in all of this.

"That's entirely up to you, Tim. I can't force you to tell them. I'd obviously prefer it if you did, but that's my opinion." She took the liberty of pouring herself another cup of tea. "I don't believe in keeping big secrets like that. Particularly when you still live under their roof. It's how I was brought up."

He nodded. "Fair enough. I do agree, though. I'll have to tell them. I don't even know how I could try and tell them, but I'll have to. I understand that."

"How do you think they'd react?" Izzy asked carefully.

He screwed his face up. "I'm not sure really. I've never had to discuss girls with them before."

Izzy looked at him incredulously. "Really? You haven't got so far as introducing a girl to your parents?"

He shook his head. "I've never had to because there haven't been any girls to discuss. I had sort of had my heart set on the girl I mentioned earlier, Hannah. I just never got around to asking her out. We were friends for a while, then Talent UK happened." He shifted a little awkwardly in his seat.

Izzy was a little shocked. "You mean you've never even had a girlfriend? Like ever? Have you even kissed a girl?"

He looked incredulously at her. "Of course, I've done that a few times."

"Just never enough with one girl to call her your girlfriend."

He shrugged. "That's right. Is that a problem?"

She considered her answer for a few moments. "No. Not at all. I'm just a bit surprised. I thought all teenagers your age would have had at least one meaningful relationship. That was how it was when I was at school. As soon as I became a teenager there was all that sort of pressure you get put under as a girl to have a boyfriend. Valentines Day was always interesting. You never wanted to be the girl that didn't get at least one card or rose."

"Were you?" Tim asked.

"Was I what?" Izzy asked, a bit lost.

"Was there a Valentines Day that went by without you getting a card?"

Izzy suddenly felt a bit shy. "No. I think the lowest number I received at school was three. That was when I was twelve."

"I don't really know what to say. I don't think I've ever sent a Valentines Day card. Is that a big thing?"

Izzy sipped her tea. "Er, yeah. Kind of. Have you really never sent a Valentines Day card? Or flowers? Or even a single rose?"

He shook his head. "I haven't had to. I never imagined a girl could think about me in the way that you do."

"I tell you what, though, Tim. If you still have a public presence early next year, you're going to be in for a hell of a shock. Teenage girls are going to inundate you with Valentines Day stuff. Particularly if you keep doing birthday messages and other noble gestures like that."

Tim looked unsure. "Really?"

"Oh, Tim. Your innocence is really something. Valentines Day is one of those days where the world goes mental for twenty-four hours, where it's suddenly acceptable for everybody to show how they feel. One thing I've learnt in life is that although you won't be attractive to everyone, you'll be attractive to someone. It's just a matter of finding them. Or them finding you."

"Do you find me attractive, then?" Tim asked.

"Yeah. I do. Even more than when I first saw you this evening. I'm not going to hold back on that. You're cute and your youthful charm makes me wonder what girls have been missing out for all your teenage years. I just find it amazing that your experience of being a teenager is so different to mine. Do teenage boys not work in the same way?"

Tim shrugged again. "Maybe. My mate Alan is a bit of a flirt. He's got a certain way with girls. I know of other guys in my year at school who've had numerous girlfriends. Guess I'm an exception. It's not that I haven't wanted one. I just haven't actively pursued one."

"Why not?" Izzy asked, intrigued.

"Music, I guess. I enjoy playing the saxophone so much, I just haven't found the time to go after girls, do college work and practise. I managed two out of those three before Talent UK put an end to my college work. I've already explained how rubbish I am with starting conversations; girls my own age seem to expect guys to be making the first move. That's what's made this whole scenario different for me. You've not expected anything of me and you've not judged me because of it either."

"They'll be in their 'bad boy' phase at that age. You don't really fit their criteria," Izzy said wisely.

Tim's puzzled face convinced her to explain.

"I swear every girl must go through that phase. I did. When you reach a certain age as a teenage girl, you feel rebellious and you suddenly find yourself attracted to boys who bring a bit of danger into your life. Maybe he has a violent streak and a criminal record. Maybe he has a motorbike. Maybe he has lots of tattoos. Whatever it is that gives him an edge, it's a huge turn-on. You can bet your parents won't like him and that makes him even more attractive."

Tim's eyes were fixed on her, which she found endearing. It was rare to find a guy who would listen as intently as he was.

"My 'bad boy' was Carl. He was the last guy I dated. I look back now and wonder how on earth I could have been attracted to such an idiot. You don't strike me as having a bad bone in your body. Carl? He was full of them. Last time I heard anything about him he'd beaten up the woman he'd cheated on me with outside a bar and was serving time."

"Wow," was Tim's only response.

"Have you got any tattoos?" Izzy asked suddenly, changing the subject.

"No. None. Never even thought about getting one. You?"

"I've got the Chinese symbol for peace on my left wrist, but my watch hides it," she said, pushing her watch up her arm to show him.

"I just don't know what I'd want to colour or pattern my body with for the rest of my life," he added.

"That's fair enough. I had mine done when my parents split up. Home life wasn't fun and so I marked myself with 'peace'."

Tim smiled at her. "I like hearing you talk about normal stuff like this. I've never really had the chance to do this with anyone apart from my friends. It's my fault, I guess, with the way I am around people I don't know."

"What other normal stuff do you want to know then? Go on, make up for all those times you've wanted to ask somebody a normal question and I'll answer it."

Tim thought about it for a few moments before asking, "Do you play any musical instruments?"

"Not any more. My parents put me through violin lessons when I was a child, but it didn't really stick. I stopped playing when I left school."

"Do you still own one?"

"It'll be in my loft somewhere."

"Do you think you can still play?" Tim asked, sounding hopeful.

"Why? You thinking of a duet?"

"Why not? At least there's something we have in common."

Izzy couldn't disagree with that. "Fair enough, it sounds like fun. I must warn you, though, I'm not great. I only agreed to play at school because there were some cute boys in the orchestra. Anything else you want to know?"

Tim asked her, among other things, about her favourite genre of music (pop), her favourite colour (spring green or orange) and lots of details in between. Izzy replied to each question openly and honestly, enjoying Tim's company immensely. She really liked having somebody interested in who she was, and not treating her like a piece of meat or a stepping-stone.

When the conversation reached a bit of a lull, Izzy turned it back towards their prospective relationship. She was sure it was now a question of 'when' and not 'if' they would get together. Tim seemed totally on board with the idea of going on a few dates to start with.

"So, I'm fairly sure we're what I'd call 'compatible'," Izzy said, pouring the last dregs of tea into her cup. "Plus, there's a six month tour coming up that will confirm that." She noticed Tim look up sharply. "What's up? Did you not realise that?"

A beaming smile spread across his face. "You mean I'd get to spend six months touring the country with you?"

She nodded. "Absolutely. I'll be on the tour too." She smiled at him. He looked like he'd just won the lottery. "It's why I wanted to have this conversation before we set off," she continued. "If you were up for having a girlfriend, we could get to know each other on tour. It would be the perfect opportunity to do that."

Tim appeared to accept that quite readily. She thought it was an offer no seventeen-year-old boy could have ever refused. An older girl offering no strings attached relationship to a teenage boy? She nearly laughed.

"We've got a couple of months before the tour gets under way, though; can we still see each other in the meantime?" he asked.

"Of course," she replied. "I'm not going to be saving it all up for the tour. From what I've heard, you don't exactly have much planned these days."

"Whereabouts do you live?"

"I live in a converted barn at Sir Andrew's manor." She noticed a disappointed look cross his face. "What's wrong?"

"I wouldn't be able to come to yours."

"Why?"

"I won't be able to get there. Well, I could cycle, but I've not been on a bike in years. And there's a few hills from what I remember in getting to Great Bournestone."

Izzy sighed, trying to prevent a smile from crossing her face. "I can drive, you know."

"I was learning to drive before I went on Talent UK, I'd had a few lessons, but I feel like I should probably book in a few. At least I could probably afford a car now," Tim said, trying to sound helpful.

"In the meantime, though, I'm quite happy driving to yours," Izzy said reassuringly.

"You'd do that?" Tim said, sounding surprised.

"Of course. Otherwise, how else would I get to see you in the next few weeks? And on that note, how are you planning on getting home tonight?"

"I normally walk. Sometimes my dad will collect me, but I almost prefer walking. He likes talking about his work, which just sounds incredibly dull."

"Fancy a lift then?"

"Seriously?" Tim said, looking hopefully at her.

Izzy nodded. "I hate to end the night, but I do have work in the morning. Plus it looks like they're closing up," she said, pointing out the chairs being put on tables. "And, I'll also get to find out where you live."

They walked to Izzy's car, parked on the opposite side of the road. She noticed him looking admiringly at it as he clambered in the passenger door.

"This must have cost a small fortune," he said, when he was strapped in.

"My dad bought me my first car when I turned eighteen. It was a second-hand BMW, a few years old. I fell in love with how they drove and how they look. Once I'd earned enough money to buy one, I bought a brand new one. This current one is my third BMW."

"It's nice," Tim said, appreciatively looking around the interior.

Izzy smiled, but said nothing. It was more than nice to her; it was a one of her favourite spaces. "So, where do I go from here?"

Tim started giving her directions, but she held her hand up. "Stop," she said, tapping the dashboard. "Built-in sat nav. What's your postcode?"

He blushed and gave her his postcode. "Sorry, Izzy. My parents don't even own a sat nav."

"Hey," she said, typing his postcode in. "I'm sorry too. I don't mean to lord it up in front of you."

"I'll get used to it," he replied, with a smile.

They spent a few more minutes making small talk; they swapped memories about school, discovering that they had actually been at the same primary school, just eleven years apart. In what felt like a matter of seconds, though, Izzy pulled up outside Tim's house. She looked out at the house, trying to see if there was any sign showing how a talented saxophonist had grown up there.

"It's home," she heard Tim say. "It's all I've really known. I know it doesn't look like much."

She turned to look at him. "I'm not judging, Tim. I've met your family, remember? They're all lovely. You're lucky. This is a great family home. And that's what you've got: a great family. It's more than I had growing up."

"But look at what you've got, Izzy. This nice car, a great job working for Sir Andrew Anderson, your clothes. What more could a girl want?"

"Thanks, Tim, that's really sweet of you. I envy you, though. You appear to have had an upbringing that I would have loved."

"Well, maybe," he said, his voice sounding shaky, "I'm just putting this out there, I know it's early days. But if things go well, we could have a family one day and we can combine the best of both worlds."

Izzy just stared at him for a few moments, scarcely believing what she had just heard. Had he really just said that? It was all of her dreams coming true at once. A family. An actual little family. She could feel butterflies in her stomach and her heart beating a calypso in her chest.

It then felt like she was being drawn towards him and his eyes widened as he seemed to grasp what was happening. Two forces appeared to be squeezing them together, millimetre by millimetre.

Izzy's head tilted slightly to the right and his went the opposite way. Their lips, slightly parted, met gently but it didn't take much time for Izzy to dip her tongue into his mouth, gently brushing against his lower teeth, searching for his tongue. Her right hand went up to cup his face, pulling him into her. Their tongues danced around each other, twirling and caressing, and Izzy never wanted this to end. Bright lights were flashing behind her closed eyes and her mind was spinning.

When the kiss did eventually end, she felt breathless. Tim looked as if he'd been transported to another planet.

"Wow," he whispered.

"Wow, yourself," Izzy replied, also whispering. "How was that for a first kiss?"

He blinked a few times and pretended to turn his nose up. "Well, you know, it was… alright."

She playfully jabbed him on the arm. "Hey! That's mean. You had some of my best work there. But kudos on the technique; you've got a lot of potential to work with."

They ended up smiling dreamily at each for a few moments. Izzy was staring at Tim trying to see if she could read what was going through his mind but she couldn't see through all the romantic emotion that was clouding her senses.

"I tell you what, Tim. Lets meet up as much as we can over the next few weeks before July comes around and see if we can build on that first kiss we just had. Then if we do discover the feelings we have are genuine, there's a whole tour to work out what those feelings mean. I'm not expecting fireworks from you to begin with. Just be honest with me, be open about what works for you, I'll do the same and we'll both be winners."

She then glanced at the clock on the dashboard. "Anyway, we've been sat here ten minutes now. Your parents will think someone's scouting the house out."

He hesitated before he opened the door and got out. He was looking at the house and Izzy noticed a light was still on in the front room. "Thanks for the lift, Izzy," he said. "And for, like, everything else that went with it," he said, through the open car door.

"No worries. Text me tomorrow and I'll see what my schedule's like."

She then blew him a kiss, which he returned.

He shut the car door carefully and she watched as he trudged into the house. He turned around again when he had the front door open and waved to her. She returned the wave, fired up the ignition and sped off down the street, reaching the country road in a few minutes. Her brain replayed the kiss the whole way home.

CHAPTER THIRTY-TWO

Friday 20th April, morning
Wright House

Joel's alarm awoke him at the usual time of seven o'clock. Even when he wasn't at college, he liked the routine of waking up at the same time every day. The last few days had been rather crazy by anybody's standards. He listened through the first song of the day, as usual, before raising himself from his bed to switch it off. He nearly trod on Alan in the process, forgetting he was on a mattress on the floor.

"Like having a permanent roommate this week," Joel muttered to no one in particular, reaching over to switch his alarm off.

The sudden silence appeared to stir Alan from his slumber with a large stretch and a groan.

"Morning, buddy," Joel said, poking Alan with a big toe.

"Is it?" Alan replied with another groan. "What time is it?"

"Well, it's like five past seven now the first song has finished."

"Oh yeah. Keep forgetting you're an early bird," Alan said, pulling a sour expression.

"It amazes me that you're not a morning person, bearing in mind your brother and your dad are always up early and having breakfast downstairs here."

"In our house it means the bathroom is always free if I'm up later."

Joel shrugged. It was fair enough; he was always used to his parents being up early and he'd never had competition for the bathroom, being an only child. He grabbed his towel off the back of his door and headed off to the bathroom for a shower.

Switching the water on and letting it warm up for a bit, he had a look in the mirror, realising he should probably shave. The events of the last few days had meant spending time in front of a mirror hadn't been a high priority.

Climbing into the shower, he let the water run off his body for a few minutes; he enjoyed soaking in the shower. Washing his hair, he turned his thoughts to the events since Amie and Hannah had appeared from behind the door to the surgery department. He didn't think he would ever forget that moment. He knew the minute that he looked at them both that the news hadn't been good. He had rung his parents and they had immediately said the twins could stay as long as they wanted.

The bus journey from the hospital back towards college was as silent as the ride had been that morning, if not more. Amie and Hannah had cuddled up to Joel and Alan on the way back, looking very tired and drained as they leaned on the boys' shoulders. Joel hadn't known what to say; what did you say to someone whose mother had just died? At least every few minutes on the bus journey he had opened his mouth to say something but hadn't found any words. He had just ended up cuddling Amie tighter every time it had happened. They got off the bus in the middle of Huntingham, giving them a ten-minute walk to Beans and Banter, also conducted in silence.

Joel's parents had left a pile of DVDs on the coffee table in their lounge, lit a few candles around the room and said that they would be in the next room if any of them needed anything. Luckily, Rick and Nicky had been downstairs and said they would happily look after the shop for them. The two regular customers had always said if Ted and Alyssa had ever needed any help with running the place, they would gladly step in; Tuesday had been one of those times.

Ted and Alyssa had also made up the beds in the lounge for the girls and insisted that they stay as long as they liked. The twins thanked them both and Joel realised that they were the first words any of them had said since leaving the hospital.

Making themselves comfy on the giant sofa, Joel chose a few DVDs off the top of the pile and had a flick through them. There was a mixture of TV series and films and he offered them to the twins to decide. He thought it was a great idea from his parents to watch something and try and take their minds off what had happened.

Wednesday and Thursday that week had been along similar lines. The girls had woken up and returned to the sofa, with Alan and Joel stumbling in a short while after seven o'clock as Joel's alarm had gone off. They carried on working their way through the discs until Thursday afternoon when Hannah suddenly turned to Alan and asked if they were still going on their date. Hannah was adamant that she still wanted to go, even without any idea what it would entail. Alan had then disappeared briefly without saying anything, and Joel was mystified as to what his best friend had planned. Amie had been probing him for information, but he honestly couldn't divulge anything.

He turned his thoughts to today. The twins had the option of going to their mum's post-mortem at the hospital that morning and then it was Alan and Hannah's date in the afternoon. He was still confused as to what Alan needed from him beforehand, but had just decided to go with the flow.

College work was just on the back burner. There was still some work he needed to do, but his head just wasn't in it. He was sure that Alan and the twins felt the same. He was hoping that at some point today him and Alan could at least do something normal together; play a song, for example. It might even cheer the twins up if they were still there.

Pulling the bathroom door open, he was surprised to see a queue.

"Well, you took your time," Amie commented, smiling when she noticed he was only wearing a towel wrapped around his waist.

"Sorry, I didn't realise you would be waiting," Joel replied, desperately hoping his towel would stay wrapped.

"We were talking about it and decided that we should probably get up and actually do something today," Hannah said, without looking at him. Amie, in contrast, was certainly making the most of the view, her eyes roaming all over Joel's body.

"Yeah, we moped around yesterday. Today's a new day and we're going to get ourselves sorted," Amie added. "We can't be sad forever. Mum wouldn't let us be like that."

"Oh right," Joel said awkwardly, hoping there would be a lull in the conversation so he could get some clothes on. Amie he wouldn't mind having a conversation with, but having them both stood there was just weird.

"Go on, Joelly, go get some clothes on," Amie said, having realised his predicament. "We'll see you in a bit." They both went into the bathroom and shut the door.

Relieved, Joel returned to his room, finding Alan had gone back to sleep and was busy snoring loudly.

"Typical," Joel muttered, searching his drawers for some clothes to wear.

Once dressed, he headed downstairs, looking for his parents. "Morning, Ma," he said, once he'd found her in the kitchen.

"Good morning, yourself," she replied, not looking up from the grill. "How is everyone this morning?"

"Yeah, alright I think. Alan's sleeping and the girls are in the bathroom."

"Great. How are the twins coping?"

"OK, I think. Thanks for letting them stay."

"It's not a problem. Honestly. Christine would have wanted us to look after them, and they're no trouble. They both work really hard here; both willing to learn, and they seem popular with the punters. Plus, I totally sympathise with them if they don't want to go home to an empty house, particularly after what happened."

Joel frowned. "I guess I hadn't thought of it like that."

"My parents took your dad in when his mum passed away. I admired them for doing that when your dad and I hadn't actually been going out for that long. I felt it was the right thing to do for the twins and we've got the room for them both."

"Well, thanks. I know I didn't ask you to take them in or anything, but thanks. It means a lot," Joel said humbly.

His mother looked up at him for the first time. "Don't mention it. So how's it going with Amie?"

"How's what going with Amie?"

"You mean… You've not taken the hint yet?"

Joel looked baffled. "What hint?"

His mother just shook her head slowly. "Honestly, boys just don't get it do they," she mumbled, but still loud enough for Joel to hear.

"Get what?"

Alyssa put the tongs down that she had been using to flip bacon and turned around to face Joel. "Seriously, I've seen you spend the best part of the last forty-eight hours with her. You've been friends for ages. Hannah and Alan are an item now. So much so, I almost want to call them 'Halan'. I just want to be stood here talking about 'Jamie'. I don't get it. How is Amie not your girlfriend?" she asked, hands on her hips, causing Joel to cringe inwardly.

"Yeah, Joelly, what's up with that," came a voice from behind him.

He turned around and saw both twins stood there smiling at him.

"Oh, Joel, you should see your face!" Amie said, while struggling to hold back laughter. "But seriously," she went on, her face becoming deadpan. "I like you. I think you like me too. Why aren't we together? Why can't we be 'Jamie'?"

Joel felt like a rabbit in headlights. He had imagined this conversation over and over in his mind for a few weeks but he had never expected to be put on the spot in the kitchen of Beans and Banter with his mother present. "I just haven't found the right moment," he said, unconvincingly. "It's never felt right and I didn't want to ask over the last couple of days in case you thought I was taking advantage of you…" He trailed off, not knowing what else to say.

"Well, now feels like the right time," Amie said, smiling coyly at him.

Joel swallowed awkwardly. "Really?"

Amie laughed. "Yes, you idiot. Just ask me the sodding question!"

Joel gulped. "OK, I guess… Are you absolutely sure?"

"Joel, I'm serious," she replied, her tone of voice growing darker.

Sensing the moment might be passing, he said the nine words he'd wanted to say since practically the moment he'd first met her. "Amie, do you want to go out with me?" he said, really quickly.

She ran and leapt on him, throwing her arms around his neck and wrapping her legs around his waist. "Of course, Joelly, of course I do," she whispered in his ear.

In that moment, Joel didn't care that Amie's twin sister and his mother were in the room. All he cared about was the girl that he was currently holding. He had finally done it. He had asked out a girl who he had fancied for longer than he cared to remember and she had said yes. In his mind, life didn't get any better than this.

Amie put her feet back on the floor, just as Alan appeared, looking dishevelled. He looked around at everybody stood in the kitchen before standing next to Hannah and putting an arm around her.

"What did I miss?" he asked, yawning.

"Joel just asked Amie out," Hannah said quietly.

"Oh right. About time, you two. Congrats," he said. "What's for breakfast?"

"Honestly," Hannah muttered, but she didn't say anything else.

Joel's mum then coughed to get their attention. "There's a few boxes of cereal out on your regular table. I'd like my kitchen back, please," she said, not unkindly.

They wandered out of the kitchen, both couples hand-in-hand and went to sit down at their table. Alyssa had laid it out with a selection of cereals, some slices of toast in a toast rack and four glasses of orange juice. Joel was really touched by the effort his mother had gone to, and headed straight back into the kitchen to give her a hug and say thank you.

He returned to his seat to find everyone else tucking in. Once he'd had a swig from his glass, he settled in next to Alan, so he was facing Amie. His girlfriend. He found it weird to think of her like that. She looked up at him and smiled. How he loved seeing that smile. He realised he hadn't seen much of that smile over the last day or so, quite understandably. The world always felt like a better place when she was flashing her teeth at him.

"What's the plan for today?" Joel asked them all.

"Well, Hannah and I are going on our date this afternoon. I just need your help beforehand still, if that's alright?" Alan said.

"Sure, no problem," Joel replied, still wondering what Alan could possibly need.

"Hannah and I have had a chat and we've decided we don't want to go to the autopsy this morning, but we'll need to go and collect the paperwork around lunchtime," Amie said.

"That's fair enough," Joel said. "I don't blame you for not going. I don't think I'd want to. What do you need to do with the paperwork you're getting?"

"We have to go to a funeral directors with it then, from what that freaky death counsellor said," Hannah replied, making Amie chuckle at her description.

"We're still alright for our date, though?" Alan asked, sounding worried.

"Sure. Wouldn't miss it for the world," Hannah replied, smiling at him.

"You don't even know what it is!" Amie exclaimed. "It could be jumping out of a plane or something horrific like that. It isn't, right?" she asked.

Alan shook his head. "I can confirm it definitely isn't jumping out a plane. Though I'm a little surprised; I'd have thought Hannah would have really enjoyed a parachute jump."

That only served to wind Amie up further and she peppered him with questions for a few minutes, establishing that the date didn't involve a long list of activities including paintballing, bungee jumping, go-kart racing or swimming.

"I have absolutely no idea then," Amie said, sounding annoyed. "Either you're lying to me or you've really, really put some effort in to this."

Joel sat there eating his breakfast, enjoying the exchange he had just witnessed. After the near-silence of the previous two days, he was grateful that the twins appeared to be talkative this morning. He understood letting them grieve as the piece of paper Amie had shown him had explained. He still couldn't imagine being in their position, though. He thought about what his own mother had done for them that morning and just couldn't imagine waking up one day with her not being there. It just made him more determined to support them through their grief.

When breakfast was finished, Alan made his excuses, saying he had to get some date things organised and that he should probably check in at his own home for a bit. He would message Joel later with details of where he needed him to be. The girls headed back to their house just to check on it and to get some fresh clothes sorted before heading to the coroner's office. Joel cleared everything away from the table, washed it all up in the kitchen and then headed back upstairs. He found it strange being on his own again; he had been getting used to having his friends around him all the time.

He thought about trying to look at some college work today, at least. Deciding he could see what was going on in the world first, he logged on to Facebook on his laptop and the news that Tim was now in a relationship greeted him. He found it surprising that the news had surprised him. He hadn't taken much notice of Tim's statuses recently so he was confused as to why seeing Tim in a relationship had puzzled him.

It then dawned on him that it was because it wasn't with Hannah. Clicking on the girl listed he looked at her profile. His frown grew deeper as he noticed the girl's age. She was a whole lot older than Tim. That was strange. He tried to figure out where Tim would have met such a girl and could only conclude that it was from Talent UK. Part of him then wondered if it was some sort of revenge for Hannah being in a relationship, but he discarded that. That would have just been stupid.

Shrugging, he then opened his coursework but felt his phone vibrate in his pocket.

Dude, I need you to meet me at one outside the church up on Manor Road.

Still unsettled by Tim's Facebook status, Joel was dealt a knockout blow by this. Why on earth would Alan want to meet him outside a church?

Al, please don't tell me you're going to get married or something. Or do funeral arrangements. That would just be crazy.

We're not going in the church, you doofus. I just need you to meet me there. What's the weather forecast like for this afternoon?

Joel pulled up a weather page on the Internet.

It's supposed to be alright this afternoon, maybe a bit overcast, but no rain showing. Is that what you need?

Yeah, cheers. I'll see you at one.

OK, see you then.

Joel shrugged again. He wracked his brain, trying to think what possible first date locations were up near Manor Road but came up blank. He trusted Alan, though, to have come up with something impressive, particularly as he had gone to such lengths to ensure the surprise remained under wraps.

CHAPTER THIRTY-THREE

Friday 20th April
Outside Beans and Banter

Hannah and Amie trudged over the road to their house. Hannah was about to put her key in the door when Amie grabbed her arm.

"Wait, Han. Just stand here a minute."

Hannah turned to her sister. "Why?" she asked.

Amie hesitated. "I know it sounds stupid but the moment we go in, our home life without Mum begins properly."

Hannah shrugged. "And? We've got to do it at some point, Amz. We can't stand out here pretending everything's fine."

Amie looked surprised. "I just wanted you to be aware, that was all," she mumbled.

"I do understand," Hannah said with a sigh. "I'm just having to face the fact that we're going to have to move on. I don't want to wallow in this grief. I did that yesterday and the day before and I'm not proud of it."

"Where's all this guts and determination coming from?" Amie asked, sounding puzzled.

"I've been reading Sir Andrew's book on and off when I can," Hannah replied, showing Amie she had it in her bag. "The counselling I had after I tried to hang myself talks about dealing with this sort of situation as well. We can't change what happened, Amz. We just have to find a way to deal with it. Do you want to smile at each other again?"

Amie nodded and it was Hannah this time that took the lead, stretching her face into the widest smile she could possibly produce.

"Thanks sis," Amie said, reaching out and giving Hannah a hug. "This book sounds amazing if it's had this sort of effect on you."

Hannah wondered if her sister was feeling a bit inadequate. "I can lend you the book if you want?" she offered.

"If it can teach me how to ignore all this anger and injustice at the world then, yeah, I'd love to borrow it.

"There is a section I found quite helpful on that." Hannah admitted. " It doesn't teach you how to ignore it though, Amz. It teaches you how to *deal* with it. I'll put a bookmark in the page where it starts."

"Thanks. I just want to find some sort of relief from all this. Shall we get this over with?"

"OK," Hannah said, turning the key in the lock and opening the front door. She struggled to push the door open. It had only been a few days but there was a small pile of regular mail on the mat. One of their mum's catalogues was the offending article making it difficult to push the door open.

"Wow," Amie said, scrabbling on the floor trying to pick it all up. "It's only been a few days. What on earth is all this?"

"No idea. Guess we'll need to have a look at it later. Right now, I just want to pack some clothes and check the house is alright."

"Do you think we should switch stuff off? Like, unplug the TV and the washing machine?"

Hannah agreed that they would do that before they left and they both headed upstairs to get changed.

Half an hour later, after switching off every appliance in the house, bar the fridge-freezer, they returned to Beans and Banter with clothes for a few more days in a suitcase. Amie had picked up the mail and they sat at the table at the back of the shop to run through it.

"It's just weird to think we'll be getting mail for someone who isn't here any more," Amie remarked, selecting the catalogue.

"Does Mum owe anything on that?" Hannah asked.

"I wouldn't know. Where would it tell me?" Amie queried, turning the catalogue over and flicking through it. "Oh, I see," she said, a few moments later. "There's a letter here."

Hannah took the piece of paper off her sister and winced when she saw the figures at the bottom. "I had no idea Mum owed this much," she muttered.

"And that's just a catalogue," Amie pointed out. "Mum's got a credit card as well. I've no idea if there's anything else."

"Like what?"

"Does Mum have a loan? We know there's the mortgage but would she have a loan as well? What about more catalogues?"

Hannah put the letter she was reading on the table. "How do you know about all this credit stuff, Amz?"

"Have you ever thought about moving out?" Amie asked.

Hannah looked shocked. "No! Why would I?"

"Did you imagine living with Mum for the rest of your life?"

Hannah hesitated. "No," she said eventually. "I guess I would have moved out one day."

"How would you have afforded it?"

"I have no idea, Amz. No idea. Apart from marrying a millionaire."

Amie chuckled. "Yeah, because you'd be that lucky. That was my plan."

"So, you've really thought about moving out?"

"I've been researching it since Dad left."

Hannah was surprised it had been that long. "Wow. Were you ever going to tell me?"

"Of course I'd have told you, when I was faced with moving out. I've found some lovely two-bedroom flats. I wouldn't have gone anywhere without telling you."

"Are you still thinking about it?"

Amie looked thoughtful. "I suppose it depends on what happens with the house. Do you reckon Dad is still connected to it?"

"I really don't know, Amz. I knew Mum worked every shift she could to make the payment on the mortgage and to pay the bills. I don't know whether Dad paid anything or not."

"No, me neither."

They both looked up as Alyssa Wright sat down with them. "Hello, girls. How are you holding up today?"

The twins shared a glance with each other. "We were just looking at the post and trying to work out if we're going to need to pay any of Mum's bills," Hannah said. "We've found a catalogue with some money owing and then we're worried about the mortgage and we don't know if Dad's paying anything..."

"OK, alright, slow down," Alyssa said, holding her hands up. "First things first. Let me see if Ted needs anything doing, and if not I'll sit down with you both and see what we can find."

She returned a few minutes later having taken her apron off. "Right, girls, I can spare about half an hour. What's going on?"

Amie and Hannah took turns in explaining what they'd discovered and what they were worried about, which Alyssa scribbled down on a note pad she'd brought with her.

"I see," she said slowly, once the girls had finished. "I can answer some of the questions but in most cases you'll need to ring the people concerned. If you have a bank statement for your mum that would help me too."

Amie and Hannah shared another look with each other and Amie left her seat. "I'll just nip over the road and see if I can find one. I'm sure Mum had a drawer she put bank statements in," she said.

Once Amie had disappeared, Alyssa looked straight at Hannah. "So, how are things?"

Hannah shrugged. "OK, I guess."

Alyssa gave her a look that suggested she didn't believe what Hannah was telling her. "Right," Alyssa said, stretching it out. "Things alright with Alan?"

"Yep."

Perhaps sensing she wasn't going to get any further, Alyssa just patted

Hannah's hand. "If you need anything, you know where Ted and me are."

Hannah just smiled. Amie then appeared and they spent some more time on sorting out the paperwork. Alyssa discovered by looking at the bank statement that Christine did appear to be paying the mortgage by herself and there were a few payments that could be a life insurance policy. There was no other money coming in apart from Child Benefit and Christine's wages.

"OK, I think we're getting somewhere," Alyssa said to the twins. "Here's a list of companies you'll need to contact. I can't say what all of the account numbers for these companies are, but you should be able to get somewhere by explaining the situation. You'll probably be asked to confirm your mum's date of birth and address. I can let you use the computer and phone upstairs to help. I need to get back to work."

Thanking her for her help, the girls headed upstairs to find some phone numbers and then to make the calls.

They returned downstairs a couple of hours later, Hannah having looked up the phone numbers and Amie having rung them. It had been a frustrating morning of being placed on hold and not having the right paperwork to hand but Amie had been able to establish that the life insurance policy their mother had had would clear the mortgage, which she considered to be one less thing to have to worry about. The mortgage company hadn't been able to confirm if their father was still named on it, which frustrated Amie; she was dreading having to call him again following her last experience.

Saying their goodbyes to Alyssa and Ted downstairs, the girls headed out to the coroners office, which was a fifteen-minute walk across the centre of Huntingham. The receptionist at the desk spent a few minutes searching her trays for their paperwork but eventually located it, with a host of apologies. The twins then had it explained to them that there needed to be an inquest into their mum's death due to the level of injuries that she had sustained, which wasn't a surprise to them. However, the receptionist explained that there was an interim death certificate available, which should help them with sorting out their mum's affairs.

Leaving the coroner's office, Amie turned to Hannah. "It's nearly date time. Are you ready?"

"As ready as I'll ever be. I just want to be able to put all this sorting out to one side for an afternoon."

"Any idea what Alan has planned?"

Hannah shook her head. "None at all."

"No, me neither. I've even asked Joel and he doesn't know. Any idea where we're going yet?"

Hannah checked her phone, discovering she had a message from Alan. "It says to meet up outside the church on Manor Road."

"Brilliant, that's just around the corner," Amie said and headed off.

Hannah followed her sister, speeding up to catch up with her. "What's near Manor Road?" she asked.

"You mean aside from the church?"

Hannah nodded.

Amie thought about it for a few seconds. "There's the lake, I suppose. Isn't the car park and the entrance to the lake all there?"

"There's not much else really is there?"

Hannah considered what Alan had told her about wearing normal clothes for the date. It did imply that there was something outdoors, so Amie could well be right. "Guess not."

"Excited now?"

Hannah smiled. "Yes. I'm still trying to work out what on earth he's got planned, though."

"There's a coffee shop and a garden centre there as well. Are you two going to be having a coffee looking out over Helton Lake?"

"Could be, I suppose. But rather than guessing, Amz, I just want to meet up with him and find out what we're doing."

Amie said nothing more, continuing to walk purposefully towards the small church building on Manor Road. As both girls turned the corner, they noticed Alan and Joel stood outside the church, deep in discussion. They both looked up as the girls approached, looking pleased to see them.

"Hey," Alan said, once they'd finished hugging. "You found us then."

Hannah smiled at him. "It turns out the coroner's office is only around the corner, so we didn't have far to go."

They both smiled at each other for a few moments until Amie coughed.

"So, what are you two going to be doing?" She then noticed Joel smiling too. "I take it you know now as well?"

Joel nodded. "It's amazing. Hannah's in for a wonderful afternoon. But I've got a question to ask you."

Amie looked puzzled. "What's that then?"

"How would you like a first date too?"

Amie's eyes widened. "Seriously?"

"Absolutely. We're not on a double date, as such, but when Alan told me his plan, I wondered if you'd be interested."

For the second time that day, Amie ran and jumped on Joel. "Of course I'm interested," she said, her voice muffled by Joel's neck. "What are we going to be doing?"

"We'd better go after Hannah and Alan then, and I'll show you," Joel replied, pointing at the other couple who were now making their way down the road. He and Amie dutifully followed.

"So, seriously, where are we going?" Amie asked, reaching for his hand to hold.

Joel tried to hide a smile. "It's a surprise."

"It's the coffee shop at the lake, isn't it?"

Joel screwed his face up. "Close, but you'll just have to wait and see how close."

Amie balled her fists in frustration. "This isn't fair! Just tell me already!"

Joel said nothing trying to prevent a smile crossing his face. They walked hand-in-hand behind Alan and Hannah for a few minutes, crossing the road together and then into the Lakeside Centre car park.

Hannah felt extremely nervous as they approached the large wooden cabin, perched at the top of a slope. There were windows on either side meaning she could see straight through to the lake on the other side. Maybe a romantic cup of coffee was what Alan had in mind after all.

She was confused a few seconds later as Alan led her straight out the other side of the building and down the path leading down to the lake.

"We're not going skinny dipping or anything like that are we?" she asked.

Alan laughed. "Not unless you want to," he said, clearly amused.

Hannah shuddered. "I don't think I'd want to do that until the weather is warmer." She noticed the surprised look on his face. "What?"

"You'd actually consider taking all of your clothes off and running into the lake?"

With her face completely deadpan, Hannah replied, "Of course. I'd just want the water to be jacuzzi temperature."

"Wow," Alan said. "I honestly never thought you'd be up for that sort of thing."

Hannah frowned at him. "Why? I'm not a prude, Alan Proctor."

He raised his hands defensively. "I never said you were!"

She shoved him playfully. "That's true, but I could tell you were thinking it," she said, carefully watching him for his reaction. She knew she had him when he just shrugged. It was then that she spotted a wooden kiosk advertising water sports equipment at the bottom of the slope. Could that be where they were heading? It certainly seemed to be. If not, there wasn't much else apart from the lake itself.

Alan cleared his throat once all four of them were stood outside the kiosk. "So, my eldest brother, Ryan, introduced us to his latest girlfriend a few weeks ago. She works as a water sports coach, which is pretty cool. She's very... athletic," he finished hurriedly when he noticed the glare Hannah was giving him. "She explained that they've recently invested in some water sports equipment up here, hoping to encourage a bit more tourism and interest in the lake. I thought spending the afternoon on the water would be different. It's not something I've ever done. I couldn't remember hearing anyone talking about it either, so I thought it would be perfect for a first date."

There was an appropriate round of appreciative noises from the girls.

"Karen's reserved us a rowing boat and a pedalo for the afternoon," he continued. "If you girls don't want to take your bags on the water there are some lockers around the back of the kiosk. Joel and I need our rucksacks for once we're out on the water," he finished, causing both girls to make an 'ooh' noise.

"We're going on the lake in a pedalo?" Hannah asked, feeling a bit nervous.

"Or a rowing boat," Alan pointed out. "We just have to wear life jackets, no matter which craft we choose."

The other three nodded and Alan walked up to the kiosk, chatted for a few moments with the blond-haired girl behind the counter and returned to them holding four life jackets.

"Here, put these on," Alan said, passing the life jackets around.

Both couples headed to the small dock, also accessed via the rear of the kiosk. Alan and Hannah chose the pedalo leaving Joel and Amie with the rowing boat. Both boys helped their respective girl into their chosen craft, untied the mooring rope and set off in opposite directions on the lake.

Joel and Amie set off quicker than Alan and Hannah, Joel pulling their boat along with the oars and before long they were a mere smudge in the distance. Alan was leisurely pedalling out towards the middle of the lake. Hannah leaned against the side of the pedalo, looking up at the sky, feeling, for the first time in a long time, utterly content with life. All the worries of the past few days seemed to be left on the shore, almost as if they weren't keen on water.

Alan stopped pedalling briefly, smiling one of his face-wide smiles at Hannah. "It's great to see you looking at peace with things. You look relaxed," he commented.

"Thanks," Hannah replied, returning his smile. "Something about the sound of the water lapping at the sides of this pedalo is quite calming. I love how quiet and peaceful it is out here. The view is stunning."

"I did alright then?"

"You did great."

"Thanks. I do have something in my rucksack, though, that's also part of the plan," Alan added casually.

Hannah just looked at him; she was curious now.

Alan reached down and unzipped his rucksack, and fished out two wine glasses and two bottles of fizzy drink. "I wasn't entirely sure which you preferred," he said, pointing to the bottles; one was lemonade and the other was cola. "What can I pour you?"

Hannah giggled. "This is actually quite romantic. Lemonade, please."

"I'm just sorry it's not wine," Alan said, handing her a glass and sounding a little regretful. "I didn't want to tempt myself with anything like that. Plus I didn't want to get drunk in the middle of a lake and get stuck or something."

"Hey," Hannah said, reaching out for his hand, "this is amazing. Who cares if I haven't got a pinot grigio in my hand? I've got a cold drink and some great company. Plus I've heard about your binges; I don't really want to have to experience one of those. Particularly marooned in the middle of a lake."

"To us," Alan said, proffering his glass.

"To us," Hannah echoed, clinking his glass with her own.

Alan smiled again and they ended up staring into each other's eyes for what felt like hours to Hannah. She debated with herself whether to lean forward and see if he would kiss her, but decided to keep her cards close to her chest. She was enjoying herself; why should she rush things? There was plenty of time for all that.

Breaking the silence, Alan said, "So, tell me Hannah French – how are you holding up? From the outside looking in, you seem to be doing really well."

"Thanks," she replied, trying to put on a brave face. "It's just very weird to think I won't see my mum again."

"Yeah, that must be awful," Alan said, nodding.

"I can't really put it into words. I just keep thinking how happy she was, the last time I saw her properly."

"Before you met up with Tim, wasn't it?" Alan asked, his tone turning darker.

"Yep. She was so happy that I was going to meet up with a boy. She did my hair and everything. She never did that for Amie; Amz was a bit jealous, if I'm honest."

"I can quite believe that," Alan added. "I can't imagine what it's like having a twin. Do you two have to share everything? Even down to experiences with your parents?"

Hannah considered this for a few moments, running back through memories in her mind. "Sort of. It was easier when Dad was at home. Amie was his favourite and Mum always favoured me. Since he left, Mum had always tried to find more time for Amz, but she just wasn't physically able to. She tried her best though; I can't fault her for the effort that she put in."

"Does your dad even know yet?"

Hannah shook her head. "No. I don't think so. Amie tried to call him the night of the accident, but he wasn't interested."

"Wow. I didn't know that. What on earth happened? How can a dad with two wonderful daughters and a great home life just leave all that behind?"

"I have no idea. If they were having problems, we never noticed. We just came home one day from college to find Mum in tears and she had to tell us he was gone and wasn't coming back. We never really knew why."

"I wonder if you'll ever find out," Alan mused.

"No idea. Amie will be the most likely to find out, I guess."

"Anyway, that's all water under the bridge. We're on our first date, of hopefully many to come. I want to know what are you looking forward to, Hannah French? What's life got in store for you?"

Hannah puffed her cheeks out, taking a few seconds to think about her answer. She then proceeded to lay out what she had wanted to do with her life, her hopes and dreams, with Alan listening intently to her. She mentioned the places she wanted to travel to that she'd imagined a couple of days ago and hoped he wanted to visit those places too.

Hannah felt at ease on the water, seemingly far away from land where all her problems were. As she started explaining, the sun appeared from behind a cloud. This made the lake surface sparkle and glisten in the sunlight and Hannah suddenly felt more positive about revealing some of her core wishes and dreams to someone else. She watched Alan while she was talking. He casually sipped from his glass, his eyes locked on hers the whole time, and offered her a refill when she had finished her own.

She then returned the question, turning the spotlight on to Alan. He was, of course, the year below her at college, but even so, she was surprised at hearing what career he wanted to be involved with; he seemed to have it all figured out. A year ago, she wouldn't have had a clue what she wanted to do with her life. She found herself watching him, with his large-rimmed glasses that stood out on his face, a few stray strands of his hair rustling in the breeze and as he talked, she liked the fact his hands were never still; he was very expressive. The passion in his eyes as he talked about the experiences he wanted to live was contagious, and Hannah found herself wanting to join him on those journeys.

Kissing Alan was in the back of her mind the whole time. She had spent a lot of time looking at the outline of his lips, wondering what kissing him would feel like. Would it be weird because she knew him as a friend? She hoped not. She saw him as much more than that now. She didn't know how to initiate a kiss with him though. She was tempted to stop him mid-sentence, put a finger on his lips, grab his face with both hands and pull him towards her. She nearly let out a giggle imagining this and thought that she risked capsizing the pedalo if she did.

She didn't want the afternoon to end, and was disappointed when Alan eventually told her they would have to head back to the shore. He began to pedal and Hannah tried to take as many mental pictures of the moment as she could; trying to remember how the lake had smelt, what the countryside that she could see looked like and how the gentle rocking motion of the pedalo she was sat in felt. She had found herself not wanting to go back, but realised she needed to find out how Amie's date had gone, desperately hoping it had at least been as good as hers.

CHAPTER THIRTY-FOUR

Friday 20th April, afternoon
Helton Lake

As Joel pulled the rowing boat to the dock and moored it, he noticed Alan and Hannah's pedalo appear into the small bay where the dock was based. He was pleased to see they were both smiling. He presumed that meant their date had gone well.

When Alan had finally revealed his plans to him earlier, he'd been surprised to say the least. He hadn't quite expected the plan to be so elaborate. Alan had merely smiled at him when he asked if he could steal the idea to use for Amie as well.

It had been worth it, though. The rowing had taken a lot out of him, but he'd been determined to do it and he'd insisted on Amie sitting there, relaxing and enjoying the experience. The only time she had complained was when she pointed out how red his face was and it was ruining her view, but she couldn't keep a straight face for long.

He had rowed Amie to the west bank of the lake before they just floated for a while. They both sat in the bottom of the boat looking up at the sky, watching the clouds pass over them. They hadn't actually said a lot to each other, both seemingly enjoying each other's company. It had been one of the best moments of his life; just sat in the boat, his arm around his girlfriend, without a care in the world. All that felt important to him during the time they spent on the water was just being there for her. He realised that he had some serious feelings for the girl sat next to him. He just didn't know how to put them into words.

It had taken Amie to say she was feeling cold for Joel to decide to row back, and he'd then remembered the drinks; another part of Alan's idea he'd stolen. There had been squeals of surprise and excitement, and it had pained him a little to say it hadn't been his idea, but Amie had still been impressed.

Feeling his shoulders, which were aching after all the effort he'd put in, he offered to give Amie a hand getting back on to the jetty.

"Thanks, Joelly," Amie said, gratefully accepting his hand. "I've had a lovely time. It was nice to get away from it all. I know we didn't go out to sea or anything, but just floating on the water and watching the clouds helped me get some perspective. I'd like to come out here again some time."

"Great idea," Joel said. "I've enjoyed it too. Though I might insist on being in a pedalo next time. I'm not sure my arms will ever be the same after today."

She smiled at him, tenderly rubbing one of his arms. "That's a shame. I thought you looked very manly rowing those oars."

Joel looked down at Amie, not quite sure how to respond, but with a smile growing across his face. "Manly?"

"Why yes, sir. Very manly," Amie said, now squeezing the bicep on his arm. "I like a manly man."

"Not quite sure why you're into me then," Joel said, trying to shrug her off.

Amie put on a stern face. "Oh I see. Playing hard to get now are we?"

Joel just looked at her, his arms now folded, one eyebrow raised.

"Well, I like my manly men to play a musical instrument or two, serve good coffee and be studious," Amie began, causing Joel's iron mask to melt into a chuckle. "They need to look good when they get out of the shower. They need to smell gorgeous and not care too much about their hair; just let it naturally fall where it falls."

"See, I'd fit that description of manly," he said, opening his arms and pulling Amie in close.

"Good," Amie replied, her voice muffled by Joel's chest. "Because you're all mine."

"Hey! A little help over here!" Joel heard Alan shout. Turning around he saw his best friend standing precariously with one foot on the dock and one on the pedalo, threatening to do the splits at any minute.

With a burst of speed, Joel ran down the dock, grabbing Alan's hand and pulling him on to the dock. They turned towards the pedalo, seeing Hannah in fits of giggles.

"Cheers, dude," Alan said, breathing heavily. "I thought I was going to end up dripping the whole way home."

"No worries," Joel replied, grabbing the mooring rope and tying it to the dock. "How did your date go?"

"Yeah, it was good," Alan said with a shrug. "Hannah's laughing. I hear that's a good sign of attraction."

Joel tried hard to keep a straight face but ultimately failed. "Well, it was pretty funny watching you do pedalo gymnastics." Amie then appeared at his side, having ambled on to the dock.

"I really wish I'd videoed that, Al," she said, a smile on her face. "That would have been a massive hit on YouTube."

"Yeah, thanks for that," Alan said, glaring at them both. "I'm going to be a bit sore in the morning," he added, gesturing towards his groin region.

"Maybe you could let Hannah know," Joel suggested, trying to keep his voice as innocent as possible.

"Let me know what?" Hannah said, having climbed out of the pedalo with relative ease compared to Alan.

The two boys looked a little awkward for a few moments before Joel blurted out, "Alan has a sore groin and he wants you to rub it better!"

Hannah's cheeks burned crimson and Amie went and put her arms around her.

"Hey, you leave my baby sister alone," Amie said, now glaring at the two boys. "None of that smutty behaviour, please."

"Sorry," they both said simultaneously, before cracking up laughing.

Amie and Hannah shared a look and before the boys could react, they both found themselves shoved unceremoniously into the lake.

"Hope it's cold enough in there to snap you both out of your dirty minds," Amie called. She then turned to her sister. "Come on, Han. Lets go and grab a drink inside and wait for those two to come and find us."

***

It was half an hour before the boys appeared at the windows of the cafe. They both looked a little bedraggled and Hannah thought that they looked sorry for themselves.

She waved at them, and they made their way in, their wet clothes clinging to their skin. Hannah thought she noticed Amie eyeing Joel up and down again, like she had that morning when he'd come out of the shower. She nudged her sister, causing her to double take, and Hannah knew that she'd caught her.

"Hey, you two," Amie said, smiling like a cat that had got the cream.

Both boys just grunted in response.

"Still want Hannah to rub your groin?"

Alan shook his head.

"Good. Hope you've learned your lesson. Both of you," Amie said with a glare.

They both nodded.

"Come on then, sit down," Amie said, gesturing at the two chairs opposite.

They both followed their orders.

"I'll tell you what," Amie continued, "I'm feeling a bit sorry for you, and you're looking *very* sorry for yourselves; would you like a drink? My treat."

"Thanks," Joel replied. "I'll have my usual, please."

"Same," Alan agreed.

Amie disappeared to get the drinks leaving Hannah sat there with them both.

"I'm sorry, Han," Joel said. "I didn't mean to embarrass you."

"It's alright. Amie and I had our revenge."

"So," Joel said, stretching it out, "how did your date go?"

"It was perfect," Hannah replied, smiling at Alan. She couldn't remember the last time she had smiled so much in one day. "I had a great time."

Alan nodded. "It all went to plan."

"I can't wait for the next date; I'm really looking forward to what Alan's got planned."

Alan looked surprised, but merely said, "No pressure then."

"There is one thing that's bugging me," Hannah said, waiting for Alan to look inquisitively at her before continuing. "You said that there was a wet-weather option; what was *that* going to be?"

Alan just smiled. "Well, if I'm under pressure for a second date, then I might just have to keep that close to my chest."

Hannah looked at Joel, who just shrugged; he obviously didn't know what Alan's other idea had been.

"Fair enough, I won't ask again," Hannah said calmly, but inside she was quite excited. What could Alan possibly have come up with?

Amie then came back to the table with their drinks. "There you go, lads," she said, watching in amusement as they both wrapped their hands around the hot mugs. "Still feeling the cold are we?"

They both nodded sheepishly.

"Where have you actually been?" Hannah asked out of curiosity.

"We got laughed at a bit by Karen at the kiosk, and she let us in to the changing room and gave us a couple of towels. She didn't have any spare clothes, though, so we've had to wring out our clothes in the lake," Alan said, looking wistfully outside.

Both girls were trying very hard not to laugh.

"We're damp more than anything else, I think," Joel added. "Though I swear my feet are squelching, still."

"So, what's the plan for the rest of the day?" Amie asked, changing the subject.

"Back to Beans and Banter?" Alan suggested.

"Possibly, possibly," Amie said, looking between just Joel and her sister now.

"I've just had an idea," Hannah said quietly.

The other three looked at her expectantly.

"You and Joel are musicians, right?" she asked rhetorically. "Our mum was a big fan of a variety of pop music. Could you put together a memorial concert or something like that after Mum's funeral?"

Joel looked the most thoughtful about the idea. "When is it?"

"We haven't got a definite date yet," Amie said, "but now we have the paperwork from the coroner hopefully it'll be in the next couple of weeks."

"We need to see about sorting out a funeral director next," Hannah added.

"Any ideas who you're going to approach?" Alan asked.

The girls confirmed that they didn't have any idea and were going to try and sort it over the weekend. They all finished their drinks and got up to leave, both Alan and Joel checking they hadn't left any noticeable puddles behind.

***

They all rocked up at Beans and Banter about thirty minutes later. Joel's parents looked strangely at the two boys in their damp clothes as they walked in. They had nearly dried out by now, but Ted and Alyssa had noticed it straight away.

The girls explained it all to them, causing much chuckling all round, and even getting a smile out of the boys. Alan and the twins went to settle at their usual table and Joel went to speak to his dad behind the counter.

"Hannah had an idea, Pops, that I wanted to run by you."

"Go on, I'm listening."

"Mrs French's funeral will be in the next couple of weeks, and Hannah wondered if Alan and I could be part of a memorial concert." Joel watched his dad carefully, as this information was processed.

"I see…" Ted said, a thoughtful look on his face.

"Could we possibly do it here?" Joel asked hopefully.

"Can other artists be involved? And did it even want to be part of the wake? We could even cater for everyone."

"You'd probably need to speak to the twins about that; I've got no idea what they've planned. And I don't see why other artists can't be involved."

"OK. If the girls come and ask about holding the wake here, then I don't see why they can't. And I asked about artists because Tim's here. He's over there with his new girlfriend," Ted said, pointing towards the front corner of the shop. "He knew Christine. I'd have thought he'd be up for something like that."

Joel turned and looked at Tim sat with his mystery girlfriend. He could only see the back of her head but he was sure it was the one from his status earlier. He was curious and found himself wandering over.

Tim looked up at him, surprise on his face as Joel put a hand on his shoulder. Joel realised it was the first time he had seen Tim in person for several months.

"Hey," Joel said, trying to keep his voice friendly; he realised he still bore a grudge about the music festival debacle and tried to not let it show.

"Hey," Tim replied, also sounding friendly. "How's things? Been ages since I last saw you."

"Yeah, I know. I'm alright, I guess," Joel said. He glanced over towards the woman sat next to Tim, who smiled at him. "Hi, by the way. I'm Joel."

"Hi, Joel. I'm Izzy," she said, with a wave.

"Nice to meet you. I saw you two made it official on Facebook," Joel commented. "Congratulations."

"Yeah, thanks, man. It's a bit weird, but in a good way," Tim said.

Joel just looked at him, waiting for Tim to expand on that and was quite surprised that Tim didn't go any further.

"Joel's parents own Beans and Banter," Tim added to break the silence.

"Ah right," Izzy said. "I really like it in here. They've done a great job with the place."

"Thanks, I presume you've met my folks. Did they do their 'routine'?"

Izzy chuckled. "Yeah, they did. Do they do that with everyone?"

"Just a bit. Pops insists it's good customer service. I find it a bit weird."

"Do you work here too?" Izzy asked.

"Yeah, occasionally. Weekends and things," Joel said, caught off guard by how pleasant Izzy appeared.

"Joel plays the odd set in here sometimes," Tim added, making Joel wonder why he was being nice about him. Surely this was Tim's opportunity to big himself up in front of his new girlfriend?

"Yeah, but I'm nowhere near as good as Tim," Joel said modestly. "On the subject of music, though, I just needed to ask you something. A bit of a favour really." Tim looked confused and Joel realised it was an odd request.

"Do you want me to sign something?" Tim asked.

Joel held back a laugh. "Not exactly. It's a bit more serious than that."

Tim was looking thoroughly baffled now. "Why? What's happened?"

"Have you not heard about the twins' mum?"

"I knew something had happened to her. How is she?"

Joel took a deep breath. "She didn't make it," he said gently. He watched as that sunk in and he noticed even Izzy looked shocked.

"No…" Tim whispered. "Surely… No… This is a joke, right?" He looked up at Joel with hope in his eyes.

"I'm afraid not," Joel said, sitting down at a spare chair at their table. "We're planning on holding a memorial concert here in the next couple of weeks. I just wondered if you'd be prepared to play in it?"

Tim's face had turned rather pale. "Of course I will," he said faintly. "No problem."

"I need to know if you'd be prepared to do some group stuff, like we used to? Or whether you'd want to do just a solo set."

Tim thought about it. "Could I do both?"

"Sure. I'll ask the girls if there's any songs in particular and we'll need to sort out a set."

"Just let me know when you want to practise and when the concert will be. I'm not exactly busy at the moment."

"Will do. Is your mobile number still the same?"

Tim confirmed that it was and Joel decided to leave him to it.

"Nice to meet you, Izzy," Joel said, waving casually at her.

"Yeah, you too," she replied with a smile.

Joel returned to the back of the shop leaving Tim looking a bit dazed. "Hey," he said to the group as he slid in next to Amie. "Tim said he'd play at the memorial concert. We just need a date to give him. And he said he'd be prepared to do an ensemble bit," he added, looking at Alan, whose eyes immediately lit up. "We're not touring with him yet, mate."

"But it's a start," Alan said excitedly.

"Did Tim say anything about us?" Hannah asked, causing Alan to frown and look away in disgust.

"No, he didn't," Joel replied truthfully. "He was shocked that your mum had died, though."

"Oh right," Hannah muttered.

"He was with his new girlfriend," Joel added, waiting to see if there was a reaction.

"Yeah, she's pretty, isn't she? Any ideas how he met her?" Hannah asked.

"None. She didn't say."

"We've been writing down a few ideas for the concert," Amie said, changing the subject and showing Joel her notebook. "Alan thinks you could probably sing all of Mum's favourites. I can try and get the sheet music from somewhere. Probably off the Internet."

"Rather than me doing all the singing, do you reckon that you'd like to join us?" Joel asked.

"But we've never sung in public before," Amie said looking shocked. Hannah, too, had a similar expression.

"And?" Joel asked. "It doesn't matter. I just wondered if you'd like to sing at the concert. You knew your mum's favourite songs better than the rest of us."

"You know what, Amz," Hannah said. "He does actually have a point."

"We've got a printer and the Internet upstairs you know," Joel went on. "Do you fancy having a look and seeing if singing is something you feel like doing? We can use Pops' piano to start with."

"I also have the Internet and a printer. Plus I have a music room, if you want to come round to mine," Alan offered.

"It's true, he's got quite a setup at his house," Joel confirmed. "It's almost a recording studio, the amount of stuff in there. Let me go and grab my guitar and we'll head over to his."

Borne on a wave of enthusiasm, the group left Beans and Banter. Joel was impressed to see that Hannah didn't look in Tim's direction once on the way out. Maybe, just maybe, she was actually over him.

CHAPTER THIRTY-FIVE

Friday 4th May, early afternoon
Huntingham Crematorium

Amie squeezed Hannah's hand. They were stood together in the front row at the crematorium, their respective boy on their other side. There was a decent-sized crowd, although there were still seats available. Amie had been surprised at the number of people that had shown up, including some of her mother's friends that they hadn't seen since they were little. Some of the staff from Fosters House were present, which Amie really appreciated. Hannah had also pointed out Wendy, the nurse from the hospital, on their way in.

She had even tried to contact their dad again, but had only reached his voicemail. She had left a message letting him know when the funeral was going to be and she left it at that. It was up to him if he decided to come or not; she had no real desire to see him after what he'd said the other night. However, she felt she should tell him that his wife of twenty-something years had died. She owed him that much.

Since they had first mooted the idea of the memorial concert, there had been a lot of work going on in the background. The day after spending the evening at Alan's, the twins had rung around the local funeral directors before settling on one that Alan's mum had recommended. The twins had found them very comforting and professional in their dealings with them and the arrangements for the funeral had been pristine, prompting the girls to choose flowers, coffin style and even what their mum would wear on the day, including jewellery. They had even asked for their mum's contacts to be able to let friends and family know about the funeral. The girls had gratefully accepted their help with that.

The trip to the crematorium had been made in silence. Alan and Joel were both dressed in their suits, while the twins were in matching long black dresses. In looking in their mum's jewellery box, they had found two similar sets of rings and earrings that they were both wearing as part of their outfits. The twins, Alan and Joel all travelled to the crematorium in a black car following the hearse and both of the twins' gazes rarely left the coffin.

Joel's parents had agreed to hold the wake at Beans and Banter, at no cost to the twins. The memorial concert was also taking shape and the girls had both enjoyed rehearsing with their boyfriends over the last two weeks. The twins had made it known that they were glad to have had something to work on and try and distract them from arranging a funeral and the increasing pressure of A Level coursework and revision. Tim had even joined them for a few rehearsals and, much to Amie's surprise, there hadn't been a shred of awkwardness between her sister and Tim, which she was grateful for. Both of them seemed happy with their new partners and didn't seem to begrudge each other for that either.

The minister stood up at the front of the crematorium, causing a hush amongst the attendees. He was of medium height, with white, receding hair and a pair of glasses perched on the end of his nose.

"Good afternoon, ladies and gentlemen," he said, with a soft, velvety voice. "Thank you for coming here today, from your various walks of life, to pay your respects to Christine French. I've been asked to let you all know that there is going to be a memorial concert this evening at the Beans and Banter coffee shop in town. It begins at seven thirty and will feature a variety of local acts playing some of Christine's favourite songs. Food is available too, according to the note I have here.

"Now, it's obvious that we've all got one thing in common here today and that is we've all been touched in some way by Christine's presence. Her twin daughters, Amie and Hannah, have told me how much joy and light their mother brought to the world, including how much she fought for them once her husband of twenty-four years had left, ensuring they all had a roof over their heads, working every hour she could get at Fosters House Care Home, where she had worked since before she was married. She was renowned for roping in the other carer's families for Christmas carols every Christmas Eve and she brought a lot of the residents together in doing so."

The minister proceeded to run through a brief history of Christine's life pieced together from the scraps of information that Amie and Hannah had found, sorting through their mum's paperwork. He finished with the Lord's Prayer and sat down again as the soft opening tones of 'The Music Of The Night' from 'The Phantom Of The Opera' came over the speakers.

A tear rolled down Amie's cheek as she stared hard at the coffin, watching it as it slowly descended from view. Their mother had taken them for their twelfth birthday to see 'The Phantom Of The Opera' in London and the chosen track had been her mother's favourite song from the show. Listening to the lyrics now, Amie realised how apt they were.

"Bless you, Mum," she whispered. "We wish you well on your final journey." She gave Hannah's hand another squeeze as she saw her sister's own eyes begin to stream.

Once the service had completed, Amie and Hannah, trying in vain to dry their eyes, trudged out into the flower courtyard and shook hands or hugged all of the attendees. Many of them said they would catch up with them later at the concert. Alan and Joel hung around the courtyard too, but kept their distance so Amie and Hannah could speak to everybody.

The last person to stop and talk to the twins was a woman that looked strangely familiar but Amie struggled to place her. She wondered if she was a resident at Fosters House, mainly due to her age. She was elderly, wizened and rather frail-looking and in the end Amie had to ask her who she was; it was bothering her that much.

The woman looked slightly amused. "I'm not surprised you don't recognise me, dear," she said, her clear voice belying her frail appearance. "Your father was strangely reluctant to ever bring you to see me. I last saw you both on your sixth birthday. And can I say, you two are still as identical now as you were when you were little; I still can't tell you two apart."

Amie felt very confused and glanced across at Hannah. Who on earth was this woman? She definitely looked familiar and obviously knew their dad. She racked her memory bank to try and remember their sixth birthday party but couldn't recall anyone strange being there.

Perhaps sensing her turmoil, the woman smiled, revealing some yellowed, cracked teeth. "I'm your father's mother, dear," the woman said. "Your grandma. My name's Elsie French."

It made sense now, and Amie realised that she was almost looking at an older version of her own reflection. "I'm Amie and this is Hannah," she said.

"I see, dear. I'll still not be able to tell you apart, so I apologise in advance. I'll be guessing who I'm talking to."

"So, did Dad send you?" Amie asked, her curiosity piqued.

"Not quite, dear. He told me when the funeral was. He never asked me to attend. I didn't think he would attend, so I came on my own accord." Amie was amused to see the woman attempt to shrug. "Sorry, my arthritis has been playing me up today," their grandma said, looking a little awkward.

"I have a lot of questions," Amie said, glancing at her sister again. "We have a lot of questions," she corrected herself. "Like, where is he? Why doesn't he love us any more? Why did he leave, even?"

Elsie held her hand up. "I can tell you what I know, but I haven't seen my son for nearly a decade. A lot of what he does is a complete mystery. He did ring me and tell me he'd left you all behind. The reason why, I don't know."

Amie felt slightly disappointed but figured that at least she might be able to put some pieces of the puzzle together for them both.

A crematorium official then appeared and informed them in a hushed tone that the next ceremony was about to begin and they would need to vacate the courtyard. Heading out of the courtyard with their grandma between them, the two girls spotted Alan and Joel waiting for them in the car park.

"What do we call you?" Amie asked.

"Please call me 'Grandma'. It's been a while since anybody called me that, dear."

"OK, can I introduce our boyfriends?" Amie asked, beckoning Alan and Joel over.

Amie watched as her grandmother narrowed her eyes when she was introduced to Joel.

"Hello again, dear," Elsie said to Joel. "Not serving today then?"

Joel shook his head. "Not today. Sadly, other duties called."

Amie was looking between them both incredulously. Now what was going on? How did Joel know her grandmother?

"Elsie's a Beans and Banter regular, Amz," he clarified. "I had no idea she was related to you."

She relaxed slightly. "So you've been visiting the coffee shop over the road for a while and didn't know we lived in one of the houses opposite? Or even that we were regulars?"

Elsie glanced between the two of them. "That's right, dear. I never did get a new address when you moved. Your dad didn't tell me these things. And I never recognised you both in the shop; it's been twelve years since I saw you last."

Amie took a deep breath to try and calm her thudding heart rate. "OK, well, Hannah and I do have a lot of questions for you. Do you fancy going to Beans and Banter now? Alan and Joel need to finish preparing for tonight's concert and we'd love to get to know you a little better."

"That sounds lovely, dear. Would you all like a lift?"

The four of them shared a glance, which Elsie spotted.

"I'm quite capable of driving, thank you. I just can't walk very far. My car's in the car park."

They all gratefully accepted and squeezed into Elsie's navy blue hatchback, only then feeling a little nervous as the car juddered out of the car park and headed towards Huntingham town centre.

**

Arriving without any mishap at Beans and Banter, the rest of the afternoon saw Amie and Hannah spending time with their grandmother while Alan and Joel were setting up the back room for the concert.

Amie realised that Elsie was in fact the only other family member, that they knew of, at the ceremony. When she mentioned this, Elsie merely gave a wry smile.

"Your dad was an only child, and your mother's sister lives in Australia with her parents now, if I recall," she said.

"That'll be Aunty Sandra won't it?" Hannah asked.

"That's right, dear."

"Did you ever meet Mum's parents?" Amie asked. "I don't think we ever have."

"At the wedding, dear. They flew over especially."

"It's a bit strange really, we don't know that much about them. Did they emigrate then, or is Mum actually Australian?" Amie pressed.

"They emigrated, as far as I know. Sandra was a young teenager when they went, if I recall correctly. Your mum had left home and had met my son, so she stayed here."

"Do they even know about Mum?" Hannah asked.

Amie nodded. "I gave the details I had to the funeral directors. They should have been informed, providing Mum had the right address and number in her book."

"Just seems strange that the only other family member that was at the funeral was Mum's mother-in-law," Hannah said, frowning. "Are there really no other family? Did Mum have any uncles or aunts or anything like that?"

"I don't know, dear. The wedding was a small affair from what I remember, but I couldn't tell you who was family or otherwise."

"So, why is Dad an only child?" Amie asked.

Elsie looked surprised, but gave a straight up answer. "Your grandpa died after your dad was born and I never remarried. That's the simple answer."

The twins fell silent.

"Your father was a difficult child. I struggled to bring him up on my own. I certainly wasn't a good mother. I missed your grandpa and resented him for leaving me to bring up a baby boy all on my own. Your dad and I mutually hated each other, I think. It's no way to bring up a child. He left home as soon as he could, moving from town to town looking for work. I was ecstatic to hear that he'd met somebody and I wondered if maybe I hadn't done a terrible job. He was very happy with your mother and she brought some stability to his life. They married and obviously you both were born. Then something changed with him and he suddenly became a person I didn't recognise."

Amie felt a little bit sorry for her in that moment, but let her grandma continue.

"He kept in touch now and again. He did say that he'd left you all last year, but he never said where he was going or why he had. He then rang me this week to say that Christine had died." Elsie sighed and looked a little melancholy. "I don't know whether he resented me for how he was brought up and that was why he never really let me see my granddaughters; I can only speculate."

"So you've been on your own since Dad was a baby?" Hannah asked.

"That's right, dear. I have my friends and I meet up at Beans and Banter with them every week. It's probably the only time I regularly leave the house now."

Once again, Elsie attempted a shrug, wincing as she did so. "I forget my body isn't what it used to be."

"I know you mentioned that something with Dad changed; do you have any inkling as to what it was?" Amie asked.

Elsie thought about it for a few moments. "I know you'd like some answers, dears, but I'm afraid I really don't have any."

"We've both just tried to work out what happened with our parents. Mum never really told us much and Dad wasn't there to ask. We'd just like to know what went wrong," Hannah stated.

"You're at that age where you realise your parents are people and that they have lives with dreams and fears and personalities all to themselves," Elsie commented. "Your mother, as the service showed today, was a wonderful woman with a great nature. Quite what she saw in my son, I'll never really understand, but she saw something in him. Your dad was always proud of his two daughters, though, I do know that. It's just a shame that you'll not get to know either of them."

"That sounds like Dad won't ever come back," Hannah said quietly.

"Come back to what, dear? You're all grown up now."

Both girls conceded this point.

"To be fair, after what he said to me this week, and his lack of contact regarding Mum's funeral, I don't care if I never see him again. But I had been wondering about what's going to happen to us," Amie said. "Like, would Social Services become involved?"

"We're eighteen, aren't we," Hannah replied. "We're considered to be adults, so it wouldn't matter."

That made sense to Amie, and she was actually quite relieved not having to worry about being sent to live with their dad.

"So, are you two going to be involved with your boyfriends in this concert tonight?" Elsie asked.

Both girls smiled. "We are," Amie said. "We're going to be singing some of Mum's favourite songs."

"I'll have to see if I can ring my friend Margaret and ask if she wants to come on down. I'd love to show her that not all my family were rotten eggs. It's not a family-only event or anything is it?"

Amie produced her mobile phone and offered it. "Not at all, it's to raise money for Mum's charity. She left a donation in her will to them. If your friend wants to come she's very welcome."

Elsie pointed to the mobile phone. "Thanks, dear. That's very kind. But you'll have to put the number in for me, I've got no idea how to use one of those confounded things."

Amie duly obliged, inputting the number Elsie read out to her from a small address book she had with her. Elsie had a brisk conversation with Margaret, who appeared interested in attending.

The twins went on to discuss the concert and their relationships in more detail, their newly-found grandma listening on intently, asking poignant questions as and when required.

Amie watched her sister interacting with Elsie and felt pleased with how well her sister was coping. There Hannah was, talking about hopes and dreams and how amazing her boyfriend was, with a woman who they had only really met properly a few hours earlier. That sort of scenario a year ago would have been unthinkable for Hannah. Amie felt quite proud of her in that moment. Hannah had come a long way since trying to take her own life; dealing with the end of her crush and now losing their mother hadn't appeared to have unsettled her at all.

***

"Testing, testing," Alan said into the microphone, tapping it a few times for good measure.

"That's coming through loud and clear, buddy," Joel called, as he flicked a switch and nearly blinding his best friend with a spotlight.

Alan put the microphone on the stand, switched it off and joined Joel on the floor. "I think that's it all done, then."

"Excellent. Did you print our set lists for tonight?"

"Sure have," Alan said, pointing towards his rucksack.

Joel smiled. "It's all quite official having a set list. Makes me feel like we're in a rock band or something."

"Did you not have them for the few gigs you've done?"

Joel shook his head. "I only play ten songs, so I didn't really see the point."

"Makes sense. When you've got a few more songs to go through, I guess it's useful."

"Can always be proper rock star and sign them at the end," Joel added.

"And give them to all our female fans in the mosh pit?"

Joel turned and looked at his best friend. "Dude, you have a girlfriend. You don't need any female attention. I was thinking we could auction the stuff off or something. Even if it made a few quid."

Alan looked a bit embarrassed. "Yeah, that's a good idea. Could even get Tim to sign it, that'll raise the value a notch."

"How do you think the concert will go?" Joel asked. "Feeling confident on your first Beans and Banter gig?"

Alan considered this for a few moments. "Well, we've rehearsed pretty much every night since we arranged it. The girls are actually better than I thought they would be. There's nothing more I can think of that we could have done so it should be amazing. I just hope lots of people are coming so we can raise some money in memory of Mrs French."

"Yeah, me too," Joel said. "So, how are things going with you and Hannah?"

"Really well. When I remember I have one, having a girlfriend is great."

"I know. Tell me about it."

"Well, it's like…" Alan began, before Joel shoved him.

"I didn't mean it like that," Joel said. "I know how great it is, dude. I can't help thinking whether I should have made a move earlier."

"That sounds like you're having regrets," Alan commented.

"I sort of am. Just regretting I could have had a girlfriend before now if I'd had the balls to ask her out."

"Joel, seriously. You don't half think weird."

Joel narrowed his eyes at his best friend. "What do you mean?"

"I mean that you're complaining about how amazing your relationship is? What's up with that?"

Joel stopped and thought about this for a few moments. "So you're saying that I should be grateful that it's worked out the way it has?"

"You're happy, right?"

Joel nodded.

"So, surely, everything's worked out alright? You've got the girl and you're happy. Who cares if it didn't happen earlier? That doesn't matter one iota. It's obviously happened this way for a reason."

Joel couldn't fault Alan's logic. "What you say makes perfect sense. I just wonder what it's like almost dating the same person as each other?"

Alan turned to him and looked Joel dead in the eyes. "You what?"

Joel suddenly felt a bit insecure. "I only meant physically. I know they're two completely separate people otherwise."

Alan grunted and appeared to let it slide, but Joel could tell he'd irked his best friend. "Do you reckon you'd ever confuse the two of them?" Alan asked eventually.

"Er, no," Joel said immediately. "Even today when they were wearing almost identical outfits, you could tell which one was which."

"True," Alan conceded.

"The idea of someone being with Hannah bothers you then?" Joel asked, semi-rhetorically.

"Definitely. I'm still not thrilled about the spectre of Tim being around, but she's never mentioned him. Even being in the same room with him, she's never shown anything, really. It's almost weird, but I'm certainly not complaining."

"Tim certainly seems to be getting on well with his new girlfriend," Joel commented, trying to change the subject.

"Yeah, she seems pretty cool, from the brief times we've seen her. Friendly."

"And very much in love."

Alan frowned at him. "Really?"

Joel laughed. "Do you not see the way that they kiss each other when he gets into her car after rehearsals? He's loved up, Al. Proper loved up."

"Well, so long as it stays that way, everything will be fine," Alan said in a way that suggested to Joel he should probably change the subject.

"Fancy a drink, Al?"

"Of course. Hard work sorting out all that wiring and getting those lights sorted. I'm parched."

Joel went to grab two drinks from behind the counter in the shop, quickly peeking at their regular table to see how Amie and Hannah were getting on. They both appeared to be getting on famously with their grandmother. Maybe discovering a family member was going to be a positive on a day where positivity had been hard to come by.

***

Sir Andrew pulled his Lexus into a street lined with terraced houses, surprised at how busy it was; parking spaces were at a premium. He wasn't used to having to fight for parking spaces. Or parking on roads for that matter.

"Is this normal?" he asked Izzy, who was sat in the passenger seat, wearing a dark green top and skinny black jeans. Sir Andrew noted how smart she appeared. She'd left her hair down around her shoulders and had put on her most expensive jewellery. He wondered if she was dressing up for someone.

"You mean the amount of cars?" she asked, to which he nodded. "It might be a little busier than normal. This concert tonight will probably be packed."

"Was Mrs French a popular woman?"

"I think it'll be more to see Tim perform. I mean, that's the reason we're going, isn't it?"

He nodded but said nothing else. It was true that as soon as Izzy had said Tim was going to be performing at a charity gig, he insisted that they both attend.

As he walked along the street, Izzy casually linked on his arm, he smiled at the people whose heads turned and whose eyes showed that flash of recognition he received whenever he appeared in public. He was accustomed to it these days, but it was always a reminder to him about how far he had reached. His tour of the Far East in a few years ago had been a

241

massive shock to him as to the scale of his success; signing autographs in the streets, meeting and greeting fans outside theatres. Seeing his books translated into a language that he didn't understand and the excited faces of a range of generations of fans really brought home to him what sort of global success he had achieved.

However, sometimes, it was difficult to be inconspicuous, as tonight was proving. He wasn't a fan of wearing hats or sunglasses as Hayden had recommended in the past, and had made the decision a while ago that he should just be gracious and put up with the attention.

Sir Andrew looked up and down the street outside Beans and Banter. There was a chalkboard advertising the night's festivities and he could hear the faint hum of activity coming from inside. He had only been inside the Red Lion a couple of times, having met Hayden for an evening drink after work. It hadn't been his favourite establishment; it had been dark and dingy and not very cheerful. He hadn't known it had been replaced by Beans and Banter and was intrigued to see what the new owners had done with the place.

**

Ted Wright appeared on the small stage, causing a hush in the packed room. He tapped the microphone a few times before saying, "Ladies and gentlemen. Thank you for being here tonight. It is a day for remembering a lady who meant a lot to many people. Christine French was also a regular punter here at Beans and Banter and my wife and I were very saddened to hear that she had died so suddenly. So, we thought we'd do a little fundraiser in aid of the local charity that she supported. There are a few local acts tonight, including my own son Joel." He paused while there was a small ripple of applause. "And some of you may have heard of him, he played his way into many people's hearts whilst on Talent UK. You know him as Tim Pointer!" Ted paused again as a few gasps went around the audience. "He's a local boy and a regular customer. He'll be doing a solo set first of all this evening and then he'll be joined by some of his friends, including Christine's daughters, to round everything off."

A greater round of applause and even some cheers came from the audience.

"So without any further ado, ladies and gentleman, it is my great pleasure to introduce to you, the one, the only… Tim Pointer!"

To great applause, Tim stepped on to the stage, raising his hand as he did so.

"Thanks, Mr Wright," Tim said, taking the microphone from him. "I'd just like to add my condolences to the long list. I've known Mrs French for a while, she was always lovely to me and she'll be sorely missed. Please donate what you can to her chosen charity; there are buckets all around this room and in the coffee shop.

"My first song tonight is a song you'll all know. It's called 'Baker Street'."

***

During the interval, having heard Tim do his solo set, Sir Andrew turned to Izzy, who was sat on the chair next to him. "Tim certainly seems to be in good spirits," he remarked. "As do you, if you don't mind me saying."

Izzy hesitated, unsure whether to tell him. But in her hesitation, she knew she had subconsciously told him that the two incidents were, in fact, linked. He was looking at her with an eyebrow raised.

"That's an interesting development," Sir Andrew commented, stroking his beard. "I'd realised you had met someone, but I certainly didn't realise it was the warm-up act for my tour."

Izzy looked at her boss, trying to read his face. She failed miserably, as she often did; he was absolutely unreadable. She couldn't tell if he was annoyed, pleased or somewhere in between. She decided to take a stab in the dark. "Well, Tim and I are very happy," she said, crossing her arms.

Sir Andrew smiled at her, which disarmed her slightly. "No need to be so defensive, Izzy. I've known you since you were a little dot and I've seen you grow into a fine, young woman. I suppose I'm just surprised; you've never really shown much interest in relationships."

Izzy opened and closed her mouth a few times before settling back in her chair. She couldn't argue with him.

"I'm presuming it was an opportunity that couldn't be missed," Sir Andrew said, trying to understand.

That made her turn and look at him again. "You're right," she said, "I think he needs someone like me in his life and to be fair, I need someone like him."

"I'm pleased for you both," Sir Andrew said, raising his mug. "I'm not used to toasting with a cup of coffee, but I suppose this is already a night for all sorts of firsts. To you and Tim."

They gently clinked their drinks together. "Thanks," Izzy said. She drained her cup and stood up. "Fancy a refill?"

"Sure, why not. Same again, please."

***

Once Izzy had disappeared to join the queue for drinks, Sir Andrew remained in his seat, looking around the room. It was strange for him to be sat in an audience. He was used to being backstage at this point in his shows. He wondered if he should try going and sitting in the seats during the interval at one of his own shows to gauge the atmosphere.

Tonight, he was picking up that everyone had been impressed with both Tim's performance and that he'd appeared for personal reasons to play. He also noted that the crowd were mentioning Tim's stupor state and that there had been no sign of him having any relapses. He gave a wry smile. Some things like that would just stick; he hoped Tim would be able to carry that burden.

He settled back in his seat and he then became aware of somebody stood next to him.

"Sorry to disturb you, sir. But are you Sir Andrew Anderson?"

Sir Andrew looked at the middle-aged woman who had appeared next to him, trying to establish if she was friend or foe.

"I am," he said, a little cautiously. He wasn't sure if it was the busy room that was affecting his judgement, but he didn't feel like he was on top of his game tonight.

The woman perched on the chair next to him. "Oh, it's an absolute pleasure. I thought I'd recognised you but my friend, Gina, said it couldn't be you."

"I see. And you are…?"

"My name's Evelyn. I'm a massive fan. Massive. Your books have got me through so many hard times. You just reach in to my head and shine a light around in there. It's amazing."

"Is there a book or anything else you'd like me to sign, Evelyn?"

"Would you, please? Oh, that'd be amazing. My husband won't believe it when I tell him. I've met somebody famous." She let out a nervous giggle and reached for her handbag.

Sir Andrew reached into his pocket for his trusty pen he used for writing autographs. It had been a present from Dorothy for his fortieth birthday and he'd had it with him ever since. He scrawled a standard message and signed off with a flourish.

"There we go, my dear. A pleasure. I hope the books keep helping you."

"No, thank *you*, sir. I'm honoured," Evelyn said with what looked like a swoon. She then melted back into the crowd.

Izzy returned at that moment, carefully carrying two cups, her purse tucked under her arm. She was then practically barged out of the way by an officious-looking, hefty woman, who came and stood next to Sir Andrew.

"Did I hear you say you were Sir Andrew Anderson? The famous author?"

Sir Andrew eyed this new stranger warily, noting Izzy's scowl. "You did."

"Could you to sign this napkin for me?"

Sir Andrew almost refused to do so unless the woman was a bit more polite about it. He waited for a few moments but realised the woman wasn't forthcoming. He just signed the napkin and hoped the woman would go away.

"Right," the woman said, sitting down in Izzy's seat. "What's it like being famous? I bet it's fascinating."

"You get to meet all sorts of people; it's a real eye-opener," he replied, trying not to sound too cynical.

"I bet you must love the attention, being recognised in the street and in places like this."

"It makes me appreciate how far my words have reached," Sir Andrew said with a shrug. Izzy was still standing behind the woman, pulling funny faces at the person sat in her seat. Sir Andrew had to try and a cover a chuckle with a cough.

"What are you doing *here*, in this crummy coffee shop? Did you know Christine?"

"I'm actually supporting my PA's boyfriend," Sir Andrew said. "He's performing. And I think this is one of the most original coffee shops I've ever visited, to be frank with you."

"Oh right, each to their own. Coming in here to drum up a bit of interest in your tour, presumably," the woman replied, apparently not listening to a word Sir Andrew was saying.

This riled him and he had to take a deep breath before he replied. "Sometimes, it's not about me. As I stated, I'm here to support my assistant and her boyfriend. I'd appreciate it if you let her sit down, actually," he said, a little snappily.

"Fascinating. Right, see you later," the woman said, and with that she got up, squeezed her considerable frame past Izzy and disappeared into the crowd.

Izzy sat down in her seat and let out a huge sigh. "Thank heavens she left when she did. She was going to end up with your coffee over her if she carried on."

Sir Andrew snorted. "Your father often says you can't choose clients. I wish I could choose my fans."

***

"Hey, sis," Amie said, appearing in the Wright's lounge above Beans and Banter. She'd been in Joel's room running through the lyrics with him, since their grandma had met up with her friend. Alan and Hannah had taken the lounge, before Alan had headed downstairs to watch Tim perform, leaving Hannah in the lounge on her own. Having seen Tim around so much recently, and with Joel's antipathy towards Tim anyway, Joel and Amie had decided to run through the lyrics one final time rather than watch him perform.

Both girls had been sleeping in the lounge, still; going home didn't feel right and Amie wasn't sure if she would ever want to go back. Joel's parents had been understanding and had insisted on them staying as long as they wanted, which helped. It had been perfect for Amie; she was practically living with her boyfriend. Hannah had been spending lots of time with Alan, but Alan's parents had some very strict rules about what happened under their roof with regards partners, so she had always ended up back in the lounge at the Wrights with her sister.

"Hey," Hannah replied with a smile.

"How you feeling? Looking forward to this?"

"Yeah, a bit. I'm nervous too. Hoping I won't get stage fright."

"You'll be fine. We're doing it together remember? I'll be right there with you."

"I know, Amz. Doesn't stop the butterflies though, does it?"

"No, I guess not," Amie muttered. A few seconds later she then piped up, "Han, I hope you don't mind, but I really want to ask you something."

Hannah frowned. "Go on."

"How's things going with Alan? Particularly with Tim being about again. I'm presuming it's going well because this is the first real chance I've had to ask you. I have to sneak out of Joel's room in the middle of the night and you're usually asleep by that point. Apart from that, we don't really spend much time with each other any more, just the two of us."

"It's going really well. He's nice, he's considerate and he's very understanding. He's like an enthusiastic puppy really."

Amie let out a laugh. "That's perfect for you; you always wanted a puppy."

"Yeah, I did," Hannah said, with another smile. "Why didn't we ever get one?"

"I think because Mum told you that you'd have to look after it, feed it and take it for all of its walks and you weren't keen," Amie said.

Hannah shrugged. "That makes sense. Mum was pretty sensible with us about things like that."

"Yeah she was. Hopefully we'll be able to remember things like that when we're bringing up our own children."

"I'm sure we will. She'll still be a part of our lives. I want our children to know who their granny was. It's just a shame they'll never get to meet her."

Amie noticed tears begin to well up in her sister's eyes. "Hey, Han, don't do that, you'll set me off too! I've not got waterproof mascara on. I'll end up looking like I'm going to be singing death metal or something."

Hannah wiped her eyes and sniffed. "Mum would have found that funny."

"She would have. It's OK to talk about her, you know. I still feel like she's here watching over us sometimes. She'll be watching the concert tonight and she'll be incredibly proud. Particularly of you. You've really come out of your shell these last few weeks. She'd have been so pleased."

Another tear escaped down Hannah's cheek. "Thanks, Amz. I feel like she's still around too. I can't quite explain it apart from I can just feel her there."

Joel bounding into the room interrupted their conversation. "Ready you two?" he asked. "This is your moment."

They nodded and followed Joel downstairs. Alan and Tim were waiting for them with Ted, who gave them a smile.

"Ready, girls? Be brilliant."

They smiled their thanks and Ted promptly turned and headed back out to the stage.

"Good evening, ladies and gentlemen," he said, pausing as everybody settled down. "I'd like to welcome to the stage your band for the rest of the show. On keyboards... Alan Proctor."

There was a polite smattering of applause as Alan ran on to the stage to sit behind his keyboard.

"On guitar... Joel Wright."

Joel was a little more casual and gave the audience a smile as he went to sit on a stool on the far side of the stage. The applause grew a little.

"On saxophone... Tim Pointer."

There was a roar as Tim appeared again.

"And finally, on vocals, it is my great pleasure to introduce to you Christine's daughters, Amie and Hannah French!"

Everyone was on their feet now, clapping enthusiastically as the twins, a little apprehensively, walked to the middle of the stage, hand in hand.

"Hi, everyone," Amie nervously said into the microphone. "Before we get on with some of Mum's favourite songs, I just wanted to say a big thank you for your support tonight. You've made an effort to be here and Hannah and I can't thank you enough. Even if you've only come to see Tim, thanks for sticking around." There were a few chuckles in the audience.

Amie continued, "There are buckets around the room and I just wanted to tell you it's for a local children's hospice that Mum supported. All proceeds will be going to them directly."

There was more polite applause.

"I also wanted to say a big thank you to Ted and Alyssa Wright for putting this concert on," Amie went on. "Their support over the last few weeks has been immense and I wanted to ask for a huge round of applause for them; they've been amazing." She then gestured for them both to come out on stage and the twins gave them both a hug as everybody stood up again, clapping.

"Now," Amie said once everyone had settled down, "to the songs. This first song was one of Mum's favourites. It's called 'Hey, Soul Sister' by Train."

***

Sir Andrew found himself clapping along with the rest of the audience during the encore as the band covered 'Livin' On A Prayer' by Bon Jovi for what turned out to be the final song. He had enjoyed himself a lot more than he thought he would when Izzy first mentioned it to him. He had revelled in Tim's performance in the first half and he was now sure he had made the correct decision in offering Tim a supporting slot for the tour.

When the concert had ended and the audience were filing out, he remained in his seat for a few minutes trying to take in as much of the atmosphere and remember the songs that he'd heard. Izzy had headed up to the front, where a few people were queuing around Tim, trying to get his attention. He smiled as Izzy was barged out of the way again as another teenager joined the queue to meet Tim.

He felt a hand on his shoulder and was rather surprised when he turned around and found one of his retired housekeepers stood there with an amused look on her face.

"Margaret? Is that you?" Sir Andrew asked, fairly sure he was right.

"Hello, sir. This was probably one of the last places on Earth I would ever have expected to bump into you. It's been a while."

"Nearly a decade I would say," he added.

"About that," she agreed.

They swapped pleasantries for a few minutes before Margaret, with a twinkle in her eye, looked straight at him. "I've got to go, sir. My friend is waiting for me. It was a pleasure to see you again. But, if you would humour me, please go and say hello to the scruffy-haired one from the band. You won't regret it."

A little surprised at such a strange request, he shrugged. "OK, Margaret, I will." It was the way she had said it that puzzled him. Was there something about the boy that was interesting? Or did it go further than that?

"Thank you, sir. Good night," she said, a strange look on her face.

Sir Andrew made his way up to meet the band members, who were busy packing away their instruments and all the wiring the boys had set up earlier. There was still a crowd around Tim, which Sir Andrew certainly wasn't going to disturb, though judging by the age of them, they probably wouldn't have known who he was anyway.

The tall one with glasses who had played the keyboards appeared to recognise him as he approached, and shook Sir Andrew's hand enthusiastically.

"Hello, Mr Anderson, I mean Sir Anderson. Actually, I don't know what I'm supposed to call you; how do you address someone who has been knighted?"

Sir Andrew laughed heartily. "Don't worry," he replied. "It's actually refreshing to be asked. 'Sir Andrew' is fine."

"Right, 'Sir Andrew' it is. I'm Alan by the way and that scruffy-looking one over there is Joel. The twins, Amie and Hannah are somewhere about. I guess you've already met Tim a few times," Alan said.

"Has Tim told you all about the tour?" Sir Andrew asked.

"Not directly. Hannah, my girlfriend, she was the one who told me originally. He'll be brilliant. He's a fantastic musician and he takes it very seriously."

"I am aware of that. He loves playing. It's the first time I've seen him live tonight as well. I can tell I've made a good choice."

"Definitely. Oh, here are the twins. Amie, Hannah? I need to introduce you to somebody," Alan said, gesturing towards Sir Andrew.

"Hello, girls," Sir Andrew said warmly. "Firstly, I just wanted to say how sorry I was to hear about your mother. She seemed like quite a lady."

"Thanks," they both said simultaneously.

"And also, your singing was very impressive. Do you do it regularly?" He could tell by the look they then shared that it wasn't. "Oh, well, you were naturals. It was brilliant."

One of the twins was staring at him with the fabled look of recognition. "Are you Sir Andrew Anderson?"

"I most definitely am."

"Stay there!" she said hurriedly. "Would you sign my book for me?"

"Of course, I'd be happy to," he said, as the girl ran off.

He was keen to meet Joel and see what Margaret had seen. He seemed very focused on ensuring his instruments were safely packed away and that the wiring was wrapped up, so much so, that Sir Andrew wasn't even sure Joel knew he was there. While waiting for the twin to return, he decided to go over to him.

"Hi," Sir Andrew said, offering his hand in greeting. "Congratulations, that was quite a set you all played."

"Thanks," Joel replied, shaking the proffered hand. "Tim's the star, though, you should be congratulating him."

Sir Andrew picked up, in that moment, the tension between Tim and his band mates, and made a mental note to ask Tim about it later. However, something had just caught his eye about the scruffy-haired teenager stood before him.

It felt like time stood still for a few long moments, as Sir Andrew looked the teenager up and down. He ended up staring into Joel's eyes. Joel was looking at him with a confused expression.

It couldn't be, he thought to himself. How had Margaret known? Had she made the connection?

But, in that instant, Sir Andrew was sure. There was no doubt in his mind. He tried to argue against it, but he just couldn't.

He was adamant that he had just met the teenage version of the baby boy he had carried out of the manor house nearly eighteen years ago.

AUTHOR'S POST-AMBLE

'Smile' is a book that has taken a lot of time to write. Lots of books take time to write, I hear you say. True. I can't deny that. I'm not saying J.K. Rowling finished her Harry Potter series overnight. But for me, my first book has been a long project.

I've been interested in writing stories since I was a child. My Aunty Pauline and Uncle Ron reminded me recently of a holiday to Portugal where I spent a lot of time writing in a notebook that I'd bought in the shop near the hotel. I was eleven at the time. Maybe I should have thought about writing a bit more in the sixteen years before 'Smile' became a reality. I'm glad technology has improved since 1997 as well. I don't think I'd have fancied writing this book out in pencil as I did back then.

I have an amazing wife. (She didn't pay me to write that, honest!) How she puts up with me, I'm not entirely sure. I've had lots of crazy ideas over the years I've known her and she replies to each one with a "You do what you think best, darling". I'm sure she was sceptical when I categorically stated I wanted to write a novel. (It has gotten me out of doing the dishes for at least seven months, so I'm definitely not complaining.) Many of those my ideas have fallen through once I realised how crazy they were, but the more I wrote of 'Smile', the more I was determined to finish it. (I mean, come on, no dishes!)

The introductory chapter was written, I think, at some point in 2013. My daughter was born in 2012 and I'm sure it was during her first few months on the planet I told my wife I wanted to write a book. The dark nights found me sat in a chair in our lounge, waiting for my daughter to cry and need a dummy putting back in and I thought to myself that I would have all the time in the world to start planning a story. That came together quickly. The introductory chapter came soon after that. But then real life kicked in and I struggled to fit it all in.

The childbirth scene is fortunately one I didn't experience first hand. Both of my children were born with no complications, one in a midwife-led unit, the other on the floor in my lounge. I know I'm incredibly lucky, as a father, to be able to say that. Having to imagine the experience that Sir Andrew went through was hard enough to write and still gets me every time I picture holding my children for that most special of all firsts. I could never have given my children away. I admire anybody who has to or has done.

I originally wrote a basic plan of twenty chapters. It gave a few details of what I was aiming to achieve. I've got no idea at what point I verged quite rapidly off that original plan, but as I wrote, ideas kept coming to me, new characters formed and storylines got more and more complex. I wanted to tackle a few issues in the book: depression being the main one, something I suffered with when I was at university (but on a much less severe level than dealt with in 'Smile'). I also wanted to write some characters with a bit of an age difference. Particularly having a girl older than the boy. Some people find it strange. I have no idea why. If it works, then it works. Where's the problem with that?

I also had a theory about plotting life's ups and downs on a graph. I reckon highs and lows happen quite close together and in a weird kind of way, they even each other out. I even went through a phase of my life where I tried to not experience life's highs so I didn't have to deal with the lows and keep everything fairly neutral. It doesn't work very well. When something good happens to you, you have to savour it. Enjoy it while it lasts. Don't fear the lows. Otherwise there's just no point in living. The lows will make you stronger. Hannah is a fine example of that.

I hate people who say: "You have to write a mega-detailed plan in order to write a book". I didn't. I started writing in my drafts on my email account. Each chapter was written in a separate email, as was the 'plan'. I had a vague storyline to start with. The rest of it just sort of appeared as I wrote. I wrote it pretty much in chronological order. I was on Chapter 23 when I decided I wanted to write the last scene and wrote it, before filling in the rest of the story.

I also changed my original plan. I decided to aim for about 2,500 words per chapter. This made completing chapters more realistic for me. 2013 went on, 'Smile' became something I touched occasionally. I was too busy with a day job that I didn't really enjoy, playing cricket at weekends and being a dad. Writing was never a priority. Then my wife became pregnant with our second child. I became determined to finish this book. I wanted to have put something on this planet that my children could refer to and read and know it only came from their dad.

2014 was a big year for me. My son was born. And I vowed to write a chapter a month. That way I would have written at least twelve chapters in the year. I think I had written eight at that point.

I did actually start doing more than a chapter a month. In the latter half of the year, I then set myself of writing at least 100 words a day. I didn't find that challenging enough and upped it to 250. I've not looked back. In January and February 2015 the rate was a chapter a week at least. It was then I decided that I had enough material to write a series. I looked back at that original twenty-chapter plan. I'd covered about six chapters of it.

If you enjoy reading, I would say try writing. I believe there's a book in everybody. Write about something that you know. You've lived your life. Take out the boring bits but mix it with dreams and things that you've always wanted to do. It's great fun researching these things. You can create characters based on people you know and have met. If there are horrible people who make your life a misery, put them in a book and have your characters be horrible to them. That's a tip I've learnt since I got to the latter stages of this story, so there's no one in 'Smile' that is solely based on a person that's negatively impacted my life.

There are echoes of my life in 'Smile'. Much of it is completely fabricated. The characters, mostly. I imagined that you could become a multi-millionaire if you wrote a series of best-selling books on depression. Further research showed that probably wasn't true, but for me it should be. Anybody who can meet people and make them better versions of themselves is a person who deserves material wealth. I wanted to create characters that were real, normal, everyday people, with their own quirks and personalities. I've no idea where they came from, or who they're based on. (Well, I do, I imagined them but they're not based on anybody I know or have met.) I can't really say why they are who they are. There's nothing more off-putting for me than opening a book filled with models. It's not real. I want to believe the story I'm reading or at least believe that it could be real. It's why my characters tend to spot personality quirks as being points of attraction.

My mum also died when I was younger. Fortunately, it wasn't in a way that was as shocking or abrupt as Christine French's demise. I was a little older than the twins but the feelings they experience were all mine. That was a particularly difficult chapter to write. I realised there were a lot of memories that had been suppressed.

I also dreamed of running a coffee shop when I was younger. (One of those 'you do what you think best, darling' moments.) I did a lot of research at that point, discovered that I should probably have experience of working in one and immediately shelved it. However, 'Smile' did allow me to bring it to life and make it successful. I feel that Beans and Banter will feature in other series I've got in the back of my mind; just as the popular TV show 'Friends' had a coffee shop as a hub, I feel that an alternative to the pub culture that is prevalent in the UK would be a good hub for other people. I have a brilliant idea for my coffee shop that I won't touch on here, because I don't want to ruin a possible storyline further down the line.

So, I've self-indulged on some of the ideas and inspiration behind my first book. I'd better crack on and start writing the sequel, 'Smiles'.

I'm usually writing updates on Twitter (@SMcClainAuthor) or my Facebook page www.facebook.com/scottmcclainauthor if you'd like to keep in touch with how it's going.

And thank you. Thanks for reading my first book. (It's absolutely wonderful to be able to write that!)